Roman
Dusk

By Chelsea Quinn Yarbro from Tom Doherty Associates

ROMAN DUSK

A NOVEL OF THE COUNT SAINT-GERMAIN

Chelsea Quinn Yarbro

A TOM DOHERTY ASSOCIATES BOOK
NEW YORK

This is a work of fiction. All the characters and events portrayed
in this novel are either fictitious or are used fictitiously.

ROMAN DUSK: A NOVEL OF THE COUNT SAINT-GERMAIN

Copyright © 2006 by Chelsea Quinn Yarbro

This book is printed on acid-free paper.

A Tor Book
Published by Tom Doherty Associates, LLC
175 Fifth Avenue
New York, NY 10010

www.tor.com

Tor® is a registered trademark of Tom Doherty Associates, LLC.

Library of Congress Cataloging-in-Publication Data

Yarbro, Chelsea Quinn, 1942-
    Roman dusk : a novel of the Count Saint-Germain / Chelsea Quinn Yarbro.—1st ed.
        p. cm.
    "A Tom Doherty Associates book."
    ISBN-13: 978-0-765-31391-1
    ISBN-10: 0-765-31391-X
    1. Saint-Germain, comte de, d. 1784—Fiction.   2. Vampires—Fiction.   3. Rome—Fiction.
I. Title.
    PS3575.A7R66 2006
    813'.54—dc22

                                                                                2006005033

First Edition: September 2006

Printed in the United States of America

0 9 8 7 6 5 4 3 2 1

For

Sharon Russell,

for hanging in there

Author's Note

This novel is set in the period of Roman history called the Decadence, which began about 160 AD, a distinction it richly deserved: social conventions had become lax; the bureaucracy was increasingly corrupt, due in large part to the privatizing of most of the civil service; the nobility were competing in luxury and excess, and were rarely held accountable for their overindulgence, either legally or politically; the Emperors were more often than not puppets for powerful families and influential plutocrats; maintenance of Roman roads, the most successful communication routes in the ancient world, was reduced or abandoned even as the Romans struggled to hold their borders; the Legions, once the heart of Roman strength, now filled their ranks with client-nation soldiers and gave high rank positions to mercenaries; the standards of education and language-use had declined and the quality of linguistic communication and literary expression was eroding; public entertainments, from the arena to the stage, were violent, sensationalistic, and debauched. The attempt to maintain a society of laws was giving way to one of political and commercial influence, and all the while the gulf between rich and poor was widening, and the legal rights of women and slaves were diminishing steadily.

On top of that, the upper classes were experiencing the genetic consequences of generations of cooking in lead-lined pots: all manner of problems from decreased birth rates to myriad physical and mental infirmities took a rising toll on those families long used to occupying positions of authority in the Empire. Even the middle-class—what there was of it—had begun to erode its generational health; for in an attempt to appear more wealthy and of higher rank than they were, many successful middle-class families sprinkled their food with powdered lead so that their food would taste as if they could afford lead pots.

Despite all these depredations from within, and although there were barbarian tribes worrying away at the edges of the Roman Empire, it still reached from the Middle East to the Atlantic Ocean, from Britain to north Africa. The first signs of a distinct east-west split were starting to develop by the time of this novel, the third century of the Christian calendar, or the tenth century of the Roman one.

At the time, Christianity was only one of many non-Roman religions gaining adherents; Mithraism was particularly popular among the Roman military, and Isis-worship was gaining supporters among Roman women as the power of the Vestal Virgins waned. Fortune-tellers and sybils had thriving clienteles in many parts of the Empire, as did any number of regional pagan practices. Christianity itself was sharply divided between the Peterine groups—who maintained most Jewish traditions but held their wives in common, in a kind of group marriage, and celebrated communal suppers—and Paulists—who did not practice strict Judaism, organized their followers hierarchically, exhorted nonbelievers in the streets, and physically attacked those they considered to be sinners, including Peterine Christians. This bipartisan rivalry was relentlessly competitive—much like siblings attempting to attract the favorable attention of a distant and baffling parent—and garnered a marked degree of public disapproval, a stance that only served to intensify both groups of Christians in a more determined practice of their versions of their faith in a display of resolve that increased the Roman condemnation of their religious beliefs as seditious.

The position of non-Romans was becoming precarious due to the barbarian incursions on Roman borders, to say nothing of Rome's increasing dependence on foreign trade. As the Empire entered its slow collapse, this first showed in the progressively aleatory postures of the internal administration of the Empire toward foreigners, especially those of substance. This was reflected in mercurial enforcement of taxation, the arbitrary enactment of customs regulations regarding imported goods, and demands of double and triple payment for such services as private security and civic repairs.

In his short, hectic reign, Heliogabalus did nothing to stop the erosion of the Roman Empire—in fact, through his systematic debasement of Roman coinage, he did a fair amount to speed it along—encouraged and abetted by the real authorities behind him: his mother and grandmother. Not that he didn't have a talent for surfeit and dissipation—he most certainly did, and he paid dearly for it. He was not alone in his avaricious exploitation of Rome and the Roman people; following Marcus Aurelius, Rome had few emperors with either the skill or the intention to secure the Empire until Constantine shifted the seat of power from Rome to Byzantium—renaming this city for himself: Constantinople—and laid the foundation for the collapse of the West.

As in *Blood Games,* I have kept the names of historical persons in traditional Roman order, but for fictional characters, I have put their family names last, as is the present style, for the sake of clarity, and to keep confusion to a minimum. For those familiar with Roman traditions of nomenclature, I ask your indulgence for this lapse in historicity.

Thanks are due to John Conner for information on the city of Rome during this period, and the shifts in Latin structure and vocabulary of the time; to Agatha Dermond for the use of her superb library on daily life in late-Imperial Rome, including extensive records on food and clothing; to David Lindenthal for allowing me to use his references on Roman roads and aqueducts of the period; to James Melchior for providing information on Roman government, laws, customs, and tax codes; and to Tracy Smith for sharing her material on the state of Roman provinces and borders in the third century. Errors and misinterpretations are mine, not theirs, and their help is much appreciated.

Also I would like to thank Lisa Eamons, Christine Sullivan, and Scott Wye, my clarity readers, at whose suggestion I have put a glossary of Roman terms at the back; to Libba Campbell and Gregory Huang, who read it for content; to the Canadian Chapter of the Transylvanian Society of Dracula, particularly Elizabeth Miller, and the Lord Ruthven Assembly, including all those who contributed to *Forgotten Gems of Horror Fiction,* for all their enthusiasm for this series of books; to Charlie and Peggy, Gaye, Megan, Steve, Maureen, Randy *in absentia,* Brian, and Alice; to Wiley Saichek for all the Internet work; to Paula Guran for getting my new Web site up and running (chelseaquinnyarbro.net); and to the Yahoo chat group. On the publishing side, thanks to Melissa Singer, my editor at Tor, and to her boss, Tom Doherty, for steadfastness. Last, thanks to you, the bookstore owners and the readers, for your ongoing support for Saint-Germain and this series—it wouldn't continue without you.

CHELSEA QUINN YARBRO
Berkeley, California
17 July, 2005

PART I

RAGOCZY GERMAINUS SANCT-FRANCISCUS

*T*ext of a letter from Almericus Philetus Euppo, freedman and mercer of Ostia, to Ragoczy Germainus Sanct-Franciscus, foreigner living at Roma outside the walls.

To the noble and well-reputed foreigner, Ragoczy Germainus Sanct-Franciscus at the villa that bears his name, to the northeast of Roma, the greetings of Almericus Philetus Euppo, freedman of Ostia, with thanks again for providing half the sum of the purchase price for the emporium on the Ostia docks where my business stores the cloth I import. May whatever god you worship show you favor, and may no other god act to your detriment.

The Coan linen has finally arrived, on the Morning Wind, *and all but two of the bales are in fine condition; one of the damaged bales cannot be salvaged, but the other can be, at least two-thirds of it. I have set my slaves to cleaning and blocking the linen to restore it, and I will see to it that the best possible results are obtained, and will provide you a record of what was done.*

You are fortunate to have so many of your ships reach port unscathed, and the cargos damaged by nothing more than weather. True, shipping has increased steadily over the last few years, which would ordinarily be cause for rejoicing, but with this increase in commerce has come increase in theft of all sorts. You may not be aware of how piracy has increased over these last few years, but most merchants have seen their losses to pirates and pilferage double since the end of the reign of Caracalla and the present, unpromising tenure of Macrinus. Reducing the pay of soldiers would appear to be a false economy to me in these times, but as Caesar, he has the right to do it, and those of us who must bear the brunt of his decision in loss of merchandise and higher taxes can only hope that he will not ruin us and leave us unguarded as well.

I do not mean to alarm you, but because of these changes in the Legions and the navy, I would advise you to consider carrying armed men on your merchant ships in future, to avoid losses to the pirates. I am enclosing a bid for your entire shipment, which I think you will find is more than fair in the current marketplace. I can supply you a letter of authorization, or funds in coin, as you prefer. The coins tend to attract more attention from footpads and other criminals, but there is a certainty in coins that cannot be denied.

According to my roster, you have three more ships due into port this month: the Neptune's Pride, *the* Northern Star, *and the* Song of the Waves. *I have nothing to report on any of these vessels, nor any of your others not yet bound for Ostia and home from any ship arrived in Ostia in the last week. I will have my scribe copy out the account provided by your captain, Getus Palmyrion, to enclose with this letter. He says the passage was relatively easy, given the time of year and the general condition of his crew and oarsmen. Again, you are fortunate to have so worthy a captain, who is alert to the needs of his men. Two days since, a ship of Pompeianus Dritto arrived with nine oarsmen suffering from fever, and half the crew also ill. They said they had taken on bad water in Tarrraco, and that the sickness came upon them at sea. Whatever the cause of their ailment, the ship and its crew and oarsmen have been isolated, and they will remain so until all have recovered or died. No amount of bribes or favors owed will change their situation; only convicted criminals are used to take food and water to the ship.*

I have a roster to send to you, from your colleague, Rugeri, from your emporia in Alexandria in Egypt, along with a sealed chest. According to what Getus Palmyrion has told me, it is a gift from a group of ancient priests who occupy some of the huge ruins near Luxor. The volumes from Rugeri are with the gift, as is his pouch of (untouched) aurei, your portion of the seasonal profits of your business in Egypt, along with his admonition to treat the carved wooden container with care. The roster is in a leather satchel and the casket from the priests is bound with lead, which will keep everyone out but those who can break or melt the lead. I have added wax and my seal to the lock on the satchel to indicate that it was undisturbed when it left my hands. If the seal is broken you will know there is a good possibility of tamperage, in which case, I recommend you notify the authorities about the crime.

It is my understanding that the spice-and-dye merchant Tercius Fortunatus Perusiano is going to send you an offer on that part of the Morning Wind's cargo. If you will be advised by me, you will wait until Petros Demetrianos has had a chance to make a bid, for he has had a recent increase in fortune and is in a position to offer you more than Perusiano will—Perusiano has a daughter about to marry, and he has had to endower her handsomely, and to take his pledged son-in-law into his business, all of which has left him with depleted funds.

Perhaps I should mention that an interesting object has arrived here, brought from a port beyond Byzantium: a very ancient sarcophagus, from the eastern crest of the Carpathian mountains. The claim is that is belongs to an ancient people, long vanished from the region, who, like the Etruscans of old, made carvings of the inhabitant of the sarcophagus as that person was in life—playing, dining, counting wealth, drinking, engaged in passion—instead of the repose of death. This particular sarcophagus depicts a man propped on his elbow and polishing a wide-bladed sword. He is smiling, and his upper leg is cocked. Knowing your interests in things from that region, I have made a bid upon it. If you wish me to pursue the matter, send me word how much you will authorize me to spend, and I will attempt to secure this object for you and have it carried to you by ox-cart, escorted, of course.

As soon as another shipment of cloth reaches my establishment here in Ostia in one of your ships, I will, as always, notify you at once, and send word by my own courier, as I have done in this instance. I intend to use my own couriers for business purposes from now on, and to send them along with at least one guard for escort. An extra expense, yes, but worth ever denarius if the messenger is protected along the way. There are many soldiers willing to hire out as escorts just now, and I recommend securing the services of a few for your couriers.

Melidulci in the lupanar has ordered nard and perfumed oils for her new establishment, and has brought in ten new girls. She has offered to receive you and any of your associates at any time you wish to call upon her. Apparently she is grateful to you for providing some medicaments to her when many of the women of the lupanar were taken with the fever of bad air, and could not work. It is always wise to have the good opinion of the women of the lupanar, is it not?

I hope you have become accustomed to Roma again, and that the demands of your move to your villa have not proven too exhausting to your body, your spirit, or your purse. There are as many drawbacks as advantages in being so close to the center of power, but, as you have lived there before, or so you said, your accommodation of Roman ways should not intrude upon you too much. Thus far, our dealings have been pleasant and profitable to us both, and I hope that they may continue to be so.

> *Almericus Philetus Euppo*
> *Freedman and mercer of Ostia*

by my own hand on the 7th day of March in the 971st Year since the Founding of Roma: with enclosures and parcels to accompany this

1

Clouds clotted the morning sky over Roma, their shadows bruising the buildings in their passing. In the Forum Romanum, such things were ignored; the Forum was alive with farmers driving their animals to the market-stalls just beyond the impressive buildings, their hogs, calves, sheep, goats, and stacked cages of chickens ready for sale. All manner of customers, from well-born women in sedan chairs accompanied by slaves to young men of rank in bigae, their horses on show as much as they themselves, to shopkeepers' wives selecting the meat for prandium, as well as Praetorian Guards, minor politicians, idlers from the baths, the curious, entertainers, speakers of all kinds, a handful of foreigners in outlandish clothing, a sprinkling of criminals and petty gamblers, slaves, and those with business to do added to the noisy confusion. The babble was loud, enhanced by the marble walls of the buildings surrounding the Forum.

Ragoczy Germainus Sanct-Franciscus strolled the edge of the Forum, his double-woven black trabea and high Persian boots in red leather marking him as a foreigner as much as the winged pectoral device he wore on a collar of heavy silver links. His dark, wavy hair was cut fashionably, and his beard was short and meticulously trimmed; he squinted in the occasional bursts of light, all the while trying to keep clear of the milling crowd. "The Swine Market is always—"

"Chaotic? Overflowing?" asked his companion, Septimus Desiderius Vulpius. "I could not agree more." He was in a good mood, enjoying himself and anticipating better to come; his toga virilis was a fashionable terra-cotta color, complementing his red-blond hair and short beard. Around his neck on a braided leather thong he wore a small silver sandal with wings, evoking the help of Mercury in today's endeavors. At twenty-nine, he was the head of his own household, well-married to Filomena Dionesia Crassens, Domina Vulpius, the father of three healthy children, and finally coming into the fortune of his uncle, which had been left to him as his uncle's only heir. In spite of everything, he thought, life was good.

"Dynamic," Sanct-Franciscus amended. "And filled to capacity. Still, it is exciting, and apparently removed from all the other problems that have weighed so heavily upon the city."

"And the Empire; our borders are beleaguered, you mustn't forget," added Vulpius, not willing to let these misfortunes mar his day.

"Yes. The Empire has not had an easy time of it," agreed Sanct-Franciscus, stepping around a group of youngsters engaged in an improvised cockfight; the two combatants were ruffling their feathers and making their first sallies at each other, to the noisy approval of their audience.

Vulpius looked around uneasily. "Caracalla did much damage."

"Yes, he did," said Sanct-Franciscus, thinking that Macrinus might not prove much better at ruling the Roman Empire than Caracalla had been.

"The Senate is divided and has done nothing to help the people," Vulpius declared.

"That is hardly surprising, given the tenor of the times." Sanct-Franciscus glanced around him at the impressive public buildings. "What would you expect the Senate to do?"

"I don't know," Vulpius admitted. "But for most Romans, the choice of Caesar is out of their hands, as it is out of so many."

Glancing at the marketplace again, Vulpius added, "And no matter who is Caesar, people need to eat."

"That they do; and judging by the crowds at the market, they will," said Sanct-Franciscus, and started up the stairs to the massive building where the law courts of the city were currently held, the Basilica Julia, distinguished by its triple colonnade and slightly old-fashioned façade.

"This should not take long; the decuriae have to earn their keep, I suppose," Vulpius said, a touch of nervousness pinching his voice.

"I have the commoda," said Sanct-Franciscus, indicating the wallet that hung from his broad belt of black leather.

Vulpius forced a laugh. "It is the merest formality, you know, for his Will was recorded four years ago without qualifications, while my uncle was still alive to endorse all the terms in it. My father-in-law vouched for it before his death."

"As you say, it is a formality," Sanct-Franciscus said calmly, nodding to the footman who stood by the door of the building to remind all those arriving to cross the threshold with their right feet. The interior was impressive, the lobby rising three stories above them at the back of the long, triple row of columns, galleries on each floor joined by wide staircases. It was as busy a place as the Forum outside, but without the livestock, and it roared like the sea from the echoes of conversations.

Vulpius went inside right foot first, and smiled. "Our success is assured."

"I had never any doubt," said Sanct-Franciscus, looking along the long lobby to the first corridor, noticing that although the people within the Basilica Julia were busy, there were fewer of them than he had expected. "It is the third door on the left, I believe?"

"So I was told," said Vulpius.

"Then 'the sooner begun, the sooner ended,'" Sanct-Franciscus reminded him. "Do you agree?"

"That old aphorism has haunted me most of my life," Vulpius admitted as he tagged after Sanct-Franciscus.

They reached the door and looked for the slave to admit them, but no one was in place to tend to that courtesy. Sanct-Franciscus made a quick scrutiny of the corridor, then shrugged. "Shall we knock?"

"I suppose we'd better," said Vulpius, and reluctantly tapped on the door. He paused and repeated the summons.

The door opened a bit, revealing a dark, wrinkled face and a slave's collar. "Your pardon, Citizen of Roma. I forsook my post." He lowered his head as if for a blow.

"If you will admit us, there is no harm done," said Sanct-Franciscus before Vulpius could speak.

"Certainly, certainly," said the slave, his accent identifying him as a native of Carthago on the north coast of Africa as much as the color of his skin. "Mind your step."

Again Sanct-Franciscus and Vulpius crossed into the room on their right feet, and Vulpius looked around, noticing the low rail that bisected the chamber, with the three writing tables on the far side of the rail. Just at present, no one occupied the tables, and that struck Sanct-Franciscus as odd, and he was about to mention this to Vulpius, when he spoke. "I am expected. Septimus Desiderius Vulpius, heir of Secundus Terentius Vulpius."

"You are expected?" the slave repeated, sounding puzzled; before Vulpius could answer, "You received a notice from this office?" the slave pursued.

"Yes. I have it with me, if you need to see it, along with my copies of the Will and letter of disposition," said Vulpius, his increasing tension making him haughty.

"No, that is hardly necessary. I shall inform Telemachus Batsho that you are here," said the slave. "If you will remain in this room?"

"Certainly," said Vulpius. "I am more than willing to wait."

"No need to be nervous," said Sanct-Franciscus in a lowered voice as the slave left them, going through a small door near the far wall. "This is only a matter of form. The Senate upheld the Will and there is just the matter of recording the transfer of titles. This man Batsho is simply a clerk with an elegant title, and an expectation of commoda for his service."

"I know; I know," said Vulpius, snapping his fingers.

"So you need not fret." Sanct-Franciscus held up his hand.

"Truly," said Vulpius with a transparent lack of conviction.

"You, yourself, Desiderius, have said that all is settled," Sanct-Franciscus reminded him; he decided not to mention the absence of clerks, assuming that the afternoon recess began early in these offices, an increasing practice in the law courts of Roma.

"No doubt," said Vulpius, and shook his head. "Pay no notice to me. I am in a state of anxiety, as you say. I am often thus when dealing with officials, even petty ones like this decuria." He cleared his throat and touched the silver winged sandal talisman. "It will pass as soon as our waiting is ended."

"Very good," said Sanct-Franciscus, and went to the nearest bench where he sat down patiently.

Vulpius began to pace, whistling softly and tunelessly between his teeth. "It was generous of my uncle to provide so well for me."

"You are his heir. It is fitting," said Sanct-Franciscus.

"My father would agree; he was the elder brother, which is why his wealth was seized by Caracalla. Fortunately, my uncle was left the vineyards, and flourished when my father was removed from office and exi— Never mind. I'm babbling, and you've heard this before." Vulpius sighed. "I will have to assume responsibility for my two cousins, of course."

"You knew you would have to," said Sanct-Franciscus, thinking of the many discussions he and Vulpius had had on this point since January, when the Will was upheld.

"I should do my best to find husbands for them, and dower them as my uncle would have wished. I know what my responsibilities are toward them." Vulpius was talking as much to himself as to Sanct-Franciscus. "They will want to marry, don't you think?"

Sanct-Franciscus thought back almost two centuries to the time when women owned property in their own right, requiring no husband, father, brother, or son to control their money and lands. When the first change had come, Sanct-Franciscus had received a flurry of outraged letters from Atta Olivia Clemens, upbraiding the Senate for depriving the women of Roma of their autonomy, and predicting that this would not be the last erosion of women's position in Roman law. "I would suppose your cousins would want to have access to their legacies however it may be accomplished."

Vulpius laughed, the edgy echoes lingering in the room. "Husbands protect their wives and daughters. That is expected. Juliana and Caia deserve the care marriage will make possible." He paced another dozen steps. "A pity my uncle chose to keep them with him for so long."

"How old are they?" Sanct-Franciscus asked.

"Juliana is twenty-three and Caia is twenty; they're pretty enough and not overly clever. Not too old, either, but far from as young as many men prefer their wives to be. They like to live in the country, so I do not have to house them with my family; that might be difficult, given the plans Dionesia has for our children." Vulpius rocked back on his heels, the thongs of his sandals groaning with the strain. "Fortunately, my daughter is still too young for such arrangements, although

Fulvius Eugenius Cnaens has spoken to me of the possible union of Linia to his son Gladius."

"How old is Linia?" Sanct-Franciscus pictured the child in her tunica and palla, hair tangled, running through the Vulpius' house.

"Nine; I have permitted her until eleven to decide for herself," said Vulpius. "The contract cannot be settled for another two years, of course, but—" He broke off as the slave returned.

"Telemachus Batsho will be with you in a moment, and bids me tell you that he will not delay you very long. He is looking for the documents you will need to sign and seal." The slave was apparently impressed with Batsho's importance, for he lowered his head respectfully as he spoke Batsho's name.

Almost without thought, Vulpius fingered the cylinder ring on his index finger. "I am ready."

"Very good," said the slave. "And your companion will serve as witness?"

"I will," said Sanct-Franciscus.

"You are a resident foreigner owning property in Roma?" The slave rattled off the question in a manner that suggested he had asked such things many times before.

"Not within the walls, but three thousand paces beyond them," said Sanct-Franciscus. "I, and those of my blood, have held the land since the days of Divus Julius. Many generations."

"Hardly a god, was Gaius Julius," muttered the slave; then, more loudly, "A goodly time. Two centuries, at least."

"So I have reckoned," said Sanct-Franciscus.

"The new law will not allow you to reside at your estate if it is outside the walls of the city. By the end of summer, you must have a residence within the walls or your lands beyond them will be subject to partial confiscation," said Batsho smugly as he came into the room. He made his gesture of respect in an off-handed way, with no attempt to hide his sizing up of the two men before him.

"A little more than a year ago the Roman state almost took my land because I was living in Egypt and ordered that I reside on my Roman lands for three years out of five in order to keep them,"

Sanct-Franciscus told the decuria. "I have complied with that order, have I not?"

"This is a honing of that provision," Batsho said in a manner that closed the subject.

Vulpius stepped closer to the slave. "Is there a problem? I was informed he is a satisfactory witness."

"That he is, so long as there is record of his property and his family's claim to it." The slave moved back from Vulpius.

Telemachus Batsho had been one of the decuriae for nearly a decade and was growing comfortably rich on the commodae he received for doing his job. He was a very ordinary man, in a very ordinary sage-green pallium, with a soft belt of braided, multi-colored wool, and two leather wallets attached to it, one for food and money, one for the badge of his office. His hair was a bit longer than fashion, of a medium-brown color that almost matched his eyes, and he was clean-shaven. He nodded to Vulpius and Sanct-Franciscus, saying as he did, "I believe you have had notification of these signings? I recall that a notice was dispatched to you? Do you have it with you?"

"That I do," said Vulpius, his chin angled upward. "It is regarding my uncle's Will. I have my copy with me."

"Oh, yes; I remember now. The official transference, without reservation, so long as the taxes are paid, and his daughters provided for," said Telemachus Batsho as if he had a long line of petitioners waiting, all of them unknown to him, all desperate for his services, and all having his four percent commoda to pay for them. "I have the Will among my pigeonholes, if you will permit me to fetch it?" He turned as if to leave, then swung back to look at Sanct-Franciscus with sudden suspicion. "And you are? I need your full name to find the proper records, since it is obvious you are not a relative of Vulpius'."

"Ragoczy Germainus Sanct-Franciscus," he answered promptly. "I have a villa beyond the city, on the northeast, some distance from the Praetorian Camp. My title to the land is of long standing, my taxes are paid, and so is my Foreigner's Fee."

The decuria studied him carefully, his hands resting on the low rail. "You fully own the villa, or have you some other arrangement for your tenancy?"

"I own it and the land around it," said Sanct-Franciscus promptly. "It has been held by those of my blood for several generations, as I have said."

"There are no monies owing on the land, either to the state or private parties?" Batsho asked.

"I own it outright, as did my predecessors."

Batsho nodded. "I see," he said flatly. "Very well. I shall ascertain your status and return with the Will and any other documents requiring signing and sealing. It is not a lengthy process, but it has to be done properly. Tuccu, go bring the sealing wax so we can attend to this."

The slave ducked his head. "At once," he said, and scurried off.

"If you will give me a moment, I will return with the Will and the Writ of Transfer, and your entitlement document." Batsho ducked out of the room, a meaningless smile smeared on his lips.

"Officious," said Vulpius quietly as soon as Batsho was gone.

"He has a high regard for his position," Sanct-Franciscus agreed. "A small man who enjoys using the power he has. He knows full well why we are here, but it pleases him to make us wait." He had encountered the type before, and had grown wary of them.

"I'll be glad when we're done." Vulpius fumbled with the buckle on his belt in order to keep his hands busy. "This is a most aggravating procedure."

"But it is in accord with Roman law," Sanct-Franciscus reminded him.

"I know, and I know it is necessary. Still, I don't like it," said Vulpius.

"It will not last long," Sanct-Franciscus soothed. "Think of the festivities this evening, when you celebrate this moment."

Vulpius opened his mouth, but said nothing as Telemachus Batsho returned, three large scrolls of papyrus tucked under his arm. "Here we are. If you would step around the rail, we will go to the second table. I think the light is best there."

"I will do so," said Vulpius promptly, relieved to have something to do at last. "What shall I sign with?"

"If you will use that ink-cake?" Batsho pointed to the lipped tray on which it was laid. "We have styluses for you to choose." He indicated a container of tarnished brass writing implements. "And Tuccu will prepare the wax for your seal." He nodded toward the slave. "Prepare a lamp, Tuccu, and have the wax ready. The honoratus is not to be kept waiting."

"My father was honoratus," Vulpius pointed out. "I am honestiorus."

"Your pardon, Patronus," said Batsho. "I had assumed the title was also yours for courtesy if not service."

"How could it be?" Vulpius asked. "I have not governed anything beyond a provincial town."

Sanct-Franciscus watched the two with a growing sense of unease; now the lack of other decuriae in the office no longer disconcerted Sanct-Franciscus, for he realized that Batsho was pursuing his own purpose; if a witness were not required for the signatures and seals, Sanct-Franciscus was convinced that Batsho would find some reason to exclude him from this meeting, and the recognition of ulterior motives made him apprehensive.

"Be good enough to ready your seal," said Batsho.

"If this is what you wish," said Vulpius, wanting to get on with it. He removed his cylinder ring.

Batsho spread out one of the scrolls. "Read this—it is your acceptance of the conditions and terms of your uncle's Will."

"I have a copy of it," Vulpius reminded him.

"Of course, of course," said Batsho unctuously. "But it is required that you read the one on file here in my presence."

Vulpius gave a single, jerky nod. "I understand." He started to read.

"This is where you sign and seal. Foreigner, if you would—?" He motioned to Sanct-Franciscus. "Come and read this and then sign and seal below this noble man's signature and seal."

Sanct-Franciscus saw Batsho's eyes narrow as he looked at him, and he had a moment's disquiet as he rose and came around the end of the railing. "Shall I stand by Vulpius, or wait until he has finished, then take the scroll to another table to read and sign?"

"Choose another table, if you would," said Batsho, as close to dismissing Sanct-Franciscus as he dared to venture.

Sanct-Franciscus selected the smaller of the two, and waited to be handed the scroll. The smell of hot wax caught his attention, and he watched as Vulpius rolled his seal through the dollop of wax on the bottom of the sheet.

"There," said Vulpius, and handed the scroll to Batsho. "What next?"

Batsho passed the scroll to Sanct-Franciscus, and said, "Witness this, foreigner."

"I will need wax," Sanct-Franciscus reminded him.

"Tuccu will attend to you," Batsho said, snapping his fingers in the direction of the elderly slave.

"Thank you," said Sanct-Franciscus. "Is there an ink-cake—"

Batsho took the one from Vulpius' writing table and handed it to Sanct-Franciscus. "Use this and give it back. The patronus has need of it."

"May I take a stylus?" Sanct-Franciscus asked.

"Go ahead," said Batsho with a burdened sigh.

"Decuria," said Vulpius in a cautionary tone, "my witness was born the son of a king. It is improper to treat him as one of the humiliora." This admonition was delivered with a faint smile. "He is one of the honestiora, as well you know."

"Son of a *foreign* king, who has had to seek refuge here," said Batsho, settling the matter with a mendacious smile. "His records say he is an exile."

"Do you suppose you could show me which scroll I am to sign next?" Vulpius offered Sanct-Franciscus a slight shrug behind Batsho's back.

"Of course, Patronus." His obsequiousness was so obvious that Vulpius had to choke back a laugh.

"This is the accounting of your uncle's fortune, a compilation of his lands and other holdings, and the makeup of his households. Please review the addition before you sign, and put your seal at the

total, to show you acknowledge the amounts as the basis of taxes."
Batsho had moved so that his shoulder was between Vulpius and
Sanct-Franciscus.

"And your commoda," said Vulpius. "Four percent—for every signature."

"That is the custom," said Batsho, working to suppress a smile.

"I am prepared, assuming your amounts coincide with my own
records," said Vulpius, another implied warning in his comment.

"And why should they not?" Batsho asked, then went silent as
Vulpius held up his hand while he reviewed the various figures on
the page. "Is all in order?"

"All but this," said Vulpius, pointing to the number of slaves
listed for the Bononia estate. "There are three more slaves than listed
here—two are coopers and one is a vine-man. I have acquired them
since this Will was filed with you." His edginess was growing worse.

"Three more, and all with skills," said Batsho, making a note on
his records.

"The transaction took place ten days ago. I can tell you what I
paid: nine aurei and four denarii for each of the coopers and eight
for the vine-man."

"A goodly sum, even for skilled workers," said Batsho. "I have
made a correction, you will sign next to it, as well as at the foot of
the scroll, and when you have the transfer in hand, you will provide
me with an authenticated copy within a week, or face penalties for
such failure. I believe you would like to avoid the penalties." He
nodded once, as if concurring with himself.

"I agree," said Vulpius. "Sanct-Franciscus will testify to it." He
signed where he was supposed to, and fixed his seal where Batsho
pointed. "Another one for you, Sanct-Franciscus," he said, holding
out the sheet.

"Should I sign and seal at the bottom only?" Sanct-Franciscus
asked Batsho.

"Of course. Unless you think the addition is incorrect." He
waited, an avaricious light shining at the back of his eyes.

"I am certain Vulpius calculated the sums accurately," said Sanct-
Franciscus, being deliberately more formal.

"Then sign under his final signature, and set your seal under his." Batsho was already opening the third scroll. "This is your verification to the Senate of your family and its position, as well as your position within it, so that your status as your uncle's heir cannot be later disputed. It sets out the validation of your claim and your heritage. Any misrepresentation is punishable as fraud."

"Should I review it?" Vulpius asked.

"If you would. If you have anything to add, append it to the foot of the page; remember each alteration has its own commoda; the law provides for it." Batsho rounded on Sanct-Franciscus. "Foreigner: is there any record of your family on file in this office?"

Sanct-Franciscus would not be goaded to a hasty reply. "If you mean in this immediate office, I cannot say, for I am not privy to the methods of you decuriae."

"You mock me," Batsho said darkly, watching Sanct-Franciscus with an expression of distaste.

"No; I proclaim my ignorance," said Sanct-Franciscus.

"Do not make light of us," Batsho said critically. "The courts depend upon our labors."

"Of that I have no doubt," said Sanct-Franciscus, aware from his manner that Batsho had taken him in dislike. "There are records of my blood's titles and lands going back more than two centuries, and I assume they are somewhere in this building," he said as he held out the second page with his signature and seal drying on it.

Batsho took the scroll and glared at it. "I will have to look into what you've said," he vowed, his muted-brown eyes seething.

"Can't we get on with this?" Vulpius complained.

Batsho turned back to Vulpius, all accommodating and exuding spurious good-will; when he handed the last scroll to Sanct-Franciscus, he glowered for an instant, then lost all expression as Sanct-Franciscus reached for the sealing-wax and lamp. "Yes, foreign exile, I will look into you."

Text of a report from Rugeri in Alexandria to Ragoczy Germainus Sanct-Franciscus at Roma, written in Greek, and carried by the merchant ship *Minerva*; delivered twenty-four days after it was written.

My master,

    You have no doubt heard that the Emperor's campaign is not doing well. Everywhere the streets are full of rumors, that Roma will fall, that Caesar is doomed, that the times are evil. We have heard such things in the past, but in this instance, I am fairly certain that there is some basis in fact for all the tattling making the rounds. I should add that Hebseret, the present High Priest of Imhotep, concurs. and not for any reason of omens or alignment of stars, but because of the diminished Roman garrison farther up the Nile, whose Legionaries have been called into Mesopotamia. Hebseret has only just been elevated by his fellows, replacing Mateheb, who died a month after your departure, to his position, and is being especially careful to guard his remaining followers from any harm or discovery. Priests of Imhotep are not much valued by the Romans—you know their distrust of Egyptians—but the Romans are not the most pressing problem they face: there are groups of Christians in this region who are becoming most zealous, and they dislike the old Roman gods as well as the older Egyptian ones.

    As you have requested, I have donated fifty aurei to the priesthood to enable them to continue their duties of treating the sick and injured. They have had to reduce their services due to lack of funds, and your gift will restore their temple once again. Hebseret has expressed his gratitude repeatedly, and I am charged with reporting such to you; he has made one journey downriver to Alexandria for the purpose of acquiring certain herbs in the market that are difficult to grow in their temple, nine thousand paces beyond Luxor.

    Trade continues brisk, and I anticipate that the Fair Wind *and the* Polaris *will soon arrive at Ostia with ample cargo as well as valuable information. They say all the signs are good for an abundant wheat harvest later in the year, so you may want to assign another ship to the Ostia-Alexandria-Ostia route come August, for we should be able to fill all holds with grain, and I will by then have the latest shipment of Syrian wine to send along. I have been informed that their harvest this year is ample, so in two years there should be many more amphorae of wine to import.*

I have acquired a new slave to deal with the records at dockside, for I am not satisfied with the accuracy of the customs agents, and rather than bribe four officials to be precise in their records, I will provide my own tally-maker. The slave is an eastern Greek from Antioch, well-versed in the skills required to do the work properly. His name is Perseus, he is twenty-three, or so he claims, and he is able to read Greek, Roman, Egyptian, and Syrian. He was formerly slave to a Byzantine merchant who lost four ships and their cargo to pirates and who, therefore, had to reduce his household. He seems able enough, and not so eager that I suspect his motives for coming to me. I have given him quarters in the second house, with two chambers for his use, and access to our shipping records.

The local decuriae have started to demand five percent instead of four for their services. Since the livelihoods of the decuriae was taken from the hands of the honestiora and put in the hands of the decuriae themselves, it is folly to assume that the decuriae will not do their utmost to ensure their position in the world. If it is happening here in Alexandria, it is likely to happen in Roma, and sooner rather than later, for I do not suppose the Senate is willing to resume the cost of keeping the decuriae at their various posts, and the courts cannot work without them.

When you write to Domina Clemens—as I assume you must do shortly—if you will, include my good wishes to her. I think it is wise that she remain away from Roma, at least until the scramble for the purple is over, and she could return without the risk of being drawn into one faction or another. If you decide to occupy her house near the Temple of Hercules, send me word. I believe it would be a wise move, not only for you, since the house is in good repair and staffed, but it would benefit Olivia as well, for it could not then be taken from her on the excuse that she has no male relatives to manage it for her. I would suppose she would be pleased to have you there, but you know what is apt to be the best disposal of your time and money in that city just now, and so you will weigh my remarks against your own observations, for they have brought you across the centuries, and should continue to do so.

Rugeri

on the 29th day of March, in the 971st Year of the City of Roma, by my own hand

2

Egidia Adicia Cortelle, Domina Laelius, was having one of her bad days: she was weak and listless, had poor control of her limbs, and she choked when she tried to swallow, all of which contributed to her resentful mood. She kept to her bed, refusing to have slaves around her, wanting only the attentions of her daughter, Pax Ignatia Laelius, whom she upbraided for every perceived fault.

"It's this horrible rain," Adicia carped. "If it weren't raining, I would improve."

Ignatia brought another pillow and put it behind her mother's shoulder. "That should make you more comfortable."

"It's lumpy," Adicia accused. "Isn't there anything softer?"

"You have four pillows to support you, Mother. Would you like me to fetch mine?"

Adicia flapped one hand, attempting to adjust the offending pillow. "No. You needn't do that."

"Mirza says the signs are for a clearing in a day or so," said Ignatia as she smoothed the covers.

"Slaves always think they know such things," Adicia muttered. "Rain in April. Who would expect such a storm in spring?"

"There is usually a late storm every spring. This one is just a little more intense than most," said Ignatia in as calm a voice as she could summon. "When the skies clear, you will be stronger."

"You would like that, wouldn't you? Then you could go about on your own, and not have to spend all day with me."

"I would like to see sunshine, and I would like you to feel better, but not for my own delight." She spoke flatly, hoping to avoid another argument.

"Why do you deny that you long for amusement?" Adicia persisted.

"I do not deny it," said Ignatia, holding on to her temper.

"If it weren't for me, you would be married by now, and tending to your own household and family. And I would be married, too, to a man who would treat me well."

"No doubt, dear Mother," said Ignatia, keeping her voice as neutral as she could, and putting a warm, damp cloth on Adicia's forehead.

"Don't bother me with such useless things," Adicia said as she took the cloth and flung it across the room. "Send for Sanct-Franciscus. He knows what to do. He cares for me, you know."

"If you are sure you want him," said Ignatia. "The last time you sent for him, you savaged him mercilessly."

"Last time I was in greater pain than I am now," said Adicia firmly. "I want him to bring me his medicaments."

Ignatia at twenty-four would have been attractive if she were not so harried; she had pretty blue-green eyes and a heart-shaped face framed by dark-blonde hair which she wore in a simple knot at her nape. In an unornamented palla of cherry and a stola of soft plum over it she could have been appealing, but only looked washed-out; she caught her lower lip in her teeth and thought before speaking. "Do you want me to go, or shall I send Octavian or Chemba?"

"You had better go, not a slave, and certainly not your brother," said Adicia at her most peevish. "Chemba may know every street in Roma, but he knows nothing about medicaments, and I have no notion of what Octavian would say to Sanct-Franciscus, if he would do as I require at all. Since he started meeting with the Christians, he has been unreliable. I'm surprised he's in the house today, rain or no rain."

"He's fourteen," Ignatia said in her brother's defense. "You can't expect him to understand your situation."

"Why not? You did. As soon as I fell ill, you cared for me, and there was no nonsense about it," said Adicia, this instance of rare praise taking her daughter by surprise.

"There was no one else to do it but your slaves," she said.

"Which is as good as saying there was no one to help me, not who could be trusted." Adicia fixed Ignatia with a hard stare. "At least you did not consent to be married to the first man who showed interest in you, as your sister did. Myrtale leaped at Quillius—it was embarrassing."

"She has been very happy with him. You've read her letters. She has so much to tell us about Naissus and Moesia: what interesting places she has seen!" Ignatia enthused, hoping to turn the conversation.

"She flaunts her happiness, and never comes to Roma." Adicia sighed. "If only your father had not been killed, or that I had died in his stead." This was an habitual lament with her, and she began to weep. "It may have been considered an accident, but I know his enemies were in the crowd and used the riot to cover his murder. But no one listens to me—no one!"

"Mother," Ignatia warned, bending over to wipe her face. "You must not do this. You'll make yourself worse."

"If it would end my suffering, why shouldn't I?" Adicia exclaimed. "There is no justice in this world. None at all."

"Then resign yourself to it," said Ignatia, renunciation in every aspect of her demeanor. "It is all that is left to do."

"You say that easily enough." Adicia's petulance made her face sag.

"Easily enough," Ignatia repeated. "Because I know whereof I speak." She reached for the jug of water and filled a cup with it. "You need to drink this."

"No," said Adicia with stubborn determination. "If I drink now, I will have to use the latrine before you return, and that would mean summoning Benona or another of the slaves to assist me. No. I will wait for you to come back."

It took all Ignatia's patience not to offer a sharp rejoinder, but she managed to say only, "You must do as you think best," before she left the room and went to get her long, oiled-wool paenula to protect her against the weather. As she started across the atrium, the rain struck her face and she dabbed at it with the sleeve of her stola. "Starus! Starus!" she called out as she reached the entrance to the house. "Ready the biga. I must go out of the city."

Starus, the steward of the house, had been a slave of the Laelius family all his life, and so he enjoyed a greater freedom than many of his fellows. "Going to get that foreign physician again, are you?"

"Yes. I'll want Philius to drive me. On a day like this, he must be in the stable, not out in the paddocks." She knew Starus wondered why she preferred the head groom to the household driver, and so explained, "Philius is a better driver than Mordeus in bad weather; he pays more attention to the horses." Ignatia smiled fleetingly at Starus. "Domina Laelius needs some relief from her suffering, and Sanct-Franciscus is the only one who can provide it, or so it seems."

Starus mumbled something about foreign concoctions as he went off toward the small stable immediately behind the house, leaving Ignatia to pace and listen to the rain.

"Going somewhere, dear sister?" The voice came out of the shadows, startling Ignatia. He pointedly ignored the display of lares; since he had become a Christian, he had little patience for household and ancestral gods.

"Octavian!" She made his name a reprimand. "I thought you were out."

Octavian was a decade younger than Ignatia; he had just reached the gangly stage of growth, all arms and legs with knobby joints, hands and feet disproportionately large. As if in accord with the rest of him, his light-brown hair was an unruly thatch, and he had the first tentative wisps of a moustache on his upper lip. He wore a heavy dark-blue woolen dalmatica over striped femoralia which were supposed to show his legs to advantage but did not, and topped it all with a dull-red tunica; a small gold fish hung from a leather thong around his neck. "I'm leaving shortly," he announced.

"Do you know when you'll be back?" Ignatia asked, certain it was useless.

"Late. Before midnight, probably." He cocked his head in the direction of Adicia's room. "Is she any better?"

"No. That's why I'm going to ask Sanct-Franciscus to treat her."

"Do you trust him—a foreigner, and one who had only our uncle to recommend him?"

"Our mother trusts him; that's all that matters," said Ignatia brusquely.

Octavian let out a bark of laughter. "She likes that foreigner; it's her flesh that she wants treated. She lies in bed, mourning our father, and wishes for someone to end her grief but cannot bring herself to find another husband, and summons the foreign physician instead."

Ignatia felt her cheeks burn. "You may think what you like, Octavian, but you will not show such disrespect inside this house." She pointed to the plaque of low-relief carvings of the family's illustrious ancestors and household gods.

"Respect? For what?" said Octavian. "There is God, the God of Christ, and no other. Nothing else deserves respect."

"Do not say so. Not here, and not—"

"Oh, stop." Octavian stepped back. "It isn't worth arguing about."

"Octavian . . . ," Ignatia began, but heard the sound of his sandals as he left her alone again. She resumed pacing, glancing at the lares occasionally, as if seeking reassurance from them. By the time Starus returned, she was calmer, and was able to say to the slave, "Have one of the women sit with my mother while I'm gone. Just see she is properly covered and fetch anything she wants except food—she is unable to swallow without great effort."

"I will send Tallia to her," Starus said. "She likes Tallia."

"Tallia will have to be gentle with her; remind her of that." Tallia baked bread every day and scrubbed the entry, chores that made her stronger than many men.

"I will," said Starus, and added, "The biga will be here shortly. Philius had Niger and Neva ready to yoke to the biga as I left the stable."

"Good. Philius can be lazy when the weather is dreary." Ignatia went to look out through the peephole in the shutters. "It hasn't let up."

"No, Doma, it hasn't." He looked directly at Ignatia. "You look tired."

"I am," she said. "Never mind. I'll retire early with a jug of hot wine. Come dawn, I'll be myself again."

"If Domina Laelius hasn't improved, you won't be able to do that," Starus warned.

"Sanct-Franciscus should do her good. He has in the past. She believes he will help her now." Ignatia swung around as the rattle of approaching hooves and wheels reached her. "Philius is here."

"Keep as warm and dry as you can," Starus recommended as he went to open the front door for her. "Do not slip in the mud. Right foot."

Ignatia crossed the threshold on her right foot and stood in the octostyle porticus waiting for Philius to come up from the stable gate, along the alley between the Laelius house and the one beyond. The location was a good one, on the north-facing slope of the Es-quilinus Hill, but in the rain it seemed dreary and unsatisfactory. She huddled into her paenula, tugging the hood as far over her head as she could, shading her eyes and concealing most of her features. She bit back a yawn just as the biga with its black and white pair turned toward her.

Philius drew rein right in front of her. He, too, was cloaked against the wet, but his Gaulish saie was of thicker, less tightly woven goat-hair cloth, and the hood was narrower than the one on her paenula. "Ready, Doma. You want to go out to Villa Ragoczy again, I'm told."

"Yes," said Ignatia as she stepped up into the biga and took hold of the handrail at the top of the high side panel.

"I'll go along the Via Thermae and out through the Porta Nova, then north on the Via Cingula, if you don't mind. The Porta Vimi-nalis is always very crowded and the streets aren't as muddy approaching the Porta Nova."

"You know what is the best route to go, and so long as we don't lose much time that way. . . ." She shrugged and did her best not to shiver as Philius put the biga in motion. In spite of the rain the streets were busy, and Philius held the pair of horses to a strict walk as they threaded their way toward the Porta Nova on the east-northeastern side of the city. They passed three small fora, one devoted to selling flowers; it was filled with new blossoms and a variety of bulbs that were brilliant with color and greenery. "Perhaps, on our return, we should stop to get hyacinths for my mother."

"Tell me on the return, Doma, and if you still wish to." He checked Niger as a donkey being led across the road balked and brayed; Neva had already stopped.

"You do this so well," Ignatia said.

"I know the horses. Neva is careful and cautious—Niger is more impulsive. For the others, Pimpona is affable, especially now that she is in foal, Raechus is eager—too eager, Farfalia is abrupt, Merius is grumpy because he is getting old, Boranda is no-nonsense, Crispus is always seeking treats, especially when none are deserved, and Statlio is determined to please, a typical gelding, as obliging as a hound." He paused, having mentioned all the household horses. "Iola, the jenny-mule? is devious and clever, as mules often are."

"Do you think we should acquire other horses? If Merius is not up to the work, should he be retired and another horse bought in his place? He could be sent to the estate at Nepete—what do you think?" Ignatia asked, tugging on the edge of her hood to keep it from flying back off her head in the freshening wind.

Philius cleared his throat, keeping his attention on the road ahead. "I would retire Merius, if he were my horse, and replace him with a younger gelding. I would purchase a second mule. I'd also buy a riding horse for Octavian of less mettle than Raechus. No matter what he thinks, your brother does not handle high-couraged horses well. A less spirited animal would suit far better than Raechus, who would thrive at Nepete, standing at stud there; his blood-line is excellent, and his confirmation is superior." Now that he had said this, Philius ducked his head. "Your pardon, Doma, but you asked."

"And I am glad to hear what you have to say," said Ignatia, wondering how she would persuade her uncle, Nymphidius Tiberius Laelius, to hand over enough money to accomplish these things. "I will not punish you for saying what you believe to be best for the horses."

"Thank you." He pulled the pair in as they reached the line at the Porta Nova.

A Praetorian centurion in full brass lorica and helmet with a broad, dyed horsehair fan atop it, was stopping every person departing the city, asking names and destinations, and occasionally ordering his scribe to make notes.

"I am Pax Ignatia Laelius, I live in the Via Decius Claudii on the Esquilinus Hill," she said when it came her turn to speak. "This is my slave Philius. We are bound for Villa Ragoczy, beyond your camp."

"The foreigner's estate; the one with the fine gate and fences. I know it," said the centurion. "Why do you seek him?"

"To summon him to treat my mother, who is an invalid," said Ignatia. "There is some urgency."

"Be sure you return through this gate, and if you delay very long, I must have the scribe make note of it," said the centurion.

"Of course," said Ignatia, and nodded to Philius. "Drive on."

The road beyond the walls was also busy, but not as much as the city streets had been; bigae and chairs carried merchants to and from the broad field where their large carpenti were left for the day, and sellers of fruits, meats, and flesh held the sides of the road, crying their wares. Philius avoided the greatest crush, and turned on the Via Cingula, then whistled his pair up to a trot and held the gait for the next thousand paces. They soon reached the Via Prenestina, and headed northeast past the Praetorian Camp. The wind picked up and the rain fell harder.

"The road to Villa Ragoczy is not far ahead. There is a stout wooden gate at the entrance," said Ignatia.

"I remember," said Philius. "I will find the place."

"Excellent," Ignatia approved shakily. She was so cold that her teeth had started to chatter and she was shivering, both of which mortified her: to show such weakness in front of a slave! She would not know what to say to her mother if Philius should speak of it among the rest of the household. Gathering her paenula more tightly around her, she pulled the hood even farther forward and did her best to keep her teeth clamped.

"This is the turn, I am certain," said Philius, slowing the pair to a walk and preparing to leave the well-paved road for a graveled one. "Best hang on with both hands, Doma."

"That I will," she said, doing her best to keep from being thrown off-balance as the biga jounced onto the loose river stones that paved the road leading to the entrance to Villa Ragoczy. She noticed that the stones had been tended recently, and this calmed her a bit, for it made the chance of an accident less than it would have been on an ill-kept road.

"The stables here once housed over a hundred horses, or so I was told when we came here in November," said Philius. "Now there are only forty or so."

"Many breeders have reduced the size of their stables," said Ignatia as if she had to convince herself of this accepted fact.

"Do you suppose the taxes are the reason?" Philius asked. "Your uncle reduced his herd because of taxes."

"I have no idea. I am not in Sanct-Franciscus' confidence," said Ignatia stiffly; her paenula was flapping open, so she took hold of it with one hand and resigned herself to having to struggle to stand.

At the gate Philius drew up, securing the reins around the brake-handle before he stepped down to approach the gate. "I will summon the warder," he said.

"Very good," Ignatia said automatically.

"You there!" came the shout from beyond the gate. "State your name and purpose here."

"I am Philius, the slave of the Laelius household. I bring my mistress, Doma Ignatia, daughter of Domina Laelius, to speak with the foreigner Sanct-Franciscus." His voice carried well against the wind.

"You are welcome," the warder announced, and drew back the heavy wooden bolt that secured the gate. "Enter, and take your biga around to the west side of the main house. One of the household will meet you there to guide you in the villa."

"Thank you," said Ignatia; a moment later Philius climbed back into the biga and took the reins again, kissing to the horses as the gate swung open.

The grounds of the villa were well-tended and prosperous-looking; the orchards just beyond the garden were coming into bloom, and the scent of apple blossoms was strong in spite of the rain.

The approach to the main house was cobbled with bricks, and had recently been raked free of debris. Only the roofs of the stables could be seen beyond the house, and they were in good repair. A groom in a hooded leather cloak was jogging toward the biga, calling out, "Draw in. I'll take them."

Philius did as he was told. "Very prompt," he said approvingly as he stopped the horses and released the reins to the groom. "If you would have their hooves picked clean as well as giving them water?"

The groom nodded as he went to the pair's heads. "Certainly."

Ignatia got out of the biga, and without waiting for one of the household slaves to offer her the protection of a rain-shield, went up the steps to the larger section of the villa, which, unlike most Roman homes, boasted two atria and two distinct sections of the building. A footman met her as she crossed the threshold. "I am here to see Sanct-Franciscus. Where may I find him?"

The footman—a young man from eastern provinces by the look of him—ducked his head, saying, "If you will follow me?"

"Of course," said Ignatia, knowing Philius would go to the stables with the biga and horses and would not accompany her.

They went down the side of the larger atrium, then through a corridor and along a peristyle on the exterior of the rear of the rambling house. At last they reached a double door located roughly at the meeting of the two sections of the house; the footman tapped on it, and waited.

Sanct-Franciscus was wearing a simple, black woolen dalmatica, deep-red femoralia, and heeled Scythian boots. He gestured welcome to Ignatia, saying, "I am surprised and happy to receive you, Ignatia Laelius. Please come into my study. Girav, if you would bring a jug of hot wine with honey? And some butter-cakes? Tell Aedius it is for my guest." He stood aside so that Ignatia could enter the room; the chamber was sizeable with windows in three walls. Most of the room was behind a segmented screen that was decorated with intricate carvings of the loves of Jupiter, with Semele dominating the center panel. There were also shelves with bound parchment sheets stored on them and a stand of pigeonholes filled with rolled scrolls.

Three painted panels from Egypt hung high on the walls, with illustrations and hieroglyphics covering them; Ignatia had seen Egyptian art before, but nothing like these panels, in which a jackal-headed figure stood with an ibis-headed one, and a wrapped mummy was rising from the ground between them, a small bird flying away from the mummy's head toward a disk with many long, golden arms. She looked around at Sanct-Franciscus. "That is most unusual. Do you know what it says?" she asked, caught by the striking images.

"Yes," he replied. "And I will tell you one day, but not now, when you have such urgent business with me." He glanced at the footman. "My guest is hungry and thirsty."

The footman hurried away after he closed the door.

"I offer my apologies for interrupting your work," she said a bit hesitantly.

"You have no reason to apologize," said Sanct-Franciscus.

"No? I would have thought you were busy, but— Your villa is wonderfully warm," said Ignatia as she let her paenula fall open.

"The holocaust has been cleaned of all ash, and the floor tiles have been taken up so that the channels could be scrubbed," said Sanct-Franciscus, who was punctilious in such matters, although cold and heat had little effect upon him. "If you want to put your paenula aside, I have a lacerna you can wear until you are warmer."

She looked at him as she threw back her hood, a touch of suspicion in her blue-green eyes. Guardedly she said, "I would like that."

"The sleeves are a little long for you: turn them back if you like," he said as he went behind the sectioned screen, to return at once with a splendid lacerna in dark-red silk. "Here, Ignatia Laelius. Let me take your paenula. I will hang it over the back of that chair"—he pointed to the one in front of the stand of pigeonholes—"until you are ready to depart."

Feeling strangely daring, she turned so that he could remove the paenula and replace it with the soft, warm, enveloping lacerna. "This is very nice, Sanct-Franciscus."

"You say that like a well-schooled child," Sanct-Franciscus said, a trace of friendly amusement in his face.

"I was taught carefully," said Ignatia, her cheeks turning rosy for no reason she could account for.

"And you are a credit to your teacher, and to your gens." As she fumbled for something to say in return, he changed his tone. "Now that you have observed the niceties, perhaps you will tell me why you have come on such a wretched day as this?"

She was somewhat taken aback by the abruptness of his question. "It *is* a wretched day, to be sure, and I realize I am intruding, but I assure you it is important, or I would not have come."

"So I assumed," said Sanct-Franciscus. "This is not a capricious call."

"No," she said. "Alas, it is not." She pulled at the sleeve of the lacerna. "I fear my mother is doing poorly, and has sent me to ask you to—"

"To provide her with such relief as I am able to," he finished for her. "I will, of course." He drew up a deeply upholstered hassock for her. "Sit. This is the most comfortable of any furniture in the room."

She regarded him dubiously, but sank obediently down onto it, and discovered it was both soft and supporting. "It is quite . . . pleasant."

"Good." He offered her a one-sided smile. "Now, if you will tell me what it is your mother requires, other than a return to health, which I fear no physician can give her?" The kindness in his eyes took the sting from his words.

Dutifully, Ignatia began her report. "Her head aches. She is suffering from weakness, lassitude; she cannot stand alone, or so she says, and so has remained in her bed. Her appetite is failing, because she claims it is hurtful to eat. She has had difficulty swallowing."

"Does she have a fever?" Sanct-Franciscus asked.

"Not that I can detect—she complained of being cold this morning, and her face appeared . . . slack." Ignatia joined her hands together. "I worry that she will not be able to eat, and will finally starve." She lowered her eyes and tried not to sneeze.

"You have reason for such concerns," said Sanct-Franciscus. "Can you tell me if she is in pain?"

"She says so." She looked up, daring to meet his eyes with hers.

"The tincture of willow-and-pansy you provided is nearly gone, but it seems to alleviate the worst of her hurt."

"Then I shall bring more with me. Pain, at least, I can alleviate." He went behind the beautiful segmented screen and came back with a small case in his hands. His dark eyes were compassionate, and he spoke soothingly. "You need not fear that your mother is dying: that will not happen for some time unless she succumbs to a putrescence that is not presently troubling her. But she has a malady that has no cure, and it is deep in her bones."

Ignatia sighed. "I can't help but worry. She grows worse, you know, and nothing has arrested the degeneration." As she said this, she felt she had betrayed her mother, and she turned away from Sanct-Franciscus. "If you say you can do nothing."

"Unfortunately, no one can heal her." He was spared the necessity of saying anything more to Ignatia as Girav rapped on the door. Opening it, Sanct-Franciscus took the tray from him, saying, "If you would, go to the stable and have Mora and Axion yoked to my new biga. And tell Raens to have my oiled-wool paenula ready—the black one with the dark-red border. Thank you." He stepped back to allow the slave to close the door, then took the tray with its jug of hot, honied wine and plate piled with butter-cakes to Ignatia.

She looked up. "How good of you," she said softly.

"Only courteous," said Sanct-Franciscus. "Now, while you recruit yourself, I will go prepare you another few vials of willow-and-pansy." With that, he went around the screen again, leaving her to pour the wine into the cup provided, and to eat a few of the butter-cakes while he completed his preparations for treating her mother.

Text of a letter from Senator Marcus Laurentius Gaius Fulvius Cneo to Telemachus Batsho; delivered by personal courier.

To the decuria Telemachus Batsho, Marcus Laurentius Gaius Fulvius Cneo, Senator of Roma, sends his greetings and his recommendation that the petition of Ragoczy Germainus Sanct-Franciscus to occupy the house of the widow Atta Olivia Clemens near the Temple of Hercules be granted acceptance without delay. Since the law now requires such foreigners as Sanct-Franciscus to live within the city walls, it is presumptive folly to prevent anyone from complying with the law. I expect this to be carried out at once, with your customary efficiency.

You have the Writ of Permission for Occupancy from the Widow Clemens, and you have the residence-transfer tax paid by Sanct-Franciscus himself, and so there is no pressing reason that his move should be delayed, and every reason for it to be expedited. Let me remind you that Sanct-Franciscus has no blood ties to any of the various barbarians raiding our borders, and no position in any other government that might compromise his dealings here. Even his dealings in Egypt are those of trade, not politics, and his alliances are strictly commercial. No one has accused him of acting against Roman interests, and since he is an exile, he has no reason to seek Roman support for his own aims.

There have been no complaints filed to Sanct-Franciscus' detriment, and for that reason alone it would seem that a speedy response in his favor is in order. If you have any doubts about his standing in the merchant community, I recommend you contact those with whom he has done business, for I suspect they will echo the good opinion he has gained among the honestiora.

It will please me and many of my fellow Senators to see this impasse at an end; I look forward to learning that all barriers to this move have been eradicated, and toward that resolution, I send you six aurei for your trouble; another six will follow when I have confirmation that this matter has been resolved to my satisfaction.

Marcus Laurentius Gaius Cneo
Senator of Roma

by the hand of the scribe Onfonius Portalio on this, the 13th day of May in the 971st Year of the City

3

Five large carts stood in the expansive courtyard of the house of Atta Olivia Clemens behind the Temple of Hercules; they were laden with crates, chests, caskets, cases, furniture, and other household goods, all flagged with tax chits and marked *paid*. The day was becoming too warm for strenuous work; even the teams of sturdy ponies pulling the carts were beginning to droop in their yokes in spite of the bucket of water provided for each of them.

Sanct-Franciscus swung down from his blue roan, calling out, "Dalio, come take my horse. Now, the rest of you: each of you carry one item into the house, then have something to eat. Then you may have your midday rest." It was times like these that he wished Rugeri were with him instead of running the Alexandrian division of his shipping business; Rugeri always made such shifts of residence as this one less of an ordeal for everyone concerned.

Holmdi, who was in charge of loading and unloading the carts, went and stood near the largest of them. "The chests here will need two men apiece, at least."

"They also need not be carried into the house at once; they can be stacked here in the courtyard and taken in later," said Sanct-Franciscus. "It is better to get the household goods first, and the chests and crates and all the rest second. Remember, I want the carts to go back to Villa Ragoczy one more time so that they may be packed tonight and carried here early tomorrow morning. Aedius," he went on to his steward, "make sure everything unloaded is inventoried. I have to present a catalogue of goods and possessions to the decuriae to compare with the officers of the Guard's records."

Aedius, who was a rangy man in his mid-thirties, ducked his head. "Yes, Dominus." It was an appropriate compromise title, one most of the slaves were willing to use.

"Be scrupulous in your accounts," Sanct-Franciscus emphasized. "The decuriae are painstaking in verifying details, and they delight in finding errors."

"Even if they have to invent them, or supply their own new taxes on the spot," said Aedius, no emotion coloring his observation.

"It is their responsibility to see the Empire is not left destitute," Sanct-Franciscus pointed out, a slight hint of irony in his voice.

"And the Empire begins with themselves," said Aedius, and looked around in sudden apprehension.

"Certainly," said Sanct-Franciscus, only his mouth smiling. "They are willing to do all they can for Roma."

"For four percent of value, I would, as well," said Aedius with a hard, single nod. "They have made their position their fortune."

Two slaves carrying chairs very nearly collided; they exchanged mild curses and continued on with their work.

"Not surprising," said Sanct-Franciscus, "since the Senate no longer provides their pay. How else are they to live?"

"Do you think they should be paid by the Senate?" Aedius asked as he watched the slaves begin their unloading.

"I think that it was a false economy, making their pay dependent upon collecting percentages from those they are supposed to assist; it opens the floodgates for corruption," said Sanct-Franciscus, and turned to the grooms. "You know where the stables are. See these ponies are watered, fed, and brushed before you nap. They deserve rest just as you do."

Three of the grooms called out, "Yes, Dominus," as they went to unyoke the tough little equines.

"Remember to list all tack and harness," Sanct-Franciscus reminded Aedius. "They are part of my holdings."

"I will," the steward said, holding up his wax tablet and stylus. "I will be as careful as you wish."

"Yes," said Sanct-Franciscus genially. "You will."

Aedius shrugged. "I could be lax on your behalf."

"I am sure you could," said Sanct-Franciscus. "And if such laxness were discovered, it would cost me double its assessment, at least. Hardly worth the risk entailed, would you think?" He cocked his head toward the house. "Go along and eat. We can attend to this later."

"And the woman? What of her?" Aedius asked. "From the lupanar?"

"Arrangements have been made," said Sanct-Franciscus obliquely. "It is my concern; do not trouble yourself about her."

"If you say so," Aedius responded, and went along for his midday meal.

Prandium was laid out in the atrium on long plank tables; there were fruits from the south, three kinds of bread, a fish stew filled with onions and green vegetables, and long slabs of pork-ribs cooked in peppers, garlic, and honey. A vat of pickled artichokes and peppers was placed precariously near the edge of the front plank. Two large barrels of Egyptian beer stood at either end of the table, and rough cups were provided. This was generous fare for slaves, and they all knew it as they fell to, nearly gorging themselves on this bounty. By the time the meal was finished, the table was a ruin of empty platters, smears of many kinds, and discarded bones.

"You fed all slaves well," said Olivia's old steward, Vitellius, the son of a condemned criminal and who was named for an Emperor. He had found himself in the odd position of having to share his position with Aedius, an arrangement about which neither man was entirely comfortable. The afternoon nap had ended and activities were starting up again in the rambling house. He had just come from the atrium and had started Olivia's slaves clearing up the disorder left over from the prandium. "Do you make a habit of it?"

"I give occasional generous meals like this, and for the most part, yes, I see that all my household has good food in sufficient amount," said Sanct-Franciscus. "I will do the same for you of Domina Clemens' household while I am here."

"You wish to make a display of your wealth?" Vitellius asked.

"Wealth and display are not my goals here: I wish to have willing servants around me, and that means providing food and shelter for them. I have learned that a man who is half-starved is a poor servant, as is one who cannot sleep well, so you will find all my slaves have double-thick straw-filled pallets for their beds. Domina Clemens will not object to that, or any other provision I wish to make regarding her slaves; she has said so in her authorization to me. This way, the slaves know they are valued, by me and by Domina Clemens, and they will live up to that value—or most will—and that is the most that I or anyone can expect of others, slave or free." Sanct-Franciscus studied Vitellius, conjecture arching his brows and lending a sardonic air to his demeanor. "I would have thought that was Domina Clemens' way, as well, to supply her slaves with good food and housing." His long association with Olivia had made him familiar with her standard of care for all her household; her absence should not have altered that.

Two slaves with a large chest held between them made their way past Sanct-Franciscus and Vitellius; one of them was breathing hard, the other less so, although he was sweating.

"She is a woman, and a Roman of the old school, one who honors all the slave laws of Augustus and Traianus; it does her much credit," said Vitellius with quiet pride. "In the many years I have been with her, I have not known her to discipline anyone unnecessarily, or to deny any reasonable care."

Sanct-Franciscus achieved a slight smile. "All to her credit."

"And you seek to emulate her?" Vitellius asked.

"Something of the sort," said Sanct-Franciscus. "My slaves will tell you how they have been treated. If it does not accord with your good opinion, you have only to tell me and I will strive to amend my ways." His voice was light but there was a glow in his dark eyes that commanded Vitellius' respect.

"A foreigner like you," said Vitellius with more daring than he had intended to use with Sanct-Franciscus.

"Precisely," was his answer.

"And the woman from the lupanar? What of her? Would Domina Clemens be willing to receive her if she were here?"

"I believe she would; she certainly would not demand that I deny myself the gratification of my . . . needs." His voice dropped, not in embarrassment but as an acknowledgment of the privacy of his requirements. "You will treat her well, and not speak against her—not you or any member of the household." A century ago, such

a precaution would not have been necessary. "Do you understand."
Then he turned to Aedius, who stood half-a-dozen paces away, and
said, "I want you to have one of this household assist you. Just at
present I require Vitellius to put his full attention here, but you will
need to discuss the division of your duties. I do not want any implication of keeping Domina Clemens' household at a distance, for
that could turn both sets of servants into camps of opposition. That
would accomplish nothing worthwhile, and so I hope to prevent it
from the beginning. Will you do your part?"

Aedius nodded. "I will."

"Very good." He glanced over at Vitellius, comparing this man
to the Caesar whose reign had lasted only a handful of weeks, a
century-and-a-half ago. This slave was circumspect in his dealings
and used his position with care and concision. Vitellius Caesar had
indulged himself recklessly and showed favor and caprice with
equal inclination; this impulsivity proved to be his undoing: his fall
had been the last of a series of short reigns, and had brought Titus
Flavius Vespasianus and his two sons to the purple. Now, once again
there was a cluster of unpopular Caesars, and Sanct-Franciscus
wondered when this spate would end.

As soon as the carts were unloaded, they were driven out of the
courtyard, bound for the Porta Viminalis and the road to Villa Ragoczy
for the last loads. The one remaining cart became a focus of activity,
its cargo of chests requiring careful handling as some contained glass
and fine stoneware, one was filled with brass instruments for measur-
ing and calculation, and others held jars and vials of medicaments and
similar substances.

"What do you think, Foreign Honoratus? Or should it be Dominus, now you have this house in Roma? Or honestiorus?" asked Urbanus, Sanct-Franciscus' twenty-six-year-old freedman clerk who
had only recently entered his employ. "Will they be back before
noon tomorrow?"

"I trust so, and I suppose it must be Dominus, or honestiorus,"
said Sanct-Franciscus. "There is a festival to be held at the Temple of
Hercules, and I hope the carts will not be caught in the celebration."

"Is that likely?" Urbanus asked. "They hold such festivities in front of the temple, not behind it. We may have to listen to the celebration, but we need not participate. Let them revel and riot as they like, it means little to us if the gates are closed." He wore three silver rings on his fingers—the highest display the law allowed him— and his silken pallium was belted in links of brass; in all, he had, as he had intended, the look of prosperity. His close-cropped brown hair shone with perfumed oil and the thin line of beard along his jaw was precisely trimmed. He was almost as tall as Sanct-Franciscus, and took great satisfaction in being half-a-head taller than most men in Roma. "Why should the celebration be a problem?"

"The celebrants will have bigae, and slaves, and they will want them near to hand. The square just beyond the gate will be a tangle," said Sanct-Franciscus.

Urbanus considered this, then said, "You're probably right. Very well. I will hope that your slaves and carts will be here before midday, and all the goods they bring bestowed before sunset."

"If that is to be achieved, the greater part of their unloading will be done before the festival is fully under way. The sacrifices are made at midday and the procession follows afterward, and then the feasting," said Sanct-Franciscus, hoping it was still true, for enough time had gone by since he had seen this celebration in Roma that he realized changes may have occurred.

"Sacrifices. Goats, sheep, and perhaps a calf or two," said Urbanus, rubbing his chin in thought. "I will be here in the morning, shortly after dawn, and you may command me as you wish."

"I am grateful for your attention," said Sanct-Franciscus, watching one of the grooms pull at the reins of the remaining empty cart. "The ponies need their rest."

"They're stubborn enough to be mules," said Urbanus.

"You have a point," said Sanct-Franciscus as he saw the ponies start to move, lured by a handful of apple-cores the groom had fetched. "Fortunately, they are bribable."

"Not only ponies," said Urbanus, clearing his throat and looking about as if expecting to be spied upon. "I have had an inquiry from one of the decuriae."

"Oh?" said Sanct-Franciscus.

"An officious fellow calling himself Telemachus Batsho. Nothing much to look at, but full of his own importance." Urbanus coughed discreetly. "He came to my insula in person, accompanied by an African slave, at the first hour after dawn. He said he'd met you with Septimus Desiderius Vulpius. He had a few questions for me regarding your business and property, and he hinted that there would be fewer questions, and fewer delays, if you would double his four percent fee for your transfer of residence."

"Did he?" Sanct-Franciscus was not surprised. "What kind of questions is he asking?"

"Mostly how much money you have outside of Roma, beyond the villa and the vineyard and the horse-farm, and how many ships you have plying the seas," said Urbanus. "I told him he should consult with your agents in Ostia about your shipping interests. Your agents there know more than I, and they have worked with you much longer than I have."

"An excellent response," Sanct-Franciscus approved.

"He wouldn't have agreed with you. I doubt he wants to divide his commission with any of the decuriae in Ostia, and that should serve to limit his searches to Roma," said Urbanus. "I suggested he wait until you are settled here and then audit your records for the Senate."

"And what did he say to that?" Sanct-Franciscus asked. He rounded suddenly on three slaves tugging at a chest in the cart. "Be careful with that. The contents are breakable."

"Sorry, Dominus," said the largest of the three. "It's pretty well wedged in."

Sanct-Franciscus sighed. "Then fetch a lever," he said. "The contents of that chest would be hard to replace."

One of the slaves paled, and all three touched their collars to show their compliance with his order.

Knowing the three were now nervous, Sanct-Franciscus said, "Have one of your fellows help you."

"Yes, Dominus," said the largest again, and motioned to the youngest to go find help.

Sanct-Franciscus turned back to Urbanus. "Pardon me."

"You are Dominus here, and by right you command," said Urbanus. "We are here to serve at your pleasure." He regarded Sanct-Franciscus a moment. "Was I wrong to make such a suggestion to that decuria? He was most insistent and curious. I thought he was looking for some excuse to confiscate your property, so I thought I should—"

"You did the right thing, Urbanus," said Sanct-Franciscus, wondering why Telemachus Batsho was so interested in him.

"You have some powerful friends who could require this Batsho to desist," Urbanus said speculatively.

"It would only increase his curiosity," said Sanct-Franciscus. "Why give him cause to investigate all my dealings." He did not add that Urbanus was privy to less than a quarter of his ventures, and that he hoped to keep it that way.

"Very well," said Urbanus, stepping back as the four slaves lugged the large chest away. "Shall I inform you of his requests?"

"If you would," said Sanct-Franciscus, shading his eyes from the rays of the westering sun as the first of six crates of his native earth was borne away to the apartments he would occupy.

"And should I apprise Batsho when I send word to you?" Urbanus asked.

"I think for now a regular report will suffice: one to him and one to me. You are a man of good sense, Urbanus; I rely upon you to know how much to reveal; I prefer you not lie, for that might come back to weigh on me." He held up his hand. "I will soon come to your office and review all the figures Aedius has supplied, and I will give you an official authorization in regard to which intelligence you may release without first obtaining my specific permission."

Urbanus offered Sanct-Franciscus a civilian salute, then started for the gate. "I will expect inventories from you in four days' time, if you think that will suffice? Better to do this quickly than to delay—that appears questionable."

"If I need more time, I will let you know, and the reason for it, so there will be no opportunity for uncertainty; I thank you for your attention on my behalf," said Sanct-Franciscus, and waited until the clerk had left before he followed the third crate of his native earth up the stairs in the atrium to his quarters on the north side of the house, where the shuttered windows admitted the least sun of any apartments in the house.

Tigilus, the understeward, stood in the largest of the three rooms set aside for Sanct-Franciscus' personal use. He held a wax tablet in one hand and a stylus in the other, and he was staring at the three crates of earth stacked against the far wall. He was no more than medium height, but so blocky that he appeared short. "Where do you want those stored?"

Sanct-Franciscus pointed to the large closet between the bedroom and this chamber. "That would seem a good place."

"As you wish. And for your body-slave, whom do you wish to serve you?" Tigilus asked.

It was all Sanct-Franciscus could do not to say Rugeri, but he stopped himself in time, and regarded Tigilus. "Would you be amenable to being in charge of my rooms? I may use my body-slave from my villa just at present, but he does not know the conduct of this house, nor its assigned uses: for that, you are much more prepared, and it would suit me to have your service, if it is suitable to you."

Tigilus blinked, and did his best to decide what would be the most advantageous decision. He studied Sanct-Franciscus, and finally asked, "You could order me to serve you—why do you permit me to decide? Or will you insist that I choose to do as you wish me to?"

"I permit you to decide so that you will know that I am willing to have it so, but not if such service is contrary to your—" Sanct-Franciscus broke off at the sound of a leather case striking the floor of the bedroom, followed by a wail of distress.

Tigilus turned and prepared to barrel into the bedroom to chastise the slave who had committed such an error. "That should earn more than a reprimand."

"At another time," said Sanct-Franciscus mildly. "But by the sound of it, all that was dropped was clothing, and the worst that may come of this is the need to have a few garments washed." He stretched out his hand, firmly blocking his way. "Let me attend to this, if you would."

"If you insist, Dominus." Tigilus was not pleased to have his authority limited, but he also was not going to press his luck with this foreigner, not given Domina Clemens' high opinion of him.

"For now, I do. Once the household has been put in order, I will not interfere with your duties, nor will I make unreasonable demands upon you. If you will wait here for me?" Sanct-Franciscus went through the dressing room to the bedroom where he saw two slaves—a young man and a girl of no more than fourteen—trying to shove three black-linen kalasirises back into the leather clothes-case they had dropped. "I hope one of you will tell me what happened."

Both began to speak at once, and both fell silent.

"One of you tell me how you came to drop the case. I am not intending to punish either of you; I simply want to know why the accident"—he emphasized the word—"happened, so we may avoid another such."

The male slave had a ridge of scars along his upper arm; he looked at Sanct-Franciscus, his expression concealing his thoughts. "I was backing up and caught my heel on the edge of that table." He pointed to the handsome, low table that stood not far from the bed.

"Well, better a dropped clothes-chest than a broken leg," said Sanct-Franciscus. "If you will be good enough to have all the clothes unpacked immediately, and hung on their pegs, I would appreciate it."

The two slaves exchanged disbelieving glances, and the girl almost sighed aloud. "At once," she said, and opened the top of the case fully, taking the fine garments out. "I have never seen such fabrics, not in all the years I have served in fine houses. I know I should not mention it, but I am astonished by the wonderful things you have," she said, almost caressing the heavy damask silk of his four trabeae. "And the colors. Not the black, but that deep-red and the black edged in silver—" She held up the garment. "This is wonderful. What is it?"

"An Egyptian kalasiris in silk. I have three of them, for hot weather."

"You wear pleated silk in summer?" the girl marveled.

"Yes," he answered, and offered no other comment.

"I will hang it with care, to keep the pleats sharp," she said.

"Thank you," said Sanct-Franciscus. "I am delighted you approve."

The girl's face froze and her cheeks went pale. "I didn't mean . . ."

"It isn't important; I am not offended that you are pleased with my clothing," said Sanct-Franciscus suddenly. "I only ask that you take good care of my things given into your care."

The two slaves nodded, and the man said, "If you will have our work reviewed before we are done, we may correct any mistakes we have made."

"Tigilus will do that," said Sanct-Franciscus.

"Very good, Dominus," said the slaves in near-unison, but with slight hesitation that revealed their uneasiness with Tigilus.

"Continue with your tasks," Sanct-Franciscus said as he left the two.

Tigilus was waiting on the other side of the dressing room shaking his head. "You will never have their respect if you do not hold them to their duty more stringently. Most Romans would beat the female for her insolence, or subdue her in other ways." He licked his lips suggestively. "She and the male were beyond their place in speaking to you as they did. They have an obligation to respect your position, even if you are a foreigner. They will take advantage of your good-will."

"Why is that?" Sanct-Franciscus asked quietly.

Although he offered no answer, Tigilus gave a put-upon sigh. "It isn't like the old days, you know, when slaves could buy their freedom and the freedom of their families. Now there must be decuriae to decide if the purchase is possible, and to have their percentage of the transaction. The only freedom purchase they cannot share in is that of gladiators."

"And why is this?" Sanct-Franciscus asked.

"Because there had been too many abuses—slaves buying their freedom for a single denarius and having nothing asked but that they allow their former masters to be their silent partners in business, which spared the former owners the burdens of taxes." Tigilus folded his arms. "The decuriae now monitor all such transactions."

"Including their commoda of four percent," said Sanct-Franciscus, with a suggestion of irony in his tone.

"They seek to turn their work to every advantage," said Tigilus with heavy, deliberate irony. Giving up trying to chasten his master for the moment, he asked, "What do you want me to do next?"

"See my bed is put in place in the outer portion of the bedroom in the position marked on the floor; the large chest topped with a mattress to go in the rear portion of the room, behind the screen, and my personal goods bestowed in chests that are being brought up. Also, if you would, be sure the two in the next room have attended properly to my clothing." Sanct-Franciscus glanced toward the door.

"May I correct their failures?" Tigilus asked, a shade too eagerly.

"If you mean may you beat them, you may not. If you think they have done things poorly or incorrectly, send for me and I will deal with them," said Sanct-Franciscus; he began to wonder if he had erred in offering Tigilus the care of his apartments.

"Of course, Dominus," said Tigilus, ducking his head and taking two steps back.

"Very good," said Sanct-Franciscus automatically. "I will be downstairs for a while; you may find me in the larder."

"Of course, Dominus," said Tigilus, bringing up his stylus and starting to write in the wax of his tablet.

"I will leave you to it, then." Stepping out onto the gallery, Sanct-Franciscus had the uneasy impression that something more than the door had closed between him and Tigilus.

Text of a letter from Brunius Tercitus Manus, secretary to Senator Juvens Gaius Horatius, to Lyllis Pulcheria, both in Roma; carried by private messenger to her house in the lupanar.

To the most highly praised and accomplished courtesan, Lyllis Pulcheria, the greetings of Brunius Tercitus Manus, on behalf of Juvens Gaius Horatius, Senator, with a few requests regarding the entertainment you have contracted to provide two nights hence:

The Senator requests that the four women to accompany her to the Senator's private banquet be no more than eighteen, preferably younger, and of a prettiness that reflects their youth. That does not mean that the Senator intends they should be beginners at their craft, for he wishes that they have all the skills and amorous accomplishments that the Senator has come to expect from the courtesan. He asks that they be elegantly attired and perfumed, and that they take care not to drink so much wine that they lose track of their purpose among his guests. The satisfaction and insouciance of all the guests should be her goal and the goal of her gracious companions. Let no attention be lacking, no act or art denied.

Three covered sedan-chairs will call at the appointed hour, when the courtesan and her women will promptly enter to be borne here. The Senator will not countenance any delay on the courtesan's part, and asks her to be ready in advance of the chairs' arrival. The bearers will be paid by the Senator, and will not accept any additional coins from the courtesan or her women, on pain of dismissal and a beating, so the courtesan must not think to gain time by offering favors to the bearers for their collusion.

Also, the Senator wishes to inform the courtesan that he has retained five youths to join the banquet, men of exceptional beauty and many talents not unlike your own. He does not wish any rivalry or unkindness to make itself apparent between the courtesan, her women, and these young men, but rather, that all should go in amity and delight. Those unwilling to participate without jealousy will be expelled without pay from the banquet and will not be asked to return at any time.

The courtesan's women will be paid at the conclusion of their service, of course, and if they have acquitted themselves well, they will be given rewards commensurate with their performance, as will the courtesan. The Senator wishes to remind her that there are other courtesans in the city, and that if she will not comply with his instructions, there are others in the lupanar who will. And while it is true that the courtesan and her women have proven satisfactory in the past, they have no cause to rest on their laurels, but instead, see that she and her women redouble their efforts, so that they may enhance their reputation and increase their worth to the Senator, on whose behalf I sign myself,

Brunius Tercitus Manus

4

"I do apologize for calling on you so late at night," said Ignatia as she faced Sanct-Franciscus across the atrium of Olivia Clemens' house; the lights from the oil-lamps made unsteady shadows on his face and hid his expression from her. She had on a long, peach-colored stola that took brightness from the lamplight, with a palla of forest-green linen over it. "I had hoped it would not be necessary, but . . ." Her words trailed away into a sigh. "Your steward was reluctant to disturb you."

"He is always most punctilious," said Sanct-Franciscus, no sign of aggravation about him, though he wished Rugeri were here; in the last century-and-a-half, Rugeri had learned his ways. Rugeri knew when to disturb him, and for whom.

"You must wonder why I am here," she began, and halted gratefully as Sanct-Franciscus shook his head.

"Your mother is doing poorly again," said Sanct-Franciscus, recognizing the worry in Ignatia's eyes.

"Yes," she said in a mix of relief and chagrin. "She has been miserable for many hours, and asking for you for almost four of them. If you were still at your villa, there would have been no expectation of bringing you to help her, but as you are now living inside the walls, she has been urging me to seek you out since sunset. I know that you believe you have an obligation to us through my uncle, but I am certain we have presumed upon your friendship so much in the last month." She made an abrupt upturn of her hands to emphasize the futility she felt. "I tried to help her without imposing on you at so late an hour, but my mother insisted, in spite of all my efforts. Nothing will ease her but your presence, or so she says." She stared at him. "I gave her the tincture you prepared, but it seems to have made little difference, and she will not be soothed, no matter how much I do for her, or what the slaves do for her."

"Have you tended her all day?" Sanct-Franciscus could see how darkly her eyes were ringed and how tired she was as she moved toward him.

"She needs someone to care for her; her weakness keeps her in her bed unable to lift a cup; her hands shake when she touches her blanket," said Ignatia, answering him indirectly. "And she doesn't trust our slaves to do what she requires."

"So the answer is yes, you have been caring for her all day." Sanct-Franciscus moved a few steps nearer to her. "You would like me to come and treat her, in part so you may have a little rest for yourself." There was only kindness in his observation, but she winced.

"I am not a feckless or ungrateful daughter," she said sharply.

"No, you are not," said Sanct-Franciscus, his hand extended to her. "You are devoted to your mother, as you were taught to be. But that does not mean that you . . . that you can continue to wait upon Adicia without aid or respite. You look worn out, and if you are, it will mitigate against the quality of your care."

Ignatia nodded fatalistically. "You have the right of it; twice I measured out the wrong amount of the syrup of poppies, and that could have been dangerous to her," she admitted.

"Who gave you the syrup of poppies?" Sanct-Franciscus asked, thinking that while it might calm Adicia, it would not benefit her for long.

"Xantheus the Athenian; Octavian brought him to the house a week ago, and he recommended syrup of poppies." Ignatia's face grew red with embarrassment. "I told him we should have sent for you, but when Octavian takes a notion, he can be stubborn."

"Octavian?" Sanct-Franciscus repeated, surprised. "I would not have expected him to do anything so conscientious."

"He did; Xantheus is one of the Christians Octavian spends his time with," said Ignatia. "He has embraced the teaching, and believes all Christians are more worthy men than those who worship other gods."

"How has your brother dealt with all this travail your mother endures, given his new religion? Beyond bringing Xantheus to minister to Adicia? I had heard Christians are merciful." He could tell that there was a lack of concern in Octavian, and that troubled him.

"My brother does not handle such misery as our mother experiences very well. It was unusual for him to bother to fetch the apothecary; ordinarily he leaves such things to me. He came to pray for her before he left for the day, but he has refused to take a turn waiting upon her. He says it isn't fitting for a grown son to tend to his mother in such intimate ways." She looked away from him. "If you cannot come, then I suppose I must try to find Artemidorus." Since the death of Galen, this Greek physician was much in demand among Roma's nobles, and known for his autocratic ways and exotic prescriptions. "Not that he is likely to call at so late an hour."

Knowing he was being goaded, Sanct-Franciscus said, "I will get my case and come with you. If you will allow me to summon a slave?" He clapped his hands, and in answer to this, Tigilus came into the atrium. "I am going with this young woman to care for her mother, who is ill. I may be gone until sunrise. If you will bring my leather-strapped chest from my second room? The one that contains my medicaments and other medicinal supplies."

"Of course, Dominus," said Tigilus, nodding as he turned away.

"Do you have your biga with you, or should I order mine readied?" Sanct-Franciscus asked Ignatia.

"My biga is outside, and Philius is walking the horses." She stared at him. "You will not wait until morning, then?"

"You say your mother is suffering now. What use is it to wait longer to alleviate her discomforts?" Sanct-Franciscus touched the silk of his Egyptian kalasiris. "I will fetch a pallium from my private room, for covering." He glanced over his shoulder. "Vitellius, if you would—bring a cup of warm honied wine for my guest? She will benefit from it, even though the night is not very chilly." He hoped it would calm her a bit, allaying her worst fears and making way for sleep to come, for clearly she needed sleep.

Coming out of the shadows, Vitellius ducked his head to Sanct-Franciscus. "Yes, Dominus."

"I will return directly," he assured Ignatia, and went to the vestibule to get his linen pallium, which he tugged over his head and let it fall over the silken kalasiris. He moved into the light from the cluster of lamps above the door.

"Leaving? And from your house instead of mine?" asked a soft voice from the broad couch in the outer part of his private room. "You have no need to escape me; I must return to my own house in a short while. My night isn't over yet."

Sanct-Franciscus paused and looked back with a rueful smile. "Ah, Melidulci," he said softly, "if I thought you would linger, so would I."

From her place amid the wonderful confusion of sheets, Melidulci laughed, a rich laugh, warm as ripe fruit. Her pale hair—a gift of nature, not of the dyer's skills—shone in the glow of the lamp-light, wheat on gold. "You have a way with words, Sanct-Franciscus, I give you that, and you don't fall on me like a ravening wolf, as so many do." She stretched out one arm to him. "It might be worth spending the night."

"You were the one who said you must be away at midnight, and I have arranged for a chair to return you to your own door," he said, smoothing the front of his pallium, adding with a regretful smile as he reached out to touch her cheek; his fingers lingered, eloquent of his reluctance to leave. "Sadly, you and I both have demands upon us. We would have had to say good-night shortly in any case."

Melidulci shook her blonde curls. "If only all my Patroni were as thoughtful as you are, my life would be far more delightful. As it is—" She glanced at the aureus on his pillow, and without seeming to pay much attention to it, said, "Oh, you are most generous, Dominus."

"It is no more than you deserve," said Sanct-Franciscus, return-ing to the bed and bending down to kiss her lovely, reddened mouth; it was an expert kiss, artful and subtle, full of promise and sensuality, awakening and tantalizing, but revealing little of either him or her.

"You are a worthy man, Patronus, for all your oddities," said Melidulci as he moved back from her.

"I thank you for your high opinion, and your lack of questions, considering everything," said Sanct-Franciscus as he once again made for the door. "And I thank you for coming to me, Melidulci. I appreciate your kindness."

"Kindness!" She laughed softly. "If you knew what I do about most men, you would do as I do every time I leave here, and thank Venus and the lares for giving me a lover who is more aware of my pleasure than his own, and who is not embarrassed to have me in his house," she said with a tinge of world-weariness in her voice. "You have no concept of how rare a thing that is."

"As I have told you, your pleasure *is* my pleasure; I have no other," he said, smiling at her. "What you achieve, I achieve, and only what you achieve."

"So you insist. And if it is so, I would every man have such affliction." She waved him out of the room. "I must dress, and that is a very unstimulating thing to watch." Unselfconsciously, she slipped out of the bed. "Odd, isn't it, when watching undressing is often the best part of the act?"

He stopped in the doorway. "Melidulci, you deserve your name. You are honey-sweet in every way."

Her laughter rippled again. "Of course it suits me: it's why I took it, although it fitted me better fifteen years ago, when I was just beginning in the lupanar." The smile she gave him was less alluring and more genuine than previous ones had been; he went to the door so she could be alone to pull on her stola and palla.

Before he left the room, Sanct-Franciscus said, "It will suit you all your life long," feeling a touch of regret that she should be so proficient in the arts of the body and so wholly indifferent to the joys of intimacy. Still, she was able to bring him more nourishment than dreaming women, and for the time being that would have to suffice.

"You present an unusual appearance," Ignatia remarked as she caught sight of him approaching.

"Well, I am a foreigner," he reminded her. "And although the night is mild, it is windy."

"And you will appear less foreign, since few will see your foreign garments with a pallium over them," said Ignatia shrewdly. "Have you had difficulty?"

"A little," he answered.

Vitellius appeared again, bearing a steaming cup. "As you ordered; it took a short time to heat."

"The humiliora are afraid of foreigners," said Ignatia, then taking the cup, held it up. "Do you keep a pot of this in the kitchen at all times? Your cooks must find that demand a hard one to meet."

"On such blustery nights as this, I like to have something to give my guests other than cool wine or broth, especially since, as you have noticed, many Romans view foreigners as uncouth. This provides me the opportunity to show them I have some graces." He was an exemplary host and both of them knew it.

"That may be so among the newest honestiora, but you are like one of the old gens," Ignatia conceded as she drank. "If you keep the old ways, you are a credit to Roma." She held out the cup to him in salute. "Thank you."

"Some Romans have excellent cause to be wary of all outsiders." Sanct-Franciscus did not point out that the lower classes and the newly elevated upper classes were not the only ones who were resentful and suspicious of foreigners; he went to the foot of the gallery stairs, waiting for Tigilus to bring him his case.

"You must tell me what I can do to assist you once you reach our house," said Ignatia, raising her voice enough to be heard.

"I will not know until I see—oh, thank you, Tigilus." He took the case from the stocky slave. "If you must send me word, I will be at the Villa Laelius."

"To Villa Laelius. Of course. I will not disturb you unless there is urgent need," said Tigilus, and ducked his head. "The sedan-chair will be here shortly. I will see your . . . package is delivered safely."

"Yes," Sanct-Franciscus agreed. "You know the destination."

Tigilus coughed discreetly. "That I do." He rubbed his hands together. "Do you have any other orders to leave with me?"

"If you will have the holocaust stoked and fired at noon, I will use the caldarium upon my return."

"Do you think you will be back by midday?" Tigilus asked.

"If I will not, I will send you word, and you may change the time you ready the holocaust." Sanct-Franciscus made a sign of dismissal and went back across the atrium to where Ignatia was finishing her wine. "When you are ready, Filia Laelius."

"So formal; that's unlike you," she said, setting the cup aside on the rim of the atrium fountain. "And I am too old to be filia," she added. "I am twenty-four, not seventeen."

"I did not want to appear overly familiar, not in front of a new

household, as this is for me; they might misunderstand. Doma Ignatia," he amended, thinking that the arbitrary severance from youth
at twenty-one was often misleading, and never more than in cases
like Ignatia's.

She nodded toward the broad corridor to the outer courtyard.
"This must have been a splendid place before it was walled. You could
see most of the grand villas on the hills, and the Tibrus."

"I suppose it was," said Sanct-Franciscus, his memories of Olivia's
house welling in his mind; for more than a century it had been one of
the most beautiful houses in the city: Olivia had transformed it over a
century ago, during the reign of Traianus, when magnificent buildings were all the rage, when she had made her first return to Roma after her death and reawakening in her tomb near the Via Appia.

Catching sight of Ignatia and Sanct-Franciscus approaching,
Philius turned his pair around and brought the biga up to them.
"They are ready to go," he declared as he got into the biga, holding
the reins lightly but firmly.

Sanct-Franciscus helped Ignatia to climb into the open chariot,
then got in behind her, setting his chest on the floor of the vehicle
between his feet. "When you like," he said, and signaled Holmdi to
open the gate for them.

The night was cool with a sharp wind out of the southwest
stroking the seven hills; the full strength of summer was not yet
upon them, and would not be for another two or three weeks, providing a pleasant prelude to the fury of July. The streets were fairly
empty except near the gaming taverns and in the lupanar, where
men continued to carouse through the dark hours. Due to riots at
the Flavian Circus earlier in the day, uniformed Praetorians moved
along the streets in small companies of four, ready to deal with any
infractions of law or peace they came upon. For the most part the
biga passed unnoticed and unchallenged, but near the Temple of
Diana-the-Huntress, a trio of Praetorians signaled them to halt.

"It's late," said their apparent leader. "Why are you abroad?"

"This young woman summoned me to treat her mother, who is
ailing," said Sanct-Franciscus. "I have done so several times before,

and I have brought medicaments with which to minister to her complaints." He patted his case.

"Is that a fact?" the Praetorian asked boldly. "Are you sure you aren't making off with an heiress?"

"If I were, why would her slave be driving, and why would I be going away from the house where I live?" Sanct-Franciscus asked pleasantly. "If you are truly concerned for her welfare, you may follow us to the Laelius house on the Via Decius Claudii."

"I know that place," said another of the Praetorians. "Has a long porticus, octostyle, I recall."

"That it does," said Sanct-Franciscus.

"A fine old house, from the time of Traianus," the first said.

"My mother is in pain, good Praetorians," said Ignatia suddenly.

One of the men laughed in disbelief. "It is a late hour for such a visit." He winked.

"All the more reason to allow us to hurry," said Sanct-Franciscus, ignoring the last implication. "The case is urgent, as the Doma says."

The leader of the trio motioned the other two aside. "Come. Let's go see if Marutius is able to stand up yet." He chuckled and reached out to slap the rump of the nearer horse. "I hope your treatment is successful, foreigner," he called after the biga as it began to move.

When they reached the end of the street and turned toward the Laelius' house, Ignatia spoke up abruptly. "Why did you let them say such things? How dared they? They suggested—I cannot think of it! I was mortified. As if I would pander for my mother!"

"You have no reason to be troubled," Sanct-Franciscus assured her. "Soldiers make a habit of such remarks; they are meaningless. By morning, they will be forgot." Had Philius not been there, he might have laid a comforting hand on her arm, but with the slave as witness, he did not want to cause Ignatia any more discomfort than she already felt. "Make sure you have hold of the handrail—you know how sharp the turn is for your villa."

They moved around onto the Via Decius Claudii and covered the last two blocks at a brisk walk. As the pair were pulled to a halt, Sanct-Franciscus took his case and stepped down from the rear of the biga, prepared to help Ignatia; a noise behind him attracted his attention: he swung around as the oil-lamps flared.

The door was opened by Starus, who looked tired and worried. "She has been weeping, Doma Ignatia," he said.

"I am sorry to hear it," said Ignatia earnestly as she got out of the biga behind Sanct-Franciscus, stepping down onto the pavement with care. "I take it she is still awake."

"And fretful," said Starus. "Tallia is with her. I sent Mirza to bed—she's so worn out, she's falling asleep where she stands."

"A wise thing to do," said Ignatia, going through the porticus into the house, taking care to cross the threshold on her right foot, for to fail in this custom would be seen as the most dreadful omen. She paused by the lares and left a coin on the narrow shelf, a token of her regard and need.

Following after her, his case of medicaments in hand, Sanct-Franciscus took a bead of amber from his wallet and placed it in a shallow dish next to the household gods. "For your mother's improvement."

Ignatia looked around at him. "The whole household thanks you."

Although he doubted this, Sanct-Franciscus kept his opinion to himself. "That is unnecessary," he said as he picked up his case and prepared to go on to Adicia's room.

"But it is," said Ignatia, walking slightly ahead of him. "I know you can find your way, but my mother would be shocked to have such a breach of manners."

"I have noticed that she prefers to keep the traditions," said Sanct-Franciscus.

"Because of her regard for her family." Ignatia's voice dropped to a whisper. "She is worried about her brother Drusus, who is fighting with the Emperor in the East."

"Word is that things are not going well," said Sanct-Franciscus, his voice also lowered.

"The Senate is abuzz with rumors," said Ignatia, a bit louder. "My mother hears the news from her visitors, and she is upset, and that makes her—"

"—more unwell," Sanct-Franciscus finished for her. "Yes; this is not uncommon."

"We have tried to advise those who call upon her to say nothing about the current scandals," said Ignatia.

"I know you are conscientious," said Sanct-Franciscus, his tone soothing.

It was as if she had not heard him. "—but she frets if she is not told the whole, and then she accuses her family and slaves of working against her—" She stopped, looking around as if hoping to discover they had not been overheard.

"Your mother's illness makes her most trying," said Sanct-Franciscus, moving toward Adicia's room.

"Oh, most trying," she exclaimed. "If only she had remained well!"

"Since that is not presently possible, I would like to suggest that you go to your own chamber, summon your own slave and be massaged so you will be able to sleep," he said. "Starus will escort me, and you will not have to worry yourself into discomposure. You have already done more than most daughters would for their mothers." He touched her shoulder, hardly more than a brush of his fingers; it held her attention. "It is unfortunate that your mother suffers, but there is no reason you must do so."

Ignatia sighed. "She will wonder why I was so lax not to escort you."

"And I will explain it to her," he said gently. "You need rest. Doma Ignatia."

She looked away from him. "You're right, I suppose."

"Go rest, Doma Ignatia," said Sanct-Franciscus softly. "You mother will manage without you—my Word on it."

She considered, then reached over to touch his hand. "You will have me wakened if anything goes ill with her?"

"Certainly," he said.

Reluctantly she nodded. "Very well. I will try to sleep. I am tired." She broke away from him and went quickly along the corridor as if she was afraid she might change her mind.

Sanct-Franciscus went along toward Domina Adicia's room, aware that the household slaves who were up kept wary eyes upon him. By the time he reached Adicia's chamber, he could hear the whispers in the dark. "Good evening, Domina," he said as he stepped through the door. "I am sorry to hear you are unwell."

Adicia smiled as she glanced at him, and although she was pale and thin, she held out her hand to him. "How good of you to come to me at this late hour. You appreciate my need."

"Your daughter was kind enough to fetch me," said Sanct-Franciscus as he came to her side. "She gives you most persevering care."

"So she would have you believe," Adicia said, pulling her hand back.

"You have no reason to doubt it," said Sanct-Franciscus as he motioned to the exhausted slave dozing at the end of the bed. "Will you bring a basin of hot water from the kitchen?"

The slave ducked her head yawning, and hurried off.

"None of my household cares what becomes of me," Adicia muttered.

"You know that is not the case," said Sanct-Franciscus as he felt her pulse, finding it hard and ragged. "You must not blame them for failing to restore your health."

"How can I not, when I continue to ail?" She reached out again and took his hand. "You don't understand how difficult this is for me. I strive to have courage, to keep my dignity, but I am—" She stopped and drew his hand to her cheek. "You know I'm still a woman, and that I truly—"

Carefully he extricated his hand from her grasp. "I know you are ill, Domina Adicia, and that you may improve if you permit me to treat you."

Adicia shook her head. "She's working on you, isn't she? She's always looking to take advantage."

Sanct-Franciscus paused in the opening of his case. "She?"

"My daughter," said Adicia as if the word were venomous. "I know what she is, and how she connives to gain the sympathy of others, so I must suffer for the loss of affection she has caused."

Taking a vial from his case, Sanct-Franciscus began to mix a potion for the wretched woman. "This is the burden of your illness speaking, Domina," he said as he poured a little tincture of pansy into the infusion of crushed nettles he had already decanted, "Your daughter has embraced your well-being and has modeled her—"

"Not she!" Adicia burst out. "She's subtle, I grant you."

"She is not the reprehensible child you think," he said, adding another ingredient to his compound. "Do not trouble yourself, Domina."

"A fine state of affairs," Adicia muttered, drawing herself under her covers. "That my own physician should not see anything so obvious. My brother is just as blind. But then, men are always fools about Ignatia."

Sanct-Franciscus held out the vial. "If you will drink this, I believe you will have enough relief to be able to sleep without pain."

"So she can work her wiles on you?" Adicia asked, but took the vial and drank the contents. "I will not relinquish your fondness to her without making an effort to keep it."

He took the empty vial. "Domina Adicia, I hope you will believe me when I tell you that whatever my feelings may be toward your daughter, they do not alter my emotions in regard to you."

There was a scratch at the door, and then another slave entered, a steaming basin of water in her cloth-wrapped hand. "For my mistress."

Adicia frowned. "Why do you need that?"

"So your slave may bathe you while you feel more comfortable. You are in need of a bath, are you not?" He indicated where the woman should set the basin down. "Keeping your body clean is important, Domina Adicia, especially when you spend so much time abed."

Her sigh this time was eloquent of ill use. "If you insist, I suppose I must." Then she flashed him a sensual smile. "You might bathe me to better purpose."

Sanct-Franciscus said nothing as he stepped away from her and went toward the door, the frown between his fine brows deepening as he went.

Text of a letter from Lucius Virginius Rufius to Marius Octavian Laelius, carried by a Greek private courier and delivered clandestinely.

To my newfound brother in Christ, the Kiss of Peace and the blessings of the glorious Apostle Paul from those of us who follow the

Paulist creed, with my fervent wish that you grow in faith and grace with every passing hour.

There is to be a meeting and a Mass at the house of Celestia Delphina Hilaria Pario, who lives off the Via Appia about two thousand paces from the walls of Roma. Tomorrow night at sunset is the time the celebration will begin. Four of us are planning to go together to this wonderful event, and returning together as well. So I have the happy task of asking you if you should care to join us. If you are able to come, bring a new loaf of bread with you, along with either a jug of wine or a basket of fresh-caught fish for the Mass and our fellowship. If you wish to travel with us, inform me if you will have your horse or will wish to ride in my biga, or the biga of my cousin, Gelasius Virginius Apollonius Metsari? If you will inform me by tonight what you intend to do, I would be most grateful.

A few of us are planning to walk about the city after Mass, to see what evils we may strive to undo. We have done this in the past occasionally, and have saved a man from being robbed, as well as prevented lewdness, and offered a mantele to a naked beggar. On one of our ventures, we spent an hour speaking to some Fora Guards bound for a tavern, exhorting them to leave their dissolute ways and join us as Christians.

Of course we will continue to pray for your mother, that God may send her a healing through your devotion. It is what we Christians must do, to demonstrate the power of our faith, and our trust in God. See that your own grace is not lost in pressing for her relief of suffering: all men must suffer, and women the more so, for the sins of Eve. Have patience, hope, and faith, and you will see your mother restored to you again, in radiant health and open heart, for the Glory of God.

Lucius Virginius Rufius

By my own hand on the 26th day of June in the 218th Year of the Christ

5

Telemachus Batsho stormed into the room Sanct-Franciscus was using for his study; his face was red from more than the heat and he moved as if he were killing vermin on the floor. "What do you mean by summoning me? And before prandium? I am to dine with my sister's husband at midday."

Behind Batsho, Vitellius stood, his head bowed in mixed exasperation and submission. "He insisted that I not announce him, Dominus."

Sanct-Franciscus paused in his putting scrolls into pigeon-hole shelves. "There is no trouble, Vitellius. I asked the decuria to call upon me; he is expected. And do not fear; this should take less than an hour—you will not miss your meal. If you will bring honied wine for my guest?" He nodded the old steward away. "You have a complaint against me, decuria?"

"That I do," huffed Batsho, in no mood to be genial. "I am not accustomed to being sent for—like a dog."

"I am sorry it seemed that way to you; it was not my intent." Sanct-Franciscus indicated an upholstered bench from Fars. "Be at your ease."

"How did you think I should react to your high-handed summons?" Batsho folded his arms and remained standing.

"I hoped you would appreciate the opportunity to review all the various records you say you need in order to make my residence here official," said Sanct-Franciscus at his most cordial, but with an air of reserve to keep Batsho from assuming he was overly impressed with the decuria's importance. "Given all the information you appear to need to accomplish this, I assumed you would want to attend to this where all is to hand. I feared I would disaccommodate you if I had to spend the day going back and forth between this house and your office, asking you to postpone your business with others; with you present, we may attend to everything with a minimal loss of time for us both." His smile was bland and urbane, quelling any hint of disrespect. "Do, please, sit down."

Batsho glared at him, his wrath giving way to puzzlement. "You may be correct," he admitted at last. "But you should keep in mind that this is not the way things are done in Roma."

"That is unfortunate, for everyone," said Sanct-Franciscus with every appearance of sympathy, knowing that if this were truly the case, it was the result of recent changes, for things were different during his last stay in Roma, when Olivia had been still alive.

"You are a foreigner; you do not understand our Roman traditions," said Batsho, his posture squaring to a more martial one.

"I fear not," Sanct-Franciscus agreed. He indicated a sheaf of fan-folded scrolls. "I believe these are where it would be most fruitful to begin."

"What documents are those?" Batsho asked heavily, as if mistrusting them. Little as he wanted to admit it, the heat had given him a headache that would undoubtedly worsen as the day dragged on.

"Various deeds, transfers, tax records, and other sorts of information regarding this property and its owner." Sanct-Franciscus held up an official letter. "This is my permit of occupancy. Next is the receipt of fees."

"All very useful," Batsho allowed. He held out his hands for the sheaf. "You may be right—this is more swiftly accomplished here." He paused. "You know my percentage is granted for each document I examine."

"So I have been told." The wryness in Sanct-Franciscus' smile was lost on Batsho. "All the more reason to attend to this here. I believe this room is cooler than the Basilica Julia is now on its upper floors."

"It will be stifling by afternoon there, yes. I understand your purpose," said Batsho as he began to read through the first document, taking great care to inspect the seals at the bottom of the text. "This appears to be in order."

"So I should hope," said Sanct-Franciscus, and looked up as Vitellius returned with a large cup of wine on a neat, round tray of hammered copper. "Put it on the ivory table," he recommended.

"Yes, Dominus," said Vitellius, taking great care not to spill any of the wine.

"It smells very good," Batsho said, lifted the cup, and hesitated. "Where is yours?"

Sanct-Franciscus lowered his head. "Alas, good decuria, I do not drink wine."

Batsho put his cup down at once. "Then I will not drink, either," he declared, the tenuous air of good will he had displayed vanishing as if by sorcery.

"Ah." Sanct-Franciscus gave a single nod of understanding. "No, good decuria; you have nothing to fear within these walls, from me or any of the household. I will force no drink or food upon you, but I assure you that you need have no fear to partake of either." He almost held his breath. "I would like to think that you would grant me the privilege of showing you hospitality."

"Hospitality has masked many acts of treachery," said Batsho grumpily. "I shall need to see the records of ownership for this domicile."

"I have them just here," said Sanct-Franciscus, taking three rolled scrolls out of the pigeon-hole shelves. "There is a fourth, which I keep in my Deeds Chest; if you want it—? I can also produce Wills, showing the line of bequests—".

"That will not be necessary," said Batsho, cutting him off. "If you have these, the Wills are redundant."

"Is there anything else you want?"

"Not that I am aware of. Yet." This last was portentous, and Batsho took delight in seeing Sanct-Franciscus duck his head as if he were little more than a slave.

"No one." he announced, "is more eager than I to see justice done for you, honestiorus. That is the reason I must see so many of your records here."

That, thought Sanct-Franciscus, and the additional commodae you are entitled to collect for the inspections you make; concealing his emotions, he said, "Of course."

For a short while Batsho read in silence, his full concentration on the scrolls before him. As he finished each page, he marked it with his sign at the bottom as proof that he had seen it. Every sign would earn him an additional two percent of his final charges, bringing the commodae he would receive to a handsome total, but it would prevent a second or third inspection being required, and the commodae being paid again; during Batsho's long scrutiny, Sanct-Franciscus returned to putting scrolls in their pigeon-holes and adding to his catalogue of what records had been put where.

"Dominus, I am needed elsewhere," Vitellius dared to say at last.

"Oh yes. You needn't linger on my account," said Sanct-Franciscus, mildly preoccupied; he, too, was aware of how much Batsho might earn for himself during this inspection, and thought back a century to a time when men of Batsho's position were paid by the Roman Senate, not by those to whose records they attended. "I will summon you when I need you, Vitellius."

Vitellius nodded and left.

"Do you allow all your household such liberty—to speak to you without your giving permission?" Batsho marveled, not entirely in admiration.

"Of course," said Sanct-Franciscus. "I would be a fool not to."

"And why is that?" Batsho asked in a tone that suggested any response must be absurd.

"Because if there is trouble in the house, I want to know of it immediately. Perhaps there is a fire in the kitchen: I would put myself and everyone under this roof in danger if the household had to wait to inform me of it until I thought to ask why I smelled smoke. If a thief should be apprehended in the act of stealing, the household should not have to detain the man for an indefinite time while I was uninformed of his presence." His manner was as open as the summer sky above them.

"Reasonable, if you are expecting trouble," Batsho conceded, and returned to reading the documents, his wine still untouched.

"What sensible man does not expect some manner of trouble?" Sanct-Franciscus asked in the same bland tone.

Batsho shrugged and went back to his reading; a short while later he asked, "What more do you have on the size and capacity of the stable here?"

"I have three records," said Sanct-Franciscus. "One for the original construction of the house, one for repairs done about a century ago, and one for the expansion of the exercise yard, thirty-five years ago." He pulled each scroll from its pigeon-hole as he spoke. "Which would you like to see?" He waited for Batsho's answer, anticipating his response.

With a sigh suggesting overwork, Batsho said, "I suppose I should see them all. You can then tell me how many horses you intend to keep here in the city."

"Seven for now, and four ponies. Also three mules." He paused. "All the rest of my livestock is at my villa outside the city walls, except for the cook's flocks of fowl."

"Birds are not livestock; there is no tax on them, for their numbers vary from day to day," said Batsho rather stiffly. "I would not like for you to have to pay more than you are required."

"I appreciate that," said Sanct-Franciscus, a wicked glint in his dark eyes. "I am prepared to pay what I owe, of course."

"No doubt you are," said Batsho, and sighed. "Do you have your record of your horses and ponies and mules?"

"On this parchment," said Sanct-Franciscus, handing the sheet to him.

Batsho barely glanced at it before putting his sign at the bottom of the page. "You have provided an inventory of household goods already. I suppose you have spices in the kitchen?"

"The cook has told me what he requires and I have provided most of it, to the limit of the markets I may use. My purchases are listed here." He handed over another sheet of parchment, and wondered what more Batsho would think of to put his mark on in order to make a bit more money from doing his duty.

"You have excellent taste, it would appear, or your cook does, and you encourage him," said Batsho as he scanned the record Sanct-Franciscus offered to him. "You are nothing if not generous with him."

"So I would hope," said Sanct-Franciscus. "My cook has a reputation to maintain."

"This is a considerable amount of spices. So much pepper! And cinnamon." He cocked his head. "How did you acquire so much, and so quickly?" The greedy twist to his features was back.

"I am a . . . a partner in a shipping company, as I must assume you know. Our ships trade in Egypt and Syria, among other Mare Internum ports. We bring Roman merchandise to and get cargo from Bithynia, Cappadocia, and Armenia as well as Chios, Byzantium, and Odessus; we have emporia in western ports as well—Narbo, Tarraco, and the Baleares Isolae, among other places, so I am able to purchase many things in quantity that others are unable to procure at all." He leaned back against the writing-table, resting on his braced hands. "I have a colleague in Alexandria just now, attending to our trading there."

"Yes. The Eclipse Trading Company," said Batsho as if to take Sanct-Franciscus by surprise.

"Yes," said Sanct-Franciscus, wholly unflustered.

"It has been a successful endeavor for you, according to the records at the Basilica Julia."

"Most years it is. Last year we lost three ships—one to pirates, two to storms—and our earnings suffered as well as our seamen." He continued to support himself on his hands.

"You ransomed three of your seamen, including your captain, from Cnossus on Creta." He frowned, then clearing his throat he added, "You know that you must bear the cost of the ransom yourself; the state cannot recompense you for what you spent?"

"I am aware of that," said Sanct-Franciscus.

Batsho tapped his fingers on the nearest sheet of parchment. "You know, there were those who said your captain was in league with the pirates, and only claimed to be a captive."

"Such things are said of all island-dwellers," Sanct-Franciscus remarked, refusing to be drawn into an acrimonious debate, as he guessed Batsho wanted him to be.

"Well, you got the fellow back, and three others." He gave a sound between a snort and a chuckle. "It was your money to spend, I suppose."

"That it was," said Sanct-Franciscus in superb neutrality.

"I see you have two new ships under construction at Ostia," Batsho went on. "You must intend to continue trading, even if it proves dangerous and costly."

"I think it is a good venture for foreigners to undertake—we have useful connections that are often to our advantage."

Batsho considered this while he read the next parchment. "I take your point," he said, deliberately unclear whether he meant the information on the sheet or Sanct-Franciscus' remarks. Signing again, he said, "This is now nineteen documents I have seen and officially noted. You will have to pay me thirty-four aurei, based on the value of your holdings described in your documents; I am entitled to receive that amount."

"You shall have the money before you leave," said Sanct-Franciscus, as if he were unaware of the inflated price. "And five aurei for your time and trouble." This last was said as if he had offered mere denarii rather than aurei.

"Most generous," said Batsho, making a note to look more closely at Sanct-Franciscus' financial dealings, for he had been expecting a protest, not an additional commoda.

"Is there anything more you will need to see, good decuria?" Sanct-Franciscus asked politely.

"Not now; I may have some other inquiries to make, at another time, and if I do, I will inform you of it. I must go to my sister's husband, as I mentioned when I arrived." He put the scrolls back in their sheaf and extended this to Sanct-Franciscus, who moved away from the table to accept them. "You have been most reasonable, honestiorus. I thank you for that."

"It is gracious of you to say so, decuria," Sanct-Franciscus answered, his demeanor revealing little of his thoughts.

"If you will permit me to take my leave?" He did his best to display official dignity, knowing it was expected of Romans.

"I would not have thought you needed my permission, but if it pleases you, you have it. I will summon my old steward to escort you as soon as I count out your aurei." He set the sheaf on the writing table and went to pull open a drawer underneath the pigeon-hole shelves, revealing a small wooden chest banded in iron. Using a key that hung on a thong around his neck, Sanct-Franciscus opened the lock, revealing a mass of gold coins. "Thirty-nine aurei is the sum, I recall?"

"That it is," said Batsho, belatedly wondering how he would carry such an amount back to his office.

As if anticipating his problem, Sanct-Franciscus held up a leather pouch. "Shall I put the coins in this?"

"I would . . . that would be . . ." Batsho floundered, torn between wanting the convenience and the fear that Sanct-Franciscus would not give him the full amount they had agreed upon.

"You shall count them and sign for them, of course, so there is no question as to the amount paid for your service," said Sanct-Franciscus, for the first time sounding a bit annoyed. "Is that satisfactory to you?"

"I am more than willing to have a record of our dealings," Batsho said promptly, taking the pouch and turning away to count the aurei. Thirty-nine aurei: whole buildings could be bought for less! "Thirty-nine, as agreed," he said, although he had counted forty. He slipped the closing straps of the pouch twice around his left wrist, hefting it. "This will do." Then he slipped the thongs off his wrist and secured them to his belt; patting the pouch, he said, "Safer this way."

Sanct-Franciscus offered a quilled stylus and an ink-cake, moist enough to use. "If you would, then?"

Batsho read the statement: *The decuria Telemachus Batsho has today received from the foreign merchant Ragoczy Germainus Sanct-Franciscus the sum of thirty-nine aurei in full and complete payment for his official inspection of documents of residence, title, occupation, and taxation status. This document stands as witness to these transactions.* "My signature and sign?"

"And the date, if you would," said Sanct-Franciscus, almost apologetically. "So there can be no confusion."

"Naturally," said Batsho, a bit huffily, for had he been able to leave off the date, he might have been able to claim a second commoda to rectify that lapse. He dipped the end of the quill into the edge of the softened ink, wrote his name and sign, and reluctantly added *19th day of July, 971st Year of the City.* "There. That should satisfy anyone, up to the Emperor himself."

"I thank you," said Sanct-Franciscus, and nodded toward the door. "Would you like one of my slaves to escort you back to your office?"

Again, Batsho was torn: he saw the advantage of added protection, but that slave could possibly overcome him, steal the pouch, and return it to Sanct-Franciscus. With the receipt he had signed, Batsho would have no recourse to regain his money, so he said, "I believe I will attract less attention on my own, honestiorus."

"As you wish," said Sanct-Franciscus, and clapped his hands. This time it was Aedius who answered the summons. "My guest is leaving. If you would see him to the gate for me?"

"Of course, Dominus," said Aedius, standing respectfully while Batsho gestured his farewell and started for the atrium. "There is someone in the rear vestibule who would like a little of your time," he added as he prepared to escort Telemachus Batsho from the house.

Something in Aedius' tone put Sanct-Franciscus on the alert. "Thank you. I will attend to it now." He called after Batsho, "You see, decuria, there are advantages in giving the household leave to speak."

Batsho, now out of the study, was able to ignore this last remark as he continued out into the atrium, his hand placed protectively over the jingling pouch he carried on a double-thong on his belt.

As soon as he was sure that Batsho was through the gate, Sanct-Franciscus left his place in the study and hastened to the rear vestibule, where he found Daniama the laundress standing guard at the door, her muscular arms folded. "I understand I have a guest," he said to the sturdy slave.

"Yes, Dominus." She ducked her head. "Aedius said I was to guard her."

"No doubt a very sensible plan," said Sanct-Franciscus. "But do you think, perhaps, I might be allowed to enter?" He waited for her to move aside, wondering as he did what—and whom—he would find inside.

"Your pardon, Master," said the slave, and stepped away quickly.

Sanct-Franciscus put his hand on the latch, calling out, "I am coming in," as he swung the door back. He found the room in shadow, the wooden blinds turned to keep out the summer sun. "Who is here?" he asked of the gloom, for although the darkness made little difference to the clarity of his sight, he knew most of the living were not so fortunate and were often troubled by his ability to see so well; he was aware his unknown guest was in the far corner, turned away from the door.

"Patronus," exclaimed Melidulci, not moving from her place.

"My delight," he exclaimed, starting toward her. "What is the matter?" For something had to be the matter: Melidulci was not behaving as Sanct-Franciscus had ever seen her act before. "What has happened?" As he reached her side, he saw her flinch. "What is wrong?"

Suddenly she burst into tears and pressed her head against his shoulder, keeping her face averted; she was trembling . "I . . . I could think of . . . of no one else to come to," she whispered, her words muffled.

"But surely within the lupanar—" he began, and felt her cringe.

"I will leave," she said suddenly, shoving him so she could step away from him. "I don't want to impose."

"No, no," he told her gently, putting his arm around the small of her back with care, for he could tell by her posture that she was in pain. "That was clumsy of me. If you have trouble, the Guard of the Lupanar should protect you—that is what they are paid for."

She broke away from his embrace, then reached out suddenly and turned the slats of the blinds, throwing the uncompromising noon light on her face: bruises and broken skin distorted her features so that she was almost unrecognizable. One eye was puffy, purple, and all but swollen shut, her lip was cracked and swollen, there were lumps on her jaw and a dribble of blood below her distended ear. Her upper arms were marred with the purple ghosts of finger dug into her flesh. "Who do you think did this?" she demanded, and her sobbing became loud and ragged. "Lupanar Guards!"

He stared at her, wanting to disbelieve, but unable to doubt her. "Why would Lupanar Guards do such a thing—and to you, of all women?"

"*I don't know!*" she wailed. "I pay them their *commoda*, and extra." A note of panic had entered her voice.

"Melidulci," Sanct-Franciscus said, folding her close to him again.

"I'm not either," she howled, twisting in his arms. "Not now!" Abruptly she collapsed, sagging into his encompassing hold. "Don't look at me!"

"Why not?" he asked her, no distress in his voice; his dark, penetrating gaze did not waver.

"Because I'm hideous!"

"No, no, Melidulci, you are injured, you are not hideous. You cannot be hideous, not to me." He supported her easily, as if she weighed no more than a child did.

"Why?" she challenged, adding angrily. "Because you love me?"

"No," he said calmly. "I like you very much and I am deeply fond of you; I know you."

This held her attention. "But you do not love me."

"No," he said, a world of kindness in his answer.

Now she was puzzled; she did her best to ignore her fear and hurts. "Why not? Almost all the men who come to me claim to love me."

"And do you believe them?" Sanct-Franciscus asked. "You do not want me to be one who claims to love you, do you."

Her ragged laughter was not as cynical as she wanted it to be. "Of course not."

"Do you believe my friendship is sincere?"

She stared at him, her eyes growing moist. "Yes," she said after a brief silence. "I do."

"Then accept it, and let me help you now." He felt her tremble, and went on compassionately, "This was done to leave marks, and to frighten you."

"Then they succeeded," she muttered, forcing her legs to support her. "One of them struck me across the back with a length of wood. I was bludgeoned more than once with it, and they struck my feet; walking here was—" She broke off.

"The Guard of the Lupanar did this, you say." Sanct-Franciscus kept her close to him, providing her the safety of his nearness.

"Or men dressed like them," Melidulci allowed, bringing her crying under control. "I didn't know their faces, and I thought I knew them all."

"Did you not?" He considered this, using the edge of the wide, square sleeve of his dalmatica to start to wipe away the dried blood from her face. "This is insufficient," he said as he examined the results. "I will order a bath, and while it is readied, I will soak your injuries with pads infused with anodyne tinctures. Once I see the whole of you, I will have a better notion of what you will need."

She stiffened. "What do you mean?"

"You know I have some skill with medicaments; you have seen the efficacy of the preparations I provide," he said without haste, his small hands moving over as much of her face and neck as he could see without adding to her distress. "I will endeavor to do my best to help your recovery; I am no Galen, but my methods have their uses." He had acquired them over centuries, beginning in the Temple of Imhotep; he looked directly into her disfigured visage. "I cannot undo all the damage, but I can keep it to a minimum."

"How!" She did not speak loudly; her anguish was all the more poignant because of it.

"There are unguents and poultices to ease the bruising and to help close the breaks in your skin with the least scarring possible," he said. "I have bandages that will also help prevent scars, and some that will keep the medicaments where they need to be to treat the hurts you have. I have syrup of poppies to diminish your pain so you may sleep. Sleep heals much more than any physician can."

She sighed. "I shouldn't. You may be in danger if you shelter me. If those men followed me—"

"So I might be," Sanct-Franciscus admitted, "but the woman who owns this house—a widow called Olivia—would never forgive me if I failed to care for you, nor would I excuse myself. You are dear to me, little as you may want to be, Melidulci, and those of my blood do not turn away from those we care for when they are in need." He thought of Periasis, less than a century ago, and winced; he clapped his hands, calling out, "Daniama, have the caldarium heated—not too hot, but enough to promote sweat. Then ask Vitellius to bring me my leather case of medicaments." Just then he missed Rugeri intensely, wishing he were here to tend to such things with only minor instruction.

From the corridor came "Yes, Master," and the sound of sandaled feet going toward the rear of the house.

"Your slaves will talk," Melidulci murmured, now sounding overwhelmed with fatigue.

"I will take care of that once I have tended to you," he assured her, and stroked her hair, his hand light as a gauze veil. "Do not fret, Melidulci."

She wiped her eyes with her palla. "I'm sorry. I can't seem to stop crying. I think I've finally finished, and then—"

"There is no error in tears. Melidulci," he told her; his next words carried their own echo, "I only wish I had my own to shed."

Text of a letter from Septimus Desiderius Vulpius, presently in Brundisium, to Ragoczy Germainus Sanct-Franciscus in Roma, carried by private messenger.

To the most excellent foreigner, the highly acclaimed Ragoczy Germainus Sanct-Franciscus at the house of the Widow Clemens near the Temple of Hercules, the affectionate greeting of Septimus Desiderius Vulpius, now on the last leg of his journey back from Pergamum:

As you suggested, I took the time to bathe in the White Fountains of Pergamum, and must tell you that they are all you claimed they would be. The stones are like snow on a river, but all is warm and pleasant. The keepers of those fountains have achieved a fine facility, with their terraces framing the baths in the springs, and their many excellent attendants. The general setting for the baths in regard to the town is also quite handsome; I spent several afternoons there, recovering from the heat of the day, and meeting men from many parts of the eastern Empire who, like me, repaired there to pass the heat of the day taking their ease.

On my travels, I was able to spend part of a day with the Syrian spice dealer you mentioned to me, and through him, I have made arrangements to import spices from Hind, to be exchanged at the

Stone Tower for nut oils and bison hides from Gaul. Little as my father would approve my increased participation in trade, he would be proud to see our fortunes thus bolstered, which would not have been possible without your help.

Which brings me to the purpose of this letter: I would like to show my appreciation to you for all you have done for me and my family—and my gens. This is to be more than a convivium: I propose to have a true banquet in your honor, with jugglers and erotic dancers to entertain. If you have a choice for a partner of your own, I will gladly do what I can to fulfill it—woman, man, girl, boy, or even goat, one, two, or three of them, I suppose, if such is to your liking. I know you will not dine with us, but you can still take your pleasure in our company. Consider what you would like and let me know upon my return. Reticent you may be, but surely you will not attempt austerity at Saturnalia?

In regard to such matters, I have bought three slaves during my travels, all three most expert in amorous skills; if you would be interested in one of them, I would be pleased to make a gift to you, either one of the women, or the youth, as a show of my regard for all you have done for me and my family. They are all three comely, well-mannered, and talented in their ways. Without a wife to tend to you, you must long for the talents of slaves like these, and the women of the lupanar can be costly. Tell me you will consider my offer, and I will think myself most fortunate to be able to express my gratitude to you.

As you must know, the fighting in Syria is worse, and there are rumors that we must look to another leader there. Severus Macrinus may have gone too far when he cut the pay of the Legions; what soldier will want to defend the Empire with insufficient weaponry and an empty belly? The Legions must be paid. Few Caesars have failed to do that with impunity, and Severus Macrinus is not popular enough to assume good opinion will carry him: he needs silver for his troops, and the support of the Senate, which I am told is wavering, if he is to continue to wear the purple. I mention this in case you should have business in Syria you may want to shift before matters get more out of hand. After all you have done for me and mine, it is time I did something worthy for you and yours.

Look for me in four or five days, in the company of Pius Verus Lucillius, who has been in Salonae for three years and is eager to see the Tibrus and the Seven Hills again. His household will follow in two or three weeks, and so he will be staying with me until they arrive. We would be delighted to have you call upon us, should that fall in with your plans. Verus is a solid man, of good character, and not given to recklessness, except in the matter of chariot races.

Until such time as I hail you myself, I extend my most sincere dedication to you and your friendship,

Septimus Desiderius Vulpius

at Brundisium on the 14ᵗʰ day of August in the 971ˢᵗ Year of the City

6

Throughout Roma the statues of Pomona and Ceres were adorned with fresh-picked apples and new-mown stalks of wheat; in their forum, farmers displayed their crops and harvests for the crowds of Romans who came to buy on this early day in September when the air was made golden with angled sunshine on hanging dust, and the clamor of the vendors crying their goods could almost be heard over the babble of shoppers bargaining with farmers. Sedan chairs and bigae carried the most ostentatious of the honestiora through the mass of those who had come to buy, but for the most part, humiliora and honestiora alike went on foot, many carrying sacks and baskets for their purchases.

"There are Games tomorrow," said Vulpius to Sanct-Franciscus, who, in a short riding dalmatica of black linen over femoria of laced deerskin, walked on Vulpius' left: to his right was Pius Verus Lucillius, all splendid in a tan-and-green-striped long dalmatica of Egyptian cotton embroidered with Roman eagles. The three men looked up at the two stories of shops and stalls that enclosed the Forum

Agricolarum. "Do you think any of those will be open when there is fighting in the Flavian Circus?"

"There will be some," said Sanct-Franciscus. "Not everyone ventures to the Games."

"I gather you do not," said Lucillius, his animated features revealing his lively curiosity. "A foreigner like you, I should think you would want to indulge in all Roman entertainments." His remark was intended to get a rise out of Sanct-Franciscus, and he was mildly disappointed when it failed to do so.

"No; I am not attracted by the spectacle. I have been in Roma long enough to have sampled most of its delights, and I have found that the Games pall quickly." Sanct-Franciscus shrugged slightly, thinking back to the reign of Vespasianus, when he had been thrown to the crocodiles as part of an aquatic venation. "No doubt a failing of mine."

"It is certainly a sign of your foreignness," said Lucillius. "I don't think any Roman would despise this display—except those unctuous Christians." He flung up his hands for emphasis. "Coming to the amphitheaters and standing with their arms raised toward the sky, singing their verses, and calling upon those who want to be diverted to join them in worship. No wonder they're being banned from so many places. And saying that their gods are the only true gods! No Jupiter, no Mars, no Mercury! No Venus, no Diana, no Minerva! No Pomona or Ceres, for that matter," he said, nodding toward a pair of statues surrounded by the bounty of orchard and field. "Where would Roma be if we all thought like that?"

"Lucillius doesn't approve of Christians," said Vulpius unnecessarily.

"And what sensible man would approve them, I should like to know?" Lucillius inquired energetically as he shoved his way past a pair of slaves loading sacks of apples onto a restive mule. "If you have so few gods as the Christians, what do you do when those few fail you? They said that their gods are powerful enough for that, but what if that isn't so? Foolish and bigoted, that's what they are. Let them stay in their tunnels and caves, and leave decent men and women alone."

"They certainly would not approve of your sheltering a prostitute," said Vulpius to Sanct-Franciscus, hoping to change the subject.

Lucillius' eyes lit up with amusement. "You? How did this come
about?" he asked incredulously. "No, they would not approve in any
way. Why should you have to shelter her? What prostitute needs
shelter, but a dishonest one? She is preying on your good nature,
mark my words. There's a Guard for the lupanar as there is for the
city, and that should suffice—"

"There is a Guard, but she tells me it was the Guard who set
upon her," said Sanct-Franciscus, his demeanor serious.

"They would not," Vulpius declared staunchly. "They are paid to
keep the women safe. Everyone knows that. The peace of the lupanar is not to be breached—and by the Guard? Absurd. That they
should so forget themse—" He stopped, unable to go on.

"Indeed," said Sanct-Franciscus. "I am concerned that a greater
problem than this incident may be behind this attack."

Lucillius thought for a long moment. "This may be an alarming
thing, if she is telling the truth. Are you satisfied that she is—
truthful?"

"I have no reason to doubt her," said Sanct-Franciscus, keeping
his tone light and steady.

"But she is a woman of the lupanar, isn't she? She may have reasons to want to avoid the place: an angry customer perhaps," said
Vulpius. "She knows her work is as much for a man's pride as his
bodily satisfaction. She has arts of deception that you have not recognized, perhaps. Most women whose work it is to please men learn
how to prevaricate most convincingly."

A group of young men carrying wide, shallow baskets filled with
all manner of nuts came shoving their way through the shoppers,
bound for the corner of the Forum Agricolarum where the growers
of nuts and berries had their stalls.

"Had you seen her, and heard her, you would not doubt her,"
said Sanct-Franciscus.

"So say all men who have been well-pleasured," said Lucillius
chuckling.

"There was no pleasure in her when she came to me, only hurt and dread; she had no strength for dissembling," said Sanct-Franciscus, beginning to climb the stairs to the second level of shops on the north side of the forum; the shadow of the huge awning sheltering the flight cast him into welcome shadow, and he felt more alert and energetic than he had done in full daylight, though the soles of his ankle-height peri had been filled with his native earth but three days ago.

"Artifice is what that was," said Vulpius. "There are men who prefer their women weeping."

"But not with swollen eyes and broken lips," said Sanct-Franciscus, driven to a sharp retort. "How is it that a Roman citizen would allow a prostitute to be so misused? It was not so a century ago."

"Perhaps not," Vulpius allowed, seeing the smolder in his foreign friend's dark eyes. "But the world is a very changed place from a century ago. Caesars—good and bad—held their titles for much longer than those we have now. There were no barbarians strong enough to stand against us: our Legions were triumphant from Britannia to Asia, from Africa to Germania. Now those same barbarians chip away at our borders, and drive back our Legions—in Germania, they—" He caught his lip between his teeth, as if worried that he might have compounded his lapse.

"I do not come from Germania; you do not offend me with your remarks," said Ragoczy Germainus Sanct-Franciscus; he was mounting the stairs ahead of Vulpius and had to look back over his shoulder to continue to be heard in the busy stairwell. "You know my home is in the Carpathian Mountains; I have told you so. Neither Germania Superior nor Inferior can claim my allegiance. Say what you will: you will not offend me or those of my blood." Amid the tangle of people thronging the market, he caught sight of a pair of men wearing the belts of Praetorian servants; he had the uneasy sensation of having seen them before, and was trying to think where it was when a man in a great hurry came pelting down the stairs from the upper floor, shoving those ahead of him out of his way.

"Thief! He's a thief!" came the bellow from above.

The fleeing man—a tall, lanky man in a long-sleeved Gaulish tunica who looked Iberian—had a stiffened arm held out before him, and, because he was of some height and strong, had been able to knock over more than a dozen shoppers; he was understandably alarmed when he battered into the moderately tall, powerful-bodied man in black, for Sanct-Franciscus did not fall, but instead reached out and took the thief by the shoulder, stopping his precipitate escape.

"By the Twins!" exclaimed Vulpius, astonished and disconcerted.

Other oaths erupted around them as the shopkeeper—a man in the clothing of Armenia—came bustling through the fallen men and women, excoriating the thief in three languages at once. He carried a slender cudgel, and he struck the thief on the upper chest hard enough to make a bone crack and the thief cry out. "You are the shrivel-dicked son of a degenerate night-hag and a mad dog!" He raised his weapon to strike again, only to have his wrist seized. "Let go of me!"

"Not if you are going to beat him again," said Sanct-Franciscus firmly, his grip on the thief tightening so that the man would not again attempt to escape. With one disputant in each hand, Sanct-Franciscus found himself in an awkward position trying to keep the two apart, and, after a brief moment of consideration, said conversationally, "Vulpius, would you mind fetching one or two of the Forum Guards? Tell them they're needed to apprehend a thief. This man needs to be taken before the Prefect for the Fora." Both the thief and the merchant protested this request, but Sanct-Franciscus remained unmoved.

"I thank you for securing this miscreant, honestiorus; you have done me a great service, but there is no need to summon the Forum Guard; the Watchmen will suffice, when I have recovered my property. This hardly requires their attention," the Armenian merchant said, making an effort at courteous persuasion. "I will deal with him in my own way."

"Meaning you will smash his hands with your staff until all the bones are broken, and then you will turn him loose to starve; that stick of yours has lead in its cap," said Sanct-Franciscus. "And what would that gain you?"

"One less thief," said the Armenian.

"That may be, but then you will have a resentful beggar, and he will be much more dangerous than this thief ever could be."

"Sanct-Franciscus—" Lucillius attempted to admonish him, then saw the warning sign from Vulpius, and fell silent, moving aside so that Vulpius could go in search of a company of Urban Guard.

The merchant glowered at the thief, rubbing the head of his weighted staff suggestively. "It would settle the matter, breaking his hands. As it is, he will be back again. You are only postponing the inevitable."

Hearing this, the thief gave one good twist in final attempt to get away; he let out a sharp cry as the ends of his damaged clavicle scraped together; Sanct-Franciscus' hold on him was not diminished.

"If you try again, you will only make it worse," Sanct-Franciscus said, no anger or threat in his remark.

The thief did not seem convinced. "They'll send me to pull an oar. Smashed hands are better than a bench on a bireme."

"It is well that you should sweat for your thievery," said the Armenian. "At least you would be doing useful work in a bireme."

Sanct-Franciscus said, "Lucillius, if you will, find out precisely what was taken so that the Guard need not spend time searching that out." He cocked his head toward the Armenian. "If you will speak with this man you have accused in a sensible way, no doubt you will soon have everything settled."

"So you claim," said the Armenian, clearly becoming annoyed.

Lucillius climbed up to the shopkeeper, took him by the elbow and pulled him out of the flow of traffic. "The honestiorus is right. You should have such information ready for the Guard."

"He'll lie," said the thief, trying again to get away; his efforts ended on a single dismayed cry. "No; no. I know how merchants are—they inflate their losses and they demand that their allegations go unchallenged." His voice roughened. "He'll say I took more than I did, that it was more valuable than what it is, so that he can get more money in recompense for his losses, and so I will be given a harsher sentence."

The Armenian looked pugnacious. "Next you will say you took nothing, that I have accused you for no reason."

"You have," the thief began, then felt Sanct-Franciscus' fingers tighten. "You have made what I have done worse than it is. I took three sandalwood boxes—little ones. That is all I took. They're in my carry-sack."

"You have an accomplice," said the Armenian loudly. "You handed the alabaster figures off to him before this man caught you."

"I don't have an accomplice," the thief insisted. "I am a solitary thief." He tried to laugh and failed utterly.

"He isn't," the Armenian insisted. "I saw him with a youth, shortly before he came in to make off with my goods. He gave that young man instructions, and the instructions were that his accomplice should receive the best of the stolen goods as he left my shop."

The thief sighed. "There was no young man helping me. I told a messenger where he could find Grodius, the pottery merchant. That's all."

Lucillius patted the Armenian on the arm. "You will be better-believed if you stay with accounts that are easily confirmed. If he has your goods on him, confine your claims to what the Prefect of the Fora can see and appraise."

"Then I lose the best of my stock," the Armenian wailed.

"Stock you never had," said the thief, and flinched as Sanct-Franciscus' grip held him in place.

There was a small crowd milling around them now, and questions were being shouted as the numbers of shoppers stopped on the stairs increased. Curiosity made the people press in, eager to hear what accusations would next be made.

The thief suddenly shouted, "I smell smoke!"

The people closing in around them stopped and turned, their attention diverted by fear. A few of them broke away from the crush and hurried toward other steps leading out of the covered shops.

"Clever," murmured Sanct-Franciscus to the thief, his hold on the man unbroken. "But reckless."

"Vesta save us from fire," Lucillius muttered. "We could not get out of here if a spark should light the awning."

The Armenian shuddered, and backed up as far as the crush of onlookers would allow, muttering an invocation to the fire-god of his people. "There was a fire in the grain emporium last week—the one behind this forum; four men were burned, and one of them died," he said, trying to control his sudden burst of panic.

"Have you paid the Guard and the Watchmen your annual fee to keep your shop from damage from fire, water, and earthquake?" Lucillius asked, as much to quiet the man as to gain information. "Have you paid your portion for the Forum Guard?"

"I have," said the Armenian, "but not all the shopkeepers in this gallery have done so, and so who knows if any of them would come? Or how much they would demand in payment before they would do their duty?" He looked around as if noticing the gathering around him for the first time. His eyes widened. "How can they get into this place, given the way it is? Too many people; too many." He shook his staff at the nearest shoppers. "Go! Be about your business. The Forum Guard is coming, and they must have a clear path. Go!"

While Lucillius tried to soothe the Armenian, Sanct-Franciscus gave his attention to the thief. "What did you take from him? Do not lie if you want my help. I know you took something."

"I told you: I took the sandalwood boxes. I still have them. I didn't see any alabaster figures on display. If he had them at all, they were out of reach." He shivered and retched. "Wait. I . . ." He was very pale now, and there was a shine of sweat on his face. "I . . . Oh, Dis release me." With a moan, his knees gave way, and had not Sanct-Franciscus held him up, he would have collapsed.

Sanct-Franciscus recognized the signs of secondary pain, and knew it could be much more deadly than the broken bone that caused it. He steadied the thief, leaning him back against the wall, and motioned for those near them to move. "This man is having an attack of chills. He needs to lie down, or he may faint."

"And good thing, too," the Armenian shouted, still trying to push his way toward his shop.

Paying no attention to the sudden buzz of questions, Sanct-Franciscus was able to lower the man almost to the paving stones; aware that he himself could impart no warmth to the cold-gripped thief, he began to look about him in the hope that he would find someone wearing a light mantele, and that he could borrow or buy it to provide the thief a little heat, for in spite of the warmth of the day, the thief's teeth were chattering. He saw no one with the garment he sought, and his efforts at a further search were stopped as three Urban Guards pushed their way up the stairs, Vulpius leading them and explaining the situation as he went.

"Which is the thief?" demanded the leader of the Guards, a good-sized fellow almost as tall as Sanct-Franciscus.

"This man, leaning against the wall," said Sanct-Franciscus. "He needs something to help warm him."

The leader of the Guard snapped his fingers and the youngest of the three tugged off his bronze-colored abolla and handed it to the leader. "Use this. Providing the thief isn't bleeding too copiously."

"Thank you," said Sanct-Franciscus, taking the abolla and wrapping it around the shivering thief. "This will help to warm you."

The thief, who had gone a pasty shade and was breathing quickly and shallowly, muttered something incomprehensible, then blinked twice.

"Hardly seems worth stealing, if you end up in this condition," said the Guards' leader. "But if he has stolen, he must be detained."

"That is my understanding," said Vulpius. He pointed to the Armenian. "That man will make the complaint."

Lucillius prodded the Armenian in the side to push him forward. "Tell the Guard what happened, and show them your staff."

The Armenian glared, but approached the Guards with an obsequious smile. "That man came into my shop. He had an accomplice out here in the gallery—I'm certain of it—and this man took sandalwood boxes and alabaster figures, then ran out to meet his comrade. I followed him, of course, to try to get my goods back, but by the time I caught up with him, he had passed along the most valuable of my merchandise to his—"

"No!" the thief managed to protest. "Only boxes. No . . . accomplice."

"He has claimed this from the first," said Lucillius, coming up to the Guard. "That he worked alone and took only boxes. He says he has no one working with him."

The leader looked directly at Sanct-Franciscus. "Is this true?"

"Yes, it is." He paused to consider. "Not that he is necessarily telling the truth."

"He is *lying!*" shouted the Armenian. "He gave the best to—"

"Not here," said the leader of the Guard. "You will have your chance to tell the Prefect of the Fora tomorrow morning. This man needs a night in which to recover himself to answer questions, which he clearly will not do at the moment." He looked about the gallery. "I will need three witnesses beyond these honestiora," he added, pointing to Lucillius, Sanct-Franciscus, and Vulpius. "You will present yourselves tomorrow morning?"

Lucillius sighed. "I suppose I must."

"I will come," said Vulpius.

"If you will permit me to visit the thief this evening, to see for myself if he has been given proper medicaments and treatment, I will gladly come to the Prefect of the Fora tomorrow," said Sanct-Franciscus.

The Guard leader shrugged. "If that suits your purpose, it will be arranged."

"Thank you," said Sanct-Franciscus. "You will do better to carry him on a litter. His clavicle is broken, and he is hurt profoundly. Have a physician treat him as soon as possible or he may not be able to appear before the Justice tomorrow."

"A litter, is it? Better than having to carry him on our shoulders," said the leader. He signaled his men to improvise a litter with their abollae, then regarded Sanct-Franciscus. "You seem to have kept this well in hand. Very commendable. I am Fulvius Ennius Castrum; use my name at the prison and you will be admitted."

"I am Ragoczy Germainus Sanct-Franciscus; you may tell the jailer to expect me."

Castrum nodded. "Very good. I will look forward to your appearance before the Justice tomorrow." With that, he went to help his men raise the thief onto their litter.

"Tomorrow. I must wait until tomorrow," the Armenian complained. "It is because I am foreign. You will see—tomorrow I will have to pay twice what the Romans pay to have my case heard."

"Very likely," said Lucillius. "That has become common practice." He laughed cynically. "Everyone decries it, but who is to challenge it?"

"Not a foreigner," said Sanct-Franciscus. "Certainly not that foreigner." He cocked his head toward the Armenian shopkeeper.

The Guards started down the stairs, Castrum going ahead of them, motioning the crowd to make way. As he reached the foot of the flight, he glanced back at Sanct-Franciscus and offered him a casual salute.

"Are you really going to check on that thief tonight?" asked Lucillius, making no apology for his incredulity.

"Yes," said Sanct-Franciscus. "He is badly hurt, and his injuries could fester inwardly."

"But why should you bother?" Lucillius pursued.

"Better to let him rot," said the Armenian.

Vulpius answered before his foreign friend could speak. "Oh, Sanct-Franciscus is meticulous in such matters; he cannot turn away from those who have no one else to help them. I don't pretend to understand it."

"An odd thing for a man in your position to do, if you'll pardon my mention of it," said Lucillius.

Sanct-Franciscus shrugged. "We exiles know the world is perilous." Lucillius shook his head. "But why—" He stopped.

"I know what it is to be in the hands of those indifferent to suffering," Sanct-Franciscus said with banked emotion before he resumed his walk toward the shop of Ebulius, the purveyor of paints and dyes, Vulpius and Lucillius following after him, chatting about the thief and the Armenian and complaining of the crowd around them.

Text of a letter from Comus Mauritanius, decuria of the Prefect of the Litigianus Prison, carried by messenger the day after it was written.

To the most worthy foreigner, Ragoczy Germainus Sanct-Franciscus, the greetings of the Prefect of the Litigianus Prison, the honestiorus Herminius Mirandus Guion, in whose name I am bidden to write to you.

First this is to acknowledge the receipt of ten aurei in payment of the fine assessed on the thief, Natalis of Thessalonika; the man has been branded on the arm and will—because of the fine Sanct-Franciscus has paid—be released after six months of labor with no further charges to answer. He will not be sent to pull an oar on a bireme or to dig roads in Gaul, unless he should steal again, and he will not be sold into slavery to cover the cost of his maintenance while in prison. Once his injuries are healed, he will be assigned to janitorial duties here until his term is finished. He has been ordered to find honest employment or to leave Roma at once and to stay away for three years, on pain of imprisonment should he return before that time. On the annual receipt of five silver denarii, I will assure Sanct-Franciscus that he will be notified of any information received here concerning the thief Natalis within the year that the amount is paid.

Second, the Prefect wishes to discuss with you what medicaments you used to treat the thief Natalis, for the recovery the man made from the corruption of the broken bone in his shoulder was remarkable, and perhaps could be used to advantage with other prisoners whose injuries show symptoms of inner rot. He is willing to pay a reasonable fee for a supply of such medicaments, or would also consider purchasing the formula for making the substance. Of course, he knows that if there are unique skills associated with the production of the medicament, he cannot expect Sanct-Franciscus to reveal them to an uninitiated man like himself.

It is an uncommon thing to see a man of property do so much for a thief, and all the more remarkable because Sanct-Franciscus is a foreigner. It creates an example that many Romans would do well to emulate. If Sanct-Franciscus is willing to set a time when he can meet with the Prefect, then the Prefect would be glad of the opportunity to thank Sanct-Franciscus face to face and in person rather than through this missive and the decuria signed below,

Comus Mauritanius
Decuria, Litigianus Prison

on the 29ᵗʰ day of September in the 971ˢᵗ Year of the City

7

Small flames danced on the peaks of a collection of beautiful bud-shaped alabaster oil-lamps, lending the room a soft glow that created a air of gauzy mystery, precisely as Melidulci intended they should. To further enhance her withdrawing room, she had set out three brass perfume pans over broad-based oil-lamps, to lend the air delectable sweetness, bestowing on her a touch of their delicate insouciance and providing a setting that would be sure to please her visitor. Most of her injuries had healed, but she was acutely aware of the scars remaining as unhappy reminders of her attack; she had no wish to reveal any more of them than absolutely necessary, and to that end she had donned her most elegant, gap-sleeved long tunica in peach-colored silk, the gaps fixed with brooches made of amber-and-gold, the clinging garment secured at the waist by a long ribbon of gold mesh. The night was cool, a bite of autumn in the air, but she had ordered the holocaust lit that afternoon, and the floor was warm from its heat, and would continue to keep them comfortable well into the night.

"So you have decided not to return to the lupanar," said Sanct-Franciscus from where he stood in the double-door facing the fountain in the center of the atrium; his black dalmatica, edged in silver eclipses, deepened the shadows in which he stood, as if he were a specter and not her honored guest.

"I believe it is best if I don't," she said, doing her best to smile at him without showing the red line running through her upper lip and toward her cheek, the most lingering reminder of the attack she had sustained; this was only the second time she had had a guest at her new house, and she felt strangely inept at performing her duties as hostess, for she had just a few slaves, chosen for their service not their appearance, to wait upon Sanct-Franciscus and her; no musicians strummed and plucked lyres and harps, no acrobats tumbled or contorted. Although she had chosen it, the simplicity of their evening unnerved her now that she was experiencing it.

"Because you do not trust the Guards of the Lupanar, and small wonder," he said, as if he had no doubt about it.

"I think it would be best if I don't return," she said more emphatically but without addressing his remark, then added, "Or not for a while, in any case."

"Have you learned who they were who attacked you?" He asked this as if he might be speaking of the turn of the seasons.

"No," she said tightly. "I won't go back until I know their names. Perhaps not even then."

"If that is truly your wish, well and good; I hope you are not being frightened away," he said, moving toward her unhurriedly.

"Why should I not be frightened?" she inquired, her question sharper than she had intended; she tried to lessen the stridency of her question. "Had I been afraid before, I might have escaped harm."

Sanct-Franciscus did not speak at once, and when he did, his voice was deep and gentle. "You would do well to be rid of fear because fear infects everything it touches, leeching the joy from life. If you are staying away to try not to be frightened, you will not succeed: fear will shadow you." He studied her face with earnest concern.

"And you think that is the case?" She attempted another smile, and managed somewhat better than before. "Why?"

"Because you have not received guests during the day, and you have offered no erotic entertainments in this new house—not as you have offered to your guests in the lupanar; you are very discreet, which is wise, but you are also striving to make yourself unnoticeable, except where you choose to be noticed," he said, coming to the end of her couch, ignoring the other couch on the far side of the low table where food would be placed.

"Do you have any objections to my methods?" She was not angry, but she could not keep from fretting.

"No," Sanct-Franciscus said. "It suits me well enough, visiting you after sundown for only the pleasure of your company, but it might not please many others, who may have different expectations of you, and who have long preferred you to all others."

"That is a matter of convenience for me, since I have no women sharing this house with me; I may have those I like call upon me, which permits me to keep to a schedule that I can accommodate. There are many who will find the evenings less . . . hasty, and they are apt to do what they must to have more time and privacy. . . ." Hearing the note of defensiveness in her explanation, she made herself stop. "I choose my company more carefully now."

"To your credit," he said, again coming a step nearer. "You may keep a closer watch on your household as you live now."

She took several heartbeats to gather her thoughts to answer. "No, it's not that. Any woman knows that mystery adds to an encounter, and night is, by its nature, mysterious."

"And more exclusive," he suggested.

She pressed her lips together, so she would not say anything too impulsive. "I do not want to become one of those women who spend the entire day with eager men, and, by evening, has no inclination to amuse herself."

"Ah." He studied her for a long, silent moment, the kindness in his dark eyes unnerving her, so that she reached for a small hand-bell, and rang it, signaling her slaves to bring in the light repast she had ordered; three slaves appeared promptly, each carrying a tray that they set down on the table next to her couch.

Melidulci had ordered scallops wrapped in bacon and broiled, boiled eggs peeled, halved, and stuffed with ground walnuts, vinegar, and olive oil mixed with the yolks, grilled eggplant, and toasted buns filled with chopped venison in a sauce of peppers, garlic, and onions; a basket of newly-baked olive-breads accompanied the meal. With this was a ewer filled with red wine from Florentia. "I suppose it is useless to ask you if you want any of this excellent food?"

"I fear I lack the stomach for it," he said in sardonic, honest dismay; he recognized all the dishes as having the reputation of increasing a man's ardor.

She motioned to the food. "It is a good convivium—not so heavy that you will be weary after eating, but not so light that you will be hungry."

"But Melidulci, you know I never dine," said Sanct-Franciscus;

he had realized more than five hundred years ago that food could be as exciting to the senses of the living as embraces or compliments, and he had learned to encourage dining as part of physical pleasances.

For a clumsy moment, she said nothing, then tried to smile. "I know it isn't your habit to eat, but I thought . . . given this occasion . . ."

Sanct-Franciscus smiled. "You are stimulant enough for me, Melidulci. Nothing you could offer could tempt me more than you do." His face softened. "If you are hungry, eat. You will not offend me."

To her astonishment, she felt herself blush. "You're most . . . gracious to say so,"

"Melidulci." He spoke softly, but something in his tone compelled her attention. "You have nothing to fear from me. I am not a monster, nor am I one who bargains in flesh. You need not placate me, or appease me—there is no cause: believe this."

"But surely . . . It is fitting that I thank you . . . After all you've done?" Her laughter was a bit too brittle to be genuine. "I should think I owe you at least a gesture of gratitude."

"You have thanked me," he said. "That is behind us."

"But I . . . you are here for enjoyment, and I . . . am no longer . . . flawless."

"Your scars do not distress me: I have more and worse of my own." He sank down on the end of her dining couch and reached to touch her arm.

"You do not show them to me," she said reproachfully. "Are you afraid they will disgust me?"

"No; they are very severe." He put his spread hand to his waist, extending his fingers. "From my thumb to my little finger."

She stared. "Scars of that sort could be deadly," she said somberly.

"So they could," he responded, adding *and so they were* to himself.

"Yet you say that flaws do not repel you?" she challenged, angling her head upward.

"No, they do not," he said tranquilly. "Flaws are often at the heart of beauty. Think of Mirabella, with her mole at the corner of her eye, or Eusacia, whose birthmark lends her face a catlike appearance. Neither of them are hampered by their flaws. Why should you be?"

"Those are gifts of birth. I have scars from a beating." She made a determined effort not to cry.

"That could make a difference to some squeamish men," he allowed. "But not to me."

She stared at him. "How can you look at me and not see me with my face swollen and broken? You must be repulsed."

"Not repulsed: saddened," he corrected her gently. "I am sorry that you have had to bear the burdens imposed upon you."

"Imposed." She looked away, trying to stop a sudden rush of tears; she very nearly succeeded, and that gave her a brief satisfaction. She used her thumb and finger to pinch the bridge of her nose and wipe away the shine of moisture on her eyelids.

"What else would you call it?" he asked, kindness suffusing his dark, compelling eyes.

"They would have been worse if not for you," said Melidulci; to distract herself she picked up a bacon-wrapped scallop and bit into it, chewed for a short while, then went on in a different tone, taking refuge in what she said. "Before my Aunt Bonascientia—she was originally named Liatris—adopted me and brought me to the lupanar, I lived with my mother and father and two surviving brothers— another brother and a sister died young—to the north of Roma, near Pisae. I was called Emera then. My father and his brother had a good-sized holding beyond the town where they bred mules for the Legions and donkeys for farmers, and we did fairly well; they were respected in the region, and their mules were always well-conformed. I'd had a marriage arranged with the son of a horse-breeder, and everything seemed set. I would probably have done well by Aquila; he was a sensible youth, and we'd grown up together. But then Swine Fever came when I was twelve, and my brothers died, and then my uncle, and a year later, my father was kicked in the head by an injured mule, which left his wits addled." She sighed and finished her scallop. "Why should I tell you this?"

"Because you will feel less alone if you do," said Sanct-Franciscus, who welcomed this effort at closeness. "Your aunt brought you here to

Roma after so much loss." It was not quite a question. "To the lupanar, where she lived."

"She did. She had been very successful in her work, and she had amassed a considerable amount of money—more than I have, and I have done quite well for myself."

"Yes, you have," said Sanct-Franciscus, encouraging her to go on.

Melidulci banished the frown forming between her brows and ordered her memories. "When she was informed about her brother's condition, she came to see for herself, and at once set about to provide for my father and mother. She took care of everything; arranged for the mules and donkeys to be sold and the land put under stewardship of Aquila's brother—the marriage had been forsworn by both families—and my mother provided for with rents from the land, so that she would not be without means in the world. When the land was dealt with, Aunt Bonascientia found slaves to take care of my father, and she paid for a Greek physician to treat him; my mother couldn't bear to do it, nor could I. Had my aunt not taken me in, my life would have been far less pleasant, and far less profitable than it has been." Wiping her hands on a square of linen set out next to a bowl of water for the purpose of cleaning greasy fingers, she continued, "I don't know why I'm telling you this . . . I don't . . . I never talk about my life before the lupanar. And when I've been asked, I haven't told the truth." She admitted this without embarrassment, but with a hint of regret. "Most men prefer a fable to the actuality."

"But I do not want a fable, I want the whole of you. I thank you for revealing so much."

"Thank me, for lamenting my misfortunes?" she asked, sounding chagrined. "What man wants to—"

"Misfortune came upon you when you were young, unaccountably, and has done so again," said Sanct-Franciscus.

She stared at him, considering what he had said. "Yes," she agreed slowly. "Yes. I suppose I hope that I will be as lucky this time as I was then, although Aunt Bonascientia has been dead more than a decade. The gods are not always kind, even to those who honor them."

"It *is* hard when all your family has died," he said, a haunted look in his eyes.

"It is," she said, with the uncanny certainty that he had endured more devastating losses than she. "I understand I have two cousins somewhere, and three other relatives, but—"

"You must not despair, Melidulci. You have prevailed," he said, lifting her hand and kissing the palm.

"I hope I have," she said, a bit unsteadily as she selected a stuffed egg-half and began to eat.

He released her hand and poured wine into one of two beautiful, costly glass goblets. "Here. You will feel better if you have wine with your food."

She took the goblet from him, holding it up to the display of oil-lamps so that she could see the brilliant red heart of the wine. "You are so kind to me."

He said nothing, reflecting that if this little courtesy was kindness, she must have been ill-used many times in the past, or she had become inured to lack of consideration, which lent even the most minor service a significance beyond its deserving. He realized it also meant that the high regard for the women of the lupanar, once unquestioned and upheld throughout the Empire, was now corroding, along with the other traditional attitudes of Romans. This unrelenting sensuality and excitation had blunted the Romans' perceptions to the point that only greater voluptuary indulgence could rouse them, and the lack of respect for the women of the lupanar was only one result of this dulled state. He sat, gazing at her, taking in every nuance of her demeanor, her manner, her expression. When she had drunk half the contents of the goblet, he took it from her and set it down on its tray, then leaned forward to gently, gently kiss her mouth. "You are all the savor I require."

This time she made no effort to hide the color that rose in her cheeks. "Wine; it heats me," she said by way of explanation, although both of them knew it was not the cause.

"Perhaps," he allowed, and kissed her again, a longer and more arousing kiss, one that seemed to touch every bit of her flesh, quickening passion and speeding her pulse. As his lips touched hers once more, he enveloped her in his arms.

"Oh, I . . . ," Melidulci exclaimed as they broke apart. Inwardly

she chided herself for behaving like a green girl: she was an experienced, successful prostitute, one of the most celebrated in Roma,
honored and praised from Egypt to Gaul, yet here she was, her
senses tingling, breathless, almost vertiginous with desire, as if she
were new to the ways of men, and learning the power of Amor for
the first time. What was it about Sanct-Franciscus that awakened so
much of her amorousness? She found it strange that this foreigner,
who used her so unlike other men, should have the power to stir her
to the depths of her desires.

"You are as beautiful as the evening star in a violet sky,
Melidulci, and nothing can change that," said Sanct-Franciscus, his
fingers trailing up her arm. At each brooch, he stopped and carefully unfastened it, exposing more of her skin. By the time he
reached the largest, at her shoulder, he could feel the frisson his
touch evoked.

She was breathing more quickly, and her eyes were lustrous as
the lamplight. As he pulled the tibia from the brooch at her shoulder, the silk slithered luxuriously down her body, exposing her breast
and pulling the material more provocatively against her. "I . . . I—"
she whispered as he began on her other arm, dropping the brooches
onto the tray next to her half-empty goblet.

"This is for you, Melidulci," he said softly, his lips brushing the
arch of her clavicle, as light and tantalizing as the feathers she sometimes used on her more adventurous clients.

"I . . ." She took a long, uneven breath as he unfastened the last
brooch, and the silk scrooped down to her waist. For several heartbeats she remained immobile, unable to bring herself to do those
things she was used to doing for her clients. Instead, she closed her
eyes so she could experience his touch more fully, her senses
heightened by his nearness, and his exhilarating, unhurried explo-
ration of her body. Gradually, she sank back on the couch, her
clothes falling away from her upper body; her increasing excitement imparted a paradoxical languor, heightening her delight in
surrender to his ministrations. She felt Sanct-Franciscus untie her
elegant belt, and almost at once her tunica was gone and she was lying naked before him. She started to sit up, to conceal her scars

with her arms, but she was stopped as Sanct-Franciscus put his hand on her shoulder, using just enough strength to keep her from trying to hide.

"You have nothing to fear," he said, one knee on the couch beside her as he bent forward to kiss her breasts.

"The scars—"

"You have nothing to fear," he repeated, and kissed her mouth with slow, delicious, insouciant torment, banishing all her unease and replacing it with steadily increasing exaltation as she gave herself once again to the bounty of gratification.

As he expanded his exquisite tantalizations, Melidulci felt the first surge of pleasure engulf her, a quivering that promised a culmination that she had rarely experienced. She tried to find something to say to Sanct-Franciscus that would lend him support, but the words slipped away, borne on ethereal wings. The only sound she offered was a soft moan of utter lightsomeness as his hands and kisses made their way down her body to the cleft at the top of her thighs. In a still, quiet part of her mind, Melidulci chided herself for surrendering so completely to Sanct-Franciscus' caresses; she had been pleasuring men for many years, and knew most of the arts that could be used to give satisfaction, yet here she was, like a girl newly taught, more willing than knowing, and filled with eagerness and novelty. It was not as if she knew nothing of the satisfaction Sanct-Franciscus' skills could impart, either, for they had lain together four times to fulfillment, but— The sensible voice was stilled as she felt his hands slide between her legs. Now she was enthralled by the expansion of her perceptions, so that the lightest touch sent waves through her body that amazed her; the flick of his tongue in the soft folds of the portal of her body shuddered through the marrow of her bones, leaving her delectably amplectant, her arms wrapped around him. The more he did to rouse her, the greater the intensity of her gratification grew, and the more she yearned for the ineffable moment when she would be transfixed with culmination. Subtle and daring at once, his hands and mouth elicited every refinement of sensual frenzy, evoking elation she had never achieved, igniting her body in escalating rapture until she cried out in release; her flesh, shaken into transports, rode the ecstatic pulse of her passion to heights that had eluded her before, but now became the apogee of her existence, leaving her all but oblivious to Sanct-Franciscus, bent over her, his lips on her neck.

While she lay replete on her couch, gradually coming back to herself, she tried to think of something to do to express her immense satisfaction. Finally, as she was able to sit up, she looked up at him. "How am I to give you fulfillment?"

He dropped on one knee beside her couch to gather up her silken tunica. "You have done so already—better than you know."

"Oh, yes," she said with a suggestion of a smile. "You always tell me that you have what I have; that your pleasure is my pleasure. I trust you will not mind if I am willing to believe you?" She stretched, her body still sinuous in the aftermath of satisfaction.

"I tell you because it is true," he said with such complete simplicity that she began to think that it was so.

"You could persuade me," she allowed as she smoothed stray damp, pale tendrils of hair back from her face.

"What reason would I have to prevaricate?" he countered, his musical voice lightly teasing.

"If you say so, I suppose I must accept it," she said, and licked her lips with the tip of her tongue; then she admitted, "I don't know if you will mind, considering what has just passed between us, but I find I'm hungry . . . still."

"Then eat," said Sanct-Franciscus, amusement lighting his dark eyes. "You mustn't exhaust yourself on my account." He rose and went to the low table, prepared to serve her wine or food.

"Would that I could," she said with a toss of her head.

"Exhaust yourself?" He gestured to the waiting dishes.

She shook her head. "No—do anything on your account. You disarm all obligation." She selected an egg-half and began to eat.

"Why would you want to do anything on my account?" he asked, mildly startled by her remark.

It took her a short while to answer. "Because you have done so much for me." She swallowed the last of the egg with a generous sip of wine.

He leaned toward her once more, his gaze compelling. "I do not expect you to keep a tally of obligation, Melidulci. I do not bargain my affections. What I offer—such as it is—I offer freely. It is not necessary for you to concern yourself with such balances, and it could come to distort our dealings together."

"I hadn't meant—" She shivered a bit, aware that this had unusual importance to him. "No, I suppose I did. For a woman in my profession . . . it is the kind of assumption we all make."

He went on, "What we have is a gift, you and I; we can touch one another. Be thankful that it exists, not the number of times and conditions under which we enjoy it."

She pressed her mouth closed, not trusting herself to speak. Finally she refilled her goblet and picked it up. "May Fortuna show you favor," she said as she took a long sip.

"And you," he responded, ducking his head in place of taking a drink.

"What are you thinking?" Melidulci asked after a brief silence; she had seen the suggestion of a frown on his brow.

"I was thinking that you may still be at risk here," said Sanct-Franciscus. "I would advise you to engage guards to protect you."

"And where might I find such dependable guards?" She was dismayed to realize that she expected him to answer her.

Sanct-Franciscus cocked his head. "Would you like me to inquire for you? I would be happy to do it."

This calm inquiry took her aback. She knew that it was something she had hoped he would help with, but the directness of his question disarmed her. "I . . . I don't know."

"Because you are unsure about wanting guards, or because you are unsure about permitting me to engage them for you?" His question was lightly asked, and the glint in his eye was affectionate, but she responded as if she had been rebuked.

"If I need guards, I will manage them for myself, Patronus," she announced, and then, to her shock, began to weep.

Sanct-Franciscus came to her side, his manner thoughtful; he laid his small, beautiful hands on her shoulders. "From your own hiring, or from mine, you would be well-advised to employ guards,

Melidulci. You cannot spend all your days in a rapture of fear. It will rob you of all you are."

She stared at him. "I'm not afraid," she insisted, although her voice shook. "I'm not."

A century ago, she could have said it and been sensible, but now, with Roma so much changed from that time, he knew that her situation was precarious. "If you deny it, you give it strength, and add to its impact."

"I must resist it," she said doggedly, dabbing with her silken tunica at her eyes. "I will not give in."

"You would do better to admit it, and to see it for what it is, and make preparation against it," he said tenderly, bending to kiss her forehead. "A goat in the night becomes a troupe of bear if you do not shine a lamp on it."

She made a terrible mull of laughing. "You always have such good advice," she said as she set the last bit of egg aside, her appetite gone as quickly as it had come.

"Not advice: concern," he corrected her gently, sitting on the couch and folding her into his arms, her pale hair brushing against his cheek as she clung to him in the deepening night.

Text of a letter from Atta Olivia Clemens at Ravenna to Ragoczy Germainus Sanct-Franciscus in Roma, carried by private courier to Roma.

To my most dear friend, currently calling himself Ragoczy Germainus Sanct-Franciscus, but who still is Ragoczy Sanct' Germain Franciscus to me, and who is abiding in my house near the Temple of Hercules in Roma, the greetings of Atta Olivia Clemens, accompanying the sworn copies of my claims to the house, as well as its history, my own records of payments for the last five years, beyond what you have there, and witnessed copies of my own registration of household.

It seems to me that you have encountered the new manner of bureaucracy which has come about in Roma since they made the earnings of the decuriae dependent on the services they render. If Roma were not corrupt before, it is so now—how could it be otherwise: this policy has made corruption almost necessary for the government to function. More fools they!

You will tell me—and beyond cavil correctly—that you have seen worse in other times and places. I do not doubt it is true, but I am most dismayed that it should happen to my city, to my home. I know that change comes to all things, but I had hoped that Roma could resist the rot a little longer. Ravenna is much the same, of course, with the addition of piracy and smuggling from the port, but it is smaller, and I have (thanks to you) more than sufficient funds to purchase my privacy and a guard for me while I live here. We still have to deal with judicial chicanery, debasement of coins, capricious taxes, and rogues in high places, but for the time being, I believe I am as safe as a woman alone may be in the Empire of Roma in this time. Ravenna may not be as splendid as Roma, but Roma has lost some of its splendor since I came to your life, more than a century-and-a-half ago.

And now, a fourteen-year-old youth from Syria is Caesar! Varius Avitus Bassianus, a self-proclaimed son of Caracalla, who is doubtless a tool of his mother, his grandmother, and who knows whomelse, is the leader of all the Empire. Grandnephew—by marriage—of Septimius Severus: a recommendation, oh, most surely. What other claims might he put forth? I would laugh if I were not a Roman. And what is this nonsense about calling himself after the Syrian sun god? Isn't Apollo grand enough for him, that he must style himself Heliogabalus. Apollonius would be audacious enough, but at least it would be Roman.

Enough of these lowering reflections. I am in no position to change what has happened, and thinking will only cause me to grieve for Roma. So: I have retained a local fellow—Catalinus by name—to serve as my steward. He is able to read and write and he knows numbers. He has no family in the region, and is in need of work; he is not uncomely, and he is taken with me, so I am fairly sure he will not cheat me too egregiously, or tell my secrets to the world. I trust he will be inclined to remain with me for some time, for I would not like to have to train a new steward again for a decade. As to the possibilities for more between us, I will tell you that I have hopes that he will not be too dismayed when he learns of my nature, and my inclinations. I grow weary of visiting men in their dreams. You told me that I would come to long for knowing embraces, and so it is.

Speaking of stewards, Rogerian—or Rugeri, as he styles himself just now—has written to me from Alexandria, saying that two of your ships have been delayed and possibly lost. I will include that letter with this one, as he has asked me to do. He believes four of his letters have not reached you, and that may be a troublesome indication, for it means that his letters are being seized, not merely lost at sea, for the ship carrying one of the letters reached Ostia and returned to Alexandria unharmed. Also, another one of your ships has been taken by pirates, and Rogerian would like you to permit him to ransom the crew. I have assured him that you would expect him to do so, in case your letter to him fails to reach him.

I must tell you that I feel a certain fellowship with Rogerian, for we came to you, each in our way, at almost the same time. In the last century and more he has shown himself to be reliable, honorable, sensible, and loyal. I do not think you could find a better bondsman anywhere, but I will admit that my opinion is not completely disinterested. I see what he does for you, and I feel a lamentable twinge of jealousy. Not that I would expect you to give up Rogerian, but I would like to have a bondsman of my own one day.

This piracy that Rogerian mentions is a growing threat, and nothing is being done to contain it. On land, gangs of bandits haunt the roads unchallenged while the Legions are beaten back on all our borders. A fine thing for Roma! Magna Mater, but I could cry for vexation, if only I had tears to shed. That such lawlessness would be allowed in the Empire, and that the people should acquiesce in it! The Praetorians swagger and boast as if Roma were still intact, as if our laws were still upheld, as if the Senate had any power beyond self-congratulations. Only the Vestal Virgins have upheld their integrity, and with the rising popularity of Christians, even that is being undermined. I must be grateful, I suppose, that these conditions did not prevail when I was alive, for then I should never have been *able to escape my husband, no matter what you may have done to help me. My death would have been the True Death, and no one would have called Cornelius Justus Silius to book for it.*

If you will permit me to repeat some of your advice to me: do not linger if the tide turns against you. Foreigners are not as welcome in Roma as they were in my breathing days, and the city is more volatile than when you were last there; as you have said yourself, there is depravity that comes from desperation everywhere— think of the zeal of the foreign religions, and the increasing numbers of soothsayers in the city—and once the people are sparked to ferocity they are more dangerous than tigers in the Flavian Circus. You encouraged me to be prepared to leave quickly, and covertly, which I have done; I also have plans to depart Ravenna, should it become necessary. I now remind you to make the same preparations, for you are as exposed as I was. Come here to me if you need a place to retreat, and I will keep you as safe as my name and gold can. It is the least I can do for you.

This carries my undying love to you, as well as my affectionate castigations, and promises you that my fealty is true, come what may. This, then, by my own hand, and with the fullness of my devotion, on the first day of November in the 971st Year of the City,

Olivia

8

"Ave Heliogabalus! Ave Heliogabalus!" the crowd roared obediently as the new emperor made his way through the foggy city, his procession being led by three gold-painted quadrigae drawn by ostriches. These elegant chariots contained half-naked young men, too drunk to be cold, who tossed handfuls of dried flowers to the people lining the streets. After the three quadrigae came a party of dancers and musicians, doing their best to perform in the daunting weather, but shivering in spite of their exertions. Behind these entertainers there was a large open carriage, gilded and jeweled, and drawn by six Iberian horses ridden by more handsome young men in skimpy Greek chlamyses; it was in this equipage that Heliogabalus rode, a golden laurel-wreath crowning him, his arms shining with bracelets, his body loosely swathed in all-but-invisible Coan linen; his genitals were painted golden-red, and he sat so that everyone could see. If he was cold, he gave no sign of it. Young as he was, there was already a cynical turn to his mouth and an air of decadence in his manner, as well as a willfulness in the set of his chin; he drank wine from a large golden goblet that was constantly refilled for him by the beautiful slave—a boy of nine or ten dressed as Bacchus—who attended upon him.

Behind him came a troupe of tumblers and dancers—all male— doing their best to perform on the slippery street; bruises and scrapes gave testimony to their lack of success. Next a contingent of Praetorians marched, their long pallia decorated with light-tan sun-disks in honor of the Emperor and his Syrian god; the Praetorians' visages were expressionless. Then came a covered quadriga in which rode Julia Maesa, Heliogabalus' formidable grandmother; she was sensibly swathed in heavy silken stolae and pallae, and she wore a vast array of golden jewelry; she nodded to the gathered Romans but neither waved nor smiled, preferring the stern demeanor of a conquering general to that of grateful parent. Next to her rode her daughter, Julia Soaemias, in brilliant silks and an ostentatious display of golden jewelry. A company of city Guards followed after the Emperor's family, just as stiff and impassive as the Praetorians. Last came a line of condemned slaves, bound for the Flavian Circus and the next day's Great Games. In spite of the chilly drizzle, Romans were out in force to see the handsome youth who had risen so high. A few in the crowd, unfamiliar with the new name, cried, "Ave, Cae-sar!" and let it go at that.

"What do you make of him?" Vulpius asked Sanct-Franciscus as the procession moved past them. He had raised the hood of his pluvial. "Comporting himself like a Greek actor, and in this weather!"

Sanct-Franciscus shrugged, recalling other figurehead leaders he had seen over the centuries. "A puppet, but an expensive one."

"They say he uses the slaves to feed his eels, which are his favorite food," Vulpius said, rolling his eyes upward. "And that he sleeps on fresh rose-petals every night. Rose-petals! In winter! He slighted the Vestal Virgins two days ago! Truth! And all those young men!" Vulpius shook his head, disappointed in the new Emperor. "It's the foreign influence—meaning no disrespect to you, Sanct-Franciscus. Romans have a taste for luxuries and male flesh, of course, but not so obsessively or exclusively. Or so flamboyantly."

"These things may mean difficulties for him, in time," Sanct-Franciscus agreed. "It would seem he is ill-advised."

"Ill-advised: a courteous phrase. There's no sense of proportion about him, not a hint of dignity—" He stopped as a young man in Iberian clothing lurched into them, mumbled an apology. "Another one following the example of Heliogabalus," Vulpius grumbled as the youth shouldered away from him.

"Heliogabalus has certainly been indulged in his life, and expects the indulgence to continue and enlarge." Sanct-Franciscus held out his hand to judge the increasing damp while he went on, "Others will want to have the same license he is granted—on that point I think you are right."

"Yes. I fear so," said Vulpius, tugging at Sanct-Franciscus' long, pleated, dark-red sagum. "Come. The crowd will soon be unruly, and you and I will want to be away from it." He glanced over his shoulder and pointed to a scuffle that had broken out among a group of on-lookers just behind the line of slaves. "See? There'll be more of that shortly. The procession has a dozen more streets to traverse, and the people will probably become raucous as it goes along; the rain won't quell their spirits. Don't you think we should be away?"

"I do," said Sanct-Franciscus. "Perhaps it is best." He stepped back into the mouth of an alley-way leading toward the small, beautiful Temple of Isis, just at present with its columns wrapped in midnight-blue linen for the dark of the year.

Vulpius hurried ahead of Sanct-Franciscus, his breath making a thicker mist before his face. "It will be raining heavily by nightfall, not just this mizzle. Tomorrow will be wet as well—all the signs are for it."

"So it seems," said Sanct-Franciscus, curious why Vulpius was so eager to put distance between them and the procession; he was aware that possible riotous behavior was not the only reason: Saturnalia would begin in a few days, and the mood of Roma was aleatory already, and would only increase in capriciousness over the next several days. He followed Vulpius, his senses sharpened.

"I am pleased that you will attend our convivium on the last night of Saturnalia," Vulpius went on, his thoughts scampering.

"With the understanding that I will not eat or drink, I have accepted," Sanct-Franciscus said genially. "I thank you for your invitation: you are most gracious to a foreigner."

"Very well, no food or drink; if you must have it so, so be it, although I wonder at any custom that keeps a man from dining in the company of his friends. Still, you say it is the tradition of those of your blood, and you do well to honor it. You will send me word when you decide what sort of slaves you want to serve you that night. I can provide you up to three." Vulpius reached a wider street, one that led to the Porta Viminalis, and he paused, still uneasy. "I am afraid that this new Caesar has come with his own army of spies."

"I would rather think his mother has," Sanct-Franciscus observed wryly.

"Yes; and even worse," said Vulpius.

"Why does that trouble you?" asked Sanct-Franciscus. "There have always been spies in Roma."

"Yes. Yes. Yet there are spies, and there are spies." Vulpius went silent, then cleared his throat. "You must know that there are those who say that the Emperor's mother is determined to destroy all resistance to her son's rule before it can start."

"I have heard something of the sort," said Sanct-Franciscus; Roma had been rife with rumors since the death of Macrinus the previous June, and now, with Heliogabalus installed in his palace, the rumors had reached the pitch and incoherence of thunder; everyone had a theory about the new regime, and everyone believed all other theories were wrong, so that each bruited his own ever more stridently.

"She is a most determined woman," said Vulpius, starting to amble in the direction of his house.

"She must be, to have advanced so young a lad to the purple," Sanct-Franciscus agreed, keeping pace with him.

"They say she disapproves of the Vestal Virgins," Vulpius added, lowering his voice as a group of young men came down the street, their abollae pulled up to help them keep dry or to conceal their faces. "They say she wants to put an end to the Vestal Virgins, banish them or disband them."

"That would not surprise me. How could she want any women to have power that supersedes her own?" Sanct-Franciscus nudged Vulpius, encouraging him to move faster. "The mist is almost rain now."

"So it is," said Vulpius, glancing at the young men who had ducked into a curbside thermopolium calling for sausages and wine. "They will be rowdy by nightfall—they, and half the city, no matter how hard it rains."

"Did you expect otherwise?" Sanct-Franciscus asked mildly.

"No. But I am growing wary of rag-tag mobs of youngsters, who are being tolerated everywhere. The Emperor encourages license of that kind, and many youths are willing to accept what Heliogabalus provides. I would rather be commanded to repel barbarians than pander to the whims of those lads. Not that the Christians, with their bands of youths preaching virtue, are preferable. Those youths have their own kind of disorderliness: they chastise those they think lack their virtues." He stopped at the corner, pointing north. "Your way is that street; I am going this way," by which he meant southeast. "I'll see you in a few days, Sanct-Franciscus, when I shall thank you properly for all you have done for me and my gens this last year. If you think of any indulgence I might be able to extend to you—?"

"It isn't necessary," said Sanct-Franciscus, holding up his hand to stop the objection that Vulpius was about to utter. "But I am honored that you would include me in your celebration."

Vulpius nodded slowly. "Very well. But at least permit me to be the one to help you put your right foot forward for the coming year."

Sanct-Franciscus smiled, knowing how important it was to Romans to cross the threshold of houses and begin the new year stepping onto the right foot. "You may do so, and with my wholehearted appreciation."

This brought a smile to Vulpius' face. "You are a most admirable friend, Sanct-Franciscus. Roman or not, you have all the true virtues."

"What can I be but flattered," Sanct-Franciscus asked, shading his eyes with his hand as the first real raindrops began to fall. He stood watching Vulpius trudge away, his shoulders hunched in his pluvial and his arms folded to help keep him warm, for a wind had kicked up, frisking maliciously down the streets and tugging at signs, clothing, and rubbish alike.

When Vulpius turned the corner, Sanct-Franciscus set out, not toward the Temple of Hercules, but toward the Villa Laelius, where he was expected. His sagum was soaked through by the time Sanct-Franciscus presented himself to Starus in proper form, saying "Domina Laelius is—"

"—expecting you. Just so," said Starus, adding automatically, "Right foot," as Sanct-Franciscus crossed the threshold; the floor was quite warm, indicating the holocaust was at full burn. "Doma Ignatia is at home. Octavian has left to join his Christian friends to harangue those watching the procession." He clicked his tongue in disapproval. "And there are guests."

"Thank you," said Sanct-Franciscus, and handed him a denarius, quite a generous commoda, but not remarkable at year's end.

"Very handsome of you, Foreign Honestiorus," said Starus, and escorted Sanct-Franciscus to the covered colonnade around the atrium. "You know the way to Domina Laelius' chambers, I believe?"

"I do," said Sanct-Franciscus, and touched the wallet hanging from his belt beneath his sagum.

"Shall I take that and hang it in the kitchen to dry?" Starus offered.

Sanct-Franciscus unfastened the sagum and slipped it off, revealing ankle-length bracae and a knee-length, belted, long-sleeved

Persian chandys in double-woven black wool ornamented at hem and sleeves with dark-red needlework; his peri were unusually thick-soled and made of tooled leather. "If you will."

"When you leave you have only to ask for it," Starus declared stoutly.

"Very good," Sanct-Franciscus said, and was about to go to Adicia's rooms when something more occurred to him. "Who is here— you said there were guests?"

"Oh, Domina Laelius' daughter Myrtale and her husband Forteus Quillius Antoninus Horaliens have come, with their two sons— Martius and Hilarius, nine and five. We have been in something of an uproar."

"They came for the procession and Saturnalia," Sanct-Franciscus guessed. "No wonder Doma Ignatia said the need was urgent."

Starus nodded, but wisely held his tongue.

Standing braziers and hanging oil-lamps lit the colonnade and the corridor beyond; Sanct-Franciscus smelled the incense burned in the braziers—a combination of sandalwood and amber—and guessed that Ignatia had ordered that as a tribute to her sister and her family.

"Sanct-Franciscus." His name was hardly more than a whisper, but it caught his attention, and he stopped where he was. "Over here." Ignatia was standing in the shadow of an alcove, dressed in palla and stola, with a ricinium over her head; all were in subdued shades of blue and gray, and unadorned, blending her in with the shadows. Her face was pale and there were smudges of fatigue around her eyes. "I need to speak with you before you see my mother."

"Doma Ignatia," said Sanct-Franciscus as he went to her side. "I came as soon as I could reasonably do so."

"Minerva and Fortuna be thanked," she said with relief and exasperation. "I fear my mother has had a difficult time of it these last three days—more than usual."

"Two grandsons can be demanding, can they not," said Sanct-Franciscus.

"Starus told you?" She saw him nod. "Yes. Glad as she is for this visit, and proud as she may be of Myrtale and her family, the boys are rambunctious and noisy, which is trying for her."

"Hardly unexpected," said Sanct-Franciscus.

"It is good you are here now; things are calmer than they were earlier, but my mother is . . . is not doing well. Myrtale and Quillius have taken the children with them to the procession, and will probably not return until they have called on some of their friends. At least," she added, "that was their plan."

"I suppose this is a welcome respite," said Sanct-Franciscus.

She nodded. "I am sorry to say so, but my sister is an indulgent parent—she has no notion the toll her boys' wildness takes on our mother."

"How could she? Your mother is thrilled to have her grandsons here, is she not? Has she admitted that they tire her?" Sanct-Franciscus asked. "I reckon your mother has not told your sister of her response."

"No, she hasn't," said Ignatia, frowning.

"Nor have you," Sanct-Franciscus added.

"It isn't my place, as I have been reminded."

"Do you intend to speak to her?" Sanct-Franciscus could feel her hand tighten. "Or have you attempted to bring such things to your sister's attention already?" If she had, he knew she had not been successful.

Ignatia sighed. "No: I haven't. It would be useless to do so."

"So your sister may think that the vitality of the children is doing Domina Laelius some good, as any proud mother is apt to do." Sanct-Franciscus took her hand, noticing it was cool and her pulse was rapid. "You are in a predicament: if you speak to your sister about your mother's distress, your mother will be angry, and if you do not speak, she will feel ill-served."

"Very likely," said Ignatia dully.

"You would do well to leave the house for a while—attend the procession if you like: it will last another hour and more; or visit friends—" He broke off as he saw her flinch.

"I have few friends," said Ignatia. "Those I have have other engagements just now, what with the procession and the preparation for Saturnalia."

"Then have Philius drive you out for an hour or so. You must have a covered biga or a city carriage he can make ready." He turned her face upward, his enigmatic gaze holding her eyes. "For your own sake, Ignatia, give yourself an abatement in your duties. You have taken too much upon yourself."

"You say this as my physician?" Ignatia achieved a half-smile.

"As your friend," he countered. "I am your mother's physician."

She pulled her hand from his. "If it weren't raining, I would take your advice," she said.

"Then go to the Forum Emporiarum, and see what the merchants are selling for Saturnalia. The walkways there are covered." He, himself, had his clerks offering bales of cloth and platters of brass at bargain prices at the Eclipse warehouse.

"If I have time, I'll go tomorrow," said Ignatia. "If Myrtale and her family are out, and I go out as well, my mother will fret."

Although he knew this was probably correct, Sanct-Franciscus made one last attempt. "I will be here at least an hour, and at the end of my visit, your mother should have some time to sleep before your nephews return. You could have that time for venturing out. Have Philius bring the covered biga around for you."

"I should not," she said dutifully.

"Ignatia, you should," Sanct-Franciscus countered.

She thought about it a long moment. "I'm going to the kitchen to get a cup of hot wine. I'll make up my mind while I'm there." She took a step away from him. "You're sure she'll be asleep?"

"Asleep or dozing," he promised her.

Ignatia considered this. "My sister should return in two hours. I ought to be here when the family returns."

"You can be," Sanct-Franciscus said. "Tell Philius; he is a steady fellow."

"Yes. Yes he is," said Ignatia, and hastened off toward the kitchen, leaving Sanct-Franciscus to make his way to Domina Adicia's rooms.

Three slaves were attending on Adicia, who was sitting up in bed, swathed in a mafortium of Cappadocian goat-wool, her covers heaped around her, and her hands wrapped in fasceae. She looked up as another household slave came in bearing a ewer of hot water with curls of orange-peel floating in it, and did not at first notice Sanct-Franciscus standing in the corridor just beyond her door. "You fool!" she snapped at the slave, her words slurring a little. "It should be lemon, not orange."

"Cook is using the lemons for his stuffed fowl for the convivium," said the slave. "I could not demand he give me any of them."

"Excuses!" Then she noticed her visitor and she modified her tone to one less severe. "Still, cook is a very temperamental fellow. I will send word to him to procure more lemons for me."

"Do you want—" the slave asked, gesturing to the ewer.

"No. Take it away," said Adicia.

"Leave it here," said Sanct-Franciscus as he came into the room. "You know that the orange-peel will do you good, Domina Adicia. There is no reason to deny yourself the benefits of oranges because they are inferior to lemons."

Adicia made a snort of ill-usage. "I am forgotten in my own house. How can I permit the cook to deprive me?" She contemplated Sanct-Franciscus for a long moment. "You are rigged out strangely, but your garb becomes you. Is it that of your native land?"

"Not precisely," said Sanct-Franciscus. "The chandys is Persian, and the rest is Roman. The clothing of my people is difficult to procure." They had all but vanished from the earth two thousand years ago; their language and customs had followed the few survivors westward from the Carpathian Mountains into the north of the Italian peninsula, but were now so scattered and so changed that neither their descendants nor their tongue was that of his people.

She smacked the nearest pillow. "The cook! What am I to do about him? I ought to have him beaten: he shows insolence in his disrespect."

"I am sure that was not his intent," Sanct-Franciscus soothed. "He must be doing his utmost to feed your daughter and her family in a manner you would approve. Have one of your slaves go to the Forum Agricolarum to buy lemons; the farmers are there in spite of the weather, and they will have lemons to sell. They're going to be costly, but you will have lemon-water before your evening meal. Be patient a while longer, and your forbearance will be rewarded." His demeanor was calm and genial, but he could see that Adicia was determined to work herself up into a state. "You would not want to have to stay away from your family because your nerves were worn, would you?" He paused an instant, then went on, "I know you want to make the most of your daughter's visit, which you will not be able to do if you're too exhausted."

Adicia reached out to touch his hand. "You do understand, don't you? You know how much I have endured. My brother made light of it, didn't he?"

"You have had much to deal with," Sanct-Franciscus said, keeping his voice level and neutral; he laid his hand on her forehead. "You are heated, Domina."

"I have said so all morning," Adicia complained, giving a look of justification to the slaves in her room.

"I believe you have agitated your humors. You house is quite warm, and you have swaddled yourself in blankets." He felt her indignation in the sudden tightening of her wasted body. "If you were to allow yourself to release some of the heat you have bottled up within you, I think you might feel better."

"Do you?" she disputed in a tone of injury.

Sanct-Franciscus softened his tone. "It is an easy thing to awaken to the cool of the morning, before the holocaust has been stoked and lit, and to wrap yourself in blankets against the chill—you are prudent to do so, Domina Adicia, for beginning the day with cold in the bones is both painful and damaging. But through the morning, your house has warmed as the holocaust has been burning; the warming is gradual, and not readily detected, so that by now, you have become accustomed to defending against cold when there is little to—"

"How can you say that, when you, of all men, know that any chill is agony to me?" She glowered toward him. "First oranges instead of lemons, now this."

Sanct-Franciscus was unflustered. "I know you are troubled by the discomfort you anticipate, but I believe you may find yourself much more easy than you are now, for you will not be overheated."

"Have you come unprepared? is that it?" Adicia demanded. "Are you trying to coddle me instead of treating me?"

"No, Domina—nothing of the sort," he assured her. "But I want the anodyne I supply to have the best chance of providing you relief, and I fear that will not be possible if you are choleric."

Adicia struggled with herself, then looked up at him, offering him a coquettish smile. "You must always charm me from my unhappiness, Sanct-Franciscus. You are a magician. Whatever my brother pays you, it isn't enough."

He studied her face. "You are too kind," he said slowly; he did not mention he accepted no payment for his services.

She shifted the heaviest blanket off her, and motioned to one of the slaves to fold it. "I will try what you suggest."

"If you begin to feel cold, drink warm honey-water. It will heat you from the inside out, which is much the better way." He opened the wallet hanging on his belt and took out a vial containing an infusion of pansy, willow, and silkflower. "I want you to drink this with your orange-water. I think it will relieve your discomfort and allow you to rest." He handed her another, smaller vial. "Then drink this. I fear the taste is not very pleasant, but it will ease you." The contents was a syrup of valerian and poppies, not a strong solution, but enough to ensure Adicia's sleep for several hours.

"I *am* tired," said Adicia, as if announcing an accomplishment. "It is good of you to do this for me. You do concern yourself on my behalf, do you not?" She smiled again, dangerously near simpering.

The rain increased from a whisper to a purr, and the wind rose enough to tap the branch of a nearby tree against the roof.

"I am your physician. It is part of my responsibility to you to be concerned on your behalf." He kept all emotion out of his voice, including his own apprehension as he poured the tincture into the cup set out for her and added orange-water from the ewer. "This first," he said as he handed her the cup.

"Very good," she said, taking the cup and giving him a long, meaningful stare as she began to drink.

"All of it; I want you to have the most benefit possible." He tried to look confident, knowing she expected that of him.

She finished the orange-water and held out the empty cup. "There—you see? I follow your orders to the letter."

He took the cup and handed her the second, smaller vial. "Now this. Drink it quickly; it does not have a pleasant taste."

"That is true of so many medicines," Adicia said. "All right." She made a face as she swallowed the contents of the vial. "Most unsavory."

"As I told you." He took the vials and put them back in his wallet.

"What then?" she asked.

"Now lie back; not with all your covers, only with a few." He watched as she complied. "I will instruct your slaves as to how they are to attend you while you rest."

"Excellent," she said, starting to close her eyes.

Sanct-Franciscus saw the slaves exchange uneasy glances; he motioned them to move to the far side of the room, where he went to tell them, "She should be drowsy shortly. Keep her head and shoulders on pillows, and bring a basin of warm camphor-water so that she may breathe freely while she sleeps. She may be a bit groggy when she wakens—if she is, prepare a mixture of apple-juice and honey with a stick of cinnamon in it, and see she drinks it slowly. Do not give her any wine until she is fully awake." He saw their doubt in their eyes. "It is for her benefit that you do this. If she dislikes it, tell her you are doing as I instructed you. I will take the brunt of her displeasure."

"She will not whip you," said the tallest of the slaves, and was hushed by her companions.

"No; and she should not whip you, either," said Sanct-Franciscus.

The slaves said nothing, but the strongest woman folded her arms and stared down at the floor.

"Be prudent," Sanct-Franciscus suggested. "She is truly unwell, and getting slowly worse; that frightens her, which turns her temper sour."

"It certainly does," said the oldest of the three.

Sanct-Franciscus nodded in sympathy. "Then blame me. It is fitting that you do so."

"Because you are her physician," the strongest one said.

"Because she likes you," said the tallest at the same time.

The oldest shook her head. "No. It is because you feel for us," she said in growing astonishment.

Sanct-Franciscus was silent, but something burned in his dark eyes that revealed more to the three women than he realized: a penetration that commanded their esteem; he patted his wallet. "I will return tomorrow, before prandium." He did not wait to see the women acknowledge this, but turned and left Domina Adicia's chambers.

Text of a letter from Lucius Virginius Rufius to Marius Octavian Laelius.

To my sweet brother in our faith, at the season of the birth of our Savior, my greetings and prayers for your deepening devotion in the year to come, numbered the two hundred nineteenth since the birth of the Christ;

In this time when the pagans of Roma hold their salacious festival of Saturnalia, I ask you to join with us, to go about the city to exhort the people to repent their many, many sins and seek redemption in Jesus the Christ. A number of us have decided to spend the last two nights of the festival trying to keep men from indulging their fleshly desires, and to that end, we will carry short whips and staves with which we may drive our lessons home. Better we should face their condemnation in this world than the disapproval of our Savior in the next.

As we have done from time to time with the disgraceful women of the lupanar, we may now seek to demonstrate our faith to those Romans who are without any hope of Grace. This extends also to those calling themselves Christians but comporting themselves in a most unseemly fashion—those who hold their wives in common, and those who maintain that the mother of Jesus is of equal majesty as her Son. Their errors are the more egregious because they have been shown the truth and have perverted it for their own base purposes, following the tenets of teachers professing to be apostles but now fully discredited as false prophets. Gelasius Virginius Apollonius Metsari, my cousin, will be with us, of course, as well as Prosperus Rufius Ursinus and Erastus Arianus Crispenus, so you will be in good company.

Send me word by the slave who carries this whether or not you will join with us, and I will be thankful to God if you decide to come along.

In Christ and in fraternity,
Lucius Virginius Rufius

9

In spite of the blustery storm that rollicked over Roma, the celebration of Saturnalia was almost unimpeded; from the gaudy extravagance of the Emperor's palace to the festive streets of the lupanar the city was alive with banquets and entertainment; even a few determined Romans were in the streets, stopping at all the major temples of the city to leave offerings for the gods and goddesses, and incense for the Vestal Virgins to burn for Roma and Romans. Gaiety offset the rattling rain, and through all but the meanest streets songs echoed merrily and cries of good wishes rang in counterpoint to the wind. Even the Watchmen and the Urban Guard took part in the festivities, enjoying drink and food at the houses of the patrician nobles on the Palatinus and Capitolinus hills instead of patrolling the rainy streets.

The house of Septimus Desiderius Vulpius was no exception to this joyousness: oil-lamps, torches, and incense-scented braziers lent their lights and perfumes to the main dining room, and to the reception room beyond where jugglers and dancers were performing unusual feats for the evening's guests to the accompaniment of a group of musicians playing popular tunes and occasional anthems to Saturn. Slaves in special holiday tunicae made their way through the attendees, bearing trays of rare, succulent appetizers and amphorae of even rarer wines. The holocaust kept the air channels under the floors so warm that where rain spattered in at the door, little wraiths of steam rose from the evaporating water, promising an evening of welcome heat for the guests.

In the alcove next to the front door, before the altar to the lares, Vulpius himself offered the traditional oranges and lemons to all, and his wife, Filomena Dionesia Crassens, Domina Vulpius, held out the plate of small loaves of bread studded with nuts, as was expected for Saturnalia in such a fine house as this one; both of them wore wreaths of gold on their heads, and their clothing was bright yellow, to mark the turn of the year from dark to light again. With slaves to escort them, all the guests were led into the house—men to the dining room, women to the withdrawing room. Only when the brass bell sounded for the convivium to begin did Vulpius and his wife forsake their positions near the vestibule and enter the dining room, preceded by six slaves holding up the first platters of the evening's food: small buns stuffed with spiced meats and preserved fruits, and plates of anchovies preserved in olive oil and garlic.

"Each of you knows your place," said Vulpius, grinning at his friends, and indicating the waiting couches, arranged in two U-formations of nine couches apiece, the opening of the U's facing each other; two long, broad tables were set in the middle of both U's, and a tall, brass-topped table occupied the opening between the two U's, on which stood great vessels of wine. "But for you," he added to Sanct-Franciscus, who stood to one side, very grand in a short silken dalmatica of dark red, embroidered in black and silver, over black Persian bracae that were gathered with bands of silver ribbon at the ankles. He had added his personal sigil—a winged eclipse—as a pendant on a silver hammered-link collar, and wore a large ruby set in silver on the first finger of his left hand. Upon his arrival,

Sanct-Franciscus had presented Vulpius with a pair of alabaster goblets, one of which Vulpius now held up as he pointed. "Most elegant; many thanks, and good fortune in the year ahead. If you will take the couch there? nearest the door to the reception room?"

"As you wish," said Sanct-Franciscus, noticing that fewer than half the couches were occupied.

"I have told the slaves not to offer you food, and I will explain that your customs forbid you to dine with us; some of my guests may remark upon your abstinence, but I assume you are used to that, since it is your custom to dine in private," Vulpius said cordially, nodding a greeting to Pius Verus Lucillius, who had just stretched out on his couch, across from Sanct-Franciscus, his white-and-wine-red toga virilis making graceful folds about him, his jewel-studded bracelets glowing in the rich light. "You are among friends here, Sanct-Franciscus, and you need not fear us." He clapped Sanct-Franciscus on the shoulder for good measure.

"Thank you," said Sanct-Franciscus, and went to sit down, though unlike the Romans, he did not recline, but sat high up on the couch, his lower back supported by the rest that was intended for shoulders and elbows.

"Delphinius Ambrosius Junian," Vulpius called out to the highest-ranking Roman in the room. "Let you name the first delight of the evening."

Junian, an abdominous fellow with a high-colored complexion and the beginning of pendulous jowls, dressed in an extravagant toga of pale-lavender silk and wearing a great many golden bracelets, sat up on his couch. "Let all the women be brought in to dine! Bring forth the women!" It was the usual first delight, and it was greeted with enthusiastic shouts.

Vulpius signaled his steward and handed him the alabaster goblet. "My wife has the other," he said, and added more loudly, "No guest is to be denied the satisfaction of his wishes; for tonight, our guests live as gods, and their desires are paramount. Do as you are commanded." He swung his arm in a gesture of anticipation and welcome, his yellow toga making him seem to glow.

The steward ducked his head and went to collect the second

goblet and to throw open the door at the back of the dining room, revealing the withdrawing room where the women guests and a few professional female entertainers were waiting. The musicians in the reception room struck up a fanfare of sorts to welcome them to the banquet, and with this to accompany them, the women entered the dining room, ready to begin the celebration. All were dressed in their newest finery, for it was good luck to celebrate the new year in fine, new clothes.

Watching them, Sanct-Franciscus could see the first signs of exhaustion, a mark of the end of Saturnalia. Five days of unrelenting festivities were taking their toll. He watched the women go to their couches, most of them across from their husbands; two of the women who were engaged for the evening selected the unoccupied couches for themselves. As host, Vulpius occupied the center couch of the U nearest the reception room while his wife occupied the center couch of the U nearest the withdrawing room, all in strict accord with Roman custom. Once the guests were settled, a group of slaves entered the dining room, one for each guest, whose job it would be to assist the guests through the banquet as well as provide any additional amusements the guest might require. All of the slaves were dressed in knee-length, pleated tunicae of fine, white wool, garments that would serve them for all festive occasions in the year to come.

"Proffer the first dishes; let the convivium commence," Vulpius ordered. "And fill the goblets with wine." He held up his own silver goblet; all his guests would take home their silver goblets as gifts.

From his post at the dining room door, Leontius, the Vulpius' steward, signaled the personal slaves to comply, while he, himself, prepared to summon the next course to the diners as soon as the first was completed.

"How delightful all this is," exclaimed Romulus Sabinus Savinus as his evening's slave held out his goblet.

"Doubly delightful for us, to end the year among such good friends," said Dionesia, and poured out a small amount of wine from her goblet onto the floor as token offering to Saturn and Janus, both of whom were the gods honored in these festivities; most of the guests did the same, and a sudden aroma of wine filled the air as the warm floors turned the red liquid to thin trails of white steam.

"The libation has been made," Junian cried out before popping one of the stuffed buns into his mouth.

"The glory of the Emperor," called out Oliverus Stephanus Tacitus Caio, spilling a generous amount of wine in honor of Heliogabalus.

The others echoed this, but with less enthusiasm, and Savinus coughed. "Is he keeping Saturnalia at all?"

Caio laughed. "Better than most. He has had feasts and entertainments from the first night until now, each more extravagant than the last. They say he has had a fountain built that pours four kinds of wine, and a device that can turn four stuffed boars over a fire-pit at the same time. His slaves are handsome young men, dressed in tunicae of cloth-of-gold. Those fortunate enough to be invited to be his guests are given golden plates to take home."

"But he slights the Vestal Virgins," said Dionesia, concerned at this impropriety. "His mother has refused to visit them, and Heliogabalus himself has only summoned them to him; he will not go to them."

"Very unseemly," said Junian.

"Well, he's foreign; he doesn't yet understand how we do things in Roma," said Caio, then glanced in Sanct-Franciscus' direction. "I mean no offense to you, of course." He took an anchovy and thumbed it into his mouth, chewing vigorously.

"Of course," said Sanct-Franciscus.

"He needs time to learn our ways," Caio went on, still chewing.

"We've offered libations to his glory," said Vulpius, raising his voice to be heard over the increasing buzz of conversation.

"That we have," said Junius, and held out his goblet to his slave to be refilled.

"Heliogabalus has been made Caesar, and we, as Romans, must hail him Emperor." This from Publicus Maximus Titanius Pereginus, who had attended an earlier celebration and whose face was already ruddy from wine; his toga was beginning to slip from his shoulder.

Caio laughed, not quite pleasantly. "So loyal you are?"

"As loyal as you," said Peregrinus, a hint of belligerence in his tone.

"Ave Caesar, then," said Lucillius, as if to put an end to the wrangling.

"He is just a youth," Peregrinus said in defense of the Emperor. "Have patience. In time he will wean himself away from his mother's influence, and we shall discover what manner—"

"Let us forsake politics for tonight," said Parthenia Orela Tallonus, Domina Caio, looking uncomfortable in her stola and palla of embroidered linen, for her pregnancy was advanced and moving had become awkward.

"My wife has expressed a wish: that we banish talk of politics," Caio said in a tone that suggested that this had been a bone of contention with them before.

"And I endorse it," said Dionesia. "You men can discuss the affairs of the Empire in the morning, when the new year dawns; tonight is only the eve of the nine hundred seventy-second Year of the City, and Saturn still reigns: Jove and Minerva will rule in the morning, and Janus, as well. Tonight we sample all the delights that flesh can know, without a care for what is to come. For tonight, we are to celebrate the time that is past, and the past is beyond our influence. Let us give no time to that which is beyond this moment's grasp."

There were a few shouts of agreement, and Bonar Datus Fabricius crowed like a cock at sunrise.

"Let each of you amuse yourself; take pleasure of the table and the slaves brought to you for your delectation," said Vulpius.

"As the Olympians do," shouted Junian.

"So it shall be for tonight," Vulpius declared, and signaled the entertainers to rest while the musicians played. "You will be kept busy later, never fear," he promised the entertainers.

One of the musicians had a small lyre from Cappodocia, and looking at it, Sanct-Franciscus had a brief, intense recollection of Tishtry, standing on her hands on the front of her racing quadriga before flipping onto the back of her favorite horse, to ride, standing, around the end of the spina in the Circus Maximus; she had bought her family's freedom with her performing before she died the True

Death on the sands. He looked away and caught Lillis Cecania Lenius, Domina Fabricius, staring at him. "Domina," he acknowledged, ducking his head.

"I have heard much about you," said Cecania, offering him a lupine smile; she was almost as tall as Sanct-Franciscus, and richly dressed in gold-shot silk; her russet hair was in an elaborate arrangement of ordered curls and golden ribbons. "So I am curious." She ran the tip of her tongue over her parted lips. "Perhaps later you will ease my curiosity?"

"Why would that be? That you are curious?" Sant-Franciscus asked politely.

"Because I have many questions about you." She caught her lower lip in her teeth and smiled. "I hope you are all I have heard you are."

"You must not believe everything you hear of me, or of anyone," said Sanct-Franciscus, his manner gracious but reserved; he read avidity in her eyes that had no hint of generosity.

"This is no night for gravitas, old Roman virtue though it may be," she admonished him provocatively. "Leave dignity behind on this last night of the year. Be willing to surrender to chance."

"As Romans do?" he suggested.

"Yes. As we do. You are our guest, you must share our—" She let her hand slide negligently down to her golden-chain belt.

"A most tempting invitation, and were I of your blood, I would be unable to resist you, lovely as you are. But, alas, I am no longer a prince of my people, and illustriata are too exalted for me," Sanct-Franciscus said, aware that this woman might find his appetites not to her liking; certainly the other guests would be appalled.

"Modest? Afraid of my husband's claim on me?" she teased, giving her husband an indulgent look. "I do not deprive him of his amusements, nor does he keep me from mine."

"Not so much modest as careful, as a foreigner is expected to be," said Sanct-Franciscus as the musicians brought out two branches of brass tintinabula and four small mallets with which to strike them; the melody they played was Greek, and soon their singer joined in, spinning out the bittersweet lyrics with little attention to their meaning.

"Not that 'Young Wife's Lament' again," said Cecania. "Everyone's heard it."

"Still, it is engaging," said Sanct-Franciscus.

Cecania gave a moue of disgust. "If such sentiments please you."

"They would," said Sanct-Franciscus, "if they were presented more appropriately. The singer does not understand the meaning of the syllables she is singing." He resisted the urge to join the musicians: perhaps later, he thought.

"So you have taste in music, do you?" Cecania inquired, making a world of possibilities fill the simple question.

"I have found it to my liking," said Sanct-Franciscus, thinking that for the first five hundred years after his death, he had no interest in the art; only after he had arrived in Egypt had he developed a fondness for songs and the sound of instruments. "Over time."

"Over time," Cecania repeated. "Then music is part of the story of your life. That must be a fascinating tale." Again she licked her lips slowly with the tip of her tongue.

"Hardly that," said Sanct-Franciscus, and watched Cecania mull over his response. It was all so predictable, he thought, their appetites and the satiation without fulfillment. How they devoured everything, and how little nourishment they gained!

She lolled back against the cushions on the rise of her couch, one arm extended as if in negligent summons. "I told Vulpius that I want a young man who might be mistaken for a gladiator—without the scars, of course, and not too brutal. What did you ask for?"

Before Sanct-Franciscus could frame his answer, Fabricius stood up and held up his goblet. "This is to wash away the old year, and to welcome the new," he announced, and drank deeply, two little rivulets of wine brimming down his chin and onto his clothing.

Vulpius signaled to Leontius. "The second course," he commanded. "See to it."

The steward nodded, ducked his head, and stepped back from the door in order to pass on the orders to the waiting slaves. "Do not intrude; do your work invisibly. Step lively, remove what is left, then serve what you have brought. Do not spill anything," he warned the six. "Bring what is uneaten out and take it with you to the kitchen."

Each tray being carried held a wide, shallow crockery bowl containing fresh mussels and seafood forcemeat in a thick, gingered sauce; this delicious offering was accompanied by stacks of buttered griddle-bread. The slaves set these down on the tables, saluted Vulpius and his wife, picked up the platters from the first course, then left the dining room promptly and in good order.

"Well done," Leontius approved once the slaves were in the corridor again. "Next, fingerbowls and napkins, then comes the squab in apricots and spiced broccoli with leeks in pepper-oil."

"After that, the shoats stuffed with chopped figs, apples, and onions," said the senior slave, a Gaul called Cepin.

"You'll need help serving them. Alert three kitchen slaves to be ready to assist you." Leontius clapped his hands to send them on their way, but called after them, "You will have your convivium when this is finished."

"Oh yes," said Cepin in happy anticipation. "Cook is making the chickens ready for spitting once the stuffed yearling calves are served, so we will not have to wait long after the masters have finished to begin our meal. We'll have the chickens and fish-and-celery stew and rabbits in gravy and anything the masters haven't eaten, as well as many breads for us, as is the custom. And we'll have the entertainers and musicians to dine with us at the end of the night—those not busy elsewhere." He grinned, showing uneven teeth, three of which were missing.

"And griddle-breads," added another slave. "Cook has a tub of batter."

"Then to your work," Leontius said, and went back into the dining room, ducking his head again to his master.

Vulpius had risen from his couch and was approaching the musicians in the reception room. "Come in with us; bring your instruments. You may play while we dine; the others may rest in anticipation of a busy time ahead."

The musicians hastened to obey; they held their instruments carefully, and stayed near Vulpius as they moved through the couches.

"I like the look of that flute-player," Lucillius said to Sanct-Franciscus, smiling expectantly. "Flute-players have agile lips and fingers."

"I suppose they must," said Sanct-Franciscus, who played the flute tolerably well himself and knew its demands. "Light, quick fingers are often needed."

"Rather like that thief you spared," Lucillius said, and laughed. "Vulpius told me you tended to his injuries at the prison."

"I did." Sanct-Franciscus waited while Lucillius had his goblet refilled.

"Why did you bother?" Lucillius asked.

"No one else was likely to do it," said Sanct-Franciscus.

"I don't imagine he thanked you," Lucillius said as one of the serving slaves came to remove the platter from the first course, and his body-slave refilled his goblet.

"Actually, he did," said Sanct-Franciscus, not adding that he had offered Natalis a position in his household upon his release from prison; he nodded toward Lucillius' wife. "This may not interest you, Domina."

"It doesn't," she said, sounding both half-drunk and bored; Docilla Adonica Tiberius, Domina Lucillius, scowled at her husband, then smiled at Sanct-Franciscus. "You could be interesting, however."

Sanct-Franciscus gestured an apology. "I ask your pardon, Domina, but it is not the custom of my people to—"

"Not another man of restraint!" she exclaimed, pursing her lips in disgust. "Are you one of those strict Christians? Not the ones who share everything, but the others, who are forever pestering decent Romans and making a display of their religion to the denigration of all the rest? They have been beating up patrons of the lupanar and the Guard there hasn't been able to stop them. I didn't think Vulpius would be so foolish as to invite anyone of that stripe to Saturnalia."

"No, I am not a Christian," said Sanct-Franciscus. "I am an exile."

Adonica considered this, sighed, and signaled the slave for more wine. "I'll have to wait for a bit, then."

"Never mind my wife—she's becoming fatigued," said Lucillius.

"After such a Saturnalia as this has been, I am surprised you are all still awake," said Sanct-Franciscus with a slight smile.

Lucillius chose to laugh at this observation. "Truly. We Romans are a hearty breed, and it takes more than a few nights of feasting and drinking to flatten us. Not even war has exhausted us." He accepted a linen square from the slave carrying the basin of lemon-water before dunking his hands into the warm liquid. While he dried his fingers, he added, "Foreigners often see our enjoyments as weakness, not what they are: the strength of the people; we have fortitude, and that requires great jollity. For as we must be powerful and resolute in purpose, so we must be able to make the most of our entertainments, in all forms, so that we do not become despotic. Just as we fight with a will, so we feast and drink with a will."

Overhearing this, Caio yelled out, "True! True!"

"Even our women are mighty," said Lucillius, glancing at his wife, who glowered at him in return.

"That they may be," said Fabricius, joining in. "But they are also the true flowers of Roma. Nothing so fair as they can be found outside our walls." Although the praise was genuine, his expression was salacious and earned him a sharp stare from his wife, which he pointedly ignored.

The slaves carried in the third course and set the broad platters down, then the plates of griddle-bread. With the musicians striking up a little march, they left the diners alone once more.

"Mussels," said Peregrinus eagerly, using a griddle-bread to scoop up the food. "You had them from—?"

"From Neapolis, preserved in brine, of course," said Vulpius.

"Ah, Neapolis," said Peregrinus, and took a large bite before calling out, "Bring me my evening's slave!"

"My guest commands," said Vulpius, and called out to Leontius, "Bring the pleasure-slaves. All of them."

"At once," said Leontius, and left his place at the door to go around the atrium, where rain was falling, to the waiting room. "You," he said to the twenty slaves waiting there; all were dressed well and had been carefully groomed and anointed with fragrant oils for the evening. "Come with me. They are asking for you."

The arrival of the pleasure-slaves was greeted with cries of delight; Leontius had already told the slaves to which couches they should go, and they passed among the guests without confusion.

Only Sanct-Franciscus remained without companionship; he watched the guests seize upon their pleasure-slaves much the same way they were guttling their food, thinking they were hungry as wolves, preferring excess to appreciation; the very touching he sought most was valued least here. He rose, so as not to be conspicuous, and went to the musicians. "Would you mind if I borrowed your lyre?"

The musician looked up, mildly startled. "It . . . it is valuable, honestiorus."

"No doubt," said Sanct-Franciscus reasonably. "I will not harm it; if it should be damaged tonight, I give you my Word I will replace it."

After a brief inner struggle, the musician surrendered his instrument. "Do you know how to play?"

"Tolerably well," Sanct-Franciscus answered as he tried the strings, and adjusted one of them to a truer pitch.

"Well, you have an ear," the musician conceded.

Sanct-Franciscus ducked his head and began to play a lively paean to the sun that he had learned from the god who changed him, more than twenty-three hundred years ago. It was fairly unsophisticated, but the tempo was quick and the tune rapturous, just the accompaniment this occasion called for.

Cecania studied Sanct-Franciscus from her couch as if trying to decide if she should make another attempt at captivating him; then, with the most minimal of shrugs, she extended her arm to the pleasure-slave who waited at her side; around her most of the other guests were beginning to engage their pleasure-slaves in titillation, except for Caio, who had a young man and a young woman already bent over him, making him ready for his gratification while he continued to dine. Vulpius and his wife had three pleasure-slaves between them—two men and a woman—trading them back and forth as they made the most of their own celebration. The household slaves continued to serve food and drink.

The night wore on, the seven courses of the banquet were served with increasing display; the guests ate to repletion, visited the vomitorium, and ate more, all the while engaging their pleasure-slaves in an increasingly wild exhibition of desire and lubricity, concupiscence mixing with gormandizing. Through it all, Sanct-Franciscus played songs from every part of the earth he had visited. When exhaustion overtook the guests, and Vulpius ordered the entertainers to perform, the musician remarked to him, "You are among the best I have heard. My lyre is privileged to have you touch it."

"How gracious of you," said Sanct-Franciscus before making his way through the tangle of guests and slaves, trays and platters and discarded garments, in order to return to his couch, the only one among the guests who was not luxuriating in the bounty of the last night of Saturnalia.

Text of a letter as written by Rugeri in Alexandria to Sanct-Franciscus in Roma.

My master,

I have been told by Domina Clemens in a letter sent three months ago that you have not been receiving the letters I have been sending you, one every other month, for all of last year. This troubled me, for it seemed more than mishap or coincidence that so many letters should fail to reach you, and I determined to discover the reasons for these failures. I began by discussing the matter with your shipping-agent, and, having seen to my satisfaction that he was not to blame, I looked closer to this household. To my chagrin, I discovered that the letters had been taken by Perseus, the clerk I bought from the Byzantine merchant, and he was selling the information in the letters to various merchants and suppliers. I apologize most earnestly for my lapse in judgment, and I ask you to pardon my inability to protect our communications as I should have.

Beyond this admission, I must also tell you that Perseus has not disclosed how many of my letters—or yours—he has taken, and so I am at a loss to know what you know of my present circumstances. Are you aware that I made a gift to Hebseret and the Priests of Imhotep in your name? Do you know that I have ransomed nine of your crew from the Aeolus, *and that all but one of them have returned to your service? Have you received a copy of the agreement I have made with the weavers of the upper Nile for linen and cotton? I ask that you send me word of what you last heard from me, and I will see you have copies of all I have sent to you since.*

I will also pledge to put all the letters into the hands of your captains myself, entrusting them to no one but the captains. This one will go to Epimetheus Bion, of the Pleiades, *who is set to depart as soon as the present weather clears. I will also send a copy to Domina Clemens, by the* Zephyrus, *which sails for Ravenna in three weeks, weather permitting.*

Perseus has been turned over to the Prefecture of Trade here, his case assigned to the chief decuria for assessment. I will inform you of any decision made in regard to his actions, and the punishment that is meted out to him. I believe it must be strict, if not severe, but I will not ask for him to be condemned to the arena unless you tell me that is your wish. Given your past treatment of slaves, I believe you would not want him to suffer anything so grievous as that.

I have a few pieces of good news to pass on to you: I have secured four full barrels of pepper and will dispatch them with Captain Bion. No doubt you will be able to sell at a handsome profit. And I have met with a physician from the East, one who has come across the Arabian Sea, and who is eager to find a place to practice his art. I have introduced him to Hebseret, who has said that Chandolar's skills will be useful to the Priests of Imhotep, and so have provided him money to purchase the herbs and other substances of his medicaments. When more is known of his abilities, I will send on to you the proportions and methods of preparation this Chandolar employs.

For now, I will say no more, in case this should fall into unfriendly

*hands in spite of all my precautions. I ask you to be circumspect in
your reply, again as a precaution. Captain Bion is expecting to carry
a message back to me from you, and has given his word to keep the
letter in a locked box for the duration of his voyage; his reliability is
known to us both, but it is as well to be discreet.*

*In all devotion, and trusting in your resolution and fairness, I
commend myself to you,*

Rogerian of Gades
Rugeri of Alexandria

*in my own hand on the 10th day of January in the 972nd Year of the
City*

The letter as received by Sanct-Franciscus.

To my master,

*I am pleased to tell you that I have secured three full barrels of
pepper and will dispatch them to you as soon as I may; the ship carrying this letter should bring the barrels as well. I have hope that we will
have more such cargos to deliver in the coming months. You should be
able to make a handsome profit in the fora with these barrels.*

*I have also dealt with the priests you have expressed interest in,
and they are now moving up the Nile to a more distant temple where
they can practice their rites unimpeded by the Romans and others
who disapprove of Egyptian sorcery. There have been many complaints about them, and this seems to me to be one way to dispel the
ill-will they have gained over the last few years. You, being in Roma,
will not have seen the rising hostility the people have of these
priests, who may not be worthy of your loyal support. I urge you to
consider ending your association with them, so that your dealings
are not tainted with their magic and malice—for whatever they may
seem to be to you, others find them malefic, which cannot accrue
to your benefit. I ask you to give this matter your full and immediate
attention.*

I was told by the local prosecutor that your taxes here are likely to be higher in the near future, due to the debasement of the denarius, the burden of which has reached all the Empire. The merchants from across the Arabian Sea have asked for gold coins only, or if they are silver, they must come from Fars, or be from the reigns no later than Marcus Aurelius. I have assured those merchants that we will deal in gold, and so I ask you to dispatch as much as you can spare so that my pledge may not be construed as false.

I will have to replace a few of the slaves in my household and those who labor for this business. Some have proven to be disloyal, and those I have given—in your name, of course—to the Legions to serve the men in any capacity they should choose. I will inform you of the new slaves when I have purchased them. One will be for my own use, as a body-servant and to fulfill my desires, something you will not deny me I am sure.

I have bought copper and tin in abundance, and struck a good bargain for the metals. I know if they are carried to you on different ships, you will not be accused of bringing materials for weapons into Roma, and you should be able to turn a handsome profit on the sale of the metals to the Praetorians, who always want new swords and shields and spears and daggers and cudgels. I will put guards on the ships carrying the metals, and I advise you to meet the ships at Ostia yourself, to make sure they are not set upon by thieves and robbers.

Your loyal factor,
Rugeri of Iberia

at Alexandria in Aegytpus on the 11th day of January in Roma's 972nd Year

10

Before the biga was entirely stopped, Ignatia had jumped out of the vehicle and was running toward the gate of Domina Clemens' house, her face flushed, her eyes reddened from weeping. She pounded on the gates, shouting for someone to admit her, while Philius brought his pair to a halt and turned them around in the space in front of the Temple of Hercules, then came back to the gate where Ignatia was still demanding to be let in, announcing her name and her mission. A waning moon imparted its gelid light from the eastern sky, marking the first clear night in the last four.

"Do you know how late it is?" a sleepy voice asked from behind the sturdy upright planks of the gate. "Call back at a sensible hour, and the master will see you, if it is convenient."

It took all of Ignatia's determination to give a sensible answer. "It's very late, I know, and I apologize. But this is urgent. *Most* urgent. I would not have come if it weren't." Toward the end of her words, she managed to steady her voice enough that her sobbing was no longer apparent.

"It is unsafe to be abroad at this hour," the voice admonished her. "Women of good character should not be abroad this late."

"That is no business of yours: you forget yourself," Ignatia yelled, no longer adhering to her discipline of a moment ago, but giving her temper free rein. "Let me in! I must see Sanct-Franciscus!"

"You could be set upon by ruffians or worse," said the slave, "riding abroad at this time of night."

"My groom carries a whip and a cudgel. Not that it is any concern of yours. What does it matter to you? We are wasting time," Ignatia said firmly, and tried to keep her tone steady. "Is Sanct-Franciscus about? I must speak with him. Now!" She bludgeoned the gate for emphasis.

"Yes, he is here. He is in his study; we are not to disturb him," said the under-steward, taking a deep breath. "You must wait until morning, I fear."

"*Let me in!*" Ignatia shouted. "My mother has fallen into a lethargy and has not awakened since early afternoon yesterday."

"Do you mean twelve hours since, or thirty-six?" the slave asked, curious in spite of the hour and the circumstances of this most unseemly demand.

"Thirty-six. *Thirty-six!* I would not bother your master for less than that," Ignatia said, her voice beginning to falter. "Let me speak with him. If he says there is no reason for concern, I will leave, I promise you. I am sorry to intrude—you may tell him that. Just let me talk with him for a little while. Please."

"I will tell him you are here, and why. If he is willing to see you, I will escort him to the gate." Tigilus coughed for emphasis. "Wait here."

"Even though it is dangerous?" Ignatia asked with an edge in her voice.

There was a pause, and then Tigilus said, "I will admit you, but you must remain in the courtyard. You may not come into the house unless the master permits it."

"Thank you for that," Ignatia said, keeping the sarcasm out of her response. She motioned to Philius. "You heard him. We're being admitted to the courtyard."

The sound of the bolt being drawn back seemed unusually loud in the night, and the moan of the hinges was like the sighing of giants. As soon as there was room enough, Philius put the biga through, Ignatia following behind. Tigilus pointed the way to the stable, saying, "There is a night-groom who will see to you and your pair. You had best stay with them until you are needed." Then he indicated a small alcove along the inner peristyle. "Wait there," he said to Ignatia; with a shrug of annoyance, he trudged off into the house, across the atrium and on to the study where Sanct-Franciscus was working at a beehive-shaped oven that had been installed at the far end of the room. The athanor was hot, the door closed and bolted shut so that the jewels being made within it would not be damaged by a sudden lessening of heat.

"What is it, Tigilus?" Sanct-Franciscus asked as the under-steward tapped at the door.

"Doma Laelius is here," said Tigilus.

"At this hour?" Sanct-Franciscus sounded more worried than surprised.

"You're right: it is too late. I will send her away," Tigilus offered.

"Did she say why she came?" Sanct-Franciscus began to bank the fires of his athanor, preparing to leave at the mention of Ignatia.

"Her mother has been in lethargy for thirty-six hours, or so she claims," said Tigilus.

"How deep a lethargy? do you know?" Sanct-Franciscus opened a tall, red-lacquer chest, and began to select unguents and vials from its pigeon-hole shelves.

"No," said Tigilus, not wanting to admit he had not asked. "She came with a groom, in a biga."

"Very sensible, and more useful than a messenger," said Sanct-Franciscus as he packed the items he had selected into a small, leather case. "Have one of the night-slaves come in here, to be sure my oven cools properly. There is a pail of water at the end of the trestle-table if he needs to stop a fire."

"Do you anticipate fire?" Tigilus could not keep from inquiring.

"No, but it is well to be prepared," Sanct-Franciscus answered. "Where is Doma Laelius?"

"In the courtyard," said Tigilus, sounding a bit uncertain.

"You should have brought her into the house, and provided her with hot wine to drink," said Sanct-Franciscus as he picked up his abolla and pulled it on, then made for the door, his leather case in hand. "She has a position in the world that must be recognized."

Tigilus stood aside as Sanct-Franciscus came out of his study and closed the door. "She is waiting."

"So I assumed," said Sanct-Franciscus. "I will go with her, of course."

"She'll be relieved," said Tigilus with a suggestion of sarcasm in his observation; he took as step back as Sanct-Franciscus turned toward him.

"Why do you slight her? Have you taken her in dislike?" Sanct-Franciscus asked.

"Slaves have no opinions on such things," said Tigilus.

"Of course you do," Sanct-Franciscus countered. "You may tell me what they are."

Tigilus hesitated. "I don't dislike her; it is only that she clings on you, so that troubles me. What manner of character has she, that she would have to do that?" He sniffed to underscore his disapproval.

"Is it that she lacks resolve in your eyes or that she depends upon a foreigner instead of a Roman?" Sanct-Franciscus did not wait for an answer, but went on, "Do not speak slightingly of that young woman. She has had heavy burdens placed upon her that she cannot hope to discharge, but which she bears nonetheless. If nothing else, her devotion deserves our respect." He continued on, his steps loud in the stillness while Tigilus fell behind, chagrined and perplexed.

"Sanct-Franciscus," Ignatia exclaimed as she saw him come out of the house. "You have decided to see me."

"I have decided to accompany you to your house," said Sanct-Franciscus, and saw her pinch her nose to keep from crying again. "Tell me about your mother."

Ignatia waved, signaling Philius to bring the biga out of the stable, and as she climbed into the open chariot, she made room for Sanct-Franciscus beside her. "My mother is in a very bad state, I fear. I hoped she would . . . that she would revive of her own inclination, but . . . It began a day-and-a-half ago." Taking a deep breath, she launched into her account. "She had been fretful all morning, and I was at a loss to ease her discomforts. She ordered Starus to beat Benona because something Benona did displeased her—he didn't, on my enjoining him not to, but now Benona has asked not to have to attend to her, and she is better in the sick-room than any of the rest. My mother refused the honied wine I had made for her, and she would not eat anything more than bread with baked marrow spread on it." She took a second, uneven breath as the courtyard gate was opened and Philius snapped the pair to a trot. "Then she became calmer, and I thought she had improved; I ordered a prandium made for her, which she refused, but which was entirely dishes she usually likes. She said she wanted to be left alone, to rest. But she soon fell into a slumber that was more than sleep. I have tried to rouse her, but without success. She continued in her dazed condition, neither sinking deeper nor emerging from it. When she did not waken after our evening meal, I became more worried, so I watched her, which is when I discovered that her eyes were open a little, showing only whites, and that is when I decided to seek you out."

"Has she urinated or—" Sanct-Franciscus began.

"Once. I ordered her sheets and blankets changed, but carefully, so she would not be disturbed. I thought she needed to sleep, you see. She had complained of not sleeping just a few days ago, and it seemed to me that she must require . . ." She made a complicated gesture, composed of distress, guilt, and a need to put it all aside. "That was yesterday, when she had been asleep for four or five hours. She has eaten so little that nothing else has left her body, and that worries me. She eats no more than a kitten, and she drinks two cups of water in a day at most."

"Insufficient to support life, if carried on for long," said Sanct-Franciscus. "That is something we must attend to, whether or not we waken her."

"You can cause her to drink though she sleeps?" said Ignatia, her dubiety making the comment into a question.

"I hope to, yes, with your help," Sanct-Franciscus answered.

Ignatia considered this, then asked, "Do you think you can— waken her?" her voice rising in near-panic.

"I trust I may," he said, taking hold of the side of the biga as it swayed around a particularly steep corner. "Do you have a slave keeping watch on her?"

"When I am not tending to her myself, I do. She prefers me to sit with her."

"No doubt," said Sanct-Franciscus, and fell silent for a short while.

"Have you ever seen this condition before?" Ignatia pursued when the quiet began to trouble her.

"A few times, yes," he said, thinking back to various forms of stupor he had observed during his centuries of service in the Temple of Imhotep. He had encountered such relentless semi-consciousness a few times since then, and was aware that the probable outcome was not what Ignatia would want, for even if Adicia recovered from her stupor, it would be likely that she would suffer a change from it, and not for the better.

"Was the outcome . . . satisfactory?" Ignatia almost held her breath.

"In two cases the sufferer made a good recovery," said Sanct-Franciscus, keeping his demeanor as calm as he was able.

"Two cases. Only two," said Ignatia.

"Three others less so," he admitted.

"And what do you think my mother will . . ." Her question faded, unfinished.

"Until I see her, I have no way to determine that," he told her gently.

The biga turned toward the Laelius house, the horses beginning to labor; Philius pulled them in to a walk, saying, "It isn't much farther to go, Doma, and they are tired."

"Niger and Neva deserve a respite," said Ignatia. "I hope they won't be harmed by this night's work."

"They shouldn't be," said Philius. "I will see they are walked before I brush them down and stall them again."

"I will tell Starus that you need not rise at dawn with the others, Philius," said Ignatia. "You have earned your rest. And so have the pair." She smiled in the direction of Neva and Niger as if the horses would recognize her gratitude.

"I thank you, Doma; I'll give them an extra measure of grain," said Philius, expertly negotiating the narrow approach to the front of the Laelius house; he pulled in his pair so that Ignatia and Sanct-Franciscus could alight.

"That's very good of you," said Ignatia, stepping down from the biga after Sanct-Franciscus had done so. "I will see you later in the morning, and you may be certain that I will reward your service."

"Thank you, Doma," said Philius as he started the horses moving toward the stable.

"Starus has waited to admit us," said Ignatia to Sanct-Franciscus as she hastened toward the door. "Half the house is awake, I venture." She rapped on the door, adding with a quivering smile, "Ironic, isn't it? that we should be awake because my mother is asleep?"

"And sad," Sanct-Franciscus said as the door was opened for them. Crossing the threshold on his right foot, he turned to Starus, and began without other salutation, "How is Domina Laelius?"

"She sleeps. Still," said Starus, and then went on to Ignatia. "Your brother's gone out. He said he is going to ask his Christian friends to pray for your mother."

Ignatia gave a little, vexed shake of her head after lighting an oil-lamp over the lares in their alcove next to the door. "Well, that may be more useful than fretting about here. At least he won't bother the household."

"He didn't say when he'd be back," Starus added.

"That cannot concern me just now," said Ignatia with an expression that revealed her irritation with her brother more than her words did. "Who is with my mother?"

"Tallia, but she is very tired, and needs to rest," said Starus. "Had you been away much longer, I was going to wake Mirza to relieve Tallia."

"I will take her place," said Sanct-Franciscus, starting toward the corridor that led to Domina Laelius' bedchamber, Ignatia keeping pace with him, Starus trudging behind. "I want a ewer of boiled water mixed with a little salt and honey brought to her room, and a basin of warm oil. In an hour I will want help from a woman with strong hands—"

"I will do whatever you require," said Ignatia.

"You may want help before this is done," said Sanct-Franciscus. "We may be working through the night and into the morning."

"I will summon help when it is wanted," Ignatia said with deep determination.

"As you wish," said Sanct-Franciscus, and made the turn into Adicia's room.

Four branches of oil-lamps provided illumination, revealing both Adicia herself, lying still beneath her covers, and Tallia, seated on a stool, chin propped on her hands, elbows on her knees, her face slack with fatigue. She rose as Sanct-Franciscus and Ignatia came into the room, rubbing her eyes carefully and trying to show herself to be ready for any task.

"You may go to bed, Tallia, Sleep as long as you must," said Ignatia, going to Adicia's bedside and bending over her. "No change, I see."

"No, Doma, none," said Tallia. "I would have told Starus had there been." She started toward the door. "When will you need me?"

"When you waken. Starus will not summon you until you rise," said Ignatia, stepping back to allow Sanct-Franciscus to examine his patient.

Sanct-Franciscus pulled one branch of oil-lamps nearer, for although his dark-seeing eyes did not require the additional light, he knew the eyes of the living did, and this difference would set him apart from those around him, leading to the kind of scrutiny he could not withstand. "She must have water with honey and salt. If you will bring a linen cloth, a moist one, and place it over her mouth, then wet it often with the water she needs, she will not suffer desiccation, which can be as deadly as this lethargy."

"Starus will bring the things you want," said Ignatia, bending over her mother once more. "Her eyes are unchanged."

"She is breathing, shallowly but steadily," said Sanct-Franciscus. "This means that she may still respond."

"Respond—not recover," said Ignatia.

"Respond is a safer assumption. Recovery is more problematic in cases like this. It will depend on how much strength she can muster, and there is no way you or I may determine that." He touched her hand—it felt like vellum, and he shook his head. "Moisture is the most pressing problem."

"I will get the linen for you. But you see?—her mouth is closed. How can she be induced to drink?"

"A small fold in the linen will part her lips, and for now, that is all that is needed."

Ignatia gave a little sigh. "Are you sure you aren't trying to soften the blow for me? You do not think she is dying?"

Sanct-Franciscus moved back from the bed to face Ignatia. "Do you mean that I think she might die? Yes, I do. But if you mean that I think she *shall* die, no, I do not: not now, not yet, not from this, not if she can take liquid." He put his hand on her shoulder. "If she continues this way for another two days without being able to drink, then there will be little chance of saving her. But we must do all we can to bring about an awakening."

"Yes. I think we must," said Ignatia, then went on in another, more matter-of-fact tone. "A box of spices was brought to her yesterday, from the Emperor's grandmother, with a most flattering note; they have been great friends in times past. When my mother is better, I will read it to her. Julia Maesa is the real power in that family, not her grandson or her daughters or daughters-in-law, so her attention will mean a great deal to my mother."

"An excellent notion," said Sanct-Franciscus. "If you will, get the linen, and I hope Starus will bring the ewer of honey-and-salt water. I will add an elixir to that, and you may begin to offer her water."

"Do you think . . . ," she began, then faltered. "No, I won't ask you any more until after dawn." She moved back from the bed. "However this turns out, I thank you from the bottom of my heart. I shall tell my uncle how much you have done for my mother." To express her sincerity, she rose on the balls of her feet and kissed his cheek. "I am in your debt."

A thousand years ago, Sanct-Franciscus thought, he might have taken advantage of her vulnerability, but he had learned how dangerous such pursuits could be; so he took her hand in his. "You owe me nothing, Doma: believe this."

Her smile was uncertain, but she left him with her mother while she went to get the linen and to urge Starus to ready the ewer of water. She felt strangely light-headed and she found it hard to concentrate. As she made her way along the corridor, she amazed herself by skipping once, then, chagrined at such a lapse, made herself walk more steadily, eyes downcast as suited this present occasion. She told herself that she was giddy from worry and enervation, but she knew that was not the whole cause; she lifted the hand Sanct-Franciscus had held and was surprised to find it unchanged. Inwardly chiding herself for such frivolity, she entered the kitchens and called out to Starus, doing her utmost to sound firm and devoted.

When she returned to her mother's room, Starus was with her, bearing the ewer. "How big a basin of oil do you need?" he asked Sanct-Franciscus as he set the ewer down.

"Not a large one," said Sanct-Franciscus; he had repositioned Adicia on her pillows so that she was directly on her back, and her lips slightly parted. "Doma, if you will?" He indicated where he had placed the stool by the bed.

"Certainly," said Ignatia, handing him a damp square of linen. "Is this what you wanted?"

"Yes. Very good," Sanct-Franciscus approved, folding the square in thirds and making a crease in the middle. He placed this over Adicia's mouth, the crease holding her mouth open, then said to Ignatia. "I will give you a measure; use it to keep the water in the crease wet enough to continue to drip down her tongue. Tell me if she doesn't swallow, but I think she will."

Concealing her doubts, Ignatia did as she was told. "Is this what Galen taught?"

"No, although he was an excellent teacher," said Sanct-Franciscus, taking a small ladle off a ring of measures hanging on his belt. "Let me put my elixir in the water"—he took a rose-colored vial from his case and poured half its contents into the ewer—"and now you are ready to begin."

Ignatia watched Sanct-Franciscus spoon out a little of the water and slowly pour it onto the crease in the linen. "I see." She took the measure from him and repeated what he had done. "Is this proper?"

"It is," he said, and went back to his case; he removed a jar of unguent and a container of powder, which he set on the table near the bed. "I am going to mix a salve that should help to increase her pulse, which is a first step in reviving her." He added to himself, *if she is able to waken.*

"Won't that be dangerous?" Ignatia asked.

"No, not in her present state. Her breath does not smell of stale meat, nor of ruined cheese, so it is likely that she will be able to have her pulse sped up without risking a seizure." He continued with his preparations. "This salve is to be applied before the warm oil is rubbed into her hands and feet."

"All right," said Ignatia, watching him with an intensity that verged on adoration; she scooped another measure of water from the ewer and dribbled it onto the folded linen; to her astonishment, Adicia swallowed. "Bona Dea!" she exclaimed.

"What?" Sanct-Franciscus asked, interrupting his work.

"She swallowed. I saw it. I felt it." She stared at him. "How did you know?"

He touched her arm. "One swallow is a good sign, but there is still a long way to go," he reminded her.

"Do you say so?" The smile that suffused her features was radiant. "It is more than I . . . hoped."

"Perhaps," he said carefully. "Let us see how she fares for the rest of the night. It is three hours until dawn. If she is still doing well by then, I think you may be encouraged for your mother's sake."

"I am encouraged already," said Ignatia.

Sanct-Franciscus looked away from her, making his final preparations for the next phase of his treatment. "Whatever the outcome, you have served Domina Laelius well."

"Because of your instruction, Sanct-Franciscus," she said, adding more treated water to the linen. She kept steadily at the task while Sanct-Franciscus made his salve and smeared it first on Adicia's hands, then on her feet, then rubbed it well into her skin with the warm oil Starus brought; in spite of the gravity of her mother's condition, Ignatia was almost overcome with happiness, and although it was an undutiful wish, she hoped the dawn would delay its arrival so that she would not have to give up this wondrous time almost alone with Sanct-Franciscus.

Text of a letter from Almericus Philetus Euppo, freedman and mercer of Ostia, to Ragoczy Germainus Sanct-Franciscus at Roma, carried by private messenger.

To the most excellent exile, Ragoczy Germainus Sanct-Franciscus living near the Temple of Hercules in Roma, the greetings of Almericus Philetus Euppo at Ostia, and the promise of delivery of spices from Alexandria, as well as private missives and two bolts of black linen, which this messenger shall have in charge.

There has been another debasing of coins, as you must know. The Emperor is too young, I suspect, to realize what damage his greed is inflicting on Roman merchants in our trading throughout the Empire and beyond. Just a month ago, I had to spend thirty percent more for a cargo of silk than I had originally bid because the denarii have been debased again. Fortunately, I still have a cache of aurei that you provided me to spend, although I paid half that increase in gold rather than silver, so as not to lose still more in the transaction.

You have expressed an interest in Barbary horses, and to that end, I have sent word to those brokers who deal in horseflesh to find out what their prices may be, and what quality of stock they may have for your consideration. You have approved the mares from Bithynia three years ago; I am prepared to deliver your agent to any port at which your ships trade, and to provide him with any assistance that I can. Perhaps you are aware that the Legions still seek out mules in great numbers, and because of that, they will put a premium on all those animals that have tested bloodlines in donkey and mare. In these uncertain times, having the good opinion of the military is a prudent measure—do you not agree?

The prices for wheat and barley have been fluctuating more than in previous years. Some claim it is the debasement of the coins that is the cause, some say it is the presence of barbarians at the edges of the Empire, who prey upon the vast farmlands in those places, that are the cause. Egypt continues to have the steadiest prices for wheat, but even there the costs are not as steady as before. If you intend to purchase barrels from the coming harvest, I would recommend settling on a price, and soon, for as the harvest draws near there may be increased instability in what is expected by the farmers, and that could mean a doubling in what is charged, and once the harvest is in, there will be no chance to bargain.

In relation to wheat, dates remain far less volatile, and for that reason you may wait until June to secure your barrels. It is also important to be careful of those agents who oversell their consigned stock, or attempt to foist inferior stock upon the purchaser. You say your man in Alexandria is reliable, and I have no reason to doubt it, but I ask you to enjoin him to be especially diligent this year, for between the monetary problems and the discontinuity of purchaser and seller, there is a great opportunity for fraud. You, and many others, will need to exercise great care in dealing with contracts, spelling out details and conditions more rigorously than in previous years.

I have recently arranged to import linen, cotton, and silk from Phoenicia and Judaea, and have contracted to supply mercers there with canvas and wool, as well as rope from Britannia. These seem not to be as much compromised by the debasement of coins, although I suspect that in time even cloth and similar goods will become as inconstant in price as foodstuffs are at present. I am attempting to prepare for that time by making my contracts now, while the markets are still holding, for I cannot persuade myself that the denarius will hold value when more than half its silver is gone to pay for the Emperor's amusements.

There has been a rumor circulating here in Ostia that the ships of Valerius Sejanus Paren have been bringing young men and women slaves to this port and Neopolis who are not truly slaves at all, but unfortunates who have been stolen from their homes and families. To hear some accounts, no attractive youth of either sex is safe. It is said that the appetency of the Emperor has fueled the license that has been increasing throughout the Empire, turning what had been an occasional lapse into a general practice among those *dealing in slaves. If this is as widespread as has been claimed, there are likely to be uprisings in many parts of the Empire, for what family will accept such rapacity without protest? You have said that your ships are not to be used to transport slaves; this is known throughout Ostia, yet many are now saying that such a posture can only result in a loss of revenue. For that reason, it may be wise to re-iterate your orders in this regard to your captains, if they are still truly your orders. Otherwise, your ships may yet be used for such purpose, if only to stay ahead of the devaluation of coins.*

May the gods give you good fortune, and look upon you with favor; may your ships' voyages be successful and profitable, and may you never have cause to regret a purchase or a choice in bed-partners. This, on the 6ᵗʰ day of February in the 972ⁿᵈ Year of the City,

Almericus Philetus Euppo
merchant and freedman of Ostia

11

For the last three days, Roma had been unseasonably warm for early March, the skies clear and limpid, the air soft, stirring the trees into buds and bringing the Romans out of their houses in great numbers, so that the fora and the streets were filled with people enjoying the burgeoning spring. Even the Emperor had joined in the occasion, escorted about the major avenues of the city by a throng of handsome young men in new tunicae with Heliogabalus' sun on their chests as a sign of affiliation.

Unmoved by the balmy weather, Telemachus Batsho hurried along the edge of the street leading to the Palatinus Hill, a leather case clasped under his arm, and a burning determination in his heart. "Thinks he'll make a fool of me," he muttered repeatedly as he went along, each step like an assault on the ground. "Using that

foreigner to hide his profits. He won't make a fool out of me."
Reaching the house of Septimus Desiderius Vulpius, he demanded
admittance from the footman at the front door, and then asked to
see Vulpius himself.

"The master is away from home just now," said the footman.

"Where is he?" Batsho asked, his patience thoroughly frayed. "I
must speak with him at once."

"You need not answer him," said a voice from the end of the
peristyle; Leontius came forward, his manner deferential but his old
eyes suspicious. "What is your purpose here, humiliorus?"

"I am the decuria Telemachus Batsho, and I have come to discuss a matter of importance with your master, having to do with
questions raised about his records," he said, making no effort to hide
his indignation: humiliorus indeed!

"I meant nothing to the decuria's discredit," said Leontius without any trace of servility. "As you have your tasks, I have mine."

"Hardly comparable," sniffed Batsho, appalled at himself for arguing with a slave.

"But equally necessary," said Leontius.

"I shall mention this to your master," Batsho threatened, wanting this most unseemly exchange to end.

"Good decuria, I regret that I must tell you my master is
presently at his estates in the north, attending to spring planting in
his orchards and vineyards, and to be present at his cousin Caia's
wedding. My master and his family will return in two weeks if all
goes well. If you would like to be notified when he is once again in
Roma, or would you prefer to dispatch a messenger to him from the
basilica?" Leontius studied Batsho in a manner not quite courteous.
"If your mission is not so pressing, I will be honored to inform my
master of your visit immediately upon his return. He will then be
able to prepare whatever accounts you want to review."

"No doubt. No doubt," Batsho said, almost spitting the words.

"If the matter is truly urgent, I am authorized to send a messenger to him—is it urgent?" asked Leontius in a tone that implied he
knew it was not.

"Not precisely urgent, no," Batsho conceded. "But it is potentially complicated, and pressing, and may require his attention for some time once he is available to answer questions."

Leontius saw the change in Batsho's demeanor, and modified his question. "How do you want me to explain your request to my master?"

"I am not going to tell a slave such things," said Batsho, trying to decide how much to impart to the steward; if this man was like most of the stewards in Roma, he knew the family's business better than they, themselves, did.

"As you wish, decuria," said Leontius, preparing to close the door.

"Be certain I shall come back once your master is at home," Batsho said, hating the lack of determination he heard in his voice—more of a whine than a clarion.

"I will inform him," said Leontius, closing the door firmly.

Batsho stood in front of the door for a short while, trying to think of what he ought to do next. He was not convinced that he should return to the Basilica Julia too quickly, for there were many—his slave Tuccu included—who might assume he had failed at his task; it stung him to think that he had. Surely there were others he could visit on official business. He paced to the end of the wall, stopped, then peered up into the sky as if seeking inspiration there. After a short while he snapped his fingers and set out to the east, away from the Forum Romanum and the Basilica Julia. There was still something he might be able to do, something that no one would question. He walked briskly toward the Temple of Hercules, gathering purpose as he went.

Vitellius admitted him to the house of Domina Clemens. "My master is busy in his study. Shall I send for him?"

This was more the reception Batsho expected, and he made himself stand as tall as possible. "Yes. He will want to talk in a withdrawing room, I believe." His smile was self-serving.

"I will have wine and bread fetched for you," said Vitellius, indicating a door across the atrium from where they stood. "It should not be long in being brought to you, honored decuria."

"Very good," said Batsho, and went briskly past the fountain to the beautiful wooden doors of the withdrawing room. He let himself in and took stock of the chamber, making note of the magnificent hanging fixture that held more than a dozen oil-lamps, and the two couches and three chairs, all upholstered in costly fabrics, reminding himself to check the records of the luxury taxes Sanct-Franciscus had paid. Two tables of glossy carved wood stood between the chairs and the couches. Certainly this foreigner was flourishing in Roma, he thought, as he dropped into one of the chairs and put his case in his lap; his heel tapped out his impatience. The shutters were open and revealed a small stand of peach trees just beginning to put out buds and leaves; Batsho only glanced at them before he again took stock of the contents of the room, mentally calculating the value of what he saw.

A discreet tap on the door announced the arrival of his refreshments, and Batsho called out, "Enter," as he shifted his position in the chair so he could reach the nearest table without effort.

Mareno brought in a tray with an amphora of wine on it, a goblet of gilded wood, and a basket of sweet buns and savory rolls stuffed with spiced cheese. He put the tray down and offered to pour the wine.

"I will attend to that," said Batsho, waving his dismissal.

With a slight bow, Mareno withdrew, leaving the door slightly ajar.

Batsho poured out a generous amount of wine and picked up one of the sweet buns, sniffing at it before he bit into it. He chewed steadily but paid little attention to the taste, thinking of what he would tell Sanct-Franciscus. So intent was he on preparing his opening salvo, he did not realize that Sanct-Franciscus had arrived until a discreet cough behind him startled him out of his contemplation. Spraying bits of masticated bun, he burst out, "What are you doing!"

"Welcoming you to the house of Domina Clemens," said Sanct-Franciscus urbanely. "I hope this means your refreshments are satisfactory?"

"You keep a good kitchen," said Batsho.

"Is that subject to taxation? I was not aware of it," said Sanct-Franciscus, coming up to Batsho.

"No, no. Not that I know of," said Batsho, forcing a chuckle. "Although, if such a tax did exist, you would have to pay handsomely, I expect."

"Then to what do I owe the honor of your visit?"

Batsho contemplated the half of the sweet bun in his fingers. "I have come about the business dealings you have with Septimus Desiderius Vulpius. There are some . . . some gaps in our records that must be eliminated."

"The records or the gaps?" Sanct-Franciscus inquired politely.

Batsho stopped the sharp retort that formed in his thoughts; instead he cleared his throat portentously. "Honestiorus, you are a man of probity, and so I come to you. You have certain business dealings that are under examination, and for that reason if no other, I come to you in the hope of reconciling the discrepancies in our accounts."

"I have provided all the information requested in regard to all my business dealings," said Sanct-Franciscus. "You yourself recorded them, and received your commoda."

Batsho blinked in surprise. "But—"

"I have your signature to that effect, or had you forgot?" Sanct-Franciscus asked, his cordiality unalloyed, but his dark eyes took on a flintiness that had not been in them a moment ago.

Trying to recover himself, Batsho managed an elaborate shrug. "If you are disinclined to assist me, then I will have to refer the matter to the curia itself, for judgment." Usually this intimation was enough to make any Roman willing to cooperate.

But Sanct-Franciscus was not a Roman. He nodded to Batsho. "I am sure the curia would be interested in what you report. As they would be interested in your attempt to solicit a bribe for your silence and complicity."

"This is not—" Batsho began, only to be interrupted.

"If I have misunderstood your purpose in coming here, pardon me for my maladroitness," said Sanct-Franciscus with icy formality. "If you are seeking to discover whether or not I am willing to bribe an official of the Roman Senate, I offer my assurance that I am not.

I will pay the taxes I am assessed, I will pay the commodae required of me, but I will not contravene Roman laws."

"Most commendable," said Batsho as he reached for the amphora to refill his goblet. "You have received me hospitably, which is to your credit."

"And suits your position, decuria."

"Just so, just so," said Batsho before he took a long draught of wine. Feeling somewhat better, he finished the sweet bun, then addressed Sanct-Franciscus again. "It is laudable that you strive to conduct your affairs correctly. Not everyone is as conscientious as you are, and for that reason, I must compare your records to some others filed in association with yours."

"Very punctilious of you," Sanct-Franciscus said.

"A man in my position must be meticulous," said Batsho, trying not to preen.

"No doubt."

Batsho cleared his throat. "You may want to review your records, to determine if what you have reported is in any way dissimilar to what Vulpius has reported."

"When Vulpius returns to the city, I will speak with him," Sanct-Franciscus said. "If we discover any divergence in our accounts, we will inform you of them, as Roman law requires."

"I . . . thank you, for your . . . cooperation and hospitality," said Batsho, although the words almost stuck in his throat.

"There is no need for thanks; I am only doing my duty as a resident of Roma." Sanct-Franciscus inclined his head. "If there is nothing else, I fear I must return to my work in the study. You may remain as long as you like; if this refreshment is insufficient, inform the steward and he will see that you have more of whatever pleases you." He gave Batsho a gesture of respect, then turned and left him alone with the wine and the basket of breads.

"Have you any instructions?" asked Aedius, who met Sanct-Franciscus outside the withdrawing room.

"Give him whatever he asks for; the more the better. Let me know when he is about to leave." Sanct-Franciscus managed a half-smile. "I would appreciate it if no one mentioned the visitor in my study. I think it best if his presence were—"

"Of course not," said Aedius, indignation raising his voice a bit. "Speak to a decuria of the household? I think not."

"I should not have doubted you. If you would prepare another tray and have it brought to the study," said Sanct-Franciscus. He turned away after handing Aedius a denarius for his service, and made for his study, where he found Natalis, his big, long-fingered hands moving restlessly as he paced. "I apologize for taking so long, particularly since you had not been here more than a few minutes when he arrived, and I have sent your refreshments to him. Had it been another, I would have asked him to wait until you and I had finished our business. But since the decuria required—"

"Decuriae are the bane of us all," said Natalis, trying to contain his temper. "I don't like being in the same house as one, I can tell you."

"Who among us does," Sanct-Franciscus said. "This one has a singleness of purpose where I am concerned."

Natalis came to an abrupt halt. "Are you suspect?"

"No; I am rich," said Sanct-Franciscus. "He would like to find a way to demand more commodae of me than the law allows, and so he pesters me and a few of my associates, hoping to force us into paying him additional sums. Unfortunately I have done so in the past, and that seems to have inspired him to regard me as a good target for his requirements: fortunately I have a record of what he has been paid, one that he has signed, and that limits his rapacity to some extent, for he would be dismissed from his post if it was revealed that he had taken bribes, or solicited additional commodae."

"They all take bribes," said Natalis. "And most of them remain at their posts."

"Yes, but not so egregiously as this Batsho: he is an avaricious little man, who uses what small power he possesses to try to enrich himself."

"Sounds like that Persian merchant. Dis take him!" Natalis slapped his fist into his hand. "I wish I had never entered his shop."

"I can understand that," said Sanct-Franciscus, continuing with delicacy, "Did you actually take anything?"

"No!" Natalis burst out, then pressed his lips together, and, under Sanct-Franciscus' penetrating gaze added, "He had nothing worth my efforts."

"Not even the alabaster figures?"

"No. They were of inferior workmanship. I have some standards; I will not risk prison for something that will fetch a few denarii, which is all those figures would have done, if I had taken any." He paused. "I still lie, occasionally."

"And the boy: does he work with you?" Sanct-Franciscus asked.

"No, he really was asking for directions. Truly. It drew the shopkeeper's attention, and that made him suspect the worst." He cleared his throat. "I do sometimes work with someone, but she is not . . . she is over forty and no one pays her much attention, so she is most effective."

"And she is . . . ," Sanct-Franciscus prompted.

"We are cousins. She is a widow of limited means, and she welcomes the extra money our efforts can bring; at forty-three, she is in no position to learn new skills—and even if she did, who would hire her?"

"Has she no other means?" Sanct-Franciscus asked.

Natalis sighed abruptly. "Her husband left her with a house, but his nephew claimed the house for his family, and the decuriae upheld his claim, so now my cousin lives in two little rooms in one of the insulae down near the slaughterhouses." He stared toward the window. "I ask you not to betray her. I might manage prison or quarry-work, but she is too old for such sentences, and I would hate to see her go to the arena."

"I will not, nor will I expose you." Sanct-Franciscus indicated one of the chairs. "Sit down. You will have food and drink shortly."

Frowning a little, Natalis moved away from Sanct-Franciscus. "That isn't necessary. I am hardly your guest."

"But of course you are," Sanct-Franciscus contradicted him with a faint smile. "I asked that you visit me upon your release. The Prefect assured me you would."

"I'm . . . I'm sorry I didn't, not at once," Natalis said, unaccountably embarrassed by this admission.

Sanct-Franciscus dismissed this with a wave of his hand. "No matter; you are here now, your injury has healed and you look fit enough."

Natalis paled. "Fit enough for what?"

Sanct-Franciscus shook his head. "Nothing that should trouble you. Nothing that would put you at odds with the law again."

"But—" Natalis began, stopping himself as a tap sounded on the door.

"Come in," said Sanct-Franciscus.

Holmdi entered the study, bearing a well-laden brass tray: a large jug of wine stood surrounded by a silver goblet, a basket of breads, a tub of soft cheese, another of fresh butter, a plate of cold sliced chicken garnished with asparagus, a dish of preserved fruits, and a bowl of pickled vegetables. This he put down on the large table in the center of the room. "I am sorry this took so long to bring, my master, but the decuria asked for more wine." He stood still, anticipating a rebuke and possibly a blow to go with it.

"Did he?" Sanct-Franciscus almost smiled. "His head will ache from so much."

"You said to serve him whatever he asked for," Holmdi reminded him.

"So I did," Sanct-Franciscus agreed. "And the household has done well in catering to him. If necessary, send for a sedan chair to carry him home."

Holmdi ducked his head and prepared to leave the study. "Is there anything more?"

"Not just now, thank you, Holmdi," said Sanct-Franciscus, and waited until the slave had left the room before turning his attention to Natalis once more. "Go ahead. Take what pleases you."

Natalis was hungry and the food smelled delicious. "I would like something to eat, and a glass of wine."

"Have as much as you want," Sanct-Franciscus said.

Ordinarily Natalis would have refused to have more than wine and bread, but he had gone two days on such fare and was famished for something more substantial. "If you don't mind."

"I will not join you. I have . . . a condition that limits my diet severely, and as those of my blood dine in private. Do not let that make you reluctant. Your pleasure is all that matters here." He watched Natalis take one of the breads, pull it open and begin to smear soft cheese in the cavity, then reach for chicken slices and pickles and stuff them into the bread.

"This is most generous, honestiorus." He turned away, as if worried that his eating might upset his host.

"Nothing more than I would offer any other guest in your situation," said Sanct-Franciscus.

Natalis, who had taken a large bite of his stuffed bread, stopped chewing. "What do you mean?"

"You have spent months in prison, and you have no employment to sustain you," said Sanct-Franciscus.

"I have not yet found . . . fitting work," said Natalis warily.

"Does nothing suit your abilities?"

"My abilities are somewhat limited," Natalis admitted.

"You mean that your skills are as a thief?" Sanct-Franciscus suggested with unruffled calm; as Natalis nodded, he went on, "You are not necessarily so constrained: that is only the application you have chosen for your talents. I would rather suppose you might do other things."

"Such as?" Natalis asked, interested in spite of himself. He resumed chewing.

"Work for me. I need someone to carry messages and to guard this house. A man of your talents should excel at both duties: you can make your way without drawing attention to yourself, and you can determine what parts of this house are vulnerable to thieves." His smile was ironic. "You do know how to do both those things, do you not?"

"Oh, yes," said Natalis. "I can do them."

"You fear such work would lack excitement?" Sanct-Franciscus proposed. "I may soon have to dispatch a messenger to Alexandria.

And many of my dealings are conducted under the rose. Do not fear that you would only fetch and carry."

After a long, thoughtful moment, Natalis said, "If I come to work for you, what then?"

"Then you will receive a place to live here, fifteen silver denarii a month for your labors, in addition to payment for every service you perform for me. I will pay you ten silver denarii today for agreeing to enter my service." Sanct-Franciscus knew the amount was generous, even in the debased coins of this time, and he expected Natalis to accept it. "My only requirement beyond your service is that while you are in my employ, you will rob no one, steal nothing. And I would prefer that you do not lie to me."

Natalis squirmed a bit. "I will make an effort to comply."

"You will do more than that, or I will not engage you. Think, Natalis: a regular wage and valuable work to do. That should suffice even you." The glint of humor in his dark eyes took the sting out of his remarks.

"And my cousin?" Natalis inquired, pouring wine before taking another bite. "Is there anything you can offer her?"

"I think I might be able to arrange something," said Sanct-Franciscus, thinking of Melidulci, who was finding it difficult to find a woman-companion to lend her the appearance of propriety at her house away from the lupanar. "I will try to find employment for her in some capacity that will not demean her. Will that suffice?"

"I can't ask more than that," said Natalis.

"Then you will accept my offer?" Sanct-Franciscus said.

Natalis considered his response. "I will do so for a year. If at the end of the year either you or I am dissatisfied, then the arrangement will end. Is that satisfactory?"

The sound of unmelodic singing interrupted them, and both Sanct-Franciscus and Natalis looked around, then realized that Telemachus Batsho was drunk and amusing himself.

"It seems reasonable," said Sanct-Franciscus, recovering himself and holding out his hand to slap palms with Natalis.

For a long moment, Natalis hesitated. "Why are you employing me: you might buy a slave to do your bidding, and spend much less in the space of a year."

"True enough," Sanct-Franciscus said. "But I have found over time that a free man is likely to prove the more loyal servant than a slave." He did not elaborate on this, but his thoughts went back to slightly less than a century before, when Srau, in Fars, had very nearly brought about Sanct-Franciscus' True Death, all in the name of seeking manumission. "I have slaves enough about me."

"Then," said Natalis, clapping his hand to Sanct-Franciscus', "I am your servant for the terms we have agreed upon, for a year."

Batsho's song grew louder.

"I accept your conditions," said Sanct-Franciscus, shaking his head. "What a wretched serenade to mark our business."

"He isn't very good at singing," said Natalis, pouring out a little wine onto the floor before drinking. "For good fortune and the favor of the gods."

"All of them," Sanct-Franciscus concurred. "Including the forgotten ones."

Text of a letter from Vettrinis the Gaul, at Vetera Castra in Germania Inferior, to Ragoczy Germainus Sanct-Franciscus in Roma, carried by merchant's courier and delivered two months after it was dispatched due to weather and being intercepted and read before it reached Roma.

To my most highly esteemed commercial partner, the greetings from Vettrinis the Gaul, with distressing news from Vetera Castra in Germania Inferior:

During the winter just past, the Cherusci came over the river and raided throughout the immediate region, seizing goods, marauding for livestock, killing, and taking slaves. The end result of this is that the shepherds with whom we have so often done business have, through no fault of theirs, no wool to sell, and so our projected earnings will be reduced by at least a third.

I am attempting to find other shepherds and farmers with fleece to sell, but many others are doing the same, and that has meant that the price for wool has risen steeply. I am at something of a loss to know what I should do, for the prices will certainly remain high in this region, and others may raise their prices, as well, to take advantage of the immediate shortages. I may return to Belgica and hope that the situation is better there, or I may go north, hoping that the wild men in the marshes have wool available. The marshes have not been raided, at least not yet, but they are nearer to danger than Gallia Belgica is, and that gives me pause. When I have decided, I will send you word of it.

The winter has been hard, which probably accounts for the raids, and spring is slow in coming. I foresee a difficult year for everyone in Germania Inferior, and probably not much better in Germania Superior. In addition, due to avalanches, and a bad flood in February, there are breaks in the road leading into Italia, and this, in turn, has slowed commerce still more. It may take this letter longer to reach you than the usual three weeks, and for that I apologize.

On your recommendation, I am trading in aurei, not denarii, and, as you predicted, I have found the few merchants and factors with whom I am dealing more willing to engage in trade for gold, since the aurei are not as debased as the denarii have been. Who would have thought that the Roman denarius could lose so much of its value, and so quickly?

There are tales being told of the young Emperor—that he is willful and extravagant beyond imagination, that he keeps favorites openly and has little interest in government, leaving such matters to his mother and grandmother while he amuses himself in outlandish feasts and festivities. He is young, and that may account for some of his thoughtlessness, but they say that he has failed to resupply many of the Legions posted on borders such as ours. If this is true, it is a sad thing for Roma and the Empire, and I fear we may expect more raids such as those of last winter. Who knows, if they are unpaid for much longer, the Legions may become the raiders, and then who will be safe?

I wish to assure you that I will do my utmost to secure enough wool to bring us both a profit this season, but that may not be possible. I ask you to hold yourself in patience while this region recovers from the troubles it has sustained. This, on the 9th day of March in the 972nd Year of the City, by my own hand,

Vettrinis
merchant of Gallia Belgica

12

With a sigh of profound satisfaction, Melidulci rolled onto her side and smiled at Sanct-Franciscus. "I wish I knew how you do that," she said contentedly, languidly, her sumptuous body still quivering in apolaustic abandon. Her bedchamber was faintly illuminated by three perfumed oil-lamps that filled the room with the scent of sandalwood and made her naked flesh shine as if dusted with powdered pearls; her hair was a glorious, disorderly nimbus on her pillow, looking dark as bronze in the dusk before sunrise. Luxuriating in the aftermath of passion, she closed her eyes as slowly as a cat, and opened them so that she would not be deprived of the vision of her partner. Beyond the windows, the first flush of dawn limned the hills in pale, luminous pinkish-gold. Birds heralded the morning, and occasionally a cock crowed. "No one has ever given me so much joy. No one has known how."

"But you have allowed me to touch you, to know you," said Sanct-Franciscus, his voice deep and gentle as his endearment.

She put her fingers to his lips to keep him from speaking. "You need not tell me that it is the same for you, because it is not: you could not know what you know without experience; I know that— you could not have learned what you know without loving many other women—and I have no complaints."

He smiled fleetingly. "You are a most understanding woman, Melidulci," he said kindly.

"I am a most *gratified* woman," she corrected him with an allur-ing smile, pulling the disordered sheet up to her chest as if to signal the end of their lovemaking. "I would thank you for all you do, but you dislike it, so I will say only that I am most fortunate that you have turned your attentions to me."

"I, too, am fortunate," he said, and kissed the corner of her mouth. His black kalasiris whispered its silken compliments to the linen of her lower sheet as he moved. "You have accepted me and my . . . limitations without question."

"I would have to be a fool to question such largesse as you pro-vide." She laughed softly. "Your so-called limitations do not trouble me, particularly since you explained your nature."

"I would repay you most cruelly if you did not know what my continued love can impart." He looked toward the open window. "Sunrise is coming. You can see the shine of it on the eastern hori-zon."

"Shortly the sun will be up, and you will need to be away." There was a kind of regret in her acknowledgment.

"I should leave," he told her. "The native earth in the soles of my peri will protect me, once I put them on, but I would like to keep as much of our night together flourishing in me as long as possible." He stroked her hair. "To do that, I must go."

"How long must I wait before you lie with me again?" She stretched, the lack of self-consciousness making this provocative in a way it would not have been had she done it deliberately. "Now that we have shared a bed as often as we have, there is no reason not to continue to do so, is there? I have passed into the shadow of your nature months ago, and nothing you can do will change it. I am pre-pared to do all that is necessary when I die to remain dead, so you need not hesitate on that account. I have no wish to live as you do, isolated amid the world of men, no remnant of my living life left to comfort me, none of my gens to remind me of my bonds. Say what you will about the Blood Bond, it isn't the same. No, thank you: I will seek my delights in life and have no regrets that death will end them."

Sanct-Franciscus touched her shoulder, his fingers moving lightly.

"I would like to spend time with you again in eight days. I have other obligations that demand my attention, and you deserve time to yourself."

"I'd rather have time with you," said Melidulci.

"You may want such a thing now, but I fear in time you would grow jaded." He was not quite serious, but there was a note of concern in his musical voice.

She lolled back on the pillows, baffled and teasing at once. "With the splendid things you do, with your generosity, with your— Very well. In time, yes, everyone grows jaded. In my work, I've seen it often. The sweetest rapture can pall, the most delectable dishes become dull to the palette: it is what makes death acceptable. Our wants and our fears are all worn out." She pulled the sheet over her shoulder. "How have you contrived not to become wearied by life?"

He shook his head a little. "Ah, but I am not alive: I am undead."

"It's the same thing," said Melidulci, stifling a yawn. "Pardon me."

"You are sleepy, and no wonder," said Sanct-Franciscus, sliding back from her. "You need rest. I'll leave you to it."

She reached for his hand. "I don't mind being tired if you're the cause."

"But you and I will have so much more to share if both of us are rested." He rolled onto his back, swung his legs over the bed and sat up. "You know what your response does for both of us."

"You mean that your pleasure increases with mine, that you can have nothing I do not experience; I understand," she said, sounding disappointed. "You've told me that before, and I will believe you, although you are the only man I have ever known who thought that."

"I think it because it is true," said Sanct-Franciscus, rising, then bending down to kiss her mouth. "I have what you have, and only what you have. Your passion is a precious gift." His lips brushed hers.

As they broke apart, she closed her eyes in resignation and somnolence. "You're probably right," she said. "I will have to hold this past night in my memory until—"

"Eight days," said Sanct-Franciscus as he found his peri and bent to put them on his feet; his feet, like his hands, were small and well-shaped. "I will send you word if there are any changes."

"I will hope that means you will come sooner rather than later," she murmured; she was already half-asleep, her breath slowing and deepening.

"You tempt me, Melidulci," he said softly.

"Good," she responded just above a whisper.

He left the room quietly, pausing at the alcove of lares and household gods to leave a small topaz on the altar, then he nudged the dozing footman awake. "Make certain that all the locks are secure," Sanct-Franciscus reminded the man. "Some beasts prowl by day as well as night."

The man blinked and nodded as he pulled back the bolt to allow Sanct-Franciscus to leave. "Fortune and favor for you today, honestiorus."

"Thank you," said Sanct-Franciscus, flipping a denarius to the footman as he went out into the morning twilight, walking as quickly as he dared, unwilling to draw untoward attention to himself. Sunrise would come shortly; already he could hear the sounds of carts and wagons lumbering in to the fora: the law required them to unload the vehicles, then drive them outside the city walls to large paddocks for the day, which made the predawn morning on a market-day a busy time in the city. Sanct-Franciscus walked more swiftly through the tangle, never allowing himself to be distracted from his purpose in spite of the confusion of traffic bound for the city gates.

A small contingent of Watchmen patrolling the streets stopped him less than five streets from Melidulci's house. "Where are you coming from and where are you bound?" asked the leader of the six men; they were armed with spears and daggers and short flagella.

"I am coming from the house of a friend and bound for the Temple of Hercules," said Sanct-Franciscus.

"Without bodyguards?" The Watchman looked askance at him.

"At this hour, with you Watchmen about, I thought it would be safer to walk by myself than to attract attention to myself with an escort of four retired gladiators." This was true enough. "Many thieves target men with bodyguards."

The Watchmen chuckled, and one with a strong Aquitanian accent said, "Too bad more honestiora don't think of that."

"The same with their dwellings," said Sanct-Franciscus. "They build on the Palatinus and the Capitolinus hills, with walled estates and many guards, then wonder why robbers know they have valuable possessions."

The leader of the Watchmen actually laughed. "Right you are."

Sanct-Franciscus could see the first, brilliant shaving of the sun emerging from behind the hills; he nodded to the Watchmen. "May I walk on?"

"Of course," said the leader, smiling cordially. "Fortune and the gods bring you your desires."

"Thank you; may Mars and Janus hold you safe." As he said this, he held out three denarii. "For all of you." While the Watchmen made approving sounds, Sanct-Franciscus strode briskly away. He was more than half-way back to Domina Clemens' house when the sun lifted above the eastern horizon, poking long, brilliant fingers among the hills and houses of Roma. As he neared the Temple of Hercules, he saw a cluster of young men and women standing before it, hands raised, all praying loudly to the Christ. Among them he noticed Marius Octavian Laelius, a skimpy beard on his chin, his clothing ornamented with designs of fish. His whole body quaked with emotion, fervor in every lineament of his being. Stopping to watch them, Sanct-Franciscus was somewhat surprised when Octavian broke off his prayers and approached him.

"Why are you watching me?" he demanded.

"I was not specifically watching you," said Sanct-Franciscus calmly. "I was observing your group."

"If you aren't watching me, what are you doing here?" His chin, with its sparse beginnings of a beard, came up.

"I live here," said Sanct-Franciscus, nodding toward the gates of Domina Clemens' house.

Octavian started to laugh and then thought better of it. "You do not—" The compelling look that Sanct-Franciscus directed at him silenced the challenge Octavian was about to deliver. "You should not live so near that temple; it is a vile, damned place," he muttered.

"Are you afraid it will influence me: I thought your Christ is more powerful than any pagan god or demi-god, and protects the righteous," Sanct-Franciscus said, irked by the presumptuous attitude of the young man.

"So long as they worship Him, He does. The rest, though virtuous, are damned."

"So your faith is an appeal for clemency?" Sanct-Franciscus suggested.

Octavian bristled. "We must proclaim the one True God and His Son, and our Savior."

"No doubt," Sanct-Franciscus said, suddenly feeling very old.

"The Last Days are coming; all the signs foretell it. The world must make ready to be Judged, and as long as there are pagan temples for the adoration of pagan gods, the Last Judgment will be one of wrath, not mercy. Paul the Apostle warned us that Christ will return very soon, so conversion must happen shortly for those who would be saved." He stood defiantly in front of Sanct-Franciscus, the shadow of the temple covering his face as the sun rose behind the hill on which it stood. "If we cannot bring redemption to all, then ours is forfeit."

"Must the end come so quickly?" Sanct-Franciscus asked, amused and saddened at once.

"Yes, it must, or so prophecy has revealed: the Blessed Paul declared that God would return in the blink of an eye; day and night we must be ready. Day and night we must strive to be worthy of His Love. All those who seek Him may hope to be raised up to join Him in glory—the rest will be cast into outer darkness. Everyone must prepare. Everyone must come to the Christ, and the worship of the True God." He touched the golden fish pectoral suspended on a leather thong around his neck. "The end will be upon us soon. No man may know the hour, but surely it will come."

Sanct-Franciscus sighed. "You are certainly sincere, but I would think you would serve your god better by helping tend to your mother than to spend the night attempting to shame a Roman temple into conversion with your prayers."

"That is not what we are doing," said Octavian hotly.

"No? Then what might it be?" He held up his hand to keep Octavian from answering. "I know something of your religion; do not think I am not aware of its precepts." He recalled the accounts of the preacher who had so offended the High Priest of the Temple in Jerusalem, proclaiming that each man was a temple unto himself. "It began as a Jewish sect, then gradually gathered Jewish, Greek, and Asianan converts, then other followers, to become a separate belief with sects of its own. Your sect within the group is the most stringent and condemnatory of those who do not agree with your faith or your interpretation of your faith: there are other sects within the Christian faithful whose beliefs and practices are less intrusive, but equally as sincere."

"The others are misled and a disgrace for the Christ, Who died to redeem all mankind." Octavian folded his arms.

"The same is believed of Mithras, and many others." Sanct-Franciscus shook his head once. "You will say that such gods are lies—only yours is true. And the others would say the same of your tenets." He gave Octavian a long stare. "Go home, Octavian. Tend to your mother, help your sister. This will not spare the world anything, and it will bring you no nearer to salvation than any other man."

"So you say! You disbeliever! *Blasphemer!*"

Sanct-Franciscus was about to turn away, but he stopped to give Octavian one last remark. "I believe to the extent that I know a man may rise from the dead, but I know also that rising does not make him a god." He had been told much the same thing when he was young and alive—that he would become one with the gods of his people, but over his two millennia of vampiric life, he had realized that was not the case, that undead existence was not divinity no matter how long he continued in that state.

Octavian took a deep breath. "You may be a physician, and a capable one for the flesh, but you have no understanding of the soul." He swung around and was about to return to his companions when Sanct-Franciscus stopped him, saying, "Perhaps not as you and your faith understand it, but I hold intimacy to be the highest expression of life one person may share with another."

The apparent leader of the praying group intervened, calling Octavian to order before that impulsive youth could continue his disputes. "Leave him alone, Octavian. God will deal with him when the time comes."

"Yes, God will judge him," Octavian said loudly enough to be certain that Sanct-Franciscus heard him. "He will know the Wrath of God at the end, when he learns what his fate is to be throughout eternity."

Sanct-Franciscus moved on toward the gate to Domina Clemens' house, calling out, "I have returned. Please let me in." The rays of the early sun touched him, promising a warm day.

Aedius, still shrugging off the last vestiges of sleep, opened the gate to Sanct-Franciscus. "Fortune favor this day, Sanct-Franciscus," he said as a matter of courtesy.

"Thank you, Aedius," said Sanct-Franciscus, stepping into the shade of the high wall around the courtyard. "Tell me, how long have those zealots been praying out there?"

"They came shortly after sundown. They had oil-lamps, but they burned out hours ago."

"Oil-lamps," Sanct-Franciscus repeated. "How provident of them." He looked around. "Has anything happened since I left last evening?"

"Someone has come," said Aedius. "I have put him in the second guest-room." He coughed discreetly. "I have told him that you will receive him upon your return."

"Is he a Roman or a foreigner?" Sanct-Franciscus asked, then added before Aedius could speak, "Never mind; I shall learn for myself."

"He comes from afar," said Aedius.

"On one of my ships, perhaps?" Sanct-Franciscus ventured.

"Perhaps," said Aedius. "I did not inquire."

"Excellent," said Sanct-Franciscus. "If this guest is awake, would you ask him to come to my study, and see he has something to break his fast."

"At once," said Aedius, and added, "Holmdi will man the gate while I do this."

"As suits you best," said Sanct-Franciscus.

"Who knows what that group of avid youths may decide to do? I have heard that they do more than exhort good Romans: the honestiorus Cyrillus Herminius Acestes had a band of them break into his house and destroy the altar and alcove of the lares, not six days ago. The Urban Guard were called out to contain them; the Watchmen were not sufficiently armed to do it."

"I would be very surprised if the group outside turned their attention to this house—they are too outraged with Hercules to demean themselves with a simple Roman abode." Saying this, Sanct-Franciscus hastened away toward his private apartments, thinking as he went that he should order the bath prepared; perhaps after he received his guest. He frowned faintly, wondering who could have come unannounced to see him; a foreigner, Aedius had said, and that was more perplexing. He made his way up the stairs to the second floor, sensing the last lingering sweetness of his night with Melidulci fade away; suddenly the eight days until their next time together seemed much too long.

In his outer chamber he stripped off his kalasiris and donned a black linen dalmatica, one that was long enough to reach his ankles. He found an ebony comb and ran it through his hair, then felt his chin and jaw to reassure himself that his beard was not too long; he had been without a reflection so long that he no longer missed referring to it, relying on touch instead of sight. Last he chose a heavy Egyptian-style silver pectoral with small disks with raised wings—his eclipse sigil—at the end of each segment of the collar, which he fastened around his neck. Satisfied, he left the room and made his way to the study, wondering afresh who might be waiting for him.

The study was sunk in half-light, for the shutters had not yet been opened. Sanct-Franciscus slipped into the room, seeing a figure wrapped in a dark-blue byrrus seated so that the visitor faced away from the door. "I am sorry you have been kept waiting on my account."

"You had no reason to expect me, my master," came the answer as Rugeri stood up and turned toward Sanct-Franciscus. A slight smile brightened his austere features.

Sanct-Franciscus recovered quickly from his astonishment. "I am delighted to see you, as always, my friend, but what brings you here—and so covertly?"

Rugeri took off his byrrus, revealing a tunica of dove-gray linen and high, laced calcea that reached almost to his knees. "I took the advice of Domina Clemens and came without notice to report to you. I borrowed one of the messengers' bigae in Ostia yesterday, and reached Roma just before the gates were closed. The Urban Guard questioned me on my business for two or three hours before permitting me to come on to this house, so I did not arrive until long after you had departed for the night."

"I hope you were received cordially," said Sanct-Franciscus.

"Luckily I brought the letter from Domina Clemens; no one here would deny hospitality to the deputy of the owner," said Rugeri.

"Olivia sent you?" Sanct-Franciscus asked, startled once more.

"Yes. She said in her letter to me that she supposed that some of our regular correspondence had been intercepted—I gather she has intimated as much to you, as well—and that to ensure you have accurate information, she advised me to come to Roma, unannounced, to speak with you. That way, she thought, we might be able to discover where the letters were being seized without alerting the culprits of our interest." Rugeri shrugged, his faded-blue eyes revealing more than fatigue. "I concurred. Ecce. I am here."

"Why do you believe that our letters are being . . . shall we say, diverted? from their destinations?" He went to open the shutters and let in the new day; light suffused the room, revealing the murals in full richness and detail, depicting the Roman gods at their pleasures, the largest of which showed Vesta and Mercury engaged in a lively debate about the happiness of home versus the excitement of commerce and travel.

"I believe it because I have asked you for decisions on certain matters that you have not addressed, and I have reason to suspect that the information you *have* received is incorrect." Rugeri held out a sheaf of fan-folded scrolls. "These are my copies of what I have sent you."

Sanct-Franciscus took the sheaf, but did not untie it or open any of the letters. "I knew something was wrong. I had a letter from you at the end of January that seemed most unlike you."

"How is that?" Rugeri asked, looking troubled.

"I will show it to you later; you will understand my apprehension," said Sanct-Franciscus. "In the meantime, tell me what has happened? There must be something specific, or I doubt you would be here."

"There are a number of matters you and I ought to discuss, and not just about your business in Alexandria." He did not wait for permission, but sat down again in the chair he had occupied when Sanct-Franciscus arrived.

"You mean there are other things bothering you?" Sanct-Franciscus took the chair opposite Rugeri's. "What has happened, that you are so troubled?"

"I wish I could tell you," said Rugeri, and lapsed into a thoughtful silence. "All the way here," he said a bit later, "I tried to decide how to explain my concerns to you, and I determined that it would be a simple matter of reporting instances of—but then, once I arrived, I realized that this would not be as easily done as I supposed." He leaned forward, elbows on knees, hands laced together. "I am certain someone managing the customs taxes in Alexandria has taken to stealing portions of your cargos after the taxes on the whole have been paid, and profiting twice—from the overpaid taxes and the purloined cargo. I am certain he must have an accomplice, either in Ostia or here in Roma, someone with direct ties to you and your trading company." He stopped, staring directly at Sanct-Franciscus.

"I gather you have mentioned these possibilities to Olivia," Sanct-Franciscus remarked. "It seems the sort of precaution you would take."

"I sent her a letter yesterday, and I used one of your private messengers at the shipping office." Rugeri's mouth pressed to a thin line. "It may be difficult to gain the kind of credibility we will have to have to persuade the Prefecture of Customs to investigate these crimes."

"True enough," said Sanct-Franciscus, sighing once. "And I do not relish making the kinds of bribes that would be needed to compensate for lack of specific evidence: such a strategy can bring about unwanted results."

"You are thinking of the Persians," said Rugeri with a single nod. "I would not like to have such an experience again."

"Nor I," said Sanct-Franciscus. He put his hands together, studying the middle distance over the tops of his fingers. "Do you think," he went on in the Persian tongue, "that someone in this household—not in the business, but this household—may be part of the trouble we have had?"

"I fear it is possible," said Rugeri. "Although I cannot guess who is behind it, or what he hopes to accomplish."

"It is most perplexing," agreed Sanct-Franciscus, beginning to stride down the room again. "You were wise to come to me yourself. We must go cautiously, I think."

"I didn't like leaving your business in Alexandria, but the Priests of Imhotep have sent their most accomplished man of numbers— Djuran is his name—to monitor all the accounts and records. Do you have anyone here you would trust with such a task?"

Sanct-Franciscus shook his head slowly. "Urbanus manages such things for this household; I have not caught him doing anything suspicious, but if he is clever, I doubt I would." He glanced toward the door. "I cannot promise we are not overheard."

"That is to be expected." Rugeri coughed and went on in Latin, "I would prefer to remain here for a time."

"I would like that as well," said Sanct-Franciscus. "I need more eyes and ears than anyone could possess, at least until I know what is going on, and why."

"I will do what I can to make your situation less confusing, although it may take some time to sort out the problem." He rose. "I will set about the work at once, my master. Do you want me to return to my duties as your body-servant?"

"I would welcome that, but I will have to arrange for Tigilus to have a new assignment, something that does not cause him disgrace." Sanct-Franciscus tapped his finger-tips together.

"Does he require such attention?" Rugeri asked.

"As much as any attentive servant does," said Sanct-Franciscus. "If I lessen his position in the eyes of the other household slaves, he will suffer for it, and hold me to blame for his misery. I need not remind you how conscious slaves are of such matters."

"He would lose his place in the household," said Rugeri; as a bondsman, he had not been subjected to the stringent order among slaves, but he had seen it work over fifteen decades, and realized Sanct-Franciscus was right.

"Unless he has something of equal importance to replace his post, yes."

"And that would distress him," said Rugeri.

"And that would distress *me*," said Sanct-Franciscus. "To lack concern for those around me lessens my humanity, and I know what desperation lies down that road." He had an appalling memory of his centuries of captivity in a Babylonian oubliette, surviving on terrified monthly sacrifices; he suppressed a shudder.

Rugeri saw the flicker of anguish in Sanct-Franciscus' dark eyes, and said, "Those times are long behind you."

"By all the forgotten gods, I hope so," said Sanct-Franciscus quietly, but with such intensity of feeling that the air seemed to shake with it.

"So," Rugeri said after a brief silence, "a new assignment for Tigilus."

"I will decide what it is to be before prandium is served," said Sanct-Franciscus.

"And you wish me to work with Urbanus."

"If you would; let us say that we wish to integrate the foreign accounts with our Roman ones," said Sanct-Franciscus. He started toward the door, then stopped and turned to look at Rugeri. "I thank you for coming, my friend. You have taken a burden off me."

Rugeri ducked his head. "Then I am pleased to be here, my master," he said.

Text of a letter from the Praetorian Centurion Fidelis Mais Paigni to Senator Valericus Hyacinthus Modestinus Vitens, carried by private messenger.

To the illustrious Valericus Hyacinthus Modestinus Vitens, Senator and member of the Curia, Ave!

On your order, we have investigated reports submitted by decuriae to the Curia for review of the foreigner, Ragoczy Germainus Sanct-Franciscus, resident in Roma at the house of the esteemed Roman widow, Atta Olivia Clemens, near the Temple of Hercules, although he also owns and maintains a sizeable villa—Villa Ragoczy— some three thousand paces beyond the Roman walls, beyond the Praetorian Camp, where he raises horses and mules. Our investigation is not complete, but so far, I must inform you, that there is nothing we have found that suggests that he has attempted to avoid paying legal taxes on any of his property or on his present leased residence, or has worked against the Emperor or the Roman State. In fact, our results thus far have revealed quite the opposite: he has on all occasions, when there was any question about amounts due, he has agreed to pay the higher assessment. This man, known to be an exile, has conducted himself with dignity and propriety, has maintained his businesses as required, paid all his taxes, occupies the Clemens house with all necessary legalities attended to, and has no complaints against him from any Roman merchant with whom he has done business.

Further, we have been informed by the Prefect of the Litigianus Prison, Herminius Mirandus Guion, that this Sanct-Franciscus has on several occasions come to the prison to treat injured or ailing prisoners, for which service he has charged nothing. The first of those he treated, a thief named Natalis, this Sanct-Franciscus has given employment, and brought into this household as a servant— his private messenger, according to the records held by the decuria Telemachus Batsho of the Basilica Julia, who has said that he believes that any exile who is as observant of Roman law as Sanct-Franciscus is must have some hidden purpose in his excessive scrupulousness. While I do not entirely concur, I and my men will continue our inquiries until you and the Curia decide that you have sufficient information to reach a conclusion pertaining to this man.

Ave, Caesar. Ave, the Vestal Virgins. Ave, the Senate and the People of Roma.

> *Fidelis Mais Paigni*
> *Centurion, Praetorian Guard*

At the Praetorian Camp on the 12th day of April, the 972nd Year of the City

PART II

PAX IGNATIA LAELIUS

T ext of a letter from Pallius Savianus, Captain of the *Evening Star,* at Ostia, to Ragoczy Germainus Sanct-Franciscus at Roma, carried by Natalis.

To the highly regarded foreign trader, Ragoczy Germainus Sanct-Franciscus, the greetings of Pallius Savianus, Captain of the trading ship Evening Star, *presently in Ostia, greetings.*

Your decision to put a small ballista aboard this ship—and others of your ships, as I understand—proved to be a most provident one. Five days out of Miletus in Asiana we were chased by a pair of pirate craft, either from Creta or one of the lesser islands; they closed on us, coming around the islands west of Achaea. They were fast ships and we were heavily laden, so our capture seemed likely, but for the ballista you provided, and which I ordered manned at once. Using the barrels of stones you had ordered carried aboard, we succeeded in driving the pirates off and doing damage to their ships, so that we had no fear of pursuit. When we arrived at Brundisium, we made a report there and I will make one here at Ostia as well.

I believe the pirates are becoming bolder, for they take chances that I have not observed taken in many years. Some say it is because Roma is growing weak, but that does not account for what is happening on the Mare Nostrum, nor does it explain the general air of degeneracy that one sees among so many Roman colonies these days. It was not so long ago that the governing posts in the provinces were held by men of distinction, of old families and high honor, but now the provinces are given as prizes to the intimates of the Emperor, or men who have done favors for the Curia, for their enrichment and pleasure, not for the Empire and its benefit.

You may be relieved, under such circumstances, that our cargo has arrived virtually intact, with all the goods we have traded still in the hold of the Evening Star. *The whole will be inventoried and assessed for taxes; then you may send word that we are to give the cargo into the hands of your teamsters who will carry it to Roma for storage in your emporia there.*

If you are going to have this ship repaired and refitted soon, I would request that all the lines be provided with new rope and brasses, for the harsh weather has worn and frayed them so that they are unreliable, and some of the brasses are pitted and roughened, so that they increase the wear on the hemp, which is not desirable for any ship. If we should have to maneuver against pirates again, I would not like to have to depend on the lines we have now, most especially given the poor state of our brasses.

And speaking of replacements, five of the sixteen oarsmen on the Evening Star *should be replaced, preferably by hardier, younger men than the slaves currently at the oars, one of whom is twenty-eight and should have been assigned to less wearing tasks two years since. If you continue your practice of finding a place for the oarsmen that is less demanding, instead of selling them, then I would say that two of these men are suffering from knots in the joints and will not be very useful as heavy laborers. The others should be able to do less constant work, although one is losing his sight, and may become completely blind in time. There are duties in your emporia to which these oarsmen may be suited. I will begin my inquiries there, and I will inform you of what I am advised by the foremen of your stackers, packers, and inventory-keepers.*

If you will authorize the purchase of slaves for the oars, I will begin my search for the best to be had; since you insist on using only freedmen as sailors, I will do my best to find two substitutes for Echirus and Dromirz, both of whom have had offers to work at the ship-building docks here in Ostia, and are glad to put the hard life of sailing behind them. As you have ordered, I will present them with two aurei each when they leave your service, and I will see that the oarsmen have three denarii for every year they served aboard the Evening Star. *I am told that there are sufficient funds at the Eclipse Trading Company here in Ostia to cover these expenses, so I will not appeal to you to supply them.*

I have in hand your bonus for a speedy voyage, for which I most heartily thank you. If all ships' owners were so generous, I doubt any captain would be inclined to make bargains with pirates. My commoda, based on the value of this cargo, set by you at five percent instead of the standard four, has already garnered me a greater fortune than I had expected when I first took command of the Evening Star, *and with this voyage should make it possible for me to purchase a villa for my wife and children, outside of Ostia, but near enough to be convenient to me while I am in port. This would not be possible had you not upheld your principles so faithfully, and for which you may be assured of my continuing allegiance, no matter where my voyages take me.*

If the lines are replaced and the hull scraped, the ship and her crew should be ready to set out again by the end of June. If you have other plans, I ask you to inform me as quickly as you are inclined to do, so that I may schedule my life to suit your purposes, and not be laggard in performing my duties while I settle my family. I am, as always, at your service, and will be so long as Neptune and Fortuna are united in my favor and the favor of your endeavors.

> *Pallius Savianus*
> *Captain of the* Evening Star

At Ostia, the 2ⁿᵈ day of May, in the 972ⁿᵈ Year of the City

1

Domina Adicia moved weakly, her right hand attempting to hold the small cup Sanct-Franciscus presented to her. "I don't need any more of that," she said, her speech slightly slurred, the right side of her face sagging; since she had come out of her stupor, she had been much weakened on the right side of her body, and she tired very quickly now, and was increasingly sensitive to fluctuations is temperature; the morning was already warm, and by midday would be hot, so that Adicia fretted under the single light blanket that covered her.

"It will do you good," Sanct-Franciscus said, aware that the benefit of his infusion was anodyne rather than healing; in his more than two millennia, he had seen this condition in many forms, and had rarely been able to provide more than palliation for those whom the malady struck.

She looked up at him, blinked slowly, then attempted a smile. "If you insist. You command me?"

"For your own sake, I do," he answered, keeping the cup near her lips. "No one can want you to suffer more than you have. The drink will ease you." He was genuinely apologetic, knowing that what was wrong with her had been bred in the bone and would not be undone.

"Someone might want me to endure more agony," she muttered, looking uneasily about the room, fixing her stare on Ignatia.

"No one that I am aware of, Domina Adicia," said Sanct-Franciscus.

"You don't know them as I do," she said darkly. "Deceivers, all of them. The household, the family, none of them care for my torment."

Knowing this discussion would lead only to more rancor, Sanct-Franciscus did his best to ignore it. "You must take care of yourself, Domina Adicia. Leave your other concerns until the time you are stronger."

She sighed. "And this will help me to do that—to be stronger?"

"It is my hope," said Sanct-Franciscus. "The tincture has been beneficial to others in the past."

"Others? You did not blend it for me?" There was suspicion in her question, and petulance.

He realized his error, and said, "This tincture has treated honorata of great rank, and helped them. I trust to the medicaments that have proven their virtue over time."

"Undoubtedly, this is a foreign concoction, no matter to whom you have administered it; I daren't ask what you give me," she said, a ghost of her old flirtatiousness asserting itself.

"If you wish to know, I will tell you," said Sanct-Franciscus, glancing briefly at Ignatia, who sat near the window, half-listening to the sea-like roar of the huge crowd milling through Roma, bound for the Flavian Circus and the Great Games scheduled to begin in three hours.

"They're unfurling the awnings," said Ignatia, recognizing the shout of approval that went up from the direction of the Flavian Circus.

"Very likely," said Adicia, sputtering on the liquid she was attempting to swallow. "This tastes like rancid grass."

Using a linen square to wipe Adicia's chin, Sanct-Franciscus said patiently, "You must not permit the noise to alarm you, Domina. Alarm can be as bad as a blow to the body when one is recuperating. You know what the Great Games are: you need not be dismayed by them."

"Dismayed?" she responded, looking affronted. "Why should I be? I have attended the Great Games since I was hardly more than a child. I loved to see the races and the battles, like any good Roman. The only thing that dismays me about the Games is that I can no longer attend them." Her expression turned resentful, the corners of her mouth curved down sharply.

"Just my point; the Games upset you—the reason for that upset is immaterial," said Sanct-Franciscus, holding the cup to her lips again, banishing her scowl for the moment. "Drink a little more—it will provide you succor."

Frowning, Adicia took another sip, then a third. "It tastes . . . not too unpleasant, now I am accustomed to it."

"It is not intended to be unpleasant," said Sanct-Franciscus as he coaxed her to drink a little more.

She batted at his hand. "Enough now; your mixture will make me euphoric if I drink any more. I must not have too much, for then it would serve to the opposite of its purposes, and I would lie in pain until well into the night. Leave off," she ordered, trying again to smile. "You have done more for me than anyone else in this household."

"I have done what I can to lessen your distress." He stepped back from her, still watching her carefully.

"Exactly," she said in something like triumph. "My slaves and my family can only wring their hands, but you—you actually seek to alleviate my misery." She looked toward Ignatia as if expecting an argument; when none was offered, she sighed. "They are all indifferent to me."

"Your daughter is not indifferent to you: quite the contrary— she has devoted herself to your care," said Sanct-Franciscus, very deliberately.

"Little do you know her, as I do, for what she is," Adicia said, her eyes flicking toward Ignatia, and then away from her.

Sanct-Franciscus set the cup down and put a protective lid over it. "You will have the rest later, when you have recovered your strength a bit."

Adicia sighed. "If you require it of me, I suppose I must."

"I must hope you would require it for yourself," said Sanct-Franciscus, taking another step back. "You should start to feel your discomfort lessen shortly, and then you may doze through the heat of the day."

"Not with those wolves howling for blood at the Flavian Circus," said Adicia, glancing toward the window again. "There must be forty thousand in the stands."

"If the noise disturbs you, I will lower the shutters," Ignatia offered.

"Perhaps, later," said Adicia with a stern gesture of her hand. "Just now the sunshine pleases me."

Sanct-Franciscus got nearer to the window. "You have a cotton blind, do you not, that you could fix across the window?"

"Yes," said Ignatia, and rose from her chair. "I'll fetch one and hook it in place."

"Very good," said Sanct-Franciscus before Adicia could object. "That will make the room less bright but not make it much hotter." He watched Ignatia leave the room, and added to his patient, "The wind may be acrid today; the blind will keep it from burning the air you breathe."

"The heat is a burden for me," Adicia said, as if it were an accomplishment.

"True enough," Sanct-Franciscus agreed. "And for that reason, we must be careful to provide for your comfort."

Adicia almost simpered at his remark. "You are good to me, Sanct-Franciscus. You are a most conscientious physician." Her smile implied that there was more to his care than the practice of medicine.

"It is gracious of you to say so," Sanct-Franciscus responded politely, and went to the far side of the room. "I am going to leave a vial of this tincture for your slave to add to the water you must drink through the afternoon."

"Why should I drink so much? I don't like sweating, or having to piss." She pressed her lips together in disapproval of her body. "If I drink less, those are not such problems."

"But the humors are out of balance when one is thirsty," said Sanct-Franciscus. "You must maintain the balance of your humors, or you will risk making yourself more ill than you have been of late. Sufficient moisture in the body is essential to that balance."

"You're trying to frighten me," she complained.

"If by doing so I can show you the importance of caring for yourself, then I hope I will succeed," he told her, doing his best to speak gently.

She made a fist of her right hand and brought it down on the blanket with all the force she could summon up. "You are being disagreeable!"

"I do not intend to be," said Sanct-Franciscus. "I am trying to care for you."

"Care for me," she repeated, musing on the words. "It is to your credit that you are willing to extend yourself on my behalf." She yawned suddenly. "You have to pardon me: your concoction seems to be working."

"Then once the blind is in place, I will leave you to rest. Which of your slaves would you like to watch you?" He saw Ignatia in the doorway, the folded blind in her hands, and motioned to her to be still.

"Oh, Rea, I suppose." She achieved a little stretch. "The knots in my joints are loosening."

"Just as they're supposed to do," said Sanct-Franciscus, motioning to Ignatia to send for the slave.

"Yes," Adicia said. "I think I will doze a little."

"Excellent," Sanct-Franciscus approved, watching Adicia carefully.

"You will remain here a while, to be sure nothing is done to me that you do not approve," said Adicia, trying to take his hand.

He allowed her to seize his fingers, then carefully moved her hand back to the edge of the blanket. "Rest, Domina. You have no need to vex yourself."

"But you *will* stay here, won't you?"

"If it will help you to rest, then I will, for a time," he said, still attempting to lull her to sleep.

With a contented sigh, she snuggled back into her pillows. "You really are most attentive to me." She blinked slowly, then opened her eyes wide as another shout went up from the Flavian Circus, followed by the metallic bray of the hydraulic organ and the beginning of the new Imperial anthem "Glorious is Heliogabalus, Sungod and Emperor."

"That's a dreadful piece of music," Adicia murmured. "Ugly and trite."

"Do not say so where Imperial spies may hear you," Sanct-Franciscus recommended, although he agreed about the pompous melody.

"What spy would bother?" Adicia asked, and opened her eyes as Rea came into the chamber, a large cup of honey-lemon water in her hands. "This is the house of an invalid widow. What could they suspect me of doing?"

"Your household protects you, whatever the trouble you may face," said Sanct-Franciscus, wanting to soothe her, and motioned to Ignatia to bring the blind in and fix it in place.

Ignatia did this as quickly as she could, saying little while she fitted the eyes in the blind over the small hooks in the window-frame. When she was finished, the light in the bed-chamber was diminished by half, and the canvas blind glowed in the brilliant May light. "I'll be in the reception room," she said softly to Sanct-Franciscus, hoping her mother would not hear her.

"Making attempts on my physician, are you?" Adicia challenged as she watched Ignatia leave the room. "Do you think he wants a paltry creature like you? I gave your father six children and three of you lived, because my blood was strong then. Myrtale at least has two living sons to carry on our line. You have nothing. Leave me alone, you wretched girl."

Inured to such abuse, Ignatia went out of the room and almost walked into Starus. "She will be asleep soon," she told the steward.

"It is her illness talking, Doma, not her dislike," Starus said, his weathered features revealing his concern for Ignatia.

"Perhaps," Ignatia allowed. "But her rebuke is justified. It is unlikely that I will have the opportunity to have children: I am too old to find a husband, and who knows what wife Octavian will bring to the house?"

"A Christian one," said Starus, disapproval in every aspect of his demeanor. "I am told Christian masters require their slaves to pray to the Christian gods, not the gods of Roma."

"Surely not," Ignatia said, starting toward the reception room on the other side of the atrium.

"Octavian has told us—the household—that we must include his god in our prayers." He paused, knowing he had overstepped his bounds. "Some of the other slaves have been offended by this. They don't want to give up their gods, who know them, for one who doesn't."

Ignatia listened with growing shock: that Octavian should have such a lapse in conduct, and at such a trying time! "You may tell them for me that they may pray to Octavian's god only if they want to. Otherwise they are to keep to their own ways, as the law provides." She stopped in the shadow of the tiled roof. "If Octavian insists, send him to me. I will remind him of the limits of our authority." There was a determined set to her mouth. "Don't let him spend too much time with our mother—she's always upset when he starts to exhort her."

"We're all on guard against that." Starus pushed open the reception room door for her. "What would you like to have for your prandium? The cooks are broiling chickens and geese, and the baker has made pillow-bread for us today. We'll have asparagus and frilled cabbage, and a wheel of cheese, in honor of the Games today, and Vesta."

"I'll have a little of the Vesuvian wine, and a platter of the meal. Oh, and ask Waloi to roast a slab of pork ribs for me, with his pepper-garlic sauce."

"Waloi will attend to it at once. Your meal should be ready in an hour or so," said Starus, watching Ignatia toss a pillow into the seat of a glossy, rosewood chair before taking her seat.

"He's a capable butcher, Waloi is," said Ignatia, picturing the rugged man from Pannonia Inferior. "You may tell him I said so."

"It will please him to hear it," said Starus, and turned to leave Ignatia alone.

"You may delay my meal if you like. The rest of the household may dine when the food is ready. I would like a little time alone with the honestiorus Sanct-Franciscus, to discuss my mother's condition. I'll summon you when he has departed." She closed her eyes briefly.

"Yes, Doma Ignatia," said Starus, and left her to supervise the prandium.

A short time later there was a tap on the door, and Sanct-Franciscus let himself into the reception room. "I think she is soundly asleep. She should continue to sleep for most of the afternoon, no matter how loud the Flavian Circus may become."

"She truly does miss the Games," said Ignatia, opening her eyes and staring at him, feeling as if she were lightly touched with fever. "You do her so much good." Her fascination increased as he approached her.

"That is what I am supposed to do, as her physician," said Sanct-Franciscus, drawing up the short bench so he could sit directly across from her. "But it seems I am failing you, Doma Ignatia."

She made herself look away from him, afraid that her interest in him was becoming too obvious. "You could not fail me." She felt his nearness like a flame in the warm room. When she laughed there was a catch in her throat, and she hurried to conceal her rush of emotion. "You've done more than anyone in this household has to make her better."

"That may be, although there is little I can do for her. You are still tired and worn, and I hope you will permit me to leave a medicament to help you to rest. You have not been sleeping, and you are pale," Sanct-Franciscus said gently. "I wish I had some means of alleviating your circumstances."

She could feel her pulse quicken; she reminded herself sternly that his remark had no hidden meaning, and that only her desires read more than courtesy into his words. "That . . . that's very kind of you."

"I know you have much to contend with," he went on, his dark eyes fixed on her averted ones. "You must not let her carping cause you despair; those who suffer from her disease often see those nearest to them as enemies, and attribute villainous motive to them for their care. That may not make her barbs more tolerable, but you need not fear there is truth in them." He did not add that those with this incurable condition usually became worse in all ways over time, and that before she died, Adicia would likely be addled and spiteful.

"I have done nothing to deserve her praises," said Ignatia, hoping she would not start to weep.

"You have done *everything* deserving of praise. No one could expect more of you than you have done. Your sister and your brother are in your debt for what you have achieved for Domina Adicia's benefit, little as they may know it." He waited until she met his gaze with her own. "You have nothing to be ashamed of—nothing."

"I don't do it for their good opinion," said Ignatia, staring at him with such yearning that he took her hand.

"You deserve it, nonetheless," said Sanct-Franciscus.

"It is what one of us must do, and I am the—" She stopped, and self-consciously pulled her hand away. "If more of us had lived . . . but honestiora do not always have children who thrive. Had there been more of us, I would not have to tend to my mother without help from any but the slaves." Her expression grew more somber. "She might like me more if others of her children shared in her care."

"That was what I meant," said Sanct-Franciscus, his compassion for this young woman making him keenly aware of every nuance of her behavior, of the despair that leached strength from her, of her hunger for him. "Your brother could help, or your uncle could send his daughters to assist you."

"They are about to be married. Both his daughters have pledged to marry." She was appalled to hear herself sniff.

Sanct-Franciscus studied her for a long moment. "As responsible as he is, your uncle is lax in not making a marriage for you."

"My uncle doesn't want his sister under his roof, and he is presently staying away from Roma, being out of favor with the Emperor's mother and grandmother," said Ignatia with a bitterness that surprised her; she put her hand to her lips. "I don't mean that he should welcome an invalid to his house. He may have three daughters, but he has only one son, and the boy is deaf."

"No doubt that provides him a reason to keep his distance—that and the state of Roman politics," said Sanct-Franciscus. "Have you any other relatives who could provide you some respite from your mother's care?"

She thought briefly. "My father's aunt lives near Neapolis. She is quite old—fifty-six, I think—and keeps to herself."

Sanct-Franciscus shook his head. "You need not trade one burden for another. Is there no one else who would welcome you for a month or so?"

"I don't know," Ignatia admitted. "My mother has driven many of our relatives off with her accusations and recriminations."

"All the more reason for you to spend a little time away from her." He rubbed his jaw, noticing that Rugeri had trimmed his beard with special care. "Tell me you will consider securing an invitation for—shall we say—September? You will have ample opportunity to arrange things for your mother during your absence. I will help you with her, so she will not hold your going against you."

"I . . . I'll try," she said, her mouth feeling unusually parched.

"Very good," Sanct-Franciscus said, and briefly laid his hand on hers, intensely aware of her pulse and her ardor. "You need time to yourself, Ignatia. You are losing flesh and there are bruises under your eyes from exhaustion."

She was barely aware of the slow tears that slipped down her face. "I am . . . rather tired."

"Then you must recuperate." He offered her a quick smile. "During your absence, your mother may come to appreciate all you do for her."

"I don't think so," said Ignatia as she used the edge of her palla to wipe her eyes. "It is generous of you to imagine she might."

He reached out and touched her chin, turning her face to his. "Then do not blame yourself for her state of mind. You have no part in it: believe this."

Before she could stop herself—had she wanted to stop herself—she leaned forward and pressed her lips to his mouth, her senses reeling at her unaccountable temerity. She felt his hand on the back of her neck, supporting her without restricting her movement, which was just as well, for after a short, delirious moment, she pulled back from him, and felt her face grow rosy with distress. "Oh . . . Oh, Bona Dea!" She rose and started across the room, away from the temptation of his nearness. "What must you think of me?"

Five centuries ago, he might have pursued her, pressed his advantage with her, but now he remained where he was, saying only, "I think you are lonely, Ignatia, and that your loneliness has worn you down."

She stepped into the deep window embrasure and stared out at the cluster of apple trees. "You're being kind to me again."

Another whoop from the hydraulic organ heralded the next booming song: "Pride of the Tibrus," a paean to Roma; the crowd in the Circus Maximus bellowed it out enthusiastically.

Sanct-Franciscus waited briefly, then told her, "It is you who are kind to me, Doma."

"I?" She studied him, searching for any hint of deceit. "Kind? To you?"

He returned her gaze steadily. "I, too, am lonely."

She dared not let herself wonder what he meant. "That must be hard."

"As you know," he answered, his voice so low it was barely audible above the crowing anthem.

She could hardly breathe; as if sleepwalking or moving in water, slowly she made her way back across the room to him, sat down once more, and held out her hands, laying them in his.

Text of a letter from Djuran in Alexandria to Rugeri in Roma, carried from Ostia by Natalis.

Greetings to the deputy of the owner of Eclipse Trading Company, the bondsman Rugeri, presently in Roma, from Djuran in Alexandria,

Most respectable Rugeri, I have done all that I may to review the accounts of the last year, and it is my unfortunate duty to tell you that a number of records are missing, some perhaps due to negligence, but most, I fear, have been removed as a means of concealing the theft the records revealed. I have also noticed that many of the accounts that should contain the seal of the Prefect of Trade have not been so marked, which leads me to two probable explanations: one—that the records were not presented to the Prefect or a decuria of the Prefect, which will double the commodae that must be paid when the lack of such seal is amended, as amended it must be; or two—that such a seal was obtained and what is in the records are either copies with misinformation, or forgeries.

That admitted, I wish to inform you that I will appear before the Prefect in a week's time to present the case to him, and to ask for consideration, given that there is ample proof of embezzlement and pilferage, all of which is traceable back to Perseus, as I will demonstrate, I trust to the satisfaction of the Prefecture. It is difficult to know what the outcome may be, for the Prefect is known to be willing to be bribed, and therefore, I am going to proceed carefully.

As you suggested, I am setting aside two hundred aurei to have in reserve to pay for any assessments that the Prefect may levy against Eclipse Trading Company. Little as the owner will like it, I have also purchased two young, beautiful slaves, accomplished and willing to devote themselves to the art of pleasing their owner, to present to the Prefect as a token of the owner's regard; I have decided to offer them to the Prefect at the next convivium sponsored by Hebseret and his priests, for they, too, would benefit from the goodwill of the Prefect. I do not know if this will result in any true advantage, but it will indicate that the owner knows how the game is played, and that can save time in settling things: the Prefect can then inform me what bribe will resolve the problem quickly so an order may be issued for Perseus' arrest. I have also informed the Prefect that the Company will compensate Iolus Ioloi for the loss of Perseus, to whom the Prefect sold Perseus upon the initial discovery of his crimes. It is my belief that now that the full extent of his malfeasance is known and his culpability is fully determined, the sentence passed on Perseus will result in him being chained to the oar of a military trireme for the rest of his life. I believe Iolus Ioloi will be relieved to have such a slave removed from his household, but he will still want recompense for giving him up, no matter how justly.

I am preparing a full set of rectified accounts, to the extent they can be reconstructed from the information on hand. I will notify you of the completion, and, at your instruction, either prepare an authentic copy for you, or await your return here to present them to you, whichever best serves you or the owner of Eclipse Trading Company. It is my earnest intention to finish this project by Roman November, which will mean the stormy season will have begun. If the weather permits, I will dispatch you word before spring, but if it is unsafe to take to the sea, I will wait until clement conditions pre-vail.

On behalf of the Priests of Imhotep and this office of the Company, I tender my sincerest respect to you and the owner,

Djuran
clerk and compiler of records

At Alexandria on the 29th day of May, AUC for Roma 972

2

As the sky faded from sunset to twilight, the torches of Roma blazed to life. On every avenue, street, and alley of the city, Watchmen set pitch-soaked staves in brackets, then lit them from their own torches, before passing on to the next corner to repeat the process. Throughout the city there were people gathering in the fora and fountain-squares to see this evening's entertainment, for this was the Summer Solstice, the Feast of Balus, the Emperor's Syrian sun-god, and he had promised a spectacular celebration to mark it, with dramatic reenactments of the story of Balus, accompanied by songs and heroic recitations—prospects that brought the Romans out in force. Already companies of musicians were cavorting among the crowds, playing their instruments and accepting copper ae for their efforts.

"They say he's ordered two hundred carpenta filled with rose-petals for the grand convivium; there are said to be more than two hundred guests invited; a carpentum of rose-petals for each guest, it appears," Vitellius remarked disapprovingly as he returned from lighting the torch by the outer gate of Domina Clemens' house; beyond the gate, the Temple of Hercules shone from the light of a dozen torches. "The boy is quite mad."

Aedius could not bring himself to disagree with Vitellius. "It is his religion. Everyone with a single god is mad."

"True enough," said Vitellius. "But two hundred carpenta of rose-petals? What kind of god wants so many rose-petals?"

"He would need an army of slaves to pluck them," said Aedius, chuckling at the thought. "Five petals to a rose . . . how many slaves would it take to fill a single carpentum, let alone two hundred?" He shoved the gate-bolt in place and started across the courtyard to the main house.

"Will you climb to the roof to watch the festivities?" asked Vitellius.

"I may," said Aedius. "If it turns out to be more than torches and noise."

"Do you think it won't?" Vitellius was both amused and disgusted. "That child is being permitted license enough to ruin him, if only he had the wits to see it. Chariot races with bears and ostriches! Who knows what he will present at his Games tomorrow?"

"Who knows what he will offer the people tonight?" Aedius said.

"His caprice is boundless," Vitellius said, shaking his head that the Emperor should set such an unRoman example.

"I think that is the intent—to show his power through whim," said Aedius, surprised that he and Vitellius were in such accord. "I think he is being turned into a distraction, a gaudy diversion so that others may work invisibly."

"It's his mother and grandmother doing that," said Vitellius.

Aedius nodded. "It will be a hard day for the Emperor if Julia Maesa and her daughter Julia Soaemias ever turn against him."

"Julia Mamaea is already against him."

"Well, she has a son of her own to advance," said Aedius. "You can't expect her to support her nephew over her own son."

"And she is truly ambitious, as all honorata and illustriata are," said Vitellius. "They are dangerous as serpents."

"Who is to hold them accountable for being that—are we?" Aedius said, and laughed.

"No, probably not; an uprising of slaves would do little to change the nobility. The Praetorians may yet take a hand in dealing with the Emperor, if they become sufficiently revolted by his actions; Heliogabalus would have to pay attention to them, and so would his mother and grandmother," said Vitellius, entering the house correctly onto the right foot. "You and I are far from such corruption."

"And that is a reason to thank Hercules and Vulcan, who protect all who labor," said Aedius with as much piety as he could summon. "Their help is always needed, and they will do much for those who burn incense to them."

"Yes, and to Carna, who guards our bodies. If she deserts us, our hearts and livers fail."

"And Verplaca—without her, there is no harmony in households." Aedius stopped walking. "We should burn incense to all of them tonight, to show that in spite of Heliogabalus, we haven't forgot them, nor lost any esteem for them." He saw Vitellius nod in agreement.

"And ask Verplaca to send wisdom to the Emperor's family, as well," Vitellius said.

"Truly. Or let the Juliae scheme amongst themselves and leave honest slaves alone," Aedius declared.

"Just so," said Vitellius, suddenly wary; it was not always safe to make a joke of the ruling family—there was no telling who might be listening. He spat to protect himself from evil, then said, "There is a fine convivium for all the household tonight. The master does well by us."

"He's foreign," said Aedius. "It helps to do the right thing when you're foreign. People notice if you don't."

"He doesn't attend the Great Games; Romans notice that," said Vitellius. "Says he has lost his taste for carnage and display."

"Foreign," Aedius repeated; the two stewards paused at the edge of the atrium. "In an hour, we dine."

"Yes," said Vitellius, feeling awkward now that their burst of camaraderie had faded quickly as it had risen. "Well, until the convivium."

"Until the convivium," said Aedius, and went off toward the dining room to supervise the final preparations for the household convivium.

Vitellius went up the stairs to the gallery and busied himself lighting the torches set in place there to provide the illumination Heliogabalus had ordered for all villas and households with gardens. He was almost at the end of the gallery when a voice spoke out of the darkness; Vitellius nearly dropped his torch.

"I prefer the stars to torches," said Sanct-Franciscus, stepping out of the dense shadows into the fluttering light of the flames. He was very grand tonight, in a Persian chandys of dual-colored silk—deep-red and black—that shone glossily; he wore bracae of fine-spun black goat-hair from Asiana, and had thick-soled peri of tooled, black leather on his feet. A silver bracelet ornamented with three large rubies was clasped to his left wrist and a silver chain around his neck held his eclipse device: displayed silver wings with a black sapphire supplying the disk. "I apologize for startling you, Vitellius."

"No matter," said Vitellius. "You . . . took me by surprise. I didn't know you were in your quarters."

"I am not, now," said Sanct-Franciscus with a trace of amusement.

"No; I can see that." Vitellius took three steps back. "I will not intrude."

"You are not intruding," Sanct-Franciscus told him. "I am about to go to my study. Rugeri and I have a few matters to discuss before I depart for the Capitolinus Hill and the official festivities."

"Will you want an escort? You are wearing jewels and there are many thieves about on such a night as this."

"Thank you; I have arranged for Natalis to accompany me; he should suffice," said Sanct-Franciscus, and saw the look of outrage that crossed Vitellius' features.

"The man is a thief, master, no matter what he may say to you. You put yourself in danger when you are in his company."

"Do you really think so?" Sanct-Franciscus asked lightly. "I would think he would keep me safe; he knows the dangers I might encounter, and can avoid them."

"Because of his trade," Vitellius muttered.

"Yes, that is why he is valuable to me." Sanct-Franciscus smiled slightly and passed on along the gallery, noting with satisfaction that the torches were making no real headway against the stars.

Rugeri was at the writing table in the study, going over a stack of folded scrolls by the light of a branch of nine oil-lamps. He was dressed in an elaborately pleated pallium of dove-gray linen belted in bands of braided rust- and straw-colored silk. As Sanct-Franciscus entered the study, he looked up, and rose respectfully, taking stock of Sanct-Franciscus' appearance. "My master. You're going to be warm tonight, I think; it will stay more hot than cold."

"Hot and cold, as you are well-aware, mean little to me, my friend," said Sanct-Franciscus, smiling slightly. "I see the records have come from Alexandria."

"This is only half of them, and they are copies. They arrived three hours ago, carried by hired courier. I provided five denarii as a commoda for him. Generous, but not remarkable." He patted the scrolls before sitting down again.

"You have begun your review of them, it appears."

"I have," said Rugeri, "and I have to agree with Djuran: Perseus was stealing from the Company at a shocking rate, and so boldly that I can only assume he had help from someone in the Prefecture. It cannot be an accident or an oversight that so much money is missing."

"That is unfortunate," said Sanct-Franciscus.

"At least for Perseus," said Rugeri. He frowned. "Do you intend to approach the Prefect of Trade on his behalf?"

"I hadn't planned on it, no, and not now if you suspect he had an accomplice there." Sanct-Franciscus studied Rugeri's demeanor. "Do you recommend it?"

"No; in his case I do not." He tapped his stylus on the table-top. "In general I understand your advocacy for slaves, and I applaud it. But in a case such as Perseus', I cannot see the use of sparing him the consequences of his crimes."

"Nor can I," said Sanct-Franciscus. "It is apparent to me that he is beyond reclamation."

"So the evidence demonstrates," said Rugeri, looking down at the two opened sheets on the table. "Do you want me to inform Djuran?"

"If you would, please, and the Priests of Imhotep," said Sanct-Franciscus, then changed the subject. "While I am out tonight, I ask that, in spite of your work here, you serve as my deputy. I know I can rely on you to keep the evening from becoming raucous. Let the slaves keep the convivium merrily, but not beyond all conduct. And with so many torches about the city and the house, be sure there are always four on watch for fire."

"There are already six barrels of water in the courtyard, my master, and men assigned to each of them, with relief to be provided two hours after sunset." Rugeri hesitated, then said, "Should I expect you back tonight?"

"I hardly know," said Sanct-Franciscus. "Since it is a celebration for all of Roma, I may not find the opportunity I seek. And the festivities may go on far into the night."

"And will you . . . feed?"

"I doubt it. There would be a high risk, with so many folk about." He looked toward the window. "It is such a strange feast they offer—flesh everywhere, and most of it willing, but without any passion beyond a short-lived thrill. It is as if in their gorging, they do not wish to be touched, not in their souls. I have had no trouble in getting adequate sustenance since I returned here, but nourishment—that intimacy that is more than the meeting of skins—that is proving to be rare."

"That is a concern of mine," Rugeri said diplomatically. "You may go hungry for too long, and that is a troublesome prospect."

"Not without cause, my friend. Melidulci occasionally approaches true closeness with me, but she does not trust the emotions that come with it." Sanct-Franciscus took a turn about the room. "If you would not mind manning the gate after midnight, my late return should not cause any comment among the household."

"I will attend to it," Rugeri promised. He cocked his head toward the window, now with the shutter half-lowered. "Should the house be secured?"

"On the lower floors, yes, until the festival is over, and then all windows should be shuttered and latched for the rest of the night. The household may spend the evening in the gallery while the celebration goes on. With the shutters open on the upper floor, the household may watch from the gallery, and the rooms along it—those that are unoccupied."

"That's . . . very generous."

"It's preferable to having them try to slip out or find places from which to watch that no one knows to secure," said Sanct-Franciscus.

"You're thinking of Persia again," Rugeri said with obvious chagrin. "I should have been more diligent."

"You did not understand the state of Srau's mind," said Sanct-Franciscus.

"It isn't an error I will make again," Rugeri vowed.

"I have no doubt of that, my friend," said Sanct-Franciscus. "Look for me after the celebration is ended and the torches are quenched."

"I will. After midnight, I'll take up the post at the gate."

"Until then, my friend, may the gods—known and forgotten—guide your labors," said Sanct-Franciscus, and left the study making for the door, the courtyard, and the gate beyond. At the gate Natalis was waiting, in a calf-length dalmatica of mauve cotton, blending him with the shadows. "Are you carrying any weapons?"

Natalis pulled a long, thin dagger from a hidden sheath in the sleeve of his dalmatica. "If needed, I am."

"Excellent," Sanct-Franciscus approved. "Let us hope you will have no cause to use it."

"Then we should keep away from the areas where the greatest numbers of people are congregating. It's too hard to maintain protection in a crowd." Natalis fell into step slightly behind Sanct-Franciscus on his left side as they made their way past the Temple of Hercules and entered the broad street leading toward the Forum Romanum.

More than six bonfires had been lit in the major fora of the city, and it was there that the greatest number of Romans gathered; Sanct-Franciscus and Natalis skirted those places, not only to avoid the conflagrations, but to stay away from the most frantic celebrants, many of whom were already drunk—not even the women who worshipped Bacchus were as delirious in their ceremonies as some of the young men who were seeking to equal Heliogabalus in the extremity of their carousing, rushing at passersby and pelting them with eggs.

"What do you make of it?" Natalis asked as they turned away from a group of youths throwing rocks at stray dogs while drinking greedily from wine-skins.

"I think it will lead to trouble," said Sanct-Franciscus. "They are rowdy now and are likely to become belligerent."

"Because they're drunk? Half the crowds at the Circus are drunk." Natalis glanced back over his shoulder as a few of the young men began to wrestle amid the approving hollers of their companions.

Sanct-Franciscus nodded once in agreement. "But at the Circus they are in the stands, with races or battles to hold their attention. Here there are no such limitations on them: excesses of their sort could easily become a riot, and not even the Watchmen, the Urban Guard, and the Praetorians could stem a wholesale orgy of violence once it got started."

"Do you think Roma is prepared for trouble?" Natalis put his hand on his knife. "On the scale they could have it?"

"I hope so: they are likely to get it," Sanct-Franciscus observed as they rounded another corner and saw the myriad torches of the Capitolinus Hill shining ahead of them. "This alone is likely to inspire mischief. They flaunt their wealth and wonder why they are robbed."

Natalis gave a knowing nod. "At one time, I would have thought those torches a beacon."

"As they probably are to others," said Sanct-Franciscus.

As the two came nearer, they noticed that the patrols of Urban Guards were more frequent, and the Guardsmen were more heavily armed than usual.

"They're expecting trouble; you're right," Natalis said, a note of regret in his tone.

"A wise precaution," Sanct-Franciscus said as quietly as the din in the streets allowed.

"Unless there is a fire. Then all the Urban Guards will be called to fight it, and the people might well panic: if that happens, then the city will be in grave danger, with people massing in the streets, attempting to get out of the gates," said Natalis, not quite shouting in the increasing noise around them. "There would be chaos if that happens."

Sanct-Franciscus motioned to him to keep his voice down, pulling him into the doorway of a closed thermopolium. "We do not want to draw attention to ourselves, not tonight."

"I understand; I'll be circumspect," said Natalis. He stood a little straighter. "While you are at the celebration, do you want me to remain in the household with the slaves, or shall I wait outside the house itself?"

"You may stay in the house, unless I send you word to leave. You will know that the instructions are mine because I will ask you to carry a message to Rugeri. If any other orders come, no matter what they may require of you, do not obey them; they will not be my intentions." Sanct-Franciscus stepped back into the street, neatly avoiding a handsome biga drawn by a flashy pair of bright bays that was bound for the same porticus as they were.

"But if they give me orders, they will expect me to leave," Natalis pointed out; they were almost to the front of the grand house that was their destination.

"Then do so, but stay where you can watch the door, and wait for me. I will join you directly." Sanct-Franciscus smiled slightly. "There will be others doing much the same thing—waiting for their masters to depart—particularly groups of bodyguards and drivers of bigae."

"Look at the Praetorians, bristling with spears and daggers. It isn't as if they are asked to wait upon the Emperor," Natalis said as they neared the porticus, pointing to the men in shining brass loricae who were taking the measure of the couple alighting from the biga.

"No, they are only guarding his aunt," said Sanct-Franciscus drily. "For reasons of her own."

"Do you expect she will ask anything of you?" Natalis could not keep from inquiring.

"Not tonight. That would be foolish, and from what I know of

Julia Mamaea, she is no fool." He saw the two bodyguards flanking the steward in the doorway, and said, "See? She leaves almost nothing to chance." He stepped up to the door and told the steward his name and the name of his freedman.

The steward, a handsome man about thirty with northern features, looked the two of them over, consulted the fan-folded scroll in his hands, and said, "Enter and turn to your right. Your freedman should continue ahead."

They did as they were told, entering a vestibule where the alcove of lares was ablaze with oil-lamps, and the scent of incense hung heavily on the air.

"I will wait for you to send for me," said Natalis, and kept on toward the atrium that was filled with many pots of blooming flowers.

Sanct-Franciscus watched him go, and thought as he did that he hoped that Natalis would not be tempted to take anything from the house, for such an outrage would lead to his execution, and nothing Sanct-Franciscus could do would spare him. He turned to the right and into the grand reception room, set up for an evening of dining and roistering. Statues of Apollo, Jupiter, Mercury, Vulcan, Mars, Diana, Venus, Minerva, and Vesta were prominently displayed, and a large sun-disk in brass hung over the center of the room, reflecting back the lights of the hundreds of oil-lamps set in brass lamp-trees around the room.

Immediately under this grand decoration on a small dais sat Julia Mamaea in stola and palla of white silk edged in gold; a sunburst tiara was set amid formal curls. She wore extravagant earrings and a necklace of hammered gold links. Her lips were rouged and her eyelashes were darkened, and she wore a perfume compounded of jasmine, rose, and amber. At her feet sat her eleven-year-old son, Gessius Bassianus, dressed in a tunica of cloth-of-gold, looking bored and annoyed. A dozen men clustered around the two of them while more circulated through the room, waiting to be summoned to greet their hostess; in a short while the women would be admitted and the evening would properly begin.

A consort of musicians hidden behind a screen were playing anthems to Roma and the historic tales of Roman heros; their tunes were familiar and the stories they told were known to almost everyone in the room. Their instruments were not loud enough to cut through the thrum of conversation, but served to underscore Julia Mamaea's position in regard to this alien festival.

"So, Sanct-Franciscus," said a voice at his shoulder. Sanct-Franciscus turned to see Dephinius Ambrosius Junian, rigged out in a brilliant yellow toga virilis, broad golden bracelets on both wrists. "I don't know if you recall me—we met—"

"—at the Saturnalia celebration. At Desiderius Vulpius' house," Sanct-Franciscus said.

"At the other end of the year," Junian said, and gave the room a swift perusal. "I reckon this occasion will be somewhat more frenetic than even Saturnalia."

"Does that displease you?" Sanct-Franciscus asked.

"If it were a Roman festival, it wouldn't. But this is a foreign god, and that troubles me." He began to walk along the edge of the room; Sanct-Franciscus kept pace with him.

"Roma has always welcomed foreign gods," he said.

"Yes, yes," Junian agreed. "But not when the Emperor puts his foreign god above all our Roman ones. Wild as he is, the Emperor is as bad as those Christians, who are forever praising their god as the only god, and decry any others. The Emperor may be as licentious as the Christians are austere, but they are equals under the skin, demanding that everyone share their faith and have no other. Romans like fond devotion, not raving monomania." He halted by a doorway that led out onto the long, narrow terrace on the north side of the grand house. "Not much of a garden, but in the city I suppose it does very well."

"And a smaller garden is easier to maintain," said Sanct-Franciscus, thinking back to the night at Nero's Golden House when prisoners had been let loose in the vast gardens in tunicae of pitch-soaked cotton that was then set blazing; even now the memory had the power to disgust him. "And they conceal less."

"True enough," said Juniun, resting his hand on his broadening paunch. "On an occasion like this, a man wants to see everything." His smirk had an air of prurience about it. "Vulpius says you know how to keep confidential things said to you."

Sanct-Franciscus' eyes flicked over the gathering. "If anything can be held secret in such a gathering."

"I take your point, Sanct-Franciscus," Junian remarked, then cleared his throat and slightly raised his voice. "They say the Emperor will dance naked for his guests tonight, and that rose-petals will fall thick as snow in the northern mountains in winter." This was clearly not what Junian had intended to say when he first approached Sanct-Franciscus. "He has declared that all Roma will join in the celebration; we can but comply."

"According to household rumors there will be excess from one end of the city to the other," said Sanct-Franciscus. "I doubt Heliogabalus would be so reckless as to endorse such overindulgence, not with his mother about, and his grandmother."

"Fierce old woman, is Julia Maesa, and raised her daughters to be the same." Junian glanced toward their hostess. "They say Julia Mamaea is hoping to see that young Syrian sprig supplanted by her own son."

"Whether it is true or not, Romans would always think such things of ruling families—not without reason." Sanct-Franciscus ducked his head as the sound of a brass gong brought the guests to attention. "The evening is about to begin."

"They'll bring in the women, and then the entertainment will start. Nothing like what the Emperor might offer, but at least something we Romans can approve," said Junian, and turned away from the open door.

Sanct-Franciscus remained there for a long moment, then joined the men clustered around Julia Mamaea's dais, all the while listening for the shouts and cries that came from the city beyond the garden.

Text of a letter from Gelasius Virginius Apollonius Metsari to Lucius Virginius Rufius, carried by one of the Christians in their group.

To my cousin and Brother in Christ, the kiss of peace, on this, the anniversary of his birth, with the wishes that the Savior guide and protect you through the coming year.

I must warn you that the Urban Guard has been about, asking questions about the fires that were lit during the appalling display on Mid-Summer Eve, when the Emperor himself paraded around his palace, naked and unashamed. A few of the Urban Guard have proclaimed that some of the fires were deliberate, and the deaths caused by them were therefore murder, a position that makes no allowance for the reasons behind the fires. The Prefect of the Urban Guard has issued orders for the arrest of anyone found to be party to setting the fires in question, and has assigned several of his men to conduct an investigation. The Praetorians also have decided to look into the reasons for the fires. So you would do well to suggest to your friends to keep to themselves, and to pray for aid from God's Christ. Any Christian found to have been party to the setting of fires will surely be sent to the arena, against which fate we must all pray. As you may not have heard, nine of the members of my own group of Christians have been sent to prison for attempting to get into the Emperor's palace during his Mid-Summer debacle for the purpose of chastising him for his carnality and luxuriousness, and are likely to be condemned to the oars of a bireme or trireme if they can avoid being sent onto the sands of the Great Games.

So far, most of those detained have been Peterines, and part of the Jewish community. They're easier to find than we are, and few of them are more than humiliora: that may be why the Urban Guard has sought them out first. The Peterines are standing firm in their assertion that Jesus was a Jewish prophet and spoke only to those of the Jewish faith, and this is making them targets for Roman condemnation. As if Salvation could be limited to Jews! Let the Peterines decrease their numbers through defying Roma. Those Peterine Jews who call themselves Christians are mistaken in their understanding. Paul has shown the way, and we, who are true to the teachings of the Christ, bear witness to his righteousness. God has given us protection in this time of tribulation, and when the Last Judgment comes—as surely it must, as we see the Last Days upon us—we will emerge among the lambs.

You and your companions have done much for our faith. I don't know who among you decided the houses to be burned, but at least three have struck a blow for Salvation: the silk merchant from Fars,

*the honoratus who was Lictor in Asiana, and the prostitute from the
lupanar all are examples of those trading on sin, and whose punishment in this life heralds what is to come for all of mankind in this
world and the next. Let the courts say what they will, they cannot
deny the justice that we have done.*

*But pious as your acts are, I advise you to discontinue them for
the time being, for it is unwise to expose our Brothers to the harsh
fate meted out by these Romans. Wait until summer is over before
you undertake any more fires, and then resume your cleansing only
after obtaining the approval of at least four Paulist groups, so that
we may make preparations to protect ourselves. Salvation is for the
devout, not the reckless, and so I ask you, in the Name of the Risen
Savior, to contain your indignation for a time, and to seek consola-
tion in prayer until we are agreed that more activity is required of
us, and where to strike.*

*May God extend His Grace to you, and may you know the Peace
Beyond the World,*

Gelasius Virginius Apollonius Metsari

*On the 10th day of July, the 972nd Year of Roma, the 219th Year of
Salvation*

3

Most of the north wall had fallen, leaving charred rubble strewn
into what small portions of the house remained standing. The front
door, burnt and askew on its hinges, revealed the street beyond
where two Urban Guards stood watch while Melidulci made her
way through the ruins, Sanct-Franciscus at her side, a large basket
slung over his shoulder on a broad leather strap; the intense heat of
early afternoon and the pervasive odor of scorching provided uncomfortable reminders of the fire.

"I know I said I wanted to take some of my things with me, but now . . ." Her disconsolate gesture finished her thought for her.

"Would you prefer to leave?" Sanct-Francisus offered, aware that nothing of value remained here.

She shook her head. "No. Not yet; I have to look," was her dazed response as she walked a short distance away from him, puzzling out what had been there only a few days ago. "That was my bedchamber, just over there," she said, pointing toward the destruction on her right. "With the window opening in that direction. The apple trees all burned. Nothing is left of the garden. Not even the bakehouse is standing. And they found Nyssa's body, didn't they?"

At the mention of Natalis' cousin, Sanct-Franciscus pressed his lips to a thin line. "Yes."

"You are certain it was she?" Melidulci looked strained.

"Oh, yes. The corpse was nothing but blackened bones, but there was a ring on her finger which held a cracked opal. Natalis identified it as hers. They—the Urban Guards—believe she hid in the pantry, hoping the bricks would protect her."

"They didn't," said Melidulci bluntly. "Nothing would have saved her."

"No," he said, remembering the look of engulfing sorrow that Natalis gave him when he realized his cousin was dead. "I have arranged for her burial, beyond the Porta Caelinus, in a simple box-tomb."

"Most Romans wouldn't do so much as that. They would arrange for the body to be carried outside the city walls and put in one of the charnel pits for dead slaves and poor men." She studied him. "Do you do this for me or for your servant?"

"For myself, and for the two of you." He caught sight of something in the rubble and bent to pick it up, rubbing the small gold object with his thumb before dropping it into the basket. "It is part of my touching that you so deplore." There was no condemnation in his observation, only a kind of desolation that was revealed in the depths of his dark eyes.

"For the same reason you will permit me to stay at your villa for many months, if I wish to." Her lower lip quivered.

"Yes," he said. "I understand how keenly you feel your loss; I wish to provide what succor I may."

"Do you?" She looked over at him, tears welling in her eyes. "I should think you would not, after your . . . But you are an exile, so perhaps . . . This is all so much changed."

"The floor is largely intact," said Sanct-Franciscus gently.

"The tiles are ruined. You can see the heating channels where the flooring buckled; all useless now," she responded. "The holocaust will have to be rebuilt if any house is to stand here. Everything will have to be rebuilt, on a stronger foundation—this one cracked." She sighed. "What will the next house be like, I wonder?"

"It is likely to be the same as yours," Sanct-Franciscus said. "Enough of the foundation remains intact to be built on. The shape of the house is clear if you—"

"If I what? If I *imagine* what my house was?" She began to cry, her sobs more like coughs than keening. Her hands were gathered into fists and though the heat was sodden, nothing could stem the emotion that poured from her more exhaustingly than sweat. "I *hate* this! I wanted to be safe here! That's why I *came* here! This house was *supposed* to be *safe*."

"It is a sad thing that you have lost your house," said Sanct-Franciscus, trying to number the dwellings he had lost since he had come to his undead life, more than two thousand years ago. Each recollection had a pain of its own, and his heart went out to her, knowing what her deprivation meant to her: to live away from the lupanar had been a brave decision, and now she feared that she had done it all for naught. Approaching her carefully, he reached for her hands.

"I'm not crying for grief," she said as her fingers tightened on his. "I'm *not!*" She blinked hard, twice, then added, "I'm crying because I'm *angry*."

He believed it. "With good reason," he told her.

She glared at the destruction around her. "The Urban Guard told me that gangs of humiliora, and worse—gangs of robbers—were looting the place before the embers were out. The Urban Guard regretted that so much was lost, but they had other fires to attend to, more dangerous than this one. They lost nineteen houses on Mid-Summer Eve." She stared at the fallen wall, saying musingly, "They had too many fires everywhere in the city to spare men to guard what had been burnt."

He continued to hold her hands. "You needn't make up your mind at once, Melidulci. You may remain at my villa outside the walls for as long as it suits you to stay there. No one would expect you to make up your mind about something so major as going to Misenum to live while you are still assuaging your losses here; I hope you do not feel compelled to commit yourself quickly, for that could bring about disappointment. I ask you to be sure of what you want to do: you may decide that you wish to stay here instead of going to Misenum." The coastal city near Neapolis was an odd choice, but one Melidulci was intent upon.

"*I* expect a swift decision of me! I have to make up my mind, not flounder like a bird with a broken wing," she responded sharply, sniffing to stop her tears and pulling her hands free. "I must find a place where I no longer fear every sound in the night. Your villa is pleasant, and your slaves and servants most attentive, but it is still *your* villa, and I am beholden to you for extending your hospitality to me."

"You make it sound as if housing you were a burden," he said, feeling a pang of sadness.

"It must be, if not at present, then in time." She looked away from him. "You will grow bored, or annoyed, or you wish to extend your . . . kindness to someone else. I know what men are, and I know you will not always want my presence, let alone my company."

"I have told you before I am not like most men," he said, almost serenely.

"You are not *that* unlike most men," she said. "You say you seek more from me than I have provided, for you want more involvement than sweet pleasures bring. In time, that will be less acceptable than you claim it is now." She frowned. "Then you will be relieved to have me gone."

"I doubt that would happen, Melidulci; I cannot force you to experience anything that does not gratify you," he said, knowing it was useless, that she had already begun to pull away from him.

She shook her head and wiped away her tears, leaving tracks of soot on her cheeks. "You need not continue to shelter me, even if you are able to. I would rather part now and continue to be friends than remain and become as tolerated as a dependent. I don't ask that support of you. I don't expect it."

He said nothing for a short while, then said, as he stared around them, "There isn't much left, is there?"

"No, not much," she said, her eyes starting to shine with tears again. "And if nothing is left, why should I bother to try to recover it? Anything worth saving has already been picked clean." She scuffed her foot on the blackened floor. "This was such a pleasant place."

"Ah," said Sanct-Franciscus. "You anticipate more trouble."

"Don't *you*?" Her eyes widened.

"I know it may be possible that there will be more disorder in the city," he said as calmly as he could. "So long as the Emperor comports himself as he does, there will be unrest among his people. If he neglects them further, they will grow ungovernable, and that would be an invitation to chaos."

"He! care for his people!" she jeered.

"He is Caesar," Sanct-Franciscus reminded her, his voice low. "His good-will is important to all those living in the Empire."

"His mother's good-will, you mean; she is the one who is Caesar, not her capricious boy," said Melidulci.

"And his grandmother's good-will. Mother and son depend upon the grandmother," said Sanct-Franciscus, and fell silent as he saw that Melidulci was not interested.

"It's useless. All of this is useless." She stood very still, her burnished hair hanging around her shoulders, limp and almost straight; her long, bronze-linen tunica clung to her where her body was wet, its hem darkened by the ash around them. "I am so tired," she said at last, her body drooping to punctuate her words.

"Then shall I appoint some of my household to come here and search for small items, or—"

"No." She held up her hands and wiped her face. "No, let it all go—all of it."

"Then if you will allow me—" He indicated the Urban Guards. "I will inform them that we are leaving."

"Yes. Yes, if you would," she said, turning toward him. "Let us leave this place." She could not bear to call it her home any longer.

"As you wish," said Sanct-Franciscus, starting toward the remnants of the door, his step firm but not too rapid, making it possible for Melidulci to keep up with him without effort over the ash and detritus of the fire. "If you want to come back again, you may. I will be glad to bring you."

"No," she said. "What would be the use?"

He nodded to her; as he approached the Urban Guards, he said, "We are finished here." He offered four denarii to both of the men, although they were not due a commoda.

"That's very gracious of you, honestiorus," said the older of the two, taking his coins and slipping them into the wallet that hung from his belt.

"I take it you didn't find anything much," said the younger as he jingled the coins in his hand before tucking them away.

"Nothing of any value. Except this." He took the gold object from the basket and held it out to them.

"A melted lump of gold. It's worth something," said the older Guard, examining it closely.

Melidulci came and stared at the gold. "It looks something like a fish. Not the sort of thing I would wear."

"Then it isn't yours?" The Guard studied her narrowly as he put the object in her palm, as if he expected her to snatch it away from him.

"I don't recognize it," she said after a brief scrutiny; she handed it back. "I would guess that most of my jewelry is gone, and not because of the fire."

The younger Guard had the ability to show chagrin. "We have to patrol, Domina, and we don't have enough men to be everywhere."

"You should have hired private guards," said the older.

"So that I could be robbed only by the guards' associates?" Melidulci suggested, going on before either man could answer. "Oh, never mind, never mind. It doesn't matter now, does it?"

"I suppose not," said the younger, and hitched up one shoulder. "We've done what we could."

"And have been paid for it," said Melidulci, her voice dulled with indifference. "I'm done here," she added, signaling to Sanct-Franciscus. "Take me back to your villa. I don't want to linger."

Sanct-Franciscus started away to where his biga waited, two handsome mouse-colored horses with black points harnessed to the chariot. He unknotted the reins from blackened tie-post, stepped into the biga, set the nearly empty basket in the large pocket on the inside front of the vehicle, then shoved the brake-lever forward and kissed to the horses to set them moving. Drawing up next to Melidulci, he reached down to help her into the chariot. "Is there somewhere you would like to stop before we—?"

"To your villa. I need to rest. This venture has tired me. I didn't realize what an effort it would be." She blinked three times as they swung away from the wreckage of her house and turned onto the cobbled street that would take them to the Porta Viminalis. "It is good of you to do this for me."

"I am sorry that it has to be done at all," he said, maneuvering between another biga and a cart drawn by a large donkey; he pulled in to a slow walk.

"And I," she said, staring toward the roof of the building at the end of the street where slaves were working to replace charred parts of the roof. "Dangerous work they're doing."

He nodded. "Many are doing similar work, throughout the city."

"How could that young fool have allowed such . . . such wildness to rule the city? Fires, and hooliganism, and more malign mischief than I would have expected of barbarians from the Dacian frontier." She shook her head, then put her hand to her lips. "I'm sorry. I keep forgetting you're from Dacia."

"But I am not a Daci; my people were gone from there well before the Daci came," he said, unperturbed; by the time the Daci had reached the Carpathians, the descendants of his people were spread through the north of the Italian peninsula. He moved his biga around the donkey-cart and started out toward the fountain-square where five streets came together.

"You don't *sound* like a Daci, that's why I don't remember—" she said, after giving the matter consideration. "Your Latin is excellent, if a little old-fashioned, but you have an accent, not pronounced, but still . . . I've never heard one like it before—and I have heard a great many of them." She paused, giving him time to respond; when he remained silent, she went on, "That's something I do miss about leaving the lupanar. I no longer meet men from the limits of the Empire. I didn't think that would bother me, but I miss it."

"You kept many of your former Patroni, did you not? You invited them to visit you at your house?" he asked, turning toward the city gate some three hundred paces up the busy street. "You have not completely set aside the favors you have enjoyed for so long, have you?"

"Yes, I have Patroni still; but they are all Romans, and not interested in talking about the ends of the earth, unless they had some claim to glory there." A touch of cynicism made her smile brittle. "Not that they didn't talk—they did, but of other things. Most of the foreigners who came to the lupanar were eager to boast of their homes and their peoples."

"What did the Romans boast of?" Sanct-Franciscus regarded her with curiosity and a trace of amusement.

"Their prowess, mostly. Then their wealth, their power, their lineage, their sons. A few would recall their victories in the field." She sighed deeply, world-weariness making her seem ancient. "I let them talk, of course, and praised them when they succumbed to doubts, or became morose . . ." Her voice trailed off, and she remained silent for a short while. "It's a terrible thing about Nyssa. She came to me for protection, and then this happened."

"You are not to blame," said Sanct-Franciscus, settling down to a place in line for the city gate.

"She was in my household. All the rest got out, slaves and freed alike. But that poor woman . . ."

"As you say, it is an unfortunate thing," said Sanct-Franciscus, watching a man with a train of four mules arguing with the Praetorian at the gate. "But you did not bring her into your household with the intention that she should burn to death, did you?"

"No, of course not." She stared at him as if she feared he was mocking her; the steady gaze of his dark eyes reassured her. "She was new to the household. No one was used to her yet. So they didn't miss her until it was too late to go and look for her."

"You had others of your household who were missing for a time, did you not?"

"Yes. Three slaves were missing for almost half the night." Fidgeting with her belt, her answer was little more than a mumble.

"Understandable in the midst of such a fire," said Sanct-Franciscus, noticing that the man with the mules was finally moving through the gate.

"Yes. I know." She bit her lower lip. "It doesn't change anything in regard to Nyssa, does it?"

"Probably not," he allowed, setting his pair in motion again.

They reached the gate, answered the usual questions put to them by the Praetorians, and were about to pass on when the centurion addressed Sanct-Franciscus. "How long will you be gone from the city?"

"I should return tomorrow," said Sanct-Franciscus. "I have matters to attend to at my villa."

"So you said," the centurion conceded. "If you are not back within two days, I must report you as missing."

This was a new stricture, and Sanct-Franciscus reacted with surprise. "Why such limits, Praetorian?"

"The Emperor has decided that foreigners must not be allowed to come and go as casually as they have done before. He fears spies." The centurion pursed his lips, revealing his disapproval of the new regulation. "More work for us, of course, and policies that the people dislike, but the Emperor demands it."

"Of course," said Sanct-Franciscus, handing over the gate-toll before signaling his pair to move out.

"That seems a bit unreasonable, asking foreigners to conduct their affairs so restrictively," Melidulci said as the biga picked up speed.

Sanct-Franciscus passed an ox-drawn carpentum laden with

fruit and melons bound for the Praetorian Camp, and then said, "It is another show of authority."

"Do you think so?" She held onto the rail as the biga swung past the Praetorian Camp.

"What else can it be?"

"An excuse for more taxes," said Melidulci, laughing sarcastically.

"That is part of the intent, without doubt," said Sanct-Franciscus, narrowing his eyes as he studied the road ahead. "It also provides closer accounts on the whereabouts of foreigners."

"You are too mistrustful. Heliogabalus is not so subtle as that."

"His grandmother is," said Sanct-Franciscus.

Melidulci shook her head and laid one hand on his arm. "You make it much too complicated. The Emperor has to pay for his extravagances somehow. And the company he keeps is expensive."

"His companions expect his indulgence," said Sanct-Franciscus.

"More fool he for keeping them," she said, leaning with the biga at the turn onto the drive that led to his villa. "Expensive boys are a luxury."

"Heliogabalus is an expensive boy himself," Sanct-Franciscus observed.

"My point exactly," she said. "Roma cannot afford him."

"Then you do expect trouble," said Sanct-Franciscus, pulling his pair to a walk in order to give his slaves the opportunity to open the main gate.

"Is there good reason not to?" She looked at him in disbelief.

"Expected or not, trouble tends to arrive," said Sanct-Franciscus, passing through into the courtyard where three grooms came running to take the biga in hand. He handed his reins to the nearest of the three. "See they are walked before you water them, then give them hay, a handful of grain, a handful of raisins, and a ladle of oil. Turn them out in their paddock when they've eaten." He stepped down from the chariot and held out his hand to assist Melidulci to alight.

"Yes, Dominus," said the groom holding the reins.

"I know I should thank you, and I do, but it is not sufficient for all you have done," she said, walking across the courtyard at his side. Her composure had returned and she spoke with the confident ease of a woman long used to dealing with men.

"Must I remind you that I need no thanks?" he countered lightly.

She kept on, determined to say what she had rehearsed mentally during their journey from her burned house to his villa. "And you mustn't think I don't appreciate all you're doing for me—"

"But?" he suggested kindly, crossing his threshold on his right foot, for luck; his vestibule was cool, and his native earth under the flooring gave him respite from the sun.

"But can't it be enough that we enjoy one another? I know you are convinced I can achieve more than I do. You are an accomplished lover, even given your . . . incapacity, and no doubt you have found that depth you seek in other women. I revel in what you offer me. Why must you always attempt to find that greater closeness you . . ." She looked about the atrium, noticing the tubs of flowers that had been moved into place in the sunlight. "I am what I am, and that may mean I lack the capacity to accomplish what you desire? Why can't you be content to bask in pleasure, like those blossoms?"

"I am not uncontent," he said, the hint of a self-deprecating smile tugging at the corner of his mouth. "Yet I know there is more to have."

"And it disappoints you that I won't seek it with you?" she asked.

"Not disappoints—saddens, perhaps." He kept in the shadow of the roof as he made his way toward the second atrium.

She stopped, tugging at the short sleeve of his black-linen dalmatica, and turning him to face her. "But you *will* come to my chamber tonight, won't you?"

His smile was filled with profound loneliness and the promise of the passion she yearned for almost as much as she sought to avoid it. "Of course I will: believe this."

Text of a letter from Ioantius Imestius Renae at Narona in Illyricum to Rugeri of Gades in Roma, carried by commercial messenger.

To the prudent and honorable Rugeri of Gades in Roma, Ioantius Imestius Renae at Narona sends his greetings along with his annual report of the commercial activities of the Eclipse Trading Company's business in this city.

As you are no doubt aware, the continuing debasement of the denarius is still eroding Roman trade throughout the eastern half of the Empire. I, myself, have followed the instruction to conduct all the Eclipse business in aurei rather than denarii, and for that reason alone I am able to report that things are not as bleak for us as they are for many other merchants not so forehanded as honestiorus Sanct-Franciscus is. When the policy was given a year ago, I thought it was overcautious and unnecessarily stringent, but no longer: I now see that the denarii are becoming as useless as ae.

I have to report that the heavy cotton canvas ordered from Tarsus has not yet been delivered, and I have received no information as to the reason for it, although I have made repeated inquiries. Neither the weather nor the engagements of the Legions can account for it. All I have received is the assurance that the order will be filled in good time, and nothing more to explain what has transpired. I am also still awaiting news from Pergamum, where a shipment of sacking has yet to arrive; with the harvest coming, sacking will be needed, and soon.

Some say that there is unrest to the east, and many goods are being confiscated by the Legions as part of their efforts to protect the Empire. While this may be true, it is also possible that pilferage and outright theft are being tolerated now as they have not been before. The loss of value of coins has caused many to fall back on direct exchange rather than the use of money. I have seen it with farmers in the fora here, and so it seems possible that there is an inclination among the people to demand value as much as substance in all dealings. In this regard, I must mention that the aurei I have on hand will not last through the year, and if this is the standard I must maintain, I will require more gold before the winter storms begin.

I know Sanct-Franciscus dislikes the slave trade, but I ask you to implore him to consider such an undertaking for a year or two, at least until the monetary problems have ended. I have consulted

*a sibyl, who has predicted that wealth can be had through trading
in slaves from the east, for it serves the Legions to have captives
sold away from their homelands, and the value of a man or woman
can be almost as certain as gold. For the sake of his trading company, Sanct-Franciscus would do well to put aside his dislike long
enough to shore up his fortunes and earn the gratitude of the Legions at the same time. Other merchants are taking advantage of
this state of affairs, and it would be wise if Sanct-Franciscus did,
as well.*

*A sworn copy of my records and accounts is appended to this re-
port, all of which I submit to you with thanks on this, the 16th day of
July, in the 972nd Year of the City. May Fortuna and Neptune desert
me if I speak false.*

> *Ioantius Imestius Renae*
> *manager of Eclipse Trading Company*
> *at Narona, in Illyricum*

4

On the arena sands, a hundred condemned women were tied to
leaning posts and were being attacked and violated by bulls, stal-
lions, lions, leopards, and wild boars, all in a state of frenzied arousal
and goaded on by their bestiarii, who used whips and long spears to
keep the animals on the women. Shrieks, screams, roars, bellows,
and shuddering groans rang through the Flavian Circus, to be
echoed by the frantic crowd; one of the women being assaulted by a
leopard had lost her arm to the beast and the gouting spray from her
shoulder was slowing, the woman hanging limply from the cat's jaws
while the bestiarius hung back, afraid to approach the aroused leopard. In the afternoon heat, the sands shimmered and the crowd
sweltered, and the odor of sweat and excitement mixed with that of
blood and entrails and animals; those fortunate enough to be in the

shade from the vast awning were spared the worst from the brassy sky, but all of Roma was stultified by the rising temperatures.

Vendors hawking sausages in buns, skewers of broiled chicken, wine-with-rosewater, honied fruit juice over chopped ice, spiced ground pork in pocket-bread, Egyptian beer, cold water, and candied flowers made their way through the stands, doing their best to be heard over the constant noise.

"I don't suppose you want anything?" Septimus Desiderius Vulpius had to lean over and almost shout at his guest while he motioned to a vendor of meats, wines, fruits, and nuts to approach; in the next box, a well-dressed young man was eagerly fondling his companion, a breathless girl just out of puberty, whose features were fervid and whose eyes glazed by the spectacle before them. The vendor reached over the pair, paying little attention to their raptures.

"No, thank you," said Sanct-Franciscus, uncomfortably aware of the slaughter as the waste and degradation it was. A quick recollection of Kosrozd, Tishtry, and Aumtehoutep came back to him. He stopped watching the cruelty on the sands and was now staring at the Imperial Box where Heliogabalus sat with six handsome young men, all of them in tunicae of yellow silk; the Emperor had painted his face, and some of the darkening around his eyes had begun to smear, leaving him with tracks down his cheeks that turned his features dissolute instead of beautiful. A wreath of roses hung around his neck and a smaller one circled his brow.

"I'm glad you finally decided to be my guest for the Games, Sanct-Franciscus." Vulpius tossed a collection of coins to the vendor and was handed a bun with a large sausage through it; he gave the vendor his cup and had it returned filled with red wine, which he sipped cautiously. "Too young, but it'll do," he said, shrugged, and drank.

Sanct-Franciscus stopped himself from saying anything about the butchery on the sands, knowing his observations would not be welcome. "Have you had this box long?"

"I had it from my father," said Vulpius with ill-concealed pride.

"This is a fine place to sit," said Sanct-Franciscus.

"You mean because you can only see the Doors of Life, not of Death?" Vulpius asked, his words muffled by the sausage-and-bun.

"That, and the shadows are deepest here," said Sanct-Franciscus, for whom the weight of the summer sun was becoming a burden in spite of the native earth in the soles of his peri.

"Oh, very true, but it also has fewer breezes," said Vulpius, leaning back against the long, bolster pillow he had brought to make his box more comfortable than the usual seat cushions provided. He licked his fingers. "Peppery. Just what I like: pepper and garlic."

"And cooked in chicken-broth, by the smell of it." Sanct-Franciscus saw Vulpius nod in agreement.

The couple in the next box shifted their cushions about so that they could recline on the marble seats; the girl was laughing excitedly, her face flushed, her lips swollen.

There was a flurry of excitement on the sands as a wild boar suddenly abandoned the woman he was straddling and charged a bull, squealing in porcine outrage, his head thrashing as he attempted to gore the flank of the bull. The bestiarii tending the two animals fled; the bull swung around, pawing and lowering his head even as his rear hooves trampled the woman beneath him.

"They'll have to answer for their cowardice," said Vulpius, using his elbow to indicate which of the bestiarii would be subject to the wrath of the crowd.

"How is it cowardice not to stand in front of a maddened animal?" Sanct-Franciscus asked at his most reasonable.

"It is what they are supposed to do," said Vulpius before taking another bite. "As you see, the crowd is displeased." Hooting echoed throughout the Flavian Circus, and in his box, Heliogabalus signaled for a Praetorian, miming a bow and arrow, which the soldier went to get for the Emperor. "I hope he knows how to shoot."

Sanct-Franciscus kept his thoughts to himself, although he found the waste of life—human and animal—appalling. He looked up toward the awning, and the beams that supported it. "They say the sails will be replaced next year."

"They need it," said Vulpius. "You can see fraying and holes in the canvas." He leaned forward as a second wild boar opened the abdomen of the woman he was on top of, his tusks shining red. Suddenly he rounded on the nearest lion, and the two big males fell into battle while the audience howled approval; a dozen arena slaves were dragging the nine dead women by their heels out through the Doors of Death. "I don't know how they'll afford it, not with the Games the Emperor is sponsoring."

"Two more days beyond this one," said Sanct-Franciscus.

"And more to come in September." Vulpius grinned, bits of sausage showing between his teeth.

"Truly," said Sanct-Franciscus, feeling slightly ill at the prospect, for the September Games were to include an aquatic venation, such as the one that had nearly resulted in his True Death, a century-and-a-half ago.

"At least that pretty puppet is Roman enough to give us Romans our Games." Vulpius finished off his sausage-and-bun and reached for his wine. "If not for that, he would be shoved from office."

"Shoved," said Sanct-Franciscus, mulling over the word. "An interesting image; you may be right."

"I know how we Romans are, and that pretty lad would do well to remember: we will tolerate many things, but not an Emperor who lacks will and vision, no matter who his mother and grandmother may be," said Vulpius pointedly, leaning back again, his attention fixed on one of the condemned. "That black-haired woman is not going to last much longer."

"No," said Sanct-Franciscus thoughtfully. "She is not." He might have added that he thought she was more fortunate than many of the others, but held his tongue, knowing that such sentiments were repugnant to Romans.

In the adjoining box, the young man was panting, his hands down the front of the girl's tie-sleeved tunica.

"There's a battle between dwarves and wolves next," said Vulpius, sounding a little bored. "They're saving the main battles for the end of the day . . . the air will be a bit cooler, and the crowd should be ready to wrawl for their favorites. It makes for a fine ending and the fighters will not be hampered by exhaustion from the heat. A man in armor can broil in the sun."

"Whom do you favor?" Sanct-Franciscus asked more out of politeness than interest.

"Mnaxder," he said promptly. "A retriarius, very deft. He belongs to Egidius Regulus Corvinus—a most fortunate master, and one of the Greens, as well. His charioteers have done well this summer."

"How many wins does Mnaxder have?"

"Thirty-nine. If he is victorious today, it will be forty, and his master has promised him his freedom. The Emperor has vowed to have a statue made in his honor." Vulpius held up his cup in anticipatory salutation to the retriarius. "I have thirty-nine aurei bet on his success, one for each previous win."

"A considerable sum," said Sanct-Franciscus, keeping his voice neutral; between horse races and combats, fortunes had been won and lost at the arena for more than four centuries.

"But as safe as if I had bought seed with it, for just as the weather, or fire, could ruin my crop, so a gladiator, or a secutor, could ruin Mnaxder and lose me my bet." His laughter was reckless, almost giddy. "I'll have another cup of wine," he bawled out, holding up his empty cup in the direction of another vendor. "Red. No honey, and no ice to water it down."

"Surely farming is less chancy than gambling," said Sanct-Franciscus, and then, seeing the expression in Vulpius' eyes, went on, "I have learned to be circumspect in such matters."

"Exiles haven't the same possibilities as we Romans do, at least not when it comes to money," Vulpius agreed, sulking a bit as he spoke. "The decuriae are always keeping track of all you buy. I can understand why you might be reluctant to act in these matters, not having the advantage of our citizenship." He paid the vendor and took his cup, now brimming with red wine.

"True enough," Sanct-Franciscus responded courteously.

Another two women were dragged away from the center of the arena, their bodies leaving bloody wakes in the sand; a number of slaves rushed out with buckets of more sand to pour over the blood while bestiarii continued to urge their animals on the remaining women; the crowd hooted derision at the flagging excitement. A few of the men in the Imperial Box threw bits of food in the direction of the women, laughing at the hopeless struggles they made.

'They say the Senate is trying some way to tax bets. So far, they haven't found a fair method for monitoring gambling reliably enough to enforce such a tax." Vulpius handed a second coin to the vendor who had refilled his cup. "Another sausage, this time with butter and cheese."

"It may be that too many Senators bet," Sanct-Franciscus suggested. "Or own charioteers and fighters."

Vulpius laughed aloud as he took the bun-and-sausage. "That may be at the heart of it," he agreed. "That, and the problems of commodae in such cases: who is to pay it, and how is the percentage to be fixed?"

In another half hour, all the women were dead and the animals were being herded back into their various cages; one of the boars was dying, and a lion had been killed, but these were minor losses, and very few in the crowd paid much heed to them. The hydraulic organ was blaring out the popular song "Onward the Legions," but almost no one was singing the lyrics.

"Would you be very annoyed if I left? Our business with Propinus and Gratians is concluded—" Sanct-Franciscus asked Vulpius as they watched the arena being made ready for the next contest. "I find this sort of battle—shall we say?—dulls my senses."

"Dwarves and wolves—I understand your lack of enthusiasm; it must be pretty tepid fare for a man who has been in battle, as you have. Go if you like; I won't be offended," said Vulpius. "You defended your homeland," he went on after a long draught of wine. "An admirable thing to do, even if you defended it against our Roman Legions."

"No; we had other enemies," said Sanct-Franciscus, an enigmatic glint in his eyes.

"Of course, of course." Vulpius waved him away. "Go, then, and do what you will. I would not wish you to be bored on my account. I thank you for coming with me today. Your company has made the afternoon more interesting."

"Thank you," said Sanct-Franciscus, "for your invitation and your company." He turned away and climbed up from the box, along the steep stairs to the covered corridor, where he threaded his way through vendors of food, drink, and other comestibles; slaves waiting for their masters; prostitutes of all descriptions and tastes; odds-makers and bet-takers; Romans from every level of society, from Senators to the lowest humiliora; and criminals from assassins to pick-pockets. The echoes of their calls and clamor mixed with the greater roar of those in the stands, so that the concrete walls offered a storm of noise to all who moved through them. Sanct-Franciscus paid little attention to the activity around him; he could not shake the feeling that he had made a mistake in visiting the Flavian Circus, and not solely for the memories it evoked: the air of the place felt tainted; he walked faster.

"My master?" Natalis ventured as Sanct-Franciscus emerged from the arched opening to the Flavian Circus.

"I apologize for keeping you waiting," said Sanct-Franciscus, shading his eyes against the fierce sunlight.

"I've kept myself amused," said Natalis, continuing hurriedly, "Not that I have stolen anything. I've been watching others steal."

"That must have amused you." Sanct-Franciscus raised his hand to summon a sedan chair.

"Most of it did, yes," Natalis admitted as a group of chairmen approached.

"The Temple of Hercules—how much?" Sanct-Franciscus asked directly.

"Fifteen denarii," said the leader of the four bearers; he was a burly man of about thirty, with callused hands and a sun-toughened face.

"I will give twenty if you can get me there in under half an hour," he said. "My servant will walk with you."

The leader bristled. "We always take the shortest route. You needn't assign one of your men to be certain we do."

"I have no doubt of it, but I think that an observer can be useful on a day like this one," said Sanct-Franciscus, his manner cordial but compelling.

"That may be," the lead chairman admitted. "Very well. He may walk beside us."

"Thank you for being reasonable."

The leader spat for luck. "On such a day as this, misunderstandings are frequent. The heat addles thought."

"Well, bring your chair, then, and we'll set off." Sanct-Franciscus gave the leader of the bearers five denarii as his comrades brought their chair in answer to the leader's summoning whistle. "This as incentive, and to assure you that you will be fully paid."

The leader hitched up his shoulder, taking the money. "The Temple of Hercules."

With the price and destination agreed upon, Sanct-Franciscus climbed into the sedan chair and leaned back on the slightly lumpy cushions provided. Before he pulled the curtain closed, he added, "Natalis, keep watch for those gangs of young zealots. I do not want to have to tangle with them."

"No, my master," said Natalis, most of his answer drowned out by a loud bellow from the crowd at the Flavian Circus.

Moving away from the huge arena, the chairmen bore Sanct-Franciscus toward the Forum Romanum, turning aside before reaching that impressive place, and instead, skirting the base of the Esquilinus Hill, passing two impressive fountains where small crowds of children and humiliora were gathered, seeking relief from the heat of the day. The bearers kept up a steady jog, not too choppy, making good time along the streets which were less crowded than usual for this time of day—most Romans were at the Flavian Circus for the Emperor's Games.

"There is a procession ahead," said the lead chairman, slowing his men and addressing their passenger. "Would you prefer we wait for it to pass or find a way around it?"

Sanct-Franciscus considered briefly, glancing out of the curtains but unable to see ahead. "What sort of procession is it?"

Natalis answered before the bearers could. "It looks to be a funeral procession, my master, bound out of the walls."

"Then find a way around it," Sanct-Franciscus recommended.

"It may slow our arrival," said the lead chairman.

"I will consider that in your payment," Sanct-Franciscus assured him. "We have no cause to disturb the dead."

"Very well," said the leader of the bearers, and took the first side-street on his left, where a pair of skinny dogs confronted the chairmen, cringing and growling at once; the leader bent and picked up a broken bit of paving-stone and shied it at the dogs, watching as they ran off. "Cowards," he said, moving forward again.

Natalis described the matter to Sanct-Franciscus, keeping pace with the bearers as they found their way through a warren of alleys and tangled streets, only to emerge less than two blocks from the Temple of Hercules a short while later.

"There is a passage here that leads to the temple," said the leader.

"Yes, there is," said Sanct-Franciscus, drawing back the curtain for the last time.

"It is less than half an hour since we took you up," the leader said as the men set the chair down conveniently near a sundial. "You promised us a bonus."

"And you shall have it," said Sanct-Franciscus, emerging from the sedan chair, coins already in hand. "You did well."

The leader counted the coins. "There are twenty-one here."

"For your extra care in going around the funeral procession," Sanct-Franciscus explained.

"Generous of you," said the leader before signaling his men to pick up their chair and turn toward the nearest forum where they might find someone in need of their services.

Natalis watched them go. "Hard work, carrying chairs," he said.

"On such a day as this," Sanct-Franciscus said. "The bearers should be careful, sweating as much as they were."

"Better this heat than rain, or worse," said Natalis. "I always worked better warm than cold."

Sanct-Franciscus started walking toward the narrow passage that led to the side of the Temple of Hercules and Olivia's house. "The streets will be wild tonight, I think."

"And tomorrow night, and the night after that," said Natalis.

"The Emperor's Games," said Sanct-Franciscus. "True enough."

"It could turn dangerous, these Games," said Natalis. "Always when the Emperor, no matter who he may be, has three days of Games, the people become unruly."

"Three days," Sanct-Franciscus repeated as he strolled toward the gate. "Why three days, and not two?"

"The people become exhausted and excitable. They lose good sense." He paused, then continued with a suggestion of pride, "When I was still a thief, I knew that the second day of Games was best for me: the people were not too keyed up, and their exhilaration had not turned to mania. By the third day, when they were exhausted but too stimulated to rest, anything would set them off. I was almost killed three years ago when I was accused of taking three loaves of bread."

"And had you taken them?" Sanct-Franciscus asked.

"No; I had stolen a small purse with ae and denarii in it, but nothing so obvious, or cumbersome, as loaves of bread." Natalis rubbed his shoulder in memory of the attack. "They threw stones, and one Urban Guard struck me with his cudgel."

Sanct-Franciscus pulled on the rope to summon one of the slaves. "How did you get away?"

"I rolled under a biga, grabbed the axle-frame and let it drag me a good distance from the crowd. The driver didn't know I was there, or didn't care: he beat the crowd off with his whip. Nyssa had seen it happen, and she came to help me." His voice dropped. "She cared for me until I healed."

"Ingenious," Sanct-Franciscus said. "And dangerous."

"Not as dangerous as continuing to be stoned," said Natalis.

Tigilus opened the gate. "Welcome, Dominus," he said, with a critical glance at Natalis.

"Good afternoon to you, Tigilus," said Sanct-Franciscus. "How do I find you and the house?"

"You find me hot," said Tigilus with unusual candor. "Since you ask."

"And the rest of the household?" Sanct-Franciscus inquired as he started across the courtyard.

"The rest of the household is hot, too. And tempers are short, as they are everywhere." He followed after Sanct-Franciscus and Natalis into the shade of the roof, and through the door into the vestibule.

"Have you distributed the ice-water I ordered?" Sanct-Franciscus stopped at the edge of the atrium.

"It wasn't delivered, Dominus," said Tigilus.

Sanct-Franciscus turned back to him, surprised and annoyed. "What do you mean?" He had a continuing arrangement with a supplier of ice, a drayer who owned four large wagons with double cargo chests lined with hay and sawdust, and maintained an emporium in the catacombs.

"I mean the drayers never brought the ice you ordered. Rugeri sent a message to the dispatcher, asking why. Severin has just returned with their answer."

"Very good," Sanct-Franciscus said, and motioned to Natalis. "If the ice is not brought shortly, I may ask him to carry a second message to the dispatcher."

"Ice on such a day as this is most welcome," Tigilus said emphatically. "It has been paid for already—the ice has, hasn't it? They should deliver or give the money back."

"Yes; I know," said Sanct-Franciscus, a frown forming between his fine brows. "Why would—"

Rugeri appeared in the doorway to the muniment room. "I have been informed by the ice-men that a decuria, Telemachus Batsho, has required that anything coming to this house be presented to him for assessment before it is released." Ordinarily he would not have spoken so directly in front of the household, but in this instance, he was keenly aware that the household was eager for news.

"Telemachus Batsho," Sanct-Franciscus repeated. "What a determined fellow he is."

Rugeri came forward, his austere features set in condemning lines. "Would you like me to send for him? You have the right to demand an explanation for this arbitrary discrimination."

"And give him another reason to deny us ice?" Sanct-Franciscus shook his head. "No; I'll prepare a purse for him, against any charges he may see fit to levy." He looked back at Tigilus. "Will you carry the purse for me?"

"You have only to give the order," said Tigilus.

"He had best go shortly," said Natalis.

"Yes; the major battles will be starting soon at the Flavian Circus, and everyone will want to be at the arena," said Sanct-Franciscus with a fleeting look of distaste. "Come, Tigilus. Let me attend to this at once." He started toward Rugeri, but looked back at Natalis. "If you want to use the tepidarium, you, and the rest of the household, may do so until the ice comes."

Natalis did his best not to appear over-eager. "That would be most . . . most pleasant."

A sudden loud shout from the distant Games shook the air, followed by a loud yowl from the hydraulic organ.

"We had best hurry; the Games are growing wilder," said Sanct-Franciscus to Tigilus. "Natalis, if you will supervise the bath—have Holmdi help you—and Rugeri, if you will prepare a message for the ice-merchant?" He was already striding toward the muniment room, wondering as he went what mischief Telemachus Batsho intended this time.

Text of a letter from Atta Olivia Clemens in Ravenna to Ragoczy Germainus Sanct-Franciscus in Roma, carried by personal courier.

To the distinguished foreigner, Ragoczy Sanct' Germain Franciscus, also known as Ragoczy Germainus Sanct-Franciscus—you see? I've remembered—the greetings of Atta Olivia Clemens to my house in Roma, near the Temple of Hercules,

I write in haste to inform you that I am about to leave Ravenna for Vesontio in Gallia Belgica. Recent troubles here make it imperative that I remove myself from this city and the accusations of some resolute followers of the Jewish Christ. I have been called a demon of the night and a sorceress, and similar appellations; they have taken to throwing stones at me when I go out of my house, and nothing the local Prefect can do will stop them. Rather than confront them and thus enrage them still further, I have decided to move rather than risk discovery of my true nature.

I have a small property in Vesontio, with good vines and a small stable, where I can live in relative comfort until Roma or Ravenna are once again safe to occupy. I plan to remain here for five years or so, and then to consider what is best to do. At least I need not fear for my survival there, as I have realized I must do if I stay here.

From all the reports I have heard of that young Syrian's caprices, I must assume Roma has endured much at his hands, and not all of it bread and circuses. It is apparent to me that until there is a Caesar worthy of the name, I would be well-advised to remain some distance from Roma—the city has become much too volatile for me, and I believe that two vampires within Roman walls could only bring trouble to us both. So in the name of self-protection, I leave my native earth to you, so long as you ship me ten crates of it as soon as I am settled at Sapientia. It is on the west side of the town, on the Via Philomena.

For the time being, I have money enough to live prosperously, and if the coins should continue to be debased, I will have wine and horses to trade, since, unlike you, I cannot make my own gold and jewels. Still, great wealth can be as much a burden as a delight; my lands will maintain me quite handsomely. Incidentally, I am learning to drive a biga, which should prove useful in the days ahead— not that I imagine myself fleeing over the country roads. One year I must learn to ride—providing in so doing I do not attract too much notice to myself.

Last week I had a letter from the regional Prosecutor, inquiring about the incidents with the so-called Christians. The man is considered well-educated and intelligent, and so I was doubly appalled at his use of Latin! If his prose is any example, the coins are not the only Roman thing being debased. I was truly shocked. I know that the humiliora and others are not careful about language—and why should they be?—but the Prosecutor is an official, and his letter was a formal one. Magna Mater! The grammar was slip-shod, the syntax was careless, and all manner of foreign usage had crept into the text.

No doubt this is a sign of my age, but I cannot help but feel that something important is lost when respect for language fails.

I will not rant any longer, and I will thank you for your understanding of the frustrations I feel. Much as I long for your company, if only through the medium of this page of vellum, I have packing to supervise and then I must purchase heavy wagons and carpenta, with oxen to pull them, and arrange for someone of good repute to occupy this house. Just writing it down is tiring, but it must be done. So I will finish this with my assurance of my

Everlasting love,
Olivia

On the 9th day of August in the 972nd Year of the City

5

"She's had a hard day—two days," Ignatia said as she met Sanct-Franciscus in the vestibule. "She hasn't been sleeping—the heat wears on her—and she is not . . ." She made a complicated gesture as Starus carefully secured the bolt on the door. "I wouldn't have sent you word so late, but she . . ."

"She has been vomiting, not much, but whenever she tries—" said Starus, holding a branch of oil-lamps so that they could more easily see one another. "Nothing she eats stays down, not even water." He spoke softly enough, for most of the household was asleep.

"I've tried poppy-water, just as you recommended, but not even that can soothe her, and she claims I want to poison her," said Ignatia, and stifled a sudden yawn. "I'm sorry. I shouldn't be so—"

Sanct-Franciscus took Ignatia's hand. "How long have you been tending Domina Adicia?" His case of medicaments was buckled to his belt, and he used his free hand to move it around to the small of his back, out of the way.

"Since before dawn yesterday," Starus said before Ignatia could answer. "Doma Ignatia has taken a few brief naps, but she is worn out with all the demands being made on her."

"Starus," Ignatia warned, staring down at her hand in his. "I have an obligation, and I will fulfill it."

"It is true, Doma," he said firmly. "And your brother's no help, going to his friends to have them pray to their Jewish god to help her. Again." He raised his chin indignantly. "I will not go back on what I've said. You have been up almost two days, and that is too much for anyone. Octavian should be here, helping to care for his mother, not with the Christians."

"He thinks their prayers will help our mother," said Ignatia, repeating what she had been saying for months.

Before the discussion became a cycle of recriminations, Sanct-Franciscus intervened. "What else is wrong with her? She cannot hold anything in her stomach, but is there anything more?"

"She complains of headache," said Ignatia, removing her hand from his.

"Hardly surprising if she is hungry and thirsty," said Sanct-Franciscus. "When did this begin?"

"More than two days ago," said Ignatia with a kind of numb fatigue that said more than lengthly explanations would.

"Why did you wait to send for me?" Sanct-Franciscus asked.

"She . . . she said . . . not to, not while she . . . could not receive you . . . properly or . . ." Ignatia's voice trailed off.

"The weather was especially hot that day, you may recall, and still, close, damp," said Starus. "Domina Laelius had not slept well, and complained that the heat was wearing her out, leeching her strength. She called for lemon-water, but—" he shook his head slowly, then went on, "She was flushed and edgy all that day, saying that her muscles were exhausted. She claimed she feared the mal aria—the bad air which is everywhere at this time of year—and insisted that incense be burned in her chamber, which made her cough."

"Did you remove the incense?" asked Sanct-Franciscus.

"No; she would not allow it. When I tried to . . . she accused me of wanting to see her die," said Ignatia, sighing. "At least most of it burned and she isn't coughing any more."

"Do you think she will want to see me, at this hour?" Sanct-Franciscus asked. "If she has not wanted my help for two days?"

"She would want to see you at any hour," said Ignatia with a fatalistic gesture. "She has been in a swither."

Sanct-Franciscus regarded Ignatia steadily. "Then it might be best if you take me to her—if you would."

"She is likely to be in a testy state of mind still," said Ignatia quietly. "She upbraided three slaves this evening. She would have beaten them if she had the strength."

"Beaten them, you say?" Sanct-Franciscus pressed his lips together thoughtfully, then, "Would it be useful if I spoke to her about that? Beaten slaves do not give good care; does she realize that."

"Probably not," said Ignatia, seconding Sanct-Franciscus' own inclination. "She hasn't paid attention to any of the household."

"Very well; I will say nothing," he said, and fell in beside her, leaving Starus to keep watch for Octavian.

"I *am* worried, no matter what she may think," said Ignatia as they crossed the atrium. "She has been demanding before, of course, but this time, she is also frightened. I see it in her eyes."

"She has been frightened before," said Sanct-Franciscus.

"Yes, but not in this way." She walked a bit more slowly, her eyes fixed on a distant place only she could see. "Before, she was angry; now the fear is stronger, and she is filled with emotions I haven't seen in her—panic, and a kind of dread."

"So you think she is worse?"

"I think *she* thinks she is worse," said Ignatia. "That frightens me, although I know I shouldn't be pulled into her . . . her . . ." Here she floundered, trying not to be condemning of Adicia.

"Her distress," Sanct-Franciscus suggested.

Ignatia nodded as they reached the door to Adicia's bedroom. "I won't go in with you; I upset her too much. I'd just as soon not cause her any more annoyance. But I would like to speak with you when you are through, if you don't mind."

"Where will I find you?" He watched her closely as she answered. "I want to speak with you, as well."

"I will be in the garden. I try to spend time in the open air every evening, and this will be my first chance since sunrise." She touched his hand. "You are good to her—better than she has any right to expect."

"That is kind of you, Ignatia," said Sanct-Franciscus before he turned to go into Adicia's room.

An angular, middle-aged woman slumped by the window, half-asleep, her slave's collar shining dully in the light of a single oil-lamp; she sat up as she heard Sanct-Franciscus' soft approach. "I am not asleep," she declared.

"No, not she; she has snored only to keep me awake," Adicia complained from her heap of pillows. A light coverlet was drawn up to her shoulders, and she had one hand clenched on its whip-sewn hem. "I thought you'd come earlier. You should have been here before sunset. I was miserable then." This rebuke was petulant, a condemnation extending beyond this occasion.

The slave sank back in her chair as if seeking invisibility.

"I did not receive word until a little more than an hour ago that you were ailing, Domina," he said tranquilly, refusing to be pulled into her anger which he was aware masked her fright. "I came as soon as I was called. You must pardon me for taking so long to get here."

"An hour?" She stared up at him.

"I had to gather my medicaments and have my horses yoked to the biga." He made this ordinary delay seem inexcusable to placate her complaint.

"At least the streets are empty tonight," Adicia remarked, fussing with the selvage of the coverlet.

"Something to be thankful for," Sanct-Franciscus said at his most soothing.

"That trollop of a daughter of mine must have thrown herself upon you again, arriving at your gate as if she were an abandoned woman," Adicia said, releasing the coverlet and fretting with the knot of her hair; she managed to pull a few tendrils free and twist them around her fingers.

"She sent your under-steward to summon me," said Sanct-Franciscus. "She preferred not to leave you." He came to the side of her bed. "They tell me the heat has been bothering you."

"It's been bothering everyone," Adicia said in disgust.

"That may be, but it is you I have come to treat, and it is you who must have my full attention." He reached for flint-and-steel to strike a spark for the nearest oil-lamps, and as their pale, wavering light sprang to life, he saw that his initial impression was right: Domina Adicia was suffering from heat exhaustion, and possibly dehydration as well for her forehead was dry. "They tell me you cannot keep food or water down: is this true?"

"Not easily," she hedged.

"Not at all, from what I was told." He took her hand to feel the pulse in her wrist. "And that is not a favorable sign," he went on, noticing her heartbeat was shallow and rapid.

"They want me to die. I've become too great a burden. That's the whole of it," Adicia said bitterly. "They are tired of me."

"They don't want you dead, Domina," Sanct-Franciscus reassured her. "They want you better."

"Hah!" She pulled her arm away from him. "Not even you believe that. You see how I am served."

"Yes, I see how carefully you are tended, and I must tell you that you are in error, thinking that anyone wishes you ill. If I thought you were in danger, I would speak to the decuriae."

"My daughter has fooled you, as she fools so many," Adicia muttered.

Sanct-Franciscus remained patient and steady, thinking back to his long years serving in the Temple of Imhotep. "It is a source of unhappiness for us all that we can give you so little relief from your suffering, but no one wants your death."

"But they do," Adicia said, pouting.

"Domina Adicia, you will chafe yourself into a fever." He put his hand on her forehead to emphasize his concern.

"I *am* in a fever," she quetched. "I am consumed with fire. My bones are hot as embers."

"I will prepare a draught for you that will ease your discomforts," said Sanct-Franciscus, doing his best to put Adicia in a better frame of mind. "Then you must rest; sleep gives more cures than a score of physicians."

Her short laughter was harsh. "You are probably the only physician in Roma who would say so."

He made no attempt to argue with her, but signaled to the slave, saying to her, "If you will fetch a pitcher of almond-milk, I will prepare my draught." The woman pushed herself to her feet, and Sanct-Franciscus noticed that the slave suffered from aching joints. "And bring a cup of water—I have some pansy-and-willow that will lessen your pain."

"I don't ask you to treat my slaves," Adicia said brusquely as the woman hurried out of the room.

"No, but I thought you would be pleased with having a woman serve you who isn't preoccupied with her own afflictions." Sanct-Franciscus let her consider this, then added, "It is to your benefit to have your slaves in good frame."

"So you say; so you say," she muttered, displeased for no reason she could describe.

He opened his case and began to set out vials and jars. "You will need a composer so that you will not vomit, and an anodyne to relieve your hurts, and something to lessen your fever. I will also include a soporific, so you may sleep." He touched his supplies as he explained, and watched her response to his recommendations.

"I need to keep my stomach settled, or all the rest will be for naught." She pressed her lips together into a thin line. "If only I knew what consumes me!" she burst out.

"Whatever it is, you have borne it a long time," he said gently.

Adicia glared at him. "As have others in my gens," she admitted with an emotion compounded of distress and pride. "My aunt died of this weakness and pain, and one of my brothers, as well, many years since."

"Such has been the case with many Romans," said Sanct-Franciscus with a suggestion of concern.

"True, very true," she said, looking away from him as the slave returned with a pitcher and a pair of cups on a tray, one of which contained water, the other of which was empty. "It has become our encumbrance for our greatness," she said so that Sanct-Franciscus would take little notice of the slave.

"Thank you," said Sanct-Franciscus, taking the tray and setting it on the bedside table next to his open case. He removed a small, deep spoon from his case and began to measure out the ingredients he had described to her into the almond-milk in the pitcher. "Do not try to drink this all at once, but take a little, wait a bit, then take a little more. You will fare better that way."

"And if I vomit—what then?" Adicia seemed almost to relish that possibility. "I may well be sick all night."

"Then your slave will hold your basin and I will try another combination of medicaments," he said.

She made a kind of scoffing sound, but held out her hand for the cup Sanct-Franciscus proffered, half-filled with almond-milk and the powders and tinctures he had mixed into it. "I had better feel improvement, or I will bar you from this house. You mustn't fail me now." There was a note of terror in her command.

He was adding pansy-and-willow to the cup of water, and so said nothing to her in response to her threat; he gave the cup to the slave and then helped steady Adicia's shoulders so that she could have a few little sips of the almond-milk without spilling any on the coverlet. When she shoved the cup back into his hand, he set it on the tray again, and began to put his jars and vials back in his case. Watching her for a short while, he ventured to hand the cup to her again, and held her in the bend of his arm to ease her swallowing. "Lie back now; let the medicine work."

She did as she was told, frowning as she settled into the pile of pillows. "You won't leave yet."

"No," he assured her. "If you have no trouble with what I have given you, I will take a turn in your garden, then return to check on you. If you are asleep, I will let you rest; if you are awake, I will prepare more of the draught for you."

"All right," she said grudgingly. "Just see you do not go."

"I will not," he said, turning toward the slave. "If you have relief from the drink, I will provide you with more."

She blinked twice at being addressed, then said, "Grateful. I am grateful."

Sanct-Franciscus indicated Domina Adicia. "Your mistress will need your close attention for the next hour or two. Stay beside her and watch for any changes in her. If she asks for water, let her have a little of the drink I have prepared, but not much. If she has not cast up any of the almond-milk, then give her water after dawn."

"Yes," she said.

"I will ask the cook to send up another pitcher for her—of water with a little salt and honey in it. That will slake her thirst once she is able to drink safely, and give her strength."

The slave stared at him, nodding repeatedly.

He moved away from the bedside, motioning to the woman to follow him. "If she starts to sweat, keep her warm until the fever is out of her. She is not so heated that she needs to be chilled, and a chill could delay her recovery."

Again the woman nodded.

"And I'll make more anodyne solution for you, that you may take later," he told her, then said to Adicia, "Domina, I am going to give you a little time to rest. I'll return to see how you are doing a bit later."

"Don't leave the house," Adicia said sharply.

"I will not go farther than your garden," said Sanct-Franciscus, making for the door, aware that both women were watching him closely.

Starus was waiting not far away; he studied the foreigner with a mixture of hope and dubiety. "Well?"

"I think she will improve in time, but right now she is losing strength, and that is a dangerous development," said Sanct-Franciscus, keeping his voice low. "I have provided her a drink to help her husband what strength she has and to lower the fever that burns in her."

"She isn't doing well, is she?" Starus dared to ask. "You think the danger is—?"

"I think it is real," Sanct-Franciscus said. "She could decline still further, and that would not be favorable. But she is not beyond recovery." He passed the steward and went along the corridor to the door leading into the garden at the rear of the house, where the scent of ripe fruit overpowered the odors from the stable and the city beyond the walls. He stood for a long moment, thinking back to the garden at Olivia's father's house, where he had sought refuge after the deaths of Kosrozd, Tishtry, and Aumtehoutep, and the succor she had provided then; he savored the memory, then reminded himself that Olivia was one of his blood now. With a slight shrug, he went toward the fountain at the intersection of three well-tended walkways, his night-seeing eyes having no trouble locating Ignatia among the pear trees. As he went toward her, she swung around to face him.

"Will she die?" The question was so blunt it surprised them both.

Sanct-Franciscus answered calmly, "Yes, as all living things will. But not just yet."

She sighed. "I don't want her to die." She took hold of the branch of the tree under which she stood, half-swinging from it as if to hold herself away from the house. "She is not easy to care for, but she is my mother, and if she dies now, everyone will say it's my fault."

He stared at her, aware of her anguish and confusion. "You must know that is untrue," he said, trying to comfort her.

"No," she countered. "No, I wouldn't know it. It might be that I—"

"You have done nothing to be ashamed of," he said, taking another step closer to her. "You have done all anyone can, and more than most would."

"My mother doesn't think so," said Ignatia, her voice forlorn.

"That is her illness, not her heart, speaking," said Sanct-Franciscus.

"Myrtale says the same."

"If Myrtale wishes to assume Domina Ignatia's care herself, then she has grounds for criticism: if she is not willing to do that, then she is also in no position to fault you." He offered his hand to her, and reluctantly, she released her hold on the branch and put her palm on his. "You must not take these things to heart, Doma Ignatia."

A faint stirring of wind made the leaves shiver above them; the sodden heat seemed to lessen with the promise of a breeze.

"I hope the weather will break," she said, staring up through the leaves at the stars. "If this still heat would end, everything would be better."

"There would be fewer mosquitos," he said, knowing how these voracious pests set upon Roma every summer.

"Everyone has welts on their arms," she said, a strange note in her voice.

"Such bites are nuisances, and may incline many to take fevers," he said, puzzled by her slight distraction. "What did you wish to see me about, Doma Ignatia?"

"I . . . I want reassurance . . . or comfort," she said distantly.

"You may have both," he said, "to the limit I can provide them."

"And that is a welcome thing," she agreed with a quick, unsteady laugh; his nearness was taking a toll on her, and she wondered how much longer she could endure his presence without making a fool of herself. She started to speak to him, to ask what he recommended for her mother's care, but to her astonishment, embraced him instead, straining to hold him to her, trying clumsily to kiss him.

Startled by her abrupt action, Sanct-Franciscus remained still as he sensed the need in her; then, slowly, he wrapped his arms around her and steadied her kisses to one that was long, exploring, arousing, answering her ardor with an intensity that surprised him: here was what he had sought for so long—passion that was more than the gratification of an evening's fancy. He felt the promise of intimacy in her urgent desire, and responded to it with fervor, taking her head in his hands so that he could help her to savor the inscience of their flesh.

"Sanct-Franciscus . . . I don't . . ." As her grip on him lessened, she gave herself over to his lips, the depths of her captivation seeming to increase with every touch, every place their bodies aligned. For an instant, she wished their clothes were on fire, so that nothing could impede their contact, that they could lie amid the last flowers of summer, naked and rapturous, but that faded at the sudden sound of chariot-wheels beyond the walls of the garden. She shoved his shoulder, forcing him back from her. "It must be . . . Octavian," she said, sounding breathless and disoriented. "He mustn't . . . not together . . . He would disapprove . . ." She struggled to neaten her clothes, aware now that she was in disarray, that her hair was mussed, and that some part of him must linger on her, a tell-tale stamp of their lubricity. Doing as much as she could to calm herself, Ignatia took three unsteady steps away from Sanct-Franciscus. "I . . . I should go in."

"Ignatia—" he began.

She stopped and held out her hand to touch him one more time, her eyes meeting his in the dark. "This isn't over, Sanct-Franciscus," she vowed before she continued on toward the fountain and the path leading back to the house.

Text of a letter from Telemachus Batsho to Septimus Desiderius Vulpius.

On this, the 4ᵗʰ day of September in the 972ⁿᵈ Year of the City, the de-curia Telemachus Batsho charges the honestiorus Septimus Desiderius Vulpius to give full and immediate answers to the following questions, with the admonishment that failure to answer in every particular may well result in action being taken against the honestiorus. These questions are in regard to the foreign honestiorus Ragoczy Germainus Sanct-Franciscus, to wit:

1) *Has the honestiorus Sanct-Franciscus ever sought to entrust gold or jewels to the honestiorus Vulpius for any reason? If he has done so, what was his stated purpose?*

2) *Is the honestiorus Vulpius aware of any irregularities in the honestiorus Sanct-Franciscus' household? If he is, what are those irregularities?*

3) *The foreign honestiorus Sanct-Franciscus is known to prac-tice healings and other medicinal skills, apparently with considerable success: is the honestiorus Vulpius aware of any cases in which those skills proved lacking, or for which he demanded excessive payment?*

4) *Does the honestiorus Sanct-Franciscus have any ties of loy-*
alty to governments presently opposed to Roma or any part
of the Empire? If he does, to what extent does he support
our enemies?

This inquiry is the first of what may be many into the activities
of this Sanct-Franciscus. You are advised to say nothing of this to
the foreign honestiorus; should you bring this to his attention, a sim-
ilar inquiry may be instigated against you and all your gens.

     Ave Heliogabalus!

Telemachus Batsho
decuria
Basilica Julia

6

Bonar Datus Fabricius stood in the doorway of Sanct-Franciscus'
study, Aedius immediately behind him. He cleared his throat and
tugged on the sleeve of his forest-green pallium of Armenian
wool, his manner suggesting he had no liking for his errand here.
"I thank you for permitting me to visit you this way, honestiorus. I
am sorry, but I am going to intrude on your hospitality still further:
Verus Lucillius will join us shortly." He glanced over his shoulder
as if to find Lucillius blowing into the house on the gusty September wind.

"Dear me," Sanct-Franciscus said serenely; he was seated at his
writing table, a sheet of vellum lying before him, a stylus and ink-
cake to his right; he presented a fine appearance: his black dalmatica
was embroidered in silver and dark red down the center of the garment in an array of interlocking winged disks, and he wore but a single piece of jewelry—a silver ring of the same eclipse design as
distinguished his garment, with a black sapphire at its center. He
smiled as he rose. "I am honored by your presence, as I will be by

Lucillius',” he said as good manners required. “But—you will pardon me—I am also somewhat nonplussed.”

“I understand why you might wonder at my coming, seeing that we have only met once, and that was at Saturnalia. I know this makes my presence now seem importunate.” He took a step into the room, his face somber. “I would have sent a messenger, but I feared he might take too long to reach you.”

“Therefore I must suppose your errand has some urgency to it?”

“Alas,” Fabricius confirmed.

“Then tell me what has brought you here, if you can do so without Lucillius. I have an engagement to visit Desiderius Vulpius in an hour, and cannot spare too much time just at present.” Sanct-Franciscus’ manner was genial but not apologetic. “I trust this will not inconvenience you or Lucillius?”

“That is one of the matters that concerns us—your appointment with our friend.” He ducked his head and tried not to appear as awkward as he felt. “It would be better for him and for you if you didn’t keep it.”

“Ah,” said Sanct-Franciscus, the first awareness of Fabricius’ intention making him more attentive. “Perhaps you had best choose a seat, illustriatus, and I will send my steward to get refreshments for you, while you explain as much of this as you are able,” said Sanct-Franciscus, then, without waiting for a response from Fabricius, turned to Aedius. “Bring breads and wine, and with them whatever savory is proper for the hour. Another guest will arrive shortly, and sustenance should be provided for him as well as for this illustriatus.”

Fabricius hesitated, waiting until Aedius was gone. “I cannot promise that you will wish me to remain once I tell you the reason for my visit. I know that what I must impart will not be greeted with delight.”

There was a slight, enigmatic smile in Sanct-Franciscus’ eyes, and his tone had an ironic edge. “You fear I would kill the messenger?”

“Something of the sort, yes,” said Fabricius, edging toward an elegant couch. “But if you would not mind?”

Sanct-Franciscus made a gesture between a salute and an invitation. "When you are comfortable, tell me what is your purpose in coming here, if you would."

"It concerns Desiderius Vulpius," said Fabricius.

"So I surmised," said Sanct-Franciscus, his affability unruffled.

"There are events taking place that may prove difficult for you, and for your friends," said Fabricius, and stopped as if afraid to go on.

"How do you mean? What is the difficulty these events pose?" Sanct-Franciscus shifted in his chair so that he almost faced Fabricius directly.

"There are questions being asked about you, at a very high level," said Fabricius. "A very high level," he repeated for emphasis.

"Why should I not be flattered by such attention," he asked as if he had no sense of the possibilities this notoriety could mean.

"Questions of this sort don't praise or benefit you," said Fabricius testily.

"What are they?" Sanct-Franciscus kept his voice level and his gaze trained on Fabricius.

"I am not truly at liberty to tell you, not as you should be told, and must wait a bit longer to discuss all that— When Lucillius arrives, we will be able to present you with our observations," Fabricius acknowledged; his expression was changing from stern to regretful.

"If you can say nothing to the point, how am I to learn what is suspected?"

"The decuriae will handle the matter once your role in the matter in question is established," said Fabricius. "In the meantime, your friends will be under the same cloud that hangs over you."

"About which you cannot tell me," Sanct-Franciscus said.

"No; none of us are permitted to tell you what the nature of the investigation is. We must report only what we know. If we speculate, we can be cited for it."

Sanct-Franciscus was silent while he considered his predicament, then asked, "How am I to diminish the danger to my friends if I am uninformed of the government's suspicions? I could easily, and inadvertently, implicate my Roman friends and associates in my danger if I have—"

"Three of your friends have been admonished to have no contact with you, which is why I am here, and Lucillius is coming." A spot of color appeared in his face, as if his admission were embarrassing.

"You are deputies, in effect," said Sanct-Franciscus. "You make it possible for Vulpius not to expose himself by visiting me. By coming in his stead, you are sparing him any greater trouble."

"That is what we hope to achieve," Fabricius admitted. "This is not how I would deal with such matters, but it is what Vulpius has asked, and I have many ties to him, as well as the tie of friendship. I could not refuse him this favor." He coughed once, as if to show his disapproval.

"Then you are a worthy friend, to do such kindness for Desiderius Vulpius," said Sanct-Franciscus, only a suggestion of wry amusement in his compliment. "I am grateful to you for your undertaking."

Fabricius blinked in surprise at this remark. "You are most gracious; this news must be unpleasant for you."

"Yes, it is, but I am not astonished by it," Sanct-Franciscus said, recollecting the many times in the past that his presence had become suddenly unwelcome, and the quick shift in loyalties that had accompanied his falls from positions of influence. "Exiles all know what it is to be at peril."

"Oh. Yes. I suppose you would," Fabricius said, and looked up as Aedius brought in a tray and the news that Pius Verus Lucillius had arrived.

"Bring him here," said Sanct-Franciscus, taking note of all that was on the tray. "A fine selection: the chopped apples in honey are a good touch."

"I'll tell the kitchen staff," said Aedius as he left the two men alone again.

"Would you like to pour the wine? There is red and white: you may choose whichever you prefer," said Sanct-Franciscus.

"Thank you," said Fabricius, his voice dropping and his demeanor becoming more relaxed; he reached for the white wine and poured a generous amount into his cup. "What will you have?"

"Alas, I do not drink wine," said Sanct-Franciscus. "It is a condition of my blood."

"How unfortunate," said Fabricius, more from good form than actual concern; all foreigners had idiosyncrasies, and Sanct-Franciscus, cultured though he was, was no exception to that rule. "I trust you have other means to satisfy your thirst?" Fabricius did not wait for an answer, and expected none; he put two rolled-and-skewered strips of lamb stuffed with herbs and garlic on the small plate provided for such use, and then took a pillow-bread from the basket, licking his fingers before he reached for the tub of mixed butter and olive oil. "This is a most satisfactory repast. You observe our ways better than most Romans."

"You are good to say so," Sanct-Franciscus told him as he rose to greet Lucillius.

"I see you have that thief working for you," Lucillius remarked as he entered the study; he was a bit windblown, the deep, shoulder-pleats of his calf-length, rust-colored pallium hanging in disarray. Tugging at his belt, he attempted to restore order to his appearance.

"Yes; he is a very useful messenger," said Sanct-Franciscus, his calm unchanged. "You are welcome to this house."

"A bad business, this," said Lucillius, his demeanor serious, his voice roughened by worry. "Enough to want me to return to the provinces again, away from the schemes and workings of Roma."

"I would be pleased to send for a mirror, if you like," Sanct-Franciscus offered as Lucillius continued to wrestle with his pallium.

"I think this will do for now," said Lucillius, glancing at the tray. "Lamb and crab. Very nice." He sat down on the Phoenician chair next to the table and poured himself a cup of red wine. "Excellent color. Where do you get it?"

"From the north; from a vineyard southwest of Florentia." Sanct-Franciscus knew that Lucillius was not being rude, but was trying to avoid the moment when he would have to address the reason for his visit. "The Widow Clemens owns that vineyard, as she owns this house."

"One of the provident women," Lucillius approved, picking up three morsels of crab and then taking some of the butter-and-oil with the small scoop provided. "And pillow-bread." With this to sustain him, he finally looked directly at Sanct-Franciscus. "I suppose Fabricius has told you the reason for our calling?"

"He said that there are inquiries being made into my affairs that may reflect badly on my friends and associates here in Roma," Sanct-Franciscus said, adding to Fabricius, "That about sums it up, or have I missed some item of importance?" He saw Fabricius nod while he ate.

"I think you have grasped the essence," said Fabricius through his chewing.

"You're an astute fellow, Sanct-Franciscus," Lucillius approved. "And it pains me to see you in such a predicament, but I fear that just at present, it can't be helped."

"Because I am a foreigner and cannot challenge the Senate's authority," said Sanct-Franciscus.

"Such is the state of affairs," said Lucillius. "And I can only hope that there will be a speedy resolution to this situation, for all our sakes, but I am afraid your contract with Propinus and Gratians has been declared void. With the decuriae investigating, it could be weeks, or months, until the matter is wholly put to rest." He took a generous sip of wine. "I think it is all overblown fussiness, but in these times, we cannot afford to have enemies in our midst."

"Certainly not," said Sanct-Franciscus.

"And while this may appear unfair to you, as a foreigner, you must understand that we Romans are in the toils of intrigue on many fronts." He drank again. "There are barbarians beyond our borders who are jealous of our Empire, and would seek to destroy it. So the decuriae have been charged with the task of revealing those working against us while living among us."

"Do you think that Sanct-Franciscus should file a petition to have the inquiry quashed?" Fabricius asked as he reached for more lamb.

"No. I fear that would only compromise him further." said Lucillius, his attention on their host. "You have done business with many Romans, haven't you?"

"I have, but most of them are associates only, hardly companions," said Sanct-Franciscus.

"But a petition would force an answer from the Curia," said Fabricius.

Lucillius glowered. "If anything, attempting to press the Curia would make the problems worse, for it could be assumed that he was seeking to conceal his dealings, which would put everyone at a disadvantage, including his most distant affiliates. The Curia will not be adjured in that manner. Now is the time when, as a foreigner, he must be forthcoming and candid, making no effort to engage others in his predicament, for honestiorus or not, he is a foreigner, and that will count against him." He cleared his throat. "So far, none of Sanct-Franciscus' business records have been confiscated, but they could be, and then everyone would have more trouble to deal with."

"You mean, there would be further inquiries among those who share in his business?" Fabricius was so transparent in the rehearsed nature of his questions that Sanct-Franciscus almost laughed aloud.

"That would be the least of it," said Lucillius, still watching Sanct-Franciscus. "If any part of his business practices are questionable, the impact on his associates could be devastating."

"So I understand," said Sanct-Franciscus, stopping Lucillius before he could launch into more of his disguised exhortations. "And I may reassure you that there is no reason for anyone with whom I have business dealings to fear that I have not observed the proprieties and the law in all I have done."

Lucillius shook his head. "There was the matter of a slave in Alexandria—"

"If you mean Perseus, you know he was stealing from me, and from those in business with me. It is all in the records of the Prosecutor of Customs." He regarded Lucillius for a moment, then went on, "If someone is hoping to hold me to blame for my own losses, I will own myself astonished."

Fabricius refilled his cup and said before taking refuge in drinking, "It is being said that the thefts were a clever ruse, to make it appear that you had been put at a disadvantage when you had not."

Stung by these implications, Sanct-Franciscus responded sharply. "But I cannot ascertain who claims this, or why, can I?"

"No; since you are not a Roman," said Lucillius.

"But it is known that you didn't pursue the slave in the courts. You allowed him to live, when you might have demanded his life." Fabricius raised his eyes again, his expression hardening.

"Is that the extent of my perfidy?" Sanct-Franciscus said, once again lightening his tone. "That I did not try to have the slave killed?"

"That is a portion of the reason," said Lucillius, suddenly cautious.

Sanct-Franciscus allowed himself a short chuckle. "And how could I—an exile in Roma—demand that the Romans in Alexandria condemn a slave for theft? I would have no authority to require such a response—if I did, it might have been assumed I wanted to silence the slave, for I no longer owned him, and that would make for harsher accusations than the present inquiry implies." He went to the window and tapped on the translucent panes of thin, polished alabaster. "I have done what would be least intrusive under Roman law, and now it seems that my very scrupulousness has brought me under suspicion."

Lucillius gestured his helplessness. "It is often so."

"At least you have been willing to abide by the laws of Roma, and respected our gods," said Fabricius, trying to put a good face on Sanct-Franciscus' predicament. "That is to your credit."

"As we must hope," Lucillius amended. "If it is determined that your compliance is actually an attempt to cover nefarious dealings, as you have proposed, well—" He shrugged.

"In any case, I can see that I am at a disadvantage," said Sanct-Franciscus, unwelcome recollections of his last sojourn in Roma reminding him of how easily and how far a foreigner could fall. "It appears that the only thing I can do for now is to wait—wait until the Curia decides."

"It will take time for all the reports on your trading enterprises to be prepared and presented to the Curia for their evaluation of your probity." Lucillius had more crab, then regarded Fabricius. "How long do you think this should take?"

"Perhaps six months," said Fabricius, "if there are no delays in securing the reports requested."

"Six months," Sanct-Franciscus repeated.

"If they get to it promptly, and all the reports provided are complete." Fabricius wiped his hands on the moist cloth provided for that purpose. "It could be twice as long."

"That is not a very pleasant prospect," said Sanct-Franciscus. "I wonder if I will be allowed to continue to trade while the Curia examines my accounts: do either of you know?"

"It may come to that," said Lucillius. "Or they may require a bond from you while their assessment is ongoing."

"In other words, the Curia and their decuriae will do their utmost to tie my hands and limit my access to them while they decide if I have been too honest or not honest enough," said Sanct-Franciscus sardonically.

"Something of the sort, I fear," said Lucillius, adding more wine to his partially empty cup; color was rising in his cheeks, and his face softened.

"And I am not to have direct contact with Desiderius Vulpius, or any of the others: Senator Italicus Romulus Primus Puero, or the illustriatus Cosimus Isidorus Crispus Horens, or Demetrius Numa Tarquinius Augustulus, or Ireaus Antonius Propinus, or Sovertius Gratians, or any other honoratus or illustriatus with whom I have had a business association, no matter how remote?" He nodded, certain of the answer. "If I am tainted, so they could be equally besmirched—is that the gist of it?"

"I understand why you are dismayed," said Lucillius, wary of the sharpness of Sanct-Franciscus' tone.

"I should hope so," Sanct-Franciscus said. "You would be outraged if the Curia should impose such restrictions upon you."

"Yes," said Fabricius. "But we are Romans, after all."

"And I am a foreigner in exile." Sanct-Franciscus paced the

length of the study, then stopped still. "Very well: so long as I am kept informed—regularly informed—of the progress of the investigation, I will abide by the restrictions placed upon me, at least for the period of a year. If the inquiry lasts longer, I will seek to find other avenues by which to resolve my predicament." He could see that his indignation was having the desired impact on his visitors, and he decided to use that response to his advantage. "If you will swear to me that you will see to it that I am given accurate reports every month, you have my assurance that I will do my utmost to assist the Curia in its inquiries."

Lucillius pressed his lips together, considering how to answer. "So you will not seek to block or oppose them? You're willing to let the probe go forth?"

"I am not in a position to stop it," Sanct-Franciscus admitted. "If it is to be brought to a swift conclusion, I will have to aid the Curia, not try to hinder its tasks."

"A most . . . reasonable position," said Fabricius, doing his best to conceal his surprise.

"Would a more belligerent one make this any easier?" Sanct-Franciscus inquired with an air of worn geniality.

"Probably not," said Lucillius.

Sanct-Franciscus regarded his two visitors narrowly. "Will you swear?"

"Of course," said Lucillius. "I have done enough business through you that I know you are forthright in your dealings. I will say as much to the Curia, and I will see that you are provided monthly reports from the decuriae assigned to your case."

"Among the decuriae, I don't suppose there is one called Telemachus Batsho, is there?" Sanct-Franciscus asked, a slight, saturnine smile tweaking the corners of his mouth.

"I don't recognize the name," said Fabricius, just a little too quickly.

"He may be one," said Lucillius, with feigned indifference. "If you want to know, I will—" He drank the last of his wine in a single, large gulp.

"No; I was only curious," said Sanct-Franciscus, convinced now that Batsho was the instigator of this punitive investigation.

He indicated the tray of viands. "Enjoy yourselves as long as you like, honestiora; my slaves will bring you more wine and food if you want them."

"But you . . . you should be with us," said Fabricius, hastily drinking wine to help swallow his mouthful of pillow-bread. "Your hospitality is exemplary, but we have no wish to impose upon you."

"You do not impose. I will return shortly; if I am not to call upon Vulpius, I must alert my stables and my staff." He nodded once and strode out of the study, making his way to his private apartments without unseemly haste. Here he found Rugeri setting out a dark-red laena in anticipation of his leaving. "Do not bother," he said in Greek.

Rugeri looked up, startled. "My master?" he said in the same tongue.

"I will not be calling upon Vulpius today." He quickly summed up what his two unexpected guests had told him, adding only, "We must be very cautious now, my friend."

"Cautious? Perhaps it would be better to visit Alexandria, or Gallia," Rugeri suggested.

"That would only confirm the Curia's worst misgivings. No. This must be handled carefully, and in full view of Roma, or I will lose my businesses and jeopardize Olivia in the process." He paused. "My various associates will have to be warned, inconspicuously, if possible."

"Then what do you propose to do?" asked Rugeri.

Sanct-Franciscus put the tips of his fingers together, saying, "I am going to write a note to my scribe at the villa; I will need Natalis to carry it for me."

"Natalis?" Rugeri was somewhat alarmed. "Do you want to trust him with such a delicate mission?"

"He can leave the city—and return—without being seen, and just now, that will be important, I believe; I dare not carry it myself, or write the letters of warning, for my handwriting would reveal that the notification came from me, and that would mean trouble if the notes are revealed to the Curia, as I must assume will happen if the Curia is determined to do a thorough inquiry. So the warnings must be anonymous, and from outside the city. For the rest, I will have to rely on Natalis' discretion." Sanct-Franciscus went to the small writing table under the window. "While I prepare the note, will you find Natalis and bring him here?"

"Without the household being made aware of it?" Rugeri ventured, and saw Sanct-Franciscus nod. "I will."

Sanct-Franciscus took an ink-cake from the drawer in the desk, and a rolled sheet of vellum from the pigeon-holes above the desk-top, then drew up a stool and prepared to write. By the time Rugeri returned with Natalis, the note was finished and sealed, and the seal impressed with Sanct-Franciscus' eclipse sigil.

"My master," the two men said almost in unison.

"Thank you for being so prompt," Sanct-Franciscus said, turning to them. "I have something for you to do, Natalis." He indicated the folded note. "It is essential that this reach Villa Ragoczy before sunset. Do you think you can do it?"

Natalis considered. "If you mean delivered there without being seen, as your manservant has told me, then I hope I can. If I can get past the Praetorian Camp, then there should be no trouble."

Sanct-Franciscus considered this. "You may remain there at the villa for the night, provided you can do so unseen. This is for my scribe, Deomadus—for him and no other. Make sure he reads it immediately. You may return before sunrise if it suits your purpose, so long as no one is aware of your coming and going." He offered the folded-and-sealed vellum to Natalis. "There will be aurea waiting for you for your efforts upon your return."

"Most generous," mumbled Natalis as he took it.

"I shall expect you before the sun has been up for two hours."

"I will be here," said Natalis. "Or I will be in prison."

Sanct-Franciscus gave a crack of laughter. "Then I will send out slaves to pay your fines, if you are."

Rugeri glanced around the room. "Do you want him to leave from here; from this room?"

"Certainly," said Sanct-Franciscus, indicating a closet on the far side of the chamber. "Use those stairs. They will bring you out behind the stable, away from the Temple of Hercules and facing the alley to the Via Castrum." He saw the surprise on Natalis' face. "You did not know about this staircase?"

"No." Natalis seemed a bit ashamed of this lapse.

Sanct-Franciscus used a key to open the closet door. "Rugeri will be here to unlock the door if I am not," he said, stepping aside for Natalis. "The lower door will be left open until the third hour after sunrise, and then I will lock it."

"I understand," said Natalis, slipping the vellum into his wallet. "I will strive to do as you wish. The note is for your scribe, who is named Deomadus. I may remain at the villa so long as I am hidden, at least until the hour before dawn."

"Precisely," said Sanct-Franciscus. "Now you must be about your errand, and I must return to my . . . guests." As he closed the door behind Natalis, Rugeri folded his arms. "What is it? You do not trust him?"

"Do you?" Rugeri countered.

"We shall see," said Sanct-Franciscus, making for the door and the gallery beyond.

"That we will," said Rugeri as he picked up the laena and returned it to its peg on the wall.

Text of a letter from Melidulci at Misenum to Ragoczy Germainus Sanct-Franciscus in Roma; carried by private courier.

To my most worthy and esteemed Patron, the honestiorus Ragoczy Germainus Sanct-Franciscus, the greetings of Melidulci from Misenum and the Villa Solea, on the north side of the town, a thousand paces from the Via Appia,

This is to tell you that I have found my home, and I should be content to remain here for the rest of my days. This estate is small— five hundred paces on a side—and producing grapes, fruits, olives, and greens, as well as grazing cattle and goats. I have five horses, a pair of mules, and a donkey, fourteen slaves, and three freemen to handle market-days for me. The setting is private, but not so remote that I might as well be in Germania Inferior. My house has ten rooms, a large kitchen-and-bake-house, a bath and a building-shed. There are two springs on the property, so water is not a problem, and the fields are drained by ditches that carry the water and offal to the sea. All in all, it is everything I could wish for, and I thank you for the loan of the money to buy it. As my fields bear fruit I will re-pay you on the terms you agreed to, for I cannot accept such an ex-travagant gift from you, not and hold my head up.

If ever you should want to visit me here, I would welcome you. I know you must have many invitations, and many must be more wor-thy than mine, but none, I assure you, is more sincere than this one, and for that reason alone, I hope you will one day permit me to offer you the same hospitality you extended to me in those hard days in Roma. We have had such pleasant moments together, we may still have one or two more, to enrich our memories.

Fortunately, I have found a scribe—a freedman, and therefore a citizen—a sensible fellow from Brundisium, who is called Lars, for the Etruscan from whom he claims descent. He has been educated in Greek as well as Latin, in keeping accounts and making records, so I will have nothing to fear from the decuriae when it is time to pay my taxes, or to deal with the officials of the region. This Lars is clean-faced and steady of gaze, of modest demeanor without being sub-servient, but he is somewhat short-sighted, which, in spite of spectacles, has inclined him to scholarly pursuits rather than a more active life. You may write to me in confidence, knowing that Lars will reveal nothing of my business to anyone.

I will never forget all you have done for me, and I will always think myself fortunate to have been afforded your good opinion when others were excoriating me for debauchery. You are most as-suredly more entitled to the honor of Romans than most Romans are.

On this, the 13th day of October in the 972nd Year of the City, and with my heart-felt gratitude,

Melidulci

by the hand of Lars, freedman and citizen of Roma

7

At the eastern end of the garden of the Villa Laelius stood the ten-year-old spring house, where water from the extension of the aqueduct to the Baths of Caracalla had been channeled to a handful of private houses for scandalous amounts that helped to pay for the construction of the monumental baths a decade ago. There was a fountain with three large, graduated stone bowls in its center, topped by a statue of the garden god, and beneath it all, a drain that funneled the water to various parts of the house. Four doors gave easy access to the fountain, with benches around the colonnade, and three couches for private dining; the walls were decorated with murals of Vertumnus and Pomona, with small panels dedicated to other numina. At the time it was built, it had been the envy of all the neighbors, but now most of the other houses got their water from new extensions of the Virgo Aqueduct, and this spring house was no longer begrudged the Villa Laelius.

Sunset was fading into twilight on this last night of October when Sanct-Franciscus arrived on foot, unseen and unannounced, at the Villa Laelius; he made his way to the garden, as silent as a shadow and as graceful. His simple black Persian chandys and black bracae lent their darkness to the coming night, hiding him from all but the most determined and alert spies. After climbing the wall, he took time to make sure the grounds were empty, then went toward the spring house, his senses attuned to the night, to the odor of wood-smoke and broiling pork from the kitchen, and the sweet-sour aroma of rotting summer fruit. The whisper of fallen leaves blowing along the gravel path accompanied him; from beyond the walls came the steady clamor of the end of market-day.

Two of the doors of the spring house were open—the north and the west ones, facing away from the main house and the stables—and the flickering light of an oil-lamp shone within the single, vaulted chamber, touching the falling water as if to turn it to bits of gold, and illuminating Ignatia, seated on the farthest couch, her plum-colored mafortium raised as if to conceal her face. She held a small book cut on broad wood-shavings in her hands, but gave no sign of reading anything written on it. At the soft sound of his peri on the marble floor, she looked up in the direction of the oil-lamp.

"Ignatia," he said as he stepped next to the fountain; the water running under the floor was a slight distraction, but his native earth in his soles prevented any serious discomfort.

She sighed at the sound of his voice, and turned toward him. "Sanct-Franciscus," she said, as if to reassure herself he was real, and not a figment of her inflamed imagination. "I was afraid you . . . wouldn't come."

He felt her hesitation struggle with her desire; two centuries ago he would have used her ambivalence to persuade her to accept him; now, he remained where he was, allowing her to reach her decision on her own. "Would you prefer I had not."

"No," she said, apparently unaware of the forlorn note in her voice. She rose and took a faltering step toward him. "If you hadn't come, I'd . . . I'd know."

"Know what, Ignatia?" He closed the distance between them, but did not touch her yet.

"That my mother was right, and that you come here because of your devotion to her; you would have no interest in me." She gave a startled blink to hear herself admit so much.

"I am her physician: I feel sympathy for her, and I have an obligation to treat her illness to the limit of my skills, but"—he took her hands in his—"were Domina Adicia not here, I would still want to be with you, to—"

Ignatia pulled one hand free and pressed her fingers to his lips. "You don't have to say that." She pulled her hand back, as if even such a minor touch as that was too personal for her.

"Why?" he asked as he took her hand again.

"Because it might not be so," she confessed, staring down at the rim of the lowest and largest bowl of the fountain.

He lifted their joined hands. His enigmatic eyes were too intense for her to meet with her own. "Do you think I would lie to you?"

"Men lie to women," she said.

"But do you think I lie to you, Ignatia?" There was no rancor in the question, no suggestion of umbrage or accusation.

She shook her head but would not look at him. "I'm scared," she whispered.

"If you are afraid of me, send me away." He felt her hands tighten in his. "If you are not afraid of me, nor think me mendacious, what *do* you fear?"

Finally she lifted her eyes to him; in the lamplight they were more green than blue. "I may want you too much."

"What is too much?"

The question startled her. "More than dignity approves," she said slowly, repeating the lessons of her childhood.

"And if you do, what then?" He waited for her answer.

"I don't know," she said in an under-voice.

"Would you rather not find out?" he asked as he released her hands.

She grabbed for him, seizing his left hand in both of hers. "No!"

"What, then?"

Lifting his hand to her face inside the circle of her mafortium, she stared over his shoulder. "I want to know—so much."

"But it vexes you to want so much," he said softly, thinking back to the first time he had met Olivia, and the fear she had shown. When Ignatia nodded, he went on. "You have denied your longing for so many years that now you wonder if you have dammed a flood in your heart, and it may drown you if you release it."

She uttered a little gasp. "You know! How can you know that?"

"It is in everything you do," said Sanct-Franciscus simply, opening his hand against her cheek; she started to turn away again, but this time he held her face gently, but with such strength that she was startled by it. "You want to know what is within you, and you are frightened of what it might be."

Astonished, she said, "Yes."

"But the desire to know is greater than your fear," he said, his voice low and compelling.

"Yes," she said, a bit uncertainly. "I want to know."

"As do I," he told her just above a whisper.

For a long moment they stood together in the wavering lamp-light, then Ignatia shivered and leaned her head against his shoulder. "You must think me a foolish woman."

"No, I think you an undiscovered woman," he corrected her in a voice that touched her soul as surely as his hand caressed her face.

"Undiscovered," she repeated. "Yes."

He eased his arms around her, supporting her against him, lending her his strength while she battled within herself to overcome her fears. "What would you like to explore first?" he asked quietly as he felt the strain go out of her body.

"I don't know," she said. "Something pleasant." She averted her face.

"Would you like me to massage your hands?" he offered.

She was startled enough to look at him. "What? Massage my hands? Why?"

"Because it is something pleasant," he answered calmly. "And, if it satisfies you, it will lead to other things."

Ignatia had been told all her life how hasty men were in sexual matters, so she was doubly surprised by his proffering. "You are going to postpone your pleasure for—"

"I postpone nothing. I have no pleasure but what you have," he said. "What fulfills you is my fulfillment as well."

Amazed, she stared at him, attempting to read his face, searching for any trace of dissimulation. "But you will have your spasm, and your release."

"Only if you do," he said as he untied her mafortium and removed it, revealing her hair, shining like turned brass in the lamp-light. "I am not like other men: my culmination comes from you. If you have no gratification, I have none. What you experience, I experience, no more and no less." He worked the tibia holding the brooch that closed the neck of her paenula; beneath it he saw her stola in soft, sea-blue cotton and her palla of blue-gray linen. "Will you be warm enough without your paenula?"

"If I am cold, we can use it as a cover," she said, shocked at her own audacity.

"Then I will spread it on the longest couch," he said, and swung the cloak off her shoulders and tossed it onto the couch.

"We can hide under it," she said, a little of her temerity fading.

"What do we have to hide from?" He took a step toward the couch, sinking down onto the end of it, and holding out his hands to her. "We are alone here."

"There are spies in the household," she said.

"But why should they follow you into the garden? What might you do here that would concern him—or anyone? It is not as if you are parading in the lupanar, is it?" he asked sensibly. "Are there not other interests to occupy them, such as your brother's activities?"

Ignatia shook her head. "My brother is out, going with his friends to 'light the fires of faith' he says. He won't be back until later unless the Watch sends him home." She paused, choosing her words carefully. "His devotion to his religion has led him to do all manner of roguery. I think he and his friends use their righteousness as an excuse for mischief." She glanced toward the open doors, as if worried he might overhear her.

"Do you think he would watch you if he were here?" Sanct-Franciscus asked.

"He might. He is constantly troubled about sin in the house. And he might set the slaves to watching for him while he's gone."

"You think you might be observed here, in your own garden, inside your own walls, at your brother's instigation?" He could feel her tension increase again as he inquired.

"I think it's possible," she said slowly, as if testing the words before speaking them.

"But why?" he asked, aware of her increasing dismay. "Why would he do it, and why would it be tolerated?"

"Because I have nothing to myself," she burst out sharply, then stared at him, aghast. "I've never said that before."

"The pity of it is that you would have to say it at all," he told her with a world of compassion in his eyes. He wrapped his arm around her shoulder. "I would it were otherwise—that you had your own assurance."

"How can I?" she asked, completely shaken by her own candor. "Where can I find it: can you tell me?"

He turned her head so he could look directly into her eyes. "You have it within you, and you can claim it for yourself."

"How?" The word hung like a barrier between them. "I want so much, and I know it will be taken from me." She put her hands on his shoulders. "If you give me what I seek, I will lose you, too."

"Only if that is what you want," he said, the kindness in his expression making the breath catch in her throat.

"Why do you want me?" she asked suddenly as his nearness became more immediate to her.

"Because you are Ignatia: that is the only reason."

Emotions that had been pent up within her for years threatened to overcome her. She pushed him back. "That is—that is more than I—" She broke off, but in the next breath she clung to him, her arms around his neck, quivering .

"Would you prefer to postpone this?" he asked gently as she grew still.

She considered this briefly. "If I say no now, I might never have courage enough to ask you again. I want you to stay. Here. With me."

"Then I will," he said, taking her hand once more, and bringing the palm to his lips.

It was as if she had been burned by a sweet flame; the sensation of his kiss rioted up her arm. Before she could stop herself, she flung herself down on the couch, her paenula spread beneath her. Reaching up to loosen her hair, she summoned the courage to say, "Whatever you want of me, I give it to you freely."

"It must be what *you* want," said Sanct-Franciscus, kneeling beside the couch and leaning forward to kiss the arch of her brow.

"That is, as you said, undiscovered," she said with an attempt at flirtatiousness. "A search may be needed."

"Then tell me what you would like to try, and I will do what I can to provide it," he said, and kissed the tail of her eye, then moved down her cheek. His lips were lingering and light, enticing in their unpressured perusal of her face. By the time his mouth reached hers, her breath was quickening, and as they broke apart, she caught her fingers in the dark waves of his hair.

"I like . . . that," she said, pulling him down to her kiss. Slowly, deliberately, joyously, she began to remove her clothes, letting them fall in a heap beside the couch. When she was down to her under-garments, she gave him a challenging look. "You do these," she said, reveling in her excitement and wanting to prolong it.

"What would you want me to do?"

"Something wonderful," she said.

He did his best not to smile. "What would be wonderful?"

This time she considered her answer. "Liberation," she said finally.

"So be it." On his knees, Sanct-Franciscus swung her around so that her back was to him and he could reach the end of the fas-cae that supported her breasts; he loosened the end and slid his hands around to take the place of the bias-cut linen, letting the weight of her breasts shape his hands to their contours, his fingers moving gently to summon the unfamiliar sensations she sought; as her passion awakened fully, her flesh grew damp in spite of the cool evening air. Rising slowly, he sat behind her on the couch, straddling it, letting her head fall back against his neck. "What more?"

"Keep doing . . . keep doing," she urged, her eyes half-closed.

He caught her nipples between his fingers, rubbing gently until they stiffened and she sighed. Then he extended his caresses down her body, along the curve of her waist and hip, then to her mani, and to the laces that held it in place. These were easily untied, but Sanct-Franciscus took his time about undoing the loop-knots, his fingers evoking sensations that left her lightheaded. "Shall I do more?" he whispered to the splendid tangles of her hair.

"Yes," she answered, her face flushed.

"As you wish," he said, bending to kiss where her shoulder and neck joined even as he pulled her mani free of her hips, and slipped his hand between her legs.

"O, Vertumnus, Pomona, my thanks," she murmured as the magic of his touch began to radiate along her veins to the limits of her flesh. Her body seemed unfamiliar now, as if it had transformed through the rapture that was filling her, displacing worry and pride and loneliness. Her breath quickened and suddenly, as Sanct-Franciscus' hands continued to stroke and search into her, to the very core of her body, a jolt went through her, so unexpected that she gasped. Then another, stronger impulse coursed from the center of her pleasure, and another; she shook with the force of her ecstasy, jubilant in the torrent of transports that flooded through her while she pressed back against him, aware of nothing but the intensity of her exaltation and his nearness. As her exaltation faded, she sank back against him, her breathing slowing and deepening, her skin still so sensitive that she was surprised it was not lambent.

"Did you—"

"Oh, yes."

"—feel that?"

His laughter was soft and low, like a purr. "As you did." He lifted her without effort, shifted his balance, and turned her to face him, her thighs atop his own, their faces hardly more than a finger-joint apart.

"How could you? You didn't penetrate me with anything but your fingers," she said, wonder in her countenance.

"My satisfaction comes from your own," he reminded her, touching the soft tendrils of hair that clung to her shining face; he could hardly see the two small spots of blood on her throat.

"But men . . . don't they . . . ?" She stopped. "I'm not complaining," she said hurriedly.

"I did not suppose you were," he said with a slight smile.

She put her arms around him and pulled herself close to him. "I wish I could brand you onto my skin, so I could never forget this."

He shook his head. "No, Ignatia—I would never want you harmed, particularly not on my account."

"But that brand wouldn't hurt me," she said, leaning back so that her breasts rose like offerings to him.

He held her with one arm, drawing her up to him, giving her long, light, slow strokes down her back. "Still."

"All right, nothing so . . . drastic as . . . a brand," she said, kissing his face with random enthusiasm.

"I thank you for that," he said, an uncomfortable memory of Hesentaton, burned and blind, fretted at him; he gave his full attention to Ignatia and the vision of Hesentaton faded.

She pulled back from him for a brief moment, tossing her head and laughing. "You asked me what I wanted, and you gave it to me, even though I didn't know what it was. I have never had so fine a gift."

"It was one you gave yourself," he said.

"No," she countered, meeting his gaze squarely. "Without you, I would not have reached so sweet a touching." She blinked, and wiped the tears that slid down her cheeks, tears she had not known were there. Slowly and deliberately she kissed him.

He answered her kiss, feeling her ardor flare again, and awakened to her desire, he began once again to rouse her with tantalizing caresses, followed by the teasing progress of his lips from her mouth to her neck to her shoulder to her breasts, unhurried, luxurious, and sublime.

She lay back, her shoulders on his knees, saying, "My bones are melting, and the air is shaking," as she surrendered to his ministrations, welcoming the gathering of passion she felt deep within her, hoping she would have another culmination as intense as the first had been.

"Sin!" came the angry shout from the southern door of the spring house.

Confusion and fear slammed through Ignatia. She grabbed Sanct-Franciscus' hands, but only to thrust them away as she turned on his lap to see her brother blocking the open door, his arms on the frame as if to close them in, despite the second open door. "Octavian," she said, reaching for the pile of her clothes and struggling to get off Sanct-Franciscus' legs.

"You have betrayed our honor!" Octavian declared, relishing his indignation.

"Oh, no," Ignatia muttered, appearing to sink into herself as she attempted to cover herself with her tangled garments.

"Do not be more of a fool than you are," Sanct-Franciscus said to the young man, unimpressed with his righteous posturing.

"This is appalling," said Octavian. "Sin and debauchery in this house!"

Sanct-Franciscus helped Ignatia to stand without rising himself. "Neither sin nor debauchery." He gestured to his own clothes.

"You disgrace us!" Octavian took an angry step forward, bringing his arms into a fighting position. "You bring your corruption within our—"

"I assure you, I do not," said Sanct-Franciscus calmly; he held out his hand to Ignatia, to help her sort out her stola and palla from her undergarments.

"I will denounce you!" Octavian proclaimed.

"That will harm your sister more than me," Sanct-Franciscus pointed out. "Or is that your intention?"

"Both of you, be quiet," said Ignatia as she bent over to secure her fascae.

"It is my duty to protect her," said Octavian, his chin rising, and paying no attention to his sister's request.

"On that we are agreed," said Sanct-Franciscus, rising and assisting Ignatia to dress.

"You have disgraced her," Octavian insisted, scowling when Ignatia began, very softly, to cry.

"I have done nothing that would," said Sanct-Franciscus, feeling weary.

"My mother will not think so," said Octavian, craftiness and something meaner showing in the line of his mouth.

"Don't tell her! Octavian—*please!*" Ignatia exclaimed as she pulled her stola over her head.

"I must," said Octavian with unctuous satisfaction.

"No, you must not," said Sanct-Franciscus firmly. "For her sake as much as your sister's. Your mother has no strength, and a shock could be bad for her."

"You recall this now, do you?" Octavian challenged. "And you, a physician!"

"Octavian, stop it!" Ignatia said, recovering her composure as she dressed. "I asked Sanct-Franciscus to come here. He obliged me."

"To ravish you," said Octavian with an expression that bordered on smugness.

"If that was his intention," said Ignatia, stung, "he did it beyond my best hopes." She started toward the door. "How did you know we were here?"

"I told Benona to watch you, and to send me word if anything untoward should occur," said Octavian with a triumphant smile.

"And what right did you have to do that?" Ignatia asked, then turned to Sanct-Franciscus. "You have done nothing to deserve this . . . this castigation from my brother, and I apologize for his bad conduct." She started toward the door. "I will see that my mother is not distressed by any rumors or other accounts."

Sanct-Franciscus managed a wry smile. "I thank you most sincerely, Doma Ignatia."

"Doma Ignatia?" Octavian mocked. "And you rutting like pigs."

Ignatia stopped on her march out of the spring house. "Rut? We most certainly did not rut. Sanct-Franciscus did nothing to compromise my virginity, if that is what you fear. He gave me pleasure because I asked him." She pointed directly at her brother. "Do not dare to accuse him of anything but what you might see at any convivium throughout Roma."

"Or worse; convivia are cesspools of sin," Octavian muttered, his momentum lost. "They are ignominy for all Romans."

"By your lights, perhaps," said Ignatia. "They are approved by the Emperor and the Vestal Virgins, and that is sufficient for me." With that, she snatched up her paenula and mafortium, dragged the paenula around her, and left the spring house by the north door, swinging it closed behind her.

Octavian, nonplussed, stared at Sanct-Franciscus. "You will not boast of this. My sister's reputation—"

"I have too much regard for Doma Ignatia to compromise her," said Sanct-Franciscus, adding with obvious meaning, "If her name is smirched, it will not be by me."

"For now, and only for my mother's sake, I will say nothing," Octavian grumbled. "But if I think there is any repetition of this shameful—"

"For your mother's sake," Sanct-Franciscus interrupted, "I thank you."

"Thanks from one who has trespassed means little." Octavian clicked his tongue and folded his arms. "I will be watching you."

Sanct-Franciscus gave a single chuckle. "You will not, I fear, be alone."

Text of a letter from Fulvius Ennius Castrum of the Forum Guard to Ragoczy Germainus Sanct-Franciscus, carried by private messenger.

To the foreign honestiorus R. G. Sanct-Franciscus, the greetings of the Forum Guard Captain Fulvius Ennius Castrum, in the hope that the honestiorus remembers me from our meeting upon the occasion of the arrest of the injured thief, Natalis of Thessalonika,

You have been most laudable in employing the said Natalis, for it has made it unnecessary for him to return to thievery. However, he has not wholly abandoned his ways, for I have recently discovered that the said Natalis has been accepting money from the decuria Telemachus Batsho for regular reports on your activities. Since it is a worthy thing for slaves to report wrong-doings on the part of their masters, and for freedmen and freemen, as citizens, to denounce crimes, I would not condemn this Natalis, but I fear it may be that your probity is being abused by his actions and reports and that inclines me to alert you to what is going on.

I hope that I am not doing a disservice to the Empire in providing you this alert, but I am convinced that you deserve to know what is being done by one who owes you his freedom and his livelihood. By Mars and Jupiter, I ask you to not betray my role in this, for that could be seen as reason to demote me. Only my strong conviction that you are the one being exploited in this matter has compelled me to inform you of what is happening.

Ave, Heliogabalus.

Fulvius Ennius Castrum
Captain, Guard of the Forum Agricolarum

by the hand of Eudoxus the scribe on the 11th day of November, in the 972nd Year of the City

8

Rugeri closed the study door quietly, but remained squarely in front of it as Natalis approached Sanct-Franciscus, who was standing beside the trestle table, sorting jars and vials in his leather medicament-case, his long-sleeved dalmatica augmented by a lacerna, as most of the household wore on sere days like this one. "My master," he said to catch Sanct-Franciscus' attention. "Natalis is here."

A slow, dreary rain was falling on Roma, so the alabaster window-panes were in place and the brazier in the corner was burning a stack of fragrant wood to add to the warmth from the floor. Five oil-lamps were lit, although it was only mid-afternoon, and their light shone on the table where Sanct-Franciscus was working. "Thank you, Rugeri," he said as he carefully closed the lid on a chalcedony jar filled with an ointment of foxglove, then gave Natalis his full attention. "Have you any notion why I asked you to come here?" he began, his demeanor carefully neutral.

Natalis hitched up his shoulder. "You have a message or some item you want taken somewhere without being noticed; I am ready to do as you order, rain or no rain," he said, but his flickering eyes revealed his apprehension. His pallium was new, made of slate-blue wool, and decorated at the hem with a band of dust-colored heavy cotton; the bracae he wore beneath were made of tan cotton, and his peri were bronze-colored leather. On the street on such a day as this, his garments would render him invisible as much as his skills as a thief.

"Not just now, I think," said Sanct-Franciscus, coming away from the table. He looked over at Rugeri. "Will the hot wine be brought shortly?"

"It will," said Rugeri.

Natalis cocked his head. "You want wine?"

"No, Natalis; you do." Sanct-Franciscus drew up a chair to the low table in the center of the room and indicated the chair opposite. "Do sit down. There is something we must talk about."

"That sounds ominous," said Natalis with a shaky chuckle as he dropped into the chair.

"Does it?" Sanct-Franciscus very nearly smiled at that. "Well, we shall see."

"I'm a bit puzzled why you want to see me, because you haven't sent for me this way before," Natalis said, ending on a note of uncertainty.

"No, I have not," Sanct-Franciscus concurred.

"I . . . I am honored that you've called me here," Natalis went on, trying to cover his growing edginess with talk. "I was thinking just this morning how what seemed to be my least fortunate day— the day I was caught in the Forum Agricolarum—became one of the most fortunate of my life. You have been most generous to me since you took me into your household: three new garments in seven months—truly beneficent of you, and I not a slave, but your servant."

"Thank you," said Sanct-Franciscus, maintaining his unnerving reserve.

"Do you have another assignment for me?" Natalis glanced at Rugeri. "Your manservant wouldn't tell me."

"I suppose you may think of this as an assignment," said Sanct-Franciscus slowly.

"Then I will ready my pluvial and be off as soon as you—"

"Your assignment today need not expose you to the weather,"

said Sanct-Franciscus tranquilly. "It is to tell me the truth. We did agree you would do that, did we not?"

Natalis went silent, his eyes moving more frantically, as if searching for a means of escape. "Certainly. Of course. The truth about what?"

"About whomever has employed you," said Sanct-Franciscus, his self-containment unimpaired.

"I work for you," said Natalis, the pitch of his voice rising.

"I certainly pay you for doing that, and you have executed your missions for me satisfactorily," Sanct-Franciscus said in the same steady voice. "But I have reason to believe that you are also accepting money from another employer, who has engaged you to report on me, someone who seeks to know more of me than I am required to tell." He looked directly at Natalis. "Is that so?"

Natalis bleated out something that might have been a laugh. "No. No. Of course no. Why would I do anything that might be against you?"

"Those are questions I have asked myself," said Sanct-Franciscus. "You must understand that I am eager to know the answers."

"I do understand," said Natalis, almost leaping out of his chair at the tap on the door.

Rugeri turned and opened the door, and took the tray Aedius held, exchanged a few words with him, and closed the door. "The kitchen sends word that the evening meal will be delayed by an hour. The breads aren't rising properly—it's the rain." He put the tray on the low table, pointing out its contents. "Hot wine in an earthenware jug, a cup, and fried cheese with bitter herbs on a plate." With a nod, he went back to the door.

"Excellent," said Sanct-Franciscus, leaning forward to fill the cup with the steaming wine, deep-red in color and smelling of spices. "You will like this, I know," he said to Natalis.

"But—"

Sanct-Franciscus held out the cup. "Drink it." Natalis took a deep sip, then started to put it down. "All of it."

"All?" Natalis asked, hesitating.

"All of it. The room is chilly, and the wine will warm you." He sat expectantly. "If you fear you might become fuddled, have some of the cheese."

Natalis stared at the cup as if he expected it to burst into flame. "I . . . I don't—"

"Drink it," Sanct-Franciscus said again, firmly but affably.

"You don't drink," Natalis said. "It is not proper that a servant should drink and the master abstain."

"You and the rest of the household know that I never—" Sanct-Franciscus reminded him, only to be interrupted by Rugeri.

"You will drink."

"All right!" Natalis hurriedly gulped down the wine, and then glared at Sanct-Franciscus. "I have drunk. How long before I die?" He set the cup on the tray, staring at it with dismay.

"That is up to you and your gods; it has nothing to do with me." Sanct-Franciscus laughed once and shook his head. "Oh, no, Natalis. You have not consumed poison. Had I wanted to be rid of you, I have other methods at my disposal not nearly so clumsy as poison."

Natalis looked shocked. "Then why insist I drink?"

"So you will not behave liked a trapped rabbit," said Sanct-Franciscus, suddenly brusque; then he softened his tone. "If you were any more jittery, you would shake your chair to flinders."

"Well, and so would you," said Natalis, summoning up the courage to bluster. "To be brought up here like a shamed apprentice, and be accused of disloyalty, then made to drink— What would you think, in my position?"

"I would think my errors in judgment had been discovered, and that would trouble me," said Sanct-Franciscus, once again calm. "Which is what I want to know: what are your errors in judgment, Natalis? I will not yet call what you have done disloyalty, but if you withhold anything"—he paused to refill the cup—"then I may have to consider that you have an inclination to—"

Natalis stared at the cup. "Not more wine?"

"If you please," said Sanct-Franciscus, handing the cup back to him.

This time Natalis made no protest, but quickly drank the contents of the cup, set it back on the tray and reached for a cube of the fried cheese, wolfing it down, then licking his fingers as he said, "Whatever it is you want to find out, you don't have to do it this way."

"There is truth in wine," said Sanct-Franciscus, watching as Natalis took a second cube of cheese. "When I say you will tell me the truth, I want it to be as bare as possible."

"Bare?" Natalis appeared baffled.

"Without modifications that might color its meaning," said Sanct-Franciscus. "Have another bite of cheese if you feel the wine too much."

Natalis took two cubes of cheese and stared at them, as if noticing the flakes of herbs for the first time. "What is in this?"

"Bitter herbs, I believe, such as are served with eggplant and asparagus, and with poached eggs," said Sanct-Franciscus with great unconcern. "The cheeses are fried in oil-with-garlic, from their aroma."

Almost defiantly, Natalis consumed them, then said, "I suppose you want me to drink more wine?"

"If you would," said Sanct-Franciscus, filling Natalis' cup a third time.

"Much more of this, and I won't be able to give you much of an answer at all," Natalis warned before he downed the contents of the cup; two bright spots were forming in his cheeks, as if he were suffering from a fever. He coughed once, and did his best to focus on Sanct-Franciscus' face. "Now what?"

"To whom do you report, and what do you tell him?" Sanct-Franciscus asked with civility.

"It's not that I wanted to," said Natalis, his words slurring a little. "I told him I didn't want to do it."

"So you were compelled," said Sanct-Franciscus. "Why and how, if you would."

"He said he would find out if I said anything to you, and he would have me arrested by the Urban Guard." Natalis squirmed in his chair.

"That only means he has other spies in my household. He will learn nothing of this from me or from Rugeri," Sanct-Franciscus assured him. "Tell me who it was who could so impose on you."

"An official, not one of high rank, spoke to me." He closed his eyes as if trying to recapture the moment in his thoughts. "How could I refuse to talk with such a man?"

"I would think you would have to oblige him, at least to hear him out," said Sanct-Franciscus. "Who was this official?"

"I was approached by a decuria—Telemachus Batsho—who said he would have me condemned to a road gang for theft if I didn't agree to report to him." He stopped, aghast at what he heard himself say.

"Ah," said Sanct-Franciscus. "And I gather he ordered you to tell me nothing."

"Yes," said Natalis, almost panting with relief at this confession.

"When did this happen?" Sanct-Franciscus asked. "When did he suborn your loyalty?"

Natalis winced, then summoned up his determination. "I will tell you the whole of it. I might as well, now." He drank the last of the wine in his cup, and continued on. "It was in July. I was returning from Ostia, with reports from your captains, and account-books. When I reached the Porta Ostiensis, the Watch detained me, they said because they had to verify the account-books; I don't know why, but I couldn't refuse the Watch, could I? If they want to look at anything being brought into the city, they have the right to do so."

"So they do. Protesting would have served only to arouse their suspicions," Sanct-Franciscus confirmed. "Continue, Natalis."

He took a deep breath, watching Sanct-Franciscus as he spoke. "While I was waiting for them to release the records, in that small chamber next to the Guard-station—you know the one?" At Sanct-Franciscus' nod, he went on. "I was sitting alone there, waiting, as I said, when this fellow Batsho approaches me, and tells me that I could be in great trouble, and so could you, if the accounts were found to be faulty."

"Why should that accrue to your discredit: you were acting as a messenger only," said Sanct-Franciscus, thinking back to the two acolytes in Persia, and their efforts, with Srau's help, in undermining of his business dealings, and then to the official in Athens—Hyres— who had found an excuse to levy double taxes on all his property as a result of slaves' gossip.

"But I am known as a thief." This cry was compounded of frustration and distress.

"You have no brand on your arm or your forehead, so his accusation would need proof, which those records would not provide him," Sanct-Franciscus observed.

"No, I am not branded, for which I offer wine in thanks to the Parcae every day. My fate would have been much changed had I ever been branded." As if the idea itself overwhelmed him, he slumped back in his chair, one hand flopping on the arm, the other reaching ineffectively for the last of the cheese.

Sanct-Franciscus picked up the plate and held it out to him. "How did he say he could do this?"

Natalis rubbed his lips together, trying to decide how to answer. "He said—He claimed he had records of other thefts I had committed, and that he would bring these before the Prefect to determine what punishment should be meted out." He took another cube of cheese, holding it between his fingers as if it were a die.

"That would seem to be a bit . . . unreasonable," said Sanct-Franciscus. "Have you been taken before a Prefect in the past?" He put the plate back down and poured the last of the wine in the jug into Natalis' cup.

"Not for years. When I was caught once, six years ago, I convinced the Prefect that there had been a mistake—that my companion had taken the items in question, and since no one found any of the . . . objects in my wallet, it was assumed I hadn't taken anything."

"But you had," said Sanct-Franciscus, pouring another measure of wine into Natalis' cup.

"I had, and passed them to my cousin. Nyssa attracted no attention from the Guard." He sobbed once, suddenly. "I miss her."

"Your cousin must have been a great help to you," said Sanct-Franciscus.

"Until the last two years, when her hands became knotted with age, she was the finest help I could have asked for," said Natalis with earnest pride and slurred words.

"And you continued to provide for her, when she could no longer help you," said Sanct-Franciscus. "Commendable."

"Until you found work for her," said Natalis, and swallowed hard. "And you arranged for an honorable burial for her." His hands gathered and his face contorted in grief and self-loathing. "I know I should have come to you at once. You have been a most upright employer, and my dealing with the decuria is shabby, I know. I know." He bit into the cheese as if to force himself to stop talking.

Sanct-Franciscus held out the cup to him. "This will make it easier."

Natalis took the cup with both hands, and drank. He sighed as he put the cup back on the tray. "Empty."

"So I see," said Sanct-Franciscus.

Natalis stared at the far wall, his eyes glazed, his features slack. Finally he looked over at Sanct-Franciscus. "I suppose you'll be rid of me now."

"No—unless you want to go," said Sanct-Franciscus.

"I don't," said Natalis, his manner at once more animated. "I want to stay here, in your service."

"Then you shall remain," said Sanct-Franciscus. "But instead of doing the bidding of the decuria, you will do mine."

Natalis sat up. "How do you mean?"

"I mean," said Sanct-Franciscus patiently, "that whenever Batsho makes a request of you, you will inform me of it—privately, of course—and you will follow my instructions, not his."

"But if he finds out—" Natalis said in a new rush of fear.

"He has other spies in this household: I know," said Sanct-Franciscus. "I think you will find I am able to deal with them so long as you are forthright with me."

Natalis was far from comfortable, but he tried to put on the appearance of satisfaction. "I think it will be satisfying to catch this bird in his own net." He belched and tried to cover his mouth with his hand.

"Yes; so do I," said Sanct-Franciscus, getting to his feet again, and motioning to Rugeri to approach as he addressed Natalis. "You have told me what I want to know, and for that I am grateful. But I warn you now that if you continue to compromise my interests, you will be cast out into the street." He saw Natalis blanch and went on more cordially. "You will want to rest a while now, I presume, so Rugeri will assist you back to your quarters. You will not be disturbed until you rise of your own accord." He stepped back so Rugeri could assist Natalis out of the chair. "Once he has lain down, come back and you and I will consider how to proceed."

"Yes, my master," said Rugeri as he tugged Natalis to his feet, supporting him with his shoulder.

"Tell me what more you learn from him," Sanct-Franciscus said as Rugeri maneuvered Natalis toward the door.

"I doubt there will be much to learn the rest of this day, or evening," said Rugeri as he reached for the latch on the door.

"Probably not," said Sanct-Franciscus as he watched Rugeri get Natalis out the door, then he crossed the room to close it behind them. Left by himself, he went to the brazier and added more wood to the wedges already burning in it; he noticed that the smoke was beginning to dull the painting on the ceiling, and decided he would put the chamber-slaves to cleaning it as soon as the rain ended. Returning to his trestle table, he set his case of medicaments on the end of the table, then took one of the fan-folded sheets of vellum from the pigeon-holes above the table and spread it open, studying its contents with careful attention. He was still going over household records when Rugeri tapped twice and stepped into the room.

"He will sleep for many hours," said Rugeri as he entered the study, taking care to check the corridor before closing the door.

"With what he consumed, I would suppose so," said Sanct-Franciscus, turning from his work.

"What was in the wine?" Rugeri inquired.

"Spices; anything more would have lacked finesse. There were herbs in the cheese that promoted a loose tongue along with a sense of repose, and will let him sleep deeply." He gave Rugeri a contemplative stare. "What do you make of this predicament, my friend?"

Rugeri weighed his response. "Assuming he was truthful, I have to say that it appears Batsho has decided to make an example of you."

"An example of what, though?" Sanct-Franciscus asked of the folded sheets on the table before him.

"A foreigner with money," said Rugeri succinctly.

"There are other foreigners with money in Roma," Sanct-Franciscus reminded Rugeri. "Why choose me, when Solon Monandos has far more money than I, and displays it far more freely?"

"Batsho may feel kinship with Greeks like Monandos," Rugeri suggested.

"Batsho is from Illyricum, hardly a region known for liking its neighbors, particularly the Greeks," said Sanct-Franciscus, thinking back to the centuries of skirmishes along the edge of the Balkans, Greeks to the south of the mountains, Illyricani to the west.

Rugeri shook his head. "You mistake my intention: you are from Dacia but not a Daci. That means you have few defenders in Roma, and may be abused with impunity."

Sanct-Franciscus laughed sardonically. "Rogerian, you have not lost your clarity of insight, nor your directness of speech." He began to put the scrolls back in their pigeon-holes. "I think," he went on in the tongue of Alexandria, "that we would be wise to step up our plans. I had thought I could remain here for another three or four years, but now I think a year-and-a-half is a more reasonable prognosis."

"As you say," Rugeri seconded. "But what of Domina Clemens? This is her house, and if you leave, she may find it confiscated."

"So she might, if it is empty. I must make it my business to see that she has an occupant for it, and a good return on their presence." He folded his hands. "I don't want this to end badly."

"No," said Rugeri. "But that may be out of your hands, my master. This Batsho is determined to make his reputation on your fall."

"It appears so," Sanct-Franciscus said, and added, "I wish I knew what his next move will be."

"No doubt he wishes the same about you," said Rugeri.

"Hence the spies in my household," Sanct-Franciscus agreed,

and went back to speaking the Latin of the time. "He has set his gaze on me, and will not relent."

"But why should he?" Rugeri asked.

"I suppose because he can—because he requires proof of the small power he possesses." Sanct-Franciscus clicked his tongue in annoyance. "I must hope that we can discover some way to prevent the worst from happening."

"Have you decided what the worst would be?" Rugeri watched Sanct-Franciscus carefully, knowing this calm remoteness concealed both anger and rapid thought.

"No. But I feel sure Telemachus Batsho has a vision for what is to come," he said, sitting down at his trestle table, and reaching for vellum on which to write. "If you will spend time with the household this evening, I would appreciate knowing what they are thinking."

"Why should they tell me anything?" Rugeri asked. "I am your manservant; they know I am loyal to you."

"They may speak if you complain of my . . . my stubbornness, perhaps," said Sanct-Franciscus, "Tell them that I am refusing to deal with trouble, and that puts you at a real disadvantage. Shared rancor can be most informative."

"They will know I'm lying," said Rugeri.

"Some may think so, but most will take complaint as being in accord with their own difficulties, and that should ease the way for you." He began to rub the ink-cake with a smooth jasper stone; the water around the cake turned dark as he worked. "I will send this to Olivia tomorrow, by courier, so that she will know of what is about to transpire here."

"Will you have Natalis carry it?" Rugeri kept his voice level.

"No; that would upset Batsho. I will hire a courier, since he will have to go a very long way. If I provide the horses and biga, I can undoubtedly find an experienced charioteer to drive the roads north." He picked up his stylus and prepared to write. "I am going out later tonight."

"To the Villa Laelius?"

"No; I will find a sleeping woman who will welcome a sweet

dream. I have no wish to put Doma Ignatia in any more danger than I have already brought her."

Rugeri ducked his head. "Just so," he said as he withdrew from the study, leaving Sanct-Franciscus to explain to Atta Olivia Clemens how his plans had changed and how they would impinge upon her.

Text of a sworn statement by Egidia Adicia Cortelle, Domina Laelius, made to Janarius Amerius Garne, Prefect of the Curia.

Ave, Heliogabalus!

On this day, the 11th of December in the 972nd Year of the City, I, Egidia Adicia Cortelle, Domina Laelius, before Jupiter, Minerva, Consivius, Astraea, and Nemesis, swear that all I say here is truthful, that I will stand before the Senate and proclaim the same to them, under penalty of beating should I in any way prevaricate or wrongfully accuse an innocent.

It gives me profound distress to have to come forth with this complaint, because it reflects badly upon our family, the lares, and our gens that these crimes have taken place under our roof. Because I am confined to my bed, it required my son, Marius Octavian, to inform me of what had taken place. My son, being only fifteen, cannot officially testify to what he saw, and therefore charges me with speaking for him, with the assurance that what he says is truthful.

As I have mentioned, I am confined to my bed. My physician is one Ragoczy Germainus Sanct-Franciscus, who has been ministering to my suffering for more than three years. Of all physicians I have engaged over the years, he is the one who has most consistently alleviated the worst of my anguish, so I am doubly distressed to have to make these misdeeds known, for his care and devotion as a physician have been beyond criticism. Yet he is the one who has so grievously trespassed against our good name and the rectitude of the gens. Little as I may want to lose so excellent a physician, I realize it is my duty to do so.

Within the household I have an unmarried daughter, now twenty-five, Doma Pax Ignatia Laelius, who has been tasked with my routine care. She has often come in the way of Sanct-Franciscus, and I have observed that she has become fascinated with him, seeking reasons to visit his house—ostensibly on my behalf—and to require his company when the household is asleep, and I am not in any need of succor. I must lay some responsibility upon her for what has taken place, for had she not thrown herself at him, I believe Sanct-Franciscus would have confined himself to my care and left my daughter alone.

My son has informed me that he surprised Sanct-Franciscus with Doma Ignatia in the spring house at the back of our garden, where they were engaged in debauched practices, she being completely naked, he about to ravish her, but still clothed, for which I must be grateful. My son did not speak of this for many days, fearing it would have a detrimental impact on my health, but he reached a point when he could no longer contain himself, for he was worried that my daughter was going to meet with Sanct-Franciscus again, and clandestinely.

I charged Doma Ignatia with her brother's suspicions as well as his account of their meeting in the spring house. I was taken aback when Doma Ignatia did not deny any part of the account I repeated, and added that she was only sorry that more had not taken place. I ordered her not to speak to him again, and to absent herself from this house on those occasions when he is here to treat me, and she refused. This defiance has led to a most lamentable rancor between us, and has contributed to my most recent crisis, from which I am only now emerging.

It is painful to say this, but my daughter, being intractable, is now declaring she will leave this house and apply to Sanct-Franciscus for his protection. This would be intolerable. Many illustriata may conduct themselves licentiously, but those of us who uphold the old values of Roma cannot countenance such dishonor: if my daughter attempts to leave this house, she must be confined to my brother's estates in Asisium until such time as she renounces her attachment for my physician. He must also be enjoined against attempting to see her or having any contact with her whatsoever.

Little as it pleases me to say it, Doma Ignatia is an ungrateful daughter, and a woman inclined to headstrongness. She cannot be reasoned with in regard to Sanct-Franciscus, and for those reasons, I fear to what excesses she may go if she is not now checked in her wildness. You have it within your power to compel her to submit to wiser minds than hers, and I urge you to do this.

Dependant as I am upon Sanct-Franciscus for what little health I now enjoy, I cannot ask you to punish him in any way, for I would surely endure agonies without his help. Once my daughter is forcibly removed from this household, he will have no reason not to resume his customary care of me, without the distraction of my heedless child. I know whatever lapses of conduct he may have committed began with her importunities: he is astute, sympathetic, and dedicated to his work. Once Doma Ignatia is beyond reach, his attention will be all that it ever has been. This is a complete and accurate transcription of the charges made by Egidia Adicia Cortelle, Domina Laelius, so I swear,

Balbinus Aranus
scribe of the Prefect of the Curia

9

In another two days, Saturnalia would begin, and Roma, for all the cold winds that frisked along its streets and fora, was vibrant with the coming celebration. With the weather clear and cold, many Romans took to the streets to make the most of the few market-days, anticipating the forthcoming festivities. On order of the Emperor, yellow ribbons flew from upper windows and galleries, invitations for the sun to return. A faint pall of wood-smoke hung over the city from the thousands of holocausts stoked to capacity in order to warm Roman houses. The dark of the year had come, and a few Romans still hung burning oil-lamps in their windows all day and all night long, as had been done in Roma five centuries ago, a custom borrowed from the Etruscans, and an observance that flooded Sanct-Franciscus' memories with the festivals at the Winter Solstice among his own, long-vanished people; in his breathing days, the end of the year and the anniversary of his own birth were heralded together in the stone fortress at the crest of the Carpathian Mountains, many centuries before the survivors had made their way west.

"So long ago," Sanct-Franciscus said aloud in his native tongue as he drove his biga carefully through the tumultuous streets, avoiding places where large numbers of people had congregated, and dark lanes where there could be trouble from some of the wandering gangs of robbers, now operating without fear of consequences, for all the Urban Guard had been ordered to protect the homes of the wealthy, and the Watch had been reduced in numbers due to another round of devaluation of coins. He reached the Villa Laelius in good time, given the route he had taken, handed the biga over to Philius, and approached the door. Using the bell to summon someone to admit him, he once again checked his case of medicaments, then pulled his Persian wool lacerna around himself as the wind picked up again.

"Enter, enter," said Starus as he flung the door open. "Enter and welcome. Right foot," he added automatically.

Crossing the threshold as ordered, Sanct-Franciscus took a moment to speak with Starus as soon as the steward had bolted the door. "How is Domina Adicia?" He removed his lacerna, revealing his black-wool dalmatica and bracae beneath.

"She fares poorly, I fear," said Starus.

"In what way?" Sanct-Franciscus inquired, trying not to press the old man, but wanting to know what he would be dealing with in a short while.

"Her breathing is noisy," he said slowly, "and her color is pasty, more than usual. Her legs have become swollen and her feet are mottled reddish."

"How swollen?" Sanct-Franciscus asked.

"I couldn't say—I haven't seen them; this is what Benona tells me," Starus said, shocked by the suggestion that he would see so noble a woman's unshod feet. "She is lethargic—which she has been before, but not so listless as she is now—and there is a strange odor about her, meaty and sweet."

"I see," Sanct-Franciscus said, doing his best to conceal the gravity this information caused; he regarded Starus directly. "I left two vials and a powder for her. How much has been used as her restorative?"

"Not much," Starus said, eyes downcast. "She will not allow Doma Ignatia near her, nor any unproven slave, so only Benona is welcome in her chamber, and Benona is worn out with caring for her. Benona does the best she can, but she cannot read the instructions you left for Doma Ignatia, and she is left with what she remembers, which she fears may not be correct." He flung up his hands. "Octavian, who could at least read your orders for Benona, is off with his fellow-Christians; he says he cannot stay in a house contaminated by sin, and that prayers will help his mother more than nostrums. He says only the fire of faith will cleanse the house, and that for the honor of his gens, he must not enter here again until the sin is gone. He claims the house stinks of shame, and wants nothing but his property out of it, as if sin were like smoke-fumes and would cling to everything. He will not listen to anyone about his mother."

"Interesting," said Sanct-Franciscus, "but not particularly useful. The Senate did Domina Adicia no service when they confined Doma Ignatia to this house yet forbade her to approach her mother."

"That may be, but Domina Laelius asked for such a ruling, and we must respect it," said Starus in a dispirited way. "Her brother is going to send a personal slave to Domina Laelius, but for now, only Benona is—" He stopped as he saw a door open at the far end of the corridor.

Ignatia stepped out of her chambers, her manner both diffident and defiant. "I must have a word with you, Sanct-Franciscus," she called out.

"That wouldn't be wise, Doma," Starus said before Sanct-Franciscus could speak. "The Senate has ordered that you receive no one—"

"I will be glad to leave my door open, or talk in the atrium, whichever suits you best," she said, paying no heed to Starus but putting all her attention on Sanct-Franciscus. "I must speak with you. It is important. I'll wait in the atrium." With that, she went toward the atrium, her paenula gathered around her; she left the door to her chambers half-open.

Starus looked down at the floor, grumbling, "As soon as Saturnalia is over, Doma Ignatia is to go to her uncle's estate, away from Roma, in Asisium. It is the only thing Domina Laelius is willing to accept for her." He stopped. "I ought not to let you speak to Doma Ignatia, but—"

"I will join her in the atrium when I am finished tending to Domina Adicia," said Sanct-Franciscus. "You may observe our conversation, if you think it prudent." The household spies would be sure to keep watch in any case, he assumed.

Relieved, Starus nodded. "The Senate believes it is necessary to protect Domina Laelius, and she agrees. As her steward and her slave, I must acquiesce in her desires. Come with me, honestiorus Sanct-Franciscus," he said formally, escorting him along the familiar route to Adicia's rooms. "I am sorry, but I must remain with you while you deal with Domina Laelius."

"In order to assure the Senate that nothing surreptitious has occurred: I know," said Sanct-Franciscus. "I thank you for your concern."

Starus looked away. "I wish I could do something . . . more."

They reached the door to Domina Adicia's room, where they paused. "What would that be?"

"I don't know," Starus admitted. "But it would be more just than what we have now."

Sanct-Franciscus regarded Starus for a short while. "I will need hot honied water and a clean cloth. Will you have someone bring it to Domina Adicia's quarters?"

"Yes, of course," said Starus. "If you will wait while I attend to that, I will be able to do as I have been commanded." He touched his collar as a reminder of his duties. "I have the household to maintain properly."

"Of course," said Sanct-Franciscus, glancing toward the opposite door, just now standing ajar. "That is Octavian's room, is it not?"

"It is. Beyond it, facing the other corridor, across from Doma Ig-natia's, is Domina Adicia's brother's quarters, for when he visits here, just opposite Doma Ignatia's . . ." His voice trailed off as he turned and made his way toward the back of the house. "I apologize for the odor; the holocaust is filled to capacity, and the whole house smells of burning."

"As does most of Roma. No doubt Octavian approves." Sanct-Franciscus lingered at Domina Adicia's door, thinking over what he had been told, and liking none of the thoughts racing in his head. There was no question that Adicia was failing, that her veins were weakening, that her body was beginning its final surrender to the ill-ness that had plagued her for so long. He wondered how much he should tell her, or her family, and decided to make no decision until he had examined her for himself. He was so sunk in contemplation that he did not hear Starus return, and was surprised when the old slave tapped his arm.

"The honied water will be brought as soon as it's warmed," said Starus, handing him a folded cotton cloth. "This should serve your purpose."

"Very good," said Sanct-Franciscus. "I will do what I may to treat your mistress." With that he opened the door and entered Domina Adicia's chamber, where he was at once struck by the scent Starus had mentioned, strong enough to be noticed over the pervasive smell of charring wood, and knew that time was grow-ing short for her; another month or two, and her body would fi-nally fail.

"Sanct-Franciscus," said Adicia, reaching up from the bed; her hands were thin and crabbed as talons and her voice rasped as she attempted to raise it above a whisper. "It is . . . good of you . . . to come."

"Domina Adicia," said Sanct-Franciscus, his tone respectful. "I am sorry to see you are not thriving."

"As if I could . . . at this stage . . . of my life." She did her best to smile at him, but her countenance had a dazed look about it, and it was apparent that she was having difficulty seeing him clearly.

He took her hand in his, noting that her pulse was rapid and her breathing, for all her effort, shallow. "I will give you a soporific, so that you may rest more comfortably, and something to lessen the swelling in your feet."

From her seat next to the window, Benona stared at Sanct-Franciscus, astonished that he should speak so immodestly. She sat more upright on her stool and glared at him. "Mind what you say," she muttered.

"I say what I must as a physician," Sanct-Franciscus told Benona without turning to face her. "I am going to make a preparation for you, Domina, and I want you to drink as much of it as you can as soon as the honied hot water I have asked for is delivered. Do not make yourself uncomfortable, but be unstinting in consuming it."

"More potions," grumbled Adicia. "At least I don't have . . . to endure my . . . daughter fussing over me."

"Your daughter's fussing, as you call it," Sanct-Franciscus said evenly, "has done you a great deal of good."

"She has you . . . ensorcelled. All men need . . . is a young woman . . . to tell them any lie. You believe . . . what she . . . what she . . ." Coughing stopped her from saying anything more.

"You are too severe, Domina Adicia," he said, knowing it was useless.

"My daughter is . . . a disgrace to her . . . gens!" Adicia was panting with effort.

Ignoring this outburst, Sanct-Franciscus said, "I am going to have Benona wash your feet and legs, and then I will have a look at them, so that I will know for myself how great your problem is, and what I should recommend for its relief."

Benona stood up, her body rigid with shock at this most improper intention. "Is it necessary? May I not tell you what I have seen, and leave it at that?"

"If you want my medicaments to provide real relief, I must know for myself with what I am dealing." He stepped back. "I will not impose upon your mistress, or you, but I must do this." Already he was planning to provide a paste of juniper berries to be taken with boiled mint. "For her next meal, I hope she will have celery root cooked with asparagus and savory."

"I dislike celery root," said Adicia.

"Perhaps," said Sanct-Franciscus, opening his case and taking out his supplies. "But for the sake of your feet, I want you to have it every day for six days."

"Hideous," said Adicia, batting at the air. "The holocaust . . . will have to be . . . cleaned—the smoke . . . is everywhere."

From the rear of the house there came excited voices, some raised, others more quiet. After a brief flurry of shouts, the disruption ceased.

"Pay them no heed," Sanct-Franciscus said calmly. "If your attention is needed, Starus will tell you." He nodded to the steward. "Find out why there is a commotion. So your mistress will not fret."

"You should not be left alone with Domina Laelius," said Starus. "The Senate would disapprove."

"I am not alone: Benona is here." He touched Adicia's forehead, remarking, "You are a bit over-warm, Domina."

"I feel cold," she countered, coughing at the end. "And my chest . . . is tight." She frowned at Benona. "She . . . doesn't do . . . anything."

"All the more reason to get something warm into you," said Sanct-Franciscus, continuing to prepare his medicaments.

Adicia stared at him. "All right. If I must."

"Go to the window, away from the Domina's bed," said Starus. "Let Benona do as you have ordered. I will have water for washing brought here." He went out into the corridor, keeping the door open so that he could observe Sanct-Franciscus; he clapped his hands: Rea answered his summons.

"I am tired of . . . the smell of smoke," said Adicia. "It seems . . . to grow stronger every . . . hour."

"Because the night is coming and the air is colder," said Sanct-Franciscus, but he noticed that Adicia was right, and that troubled him.

Starus came back into the room, and closed the door again. "Rea tells me that Octavian came to the stable to get his horse, but would not see his mother. He ventured only as far as the kitchens. A few of the household were ordered to help him to gather his things."

"That is certainly petty of him," said Sanct-Franciscus. "If he has his mother's interests at heart, he would visit her, if only to learn for himself how she is doing."

Starus shook his head and stifled a sneeze. "I should not speak against him, but he has become so arbitrary in his conduct, claiming that his religion requires him to avoid this house out of shame."

"But he returns to claim a horse?" Sanct-Franciscus asked. "How does his religion accommodate that?"

"Still keeping away from me," Adicia sighed. "The selfless devotion of . . . piety is for . . . our gens, not our . . . religions."

A clamor of outcries rose suddenly once again, and this time there was terror in the sound. Starus glanced around, as if trying to discern the cause for this disturbance.

"Octavian?" Adicia asked.

"Possibly," said Starus. "If there is any more—"

"Now what does that boy—" Adicia burst out.

"Fire! *Fire!*" The scream was accompanied with energetic banging on the kitchen-gong, and was met with yells and a rush of feet.

"Fire?" Starus exclaimed, rushing to open the door; a billow of smoke met him, swirling into Adicia's chamber before he could react.

Benona screamed, and Sanct-Franciscus set his medicaments down. "Take Domina Laelius out into the garden," he said to Starus.

"The cooks will put it out," Adicia declared. "It is just . . . too much wood . . . in the holocaust. No one . . . should leave. Stay here. All of you."

The shouts increased, and more of the household could be heard to be running toward the front or garden doors.

"Get everyone outside," Sanct-Franciscus countermanded. "It is not safe to stay here. Once the fire is out, everyone may return."

"But what—?" Starus asked blankly, belatedly closing the door.

"Move! Open the door!" Sanct-Franciscus ordered.

Benona held up her hands. "Bona Dea!"

"I should have the Domina's chair brought," Starus muttered, glancing from Adicia to the corridor and back again.

"That is not important just now," said Sanct-Franciscus, taking Starus by the arm and shaking him. "Get everyone out. Now. I will take Domina Laelius out of the house. Hurry. Fire is voracious. Summon the Urban Guard at once!" With the streets so crowded, Sanct-Franciscus doubted that they would be able to mount an effective defense against the flames in time to save the house.

Starus nodded repeatedly, opened the door, and reached to drag Benona through it. The sounds of the fire were louder now, and the smoke was more intense. Shouts and the clap of running footsteps echoed along with the roar of the fire. Frightened, Starus bolted for the door, Benona rushing after him, howling in panic.

Someone bellowed "It's cracking the floor!" and another shouted "Make for the street!"

A loud clatter of buckling masonry heralded the break in the floor, and at once shrieks rang through the fire. From the stables whinnies and brays added to the clamor.

"What is happening?" Adicia cried out, as if her danger was not yet apparent to her.

"I must get you out of here," said Sanct-Franciscus, bending to pick her up; now that he was unobserved, he made no attempt to conceal his remarkable strength, and he carried Adicia as if she weighed no more than a puppy. "Put your arms around my neck, Domina." He slapped out the first embers that touched her bedclothes.

"Why should I? I am not . . . a helpless . . . trull." She glared at the smoke. "Starus will . . . answer for—"

"Starus did nothing to cause this," Sanct-Franciscus said as he made for the door, taking care to tread warily, for the smoke was thick as mid-winter fog, and through it, he could see ripples of flames going up the walls outside Octavian's room. "Best try the garden," he said as he changed direction, going away from the atrium and the front of the house and toward the rear door; the stinging sensation in his feet grew hotter and more painful as he hurried toward the garden. He began to move without thought, only seeking to get away from the menace of the flames.

Adicia was clenching her hands to his neck, her breathing strained and interspersed with coughs as the smoke surged around them. The corridor was hot, the air acrid. "This . . . is . . ."

"Do not try to talk," Sanct-Franciscus said, moving as quickly as he dared; he could hear the fire as well as feel its sizzling breath. A loud crash ahead of them stopped him; a chasm opened in the floor, revealing the burning pantry below. In the brilliance of the fire it looked as if the kitchen and the storeroom as well as the pantry were completely lost. Skittering on the edge of the break, Sanct-Franciscus felt the heat beginning to singe his clothing; his feet were blistering, and his skin ached.

"We'll . . . die!" Adicia wailed, and gave a series of hacking coughs, growing steadily weaker.

That was an imminent possibility, Sanct-Franciscus realized; the skin on his hands was blackened and fissured, and his face felt scoured. Once fire consumed his flesh, he would be beyond all regeneration: vampires could burn as truly as any living being. He did his best to calm himself, blinking against the smoke and seeking a way out; sparks and bright cinders swarmed in the smoke like incendiary bees. On impulse, he bolted back into Domina Adicia's chambers, the part of the house the fire had not yet entirely reached, and made for her dressing-room; there was a door and a narrow balcony beyond, half a story above the small side-garden. Knowing his clothes were starting to burn, he struggled to lift Adicia over the balcony railing, and did his utmost to lower her as far as he could, leaning over the railing until he was bent double. Finally, his dalmatica smoking and small knots of flame catching the fabric alight where sparks landed, Sanct-Franciscus released his hold on Adicia's hands, watching her drop half her height into a myrtle bush. Almost at once, he righted himself and jumped after her, his hair smoking, his clothes spotted with fire, his flesh feeling peeled. He struck the ground, and rolled, hoping to extinguish the fire that was almost engulfing him, and at once let out a moan of agony as patches of skin pulled off, along with the ruins of his dalmatica and bracae; above him, flames were chewing at the balcony where he had just stood.

Roof-tiles began to fall, and this goaded Sanct-Franciscus to action. Striving against the hideous pain carousing through him, he managed to get to his feet and staggered toward Adicia, who was still lying in the myrtle bush, hair and eyebrows scorched, clothing half-burned away.

"Who—?" Her reddened eyes opened a little, but there was no shine of recognition in them.

"We must move," he gasped, reaching to try to lift her.

She keened as bits of blackened skin fell on her. "Get . . . away!"

"But the roof—it is going to fall," he warned her, making a second attempt while glancing up at the spreading flames.

"No!" She struck out with what little strength she had.

He made a last grab for her and tugged her out of the myrtle bush; an instant later a large number of roof-tiles smashed down on the bush. Half-carrying, half-dragging her, he fought free of the side of the house to the side-garden wall, his pain so intense that it muffled all other considerations, so that he was only vaguely aware of the tumult beyond the walls. As his strength began to surrender to his burns, Sanct-Franciscus bent protectively around Adicia's supine form and felt himself slipping into oblivion.

From the nearest neighbor came shouts and frantic activity; household gongs were clanging from all around the Villa Laelius. The clatter of horses' hooves in the street were barely audible amid the thunder of the fire and the confusion of those who had escaped the Laelius house.

"There's someone in the side-garden!" Philius bellowed as he tugged the last of his panicky horses to the relative safety of the rear-neighbor's stable-yard.

"Just burned beams," said the steward of the Nevius house.

"No, not beams. I think Domina Laelius' slave threw herself out the window," said Philius. "She couldn't get out any other way. Fetch a ladder. I'll go look, if someone will take this lead?" He held out the rope, noticing for the first time that his hands were shaking badly.

The steward rapped out orders, and while most of the Laelius slaves joined the Nevius slaves in starting a bucket-line to fight the fire, Philius was provided a ladder, and a young Germanian boy to steady it. "We'll try to throw a rope over, for you to climb out."

"You think I'm a fool, don't you? But I must try," Philius said, and did not wait for a response; he was half-way up the ladder when a loud crash and an eruption of sparks redoubled his efforts, sending him over the wall as quickly as he could move; dropping into the side-garden was a terrifying fall into blackness, leaving him in sooty murk where he could barely see half an arm's-length ahead of himself, and that distance made his eyes smart and his lungs scathe. He found Sanct-Franciscus by accident, treading on his arm and evoking a tortured groan. "There's someone!" he yelled, and gasped as the contents of a water-bucket sloshed over them all.

"Alive?" the Nevius' steward shouted back.

"Enough to hurt," Philius answered as he pulled at Sanct-Franciscus' raw shoulder. "Two of them!" he corrected, then began to cough uncontrollably, while on the other side of the wall, five slaves scrambled to get another pair of ladders to scale the wall before the back of the Laelius house fell in.

Text of a letter from Rugeri in Roma to Atta Olivia Clemens in Vesontio, Gallia Belgica, carried by private courier.

To the most worthy, most excellent Roman widow, Atta Olivia Clemens, at her estate Sapientia on the Via Philomena in Vesontio in Gallia Belgica, the greetings of Rogerian of Gades at Villa Ragoczy, three thousand paces east-by-north of Roma.

Not that you do not know this place, for you most certainly do, but so that you will appreciate what I have to tell you, on this, the beginning of Saturnalia at the end of the 972ⁿᵈ Year of the City.

Two days ago my master, known presently as Sanct-Franciscus, was caught in a house-fire in Roma. In his efforts to save the Domina, his patient, he was severely burned. Do not despair; he is alive, but in great pain and much in need of recuperation away from the scrutiny of Roma, since any breathing man must perish from such burns as he has suffered. He will not perish, but it may be a year or two before he has truly recovered. For that reason, I will accompany him to Misenum, to the house of Melidulci, whose house in Roma also burned, some months ago. She has sent a messenger just today to extend her hospitality for as long as it may be needed. Since she is aware of my master's true nature, she is prepared to do what she can to help his recuperation.

I am saddened to tell you that his patient, Domina Laelius, who had long suffered from failing health, died yesterday, never having regained consciousness once the smoke from the fire overcame her. Her brother has made arrangements for her to be entombed with her parents in their mausoleum on the Via Appia—a place you must remember with mixed emotions—and her daughter is arranging the rites for her interment.

The Urban Guard did what they could to save a portion of the Villa Laelius, but in the end they only preserved the bake-house and the stables. These are no doubt worth saving, but they leave the household without shelter in the harshest days of the year. I have opened your house to them, since my master has been given permission to leave the city for treatment, and I have supposed this is what you would want done for those unfortunates. There is a daughter, twenty-five, who cared for her mother and is in great distress; also a son, who refuses to enter your house for fear it will contaminate his religion, so close as it is to the Temple of Hercules.

My master's friends and those of the Laelius gens are preparing a petition to the Curia for an investigation of the fire that destroyed the Laelius house, because although the holocaust was in its most concentrated use, the under-cook, who got himself and his staff out just before the upper floor fell in, insists that the fire first began near the pantry, next to the access to the holocaust, and that there was also another fire in the rooms at the back of the atrium. This may be nothing more than the invention of terror, but knowing that many fires have been set in Roma of late, the Curia may order just such an inquiry, as they have in the case of several similar fires of late. In the meantime, I have engaged a private guard for your house, and doubled your night watch.

I pledge to keep you informed of my master's progress during his months of convalescence, and to have your staff inform you of the state of your Roman house. I also pledge to notify you of any decision the Curia reaches in regard to the Laelius fire, and the decisions of the Urban Guard, should they decide to investigate the fire. If there are other issues which you wish to be made cognizant of, you have only to let me know, and I will attend to them promptly.

With high regard and enduring respect,
Rogerian of Gades,
called Rugeri

By my own hand and under the seal of the Eclipse

10

Spring was in full and glorious riot along the Mare Tyrrhenum; from Neapolis to Ostia the hillsides glowed with blossoms and the glowing green frills of new leaves. The first of the season's foals were romping in paddocks with their dams, with lambs and calves in the pastures with ewes and cows, kids clambered through the stable-yard with goats, and shoats rooted in the new, heavily fenced sties with sows. Bees droned among the flowers, and the first wasps' nest was under way beneath the eaves of the spring house. Peasants and slaves busied themselves with planting and spring pruning, while the seas once again were filled with ships and sails.

Melidulci strolled along the broad path that led to her small bath-house behind her villa, dressed in a light tunica of pale-blue Egyptian linen that matched the mid-morning reflected sky in the stream that ran beside the pathway; Rugeri followed a pace behind her. She stretched up her hands as if to embrace the merry breezes as they frolicked by. "The rains are over for a time, I think."

"They're usually gone by the Equinox," said Rugeri, adjusting the soft cotton paenula he carried over his arm so none of it would drag on the ground.

"There will be thunderstorms in summer, of course," she went on, "but they don't last long, and they keep down the flies." She picked a spray of blooms and set it on the base of a small statue of

Copia. "She has shown me her abundance since I came here; I want to keep her favor."

"Always useful," said Rugeri.

"Does Sanct-Franciscus make offerings to any gods?" Melidulci asked, only mildly curious.

"Only his forgotten ones," said Rugeri, descending the four broad steps to the portico of the bath-house, entering it after Melidulci; his voice echoed through the handsome stone building which was nearly as large as the villa itself.

"I would guess that he's still in the frigidarium," she said, glancing toward her tepidarium, which was large enough for a dozen adults to swim in, and lined with decorative mosaics depicting the War of the Centaurs. "Well. Time for my swim."

"So I would expect," said Rugeri, and stepped away to permit her to undress alone; he entered a short corridor that led back into the rise of the hill, where the small, stone-enclosed frigidarium could be kept cool through the heat of summer. "My master?" he called as he tapped on the door.

"Yes, Rugeri. Come in." His voice was still weak but significantly improved from the fourth day of Saturnalia when they had arrived here in the end of a gale, Sanct-Franciscus looking then like boiled rawhide with bleeding sores. He had said then his healing would be long and difficult, and so it was proving to be; for the duration of winter he had kept to his room, but once the season turned, he began to venture out of his quarters; in the last ten days he had been taking cold baths in the early afternoon, declaring that they eased his soreness, which remained omnipresent. For the most part, he endured his pain stoically, but occasionally it made him brusque.

"I brought your paenula," said Rugeri, holding up the garment. He still found it difficult to look at Sanct-Franciscus, for although his skin had at last begun to heal, it appeared raw and overly tight on his bones and sinews. His hair, eyebrows, and eyelashes had started to grow again and no longer looked like shriveled miniature cocoons, or fried larks' tongues.

"Thank you, old friend," said Sanct-Franciscus, sitting up in the darkened room carved into the rock. He moved toward the edge of the deep, cool basin in which he sat, and paused to squeeze a sponge over his head and face, the water running down his body as he moved to get out of the frigidarium. His demeanor was coolly cordial, reserved without being alienating; he remarked, over the splash of the chilly water, "I believe the afternoon is warm."

"Warm enough, but not yet hot," said Rugeri.

"And Melidulci?"

"Domina Melidulci is in the tepidarium just now, taking her afternoon swim," said Rugeri as he held out a drying sheet that lay folded on the stone bench at the edge of the basin. "She is expecting to see you."

"I will not bother her with my company until I am bound for the villa, and dressed," said Sanct-Franciscus, looking down at the broad swath of white scar tissue that ran from the base of his ribs to the top of his pubis, the token of his first death from disemboweling. "I am hideous enough as it is." He turned away as he stood up, reaching for the drying sheet.

"Is your skin getting better?" Rugeri asked as he watched Sanct-Franciscus close the drying sheet around him.

"Slowly, it is," he said. "In another two months, I will look less like a peeled corpse. In two years, no trace of the burns will remain; no injury since the one that killed me has left an enduring mark upon me, but that does not mean there is never any damage, or that I am not marked by it; this is some of the worst I have had." He looked over his shoulder at Rugeri, his expression inscrutable. "Those of us who have died and risen again take longer than breathing men to heal."

"You have said so," Rugeri reminded him.

"But did you believe me, until now?" Sanct-Franciscus countered.

"Not as I do since you were burned," said Rugeri. "I recall how long you needed to recover from Srau's attack."

"And it is thus with all who come to my life," said Sanct-Franciscus with underlying fatigue.

"Does that apply to me, as well? I am not a vampire, my master, only a ghoul." He studied Sanct-Franciscus, not expecting a reply, and so was mildly surprised when Sanct-Franciscus answered him.

"You heal more rapidly than I, but more slowly than the truly living, just as you can eat meat so long as it is raw, while I must subsist on nourishment more . . . shall we say? ephemeral and intimate. Your nature is closer to that of the living than mine is, and your body reflects that." He turned around, his drying sheet draped like a toga, and added, "How do you suppose I would look to the Curia just now? Would my appearance upset them, do you think?"

The questions surprised Rugeri, and he paused before he answered them. "If they could see you, they would marvel to find you among the living."

"Although my skin is chafed, taut, and . . . incomplete?"

"Your aspect would be alarming to some, if they had the opportunity to peruse your appearance," said Rugeri as diplomatically as possible. "Some might wonder at your condition, but others would not let such things trouble them, particularly those who have led troops in battle and have seen the scathing a man may sustain and yet live."

Sanct-Franciscus considered this. "Doubtless, you are correct."

Taking advantage of this concession, Rugeri added, "At least you are recognized as a physician; many would assume you have cures known only to you."

"Just so," said Sanct-Franciscus with an unsuccessful attempt at a wry smile; his skin stretched and twisted to a rictus. "Medical skills or not, most, I fear, would be troubled by my survival, and they would wonder at my laggardly recovery, and that might lead to more questions than I would prefer. I am reluctant to create doubts in their minds, for thanks to Telemachus Batsho, they are already mired in them."

"As you say, my master." Rugeri's expression remained neutral as he attempted to discern what Sanct-Franciscus' intentions were.

"What do you reckon they would do if they suspected the truth?" Sanct-Franciscus inquired, then motioned Rugeri to silence. "Do not bother. You and I know I cannot return to Roma as myself again, not for a good many years."

"What do you mean?" Rugeri asked uneasily.

Sanct-Franciscus went on as if he had not heard Rugeri's question. "But I have unfinished business in Roma, and I must attend to it myself before the Curia completes its investigation—private business. Which is why I have sent for Natalis."

Rugeri stared at him. "Natalis?"

"Yes. He should arrive some time this afternoon," said Sanct-Franciscus, then saw Rugeri's appalled visage. "Do not fret, old friend: Natalis has been told to leave and return to Roma unofficially, and so he shall. No one will know he has left Olivia's house."

Rugeri considered all of this. "Why entrust such a mission to him?"

"Because he is determined to make up for his earlier disloyalty; he wants to prove himself worthy of trust again," said Sanct-Franciscus, methodically toweling himself dry. "He continues to blame himself for being suborned as he was; I am willing to provide him an opportunity for expiation." He held out his hand, flexing the fingers, watching the tight skin stretch. "Slowly better," he whispered.

"And that is to the good," said Rugeri, then added more sharply, "Why should you risk anything just now, when you are safely away from Roma, and protected? Wouldn't it make more sense to postpone—"

Sanct-Franciscus cut him short. "Because I am certain that the fire that killed Domina Adicia was no accident, for I believe, from what I saw, that it flared in two places at almost the same instant, which would mean it was set, and that indicates that it was an act of deliberate malice; I cannot permit that to go unanswered," he said with terrible calm. "Someone attacked an invalid in her bed, and was willing to kill all the household."

"And you," Rugeri reminded him.

"Yes, old friend: and me." Sanct-Franciscus dropped his drying sheet and reached for his soft paenula, shrugging into its folds with more ease of motion than he had shown since the fire.

"How long do you think you will need before you are ready to deal with whomever set the fires—if, indeed, someone did?" Rugeri inquired, curious to discover why Sanct-Franciscus was so certain about the miscreant.

"I think by mid-summer I will be sufficiently recovered to be able to do what I have in mind. And I will need my arrangements in place in advance, or I will risk discovery." He fastened the closures on the paenula and looked toward the door leading to the tepidarium. "You say Melidulci is bathing?"

"Swimming," said Rugeri.

"I should have a word with her before I go back to the house," he said, pushing the door open and stepping, barefoot, onto the broad, tiled rim of the pool. He waited, watching Melidulci swim the length twice, then called out, "My kind hostess, may I have a moment?"

Melidulci, her wet hair trailing around her like sirens' seaweed, let her feet settle onto the floor of the pool, her arms rising to float, extended, on the surface of the water. "Yes. What is it?" Before he could speak, she added, "You are looking a little better at last."

"You reassure me," said Sanct-Franciscus. "I was beginning to think I would never be restored."

"You said it would take time, and I have done what I could to provide it," she reminded him. "Is that what you wanted to know?"

"No; my servant Natalis should be here later today, and I assume he will be here for a day or two. I will provide for his food and care."

She laughed. "If you like, I won't refuse your gold. But, considering I could not have bought this place without your generosity, I imagine I can support your servant for a day or two." She lolled back in avid water, floating lazily. "Will you come to my room tonight? I have missed you these last five evenings."

"Would you like that?" Sanct-Franciscus gave her time to answer.

"I would, if it is no imposition on you." She began, very slowly, to swim again. "I am always glad of your company, and of the joys you bring to me."

"Even burned as I am?"

"I have seen almost as bad, including two with the White Disease," she said indifferently. "You tell me that our lovemaking helps you to heal, and that pleases me, although the lovemaking pleases me more. The four times I have come to your room here were for sympathy in your plight, yet still were not unsatisfactory to me. Since you have come to my apartment, I have nothing—nothing—to regret in your company. Injured as you are, you still surpass most men in giving me insouciance and gratification—whatever your reason for seeking me out, I am delighted to accommodate you." She rolled back in the water so her breasts rose above the surface of the pool. "If you and I were taken in great passion, no doubt I would be unable to disregard your hurts, but as our arrangement has always been more pragmatic, well . . ."

"Then I thank you, and I look forward to the time we spend together," he said with some of his old elegance of manner.

Her smile was eager but without avidity; she caught her lower lip between her teeth and looked at him through her lashes in unmistakable invitation. "I, too, look forward to our time together."

"And I thank you," he said, turning away from her and going to the path leading to the house, mincing as the soles of his bare feet trod on the crushed pebbles.

"I should have brought your peri," Rugeri said as he watched Sanct-Franciscus make his precarious way back to the shadow of the broad eaves of the villa.

"No, you should not," said Sanct-Franciscus. "You are doing precisely what I would like you to do." As he reached the rear door, he stopped still, saying, "I have no wish to be coddled; it does me no good, and it spares me nothing worthwhile."

"It spares you pain," said Rugeri.

"A little, perhaps, but it lengthens the time I will feel it," Sanct-Franciscus explained.

Rugeri nodded. "You will let me know if you change your mind, won't you?"

"Of course," said Sanct-Franciscus, and opened the door.

After a long moment of hesitation, Rugeri followed after, climbing to the second floor where Sanct-Franciscus had been allocated three rooms for his use on the north side of the house. As he went into the room, he found Sanct-Franciscus unfastening his paenula while contemplating the garments hanging from pegs on the far wall. "What do you want to wear?"

Sanct-Franciscus cocked his head. "I have not decided," he told Rugeri. "I think perhaps the black-and-red chandys; it covers more of the burns, and it is soft to the touch."

Rugeri reached for the handsome silken garb, adding black-linen bracae to it. "I think this will suit you, my master."

"I think so, as well." He sat down and reached for the bracae, pulling them on his left leg and then his right. "I will want to purchase a few more pair of these now that I can wear them without agony," he said, glancing at Rugeri. "From whom did you buy them—do you recall?"

"The spinner from Fars," said Rugeri. "Her stall is in Roma, near the Baths of Caracalla,"

"Where the foreign weavers and spinners congregate?" Sanct-Franciscus inquired as he secured the mani and the waist-ties. He stood up with only a little visible effort, reaching for his chandys as he did.

"Would you like me to help you don that?" Rugeri asked, perplexed by the polite distance Sanct-Franciscus had maintained since he had been carried to Olivia's house in Roma in a chair, barely conscious enough to moan.

"If you will pull it down for me, I would appreciate it," said Sanct-Franciscus as he gathered the chandys and tugged it over his head, thrusting his arms into the capacious sleeves. "I will want a pallium made in a shade of soft ochre, a very ordinary linen pallium, mid-calf length, no decoration on it, moderate sleeves from the pleats," he went on as Rugeri took hold of the hem, loosening it so that the chandys would fall to his knees. "And short bracae in rust-colored cotton, such as a shop-keeper might wear," he added.

"In other words, a disguise," said Rugeri.

"A disguise," Sanct-Franciscus confirmed. "I should probably have one of those wide-brimmed straw hats, too, such as the forum hawkers have."

"To shade your face," Rugeri said.

"From the sun and from prying eyes," said Sanct-Franciscus. "Sunlight is a discomfort, even when I stand on my native earth, and just now, my skin is sensitive."

"And how soon will you want this?" Rugeri inquired.

"Two months or so," said Sanct-Franciscus, smoothing the front of his chandys gingerly, for his hands still showed the damage of blistering.

The implied delay relieved Rugeri, who assured his master he would attend to it, then left him alone until shortly before sunset, when he once again went to Sanct-Franciscus' quarters to inform him that Natalis had arrived. "He is in the small reception room."

"I will come down," said Sanct-Franciscus, setting aside the papyrus scroll he had been reading. "If you will light the lamps after you dine?" The slanting, afternoon shadows had cast one side of the chamber into soft purple obscurity.

"Of course," said Rugeri, and held the door for Sanct-Franciscus. "Shall I remain with you while you speak with Natalis?"

"Not if it will bother you," said Sanct-Franciscus mildly. He was half-way down the stairs when he stopped. "My intentions toward the arsonists are not kindly."

"So I realize," said Rugeri, then dared to continue, "But I fear that in your zeal for vengeance—"

"Justice," Sanct-Franciscus corrected.

"Vengeance, justice, whatever it may be, that you will put yourself at great risk again, and might not be as fortunate as you were at the Villa Laelius." Now that he had spoken his misgivings, he felt less apprehensive, as if his words had banished some of the danger. When Sanct-Franciscus said nothing and resumed his descent, Rugeri stayed close behind him. "If you want my help, it is yours."

"I thank you, Rugeri, yet I will also do my utmost to keep you out of it." His grim tone vanished as he said, "Besides, I will need you to make the arrangements to get us from Brundisium to Alexandria. I could not risk having you taken into custody in Roma."

"If that is your wish, my master," said Rugeri, trying to mask his disappointment as they reached the bottom of the stairs.

Sanct-Franciscus stood still. "It is enough that I must do this, old friend. I will not, and cannot, add your life to the stakes in this game." There was an implacable note in his tone that was uncompromising. "If I fail in my intent, I will comfort myself with the certainty that no one but I had to pay the price of that failure." He moved off toward the small reception room to where Natalis was waiting.

Text of a record from Ulixes Lenus Varian, Prosecutor of the Urban Guard, delivered to the Curia in private session; sent by Natalis in Roma to Sanct-Franciscus at Melidulci's house near Misenum by private courier.

Ave, Heliogabalus.

On this, the 14ᵗʰ day of May in the 973ʳᵈ Year of the City, I, Ulixes Lenus Varian, Prosecutor of the Urban Guard for Roma, submit to the Curia the findings of our investigation of the fire at the Villa Laelius that claimed the lives of four people, including the Domina, Egidia Adicia Cortelle, Domina Laelius.

Upon the order of the Curia, we have taken testimony from surviving household members and we have examined the ruins of the house, and we offer our conclusions now, with such support as we have determined is appropriate for the completion of our commission, and we offer these as part of this summary.

From the groom-slave Philius, we have learned that the son of the household, Marius Octavian Laelius, who is currently residing with Erestus Arianus Crispenus, a known Christian and one who has been interviewed before during investigations of fires thought to be set by Christians, was at the Villa Laelius on the night it burned. He had come to claim his horses, and spent time by himself at the bake-house, next to the access to the holocaust, or so he told Philius he had done. The fire that consumed the house began shortly after he left. Philius was occupied getting their horses, mules, and donkeys out of their stable to notice where any of the rest of the household was until he was summoned to help find any who might have escaped into the garden, which he did with all celerity, and found Domina Laelius and her physician, the foreigner Ragoczy Germainus Sanct-Franciscus, by the side-garden wall, almost beneath Domina Laelius' quarters.

Starus, the steward-slave of the household, was the one who did his best to get those in the house out of it. He personally escorted the daughter of the family, Pax Ignatia Laelius, to safety, and for which she is preparing to free him with a stipend for life, assuming her uncle, Albinus Drusus Cortelle, recently returned from Syria, will approve her doing so. Starus declares that the fire broke through the floor from the kitchen in several places, and he could not determine if it was because of one fire or more than one. He has suffered from a severe cough since the fire, and thus far, he has not made a good recovery, so his testimony must be by report rather than appearance.

Pax Ignatia Laelius has said that she believes that the fire broke out in two places at almost the same time, and that it spread with terrible quickness. She has said that she does not know who would do such a thing, but she is aware that there have been many fires set in Roma through mishap and miscalculation as well as malice, and so it may be with this one. She has supervised the clearing of the burned house, and the obsequies for her mother, who is now in the Cortelle tomb on the Via Appia.

Idicoris, the under-cook, swears that the fire burst the kitchen walls and had to be more than the holocaust breaking from the constant heat. It is his belief that the fire was a deliberate one, and that it was set on the main floor as well as the lower-levels to burn rapidly and with the intention of causing the house to be destroyed, for in following the heating channels under the floors, once the upper tiles failed, the fire would have to consume the building totally and quickly. He received burns on his hands and arms in his effort to save the house, and for this, he has been paid a generous commoda and the promise of a stipend when his working days are done.

Waloi, the regular cook, was not so fortunate; he was in his room when the fire broke out, and in spite of his efforts to escape, he died in the fire itself. It is curious that the entrance to the slaves' quarters should have been burning so fiercely at the beginning, for that would support Idicoris' belief that the fire began in more than one place, the slaves' quarters being on the opposite of the house from the holocaust access.

The son, Marius Octavian Laelius, avers that he was away from the house by the time the fire broke out, and that, while he mourns his mother as a martyr, had she been Christian, he is certain that the house deserved burning, much as it was imbued with sin and corruption. He continues to wear ribbons for his mother, and to offer prayers for her among the Christians. However, we discovered that according to a man two streets away, Marius Octavian Laelius watched the fire from the rise behind the neighbor's house. This neighbor, one honoratus Regulus Vitus Sextus Vincens, claims to have observed Laelius for some time after the flames erupted from the Villa Laelius.

As has been reported elsewhere, Domina Laelius succumbed to smoke and burns, and was interred with her ancestors. Of Ragoczy Germainus Sanct-Franciscus we have no final report, for although he most certainly carried Domina Laelius from her house, he was claimed that very night by his own household and taken out of the city for recuperation. I have heard three accounts of his burns, and I must tell you here that I have never known anyone so badly blistered and blackened as he to live long—nor would anyone want life for him, for his sake. Still, I have left word at the house he occupies behind the Temple of Hercules, which he has from a Roman widow, Atta Olivia Clemens, currently abiding in Gallia Belgica, that should any word be brought from him, I am to be notified of it at once, and any information he may have to offer in regard to the fire be entered as part of the official inquiry.

I cannot be wholly certain that the fire at the Villa Laelius was deliberately set, but I believe there is reason enough to continue the investigation, in the event that other information may come to light that would provide the necessary intelligence to resolve our remaining questions beyond the requirements of law. I recommend that Albinus Drusus Cortelle be entered as the provisional owner of the burned house, and that all matters of taxation and disposal be his, for the benefit of Domina Laelius' two unmarried children: her daughter, Pax Ignatia Laelius, twenty-five, and Marius Octavian Laelius, sixteen. They will eventually receive the full value of their mother's estate, but only after the cause of the fire that killed her is established. On arrangements with Atta Olivia Clemens, they *presently occupy her house near the Temple of Hercules that Sanct-Franciscus had hired from the widow.*

Submitted under the pain of whipping if any portion is a deliberate falsehood or unsubstantiated conclusion,

Ulixes Lenus Varian
Prosecutor of the Urban Guard of Roma

11

Although the procession earlier that day was officially meant to honor the Emperor whose month it was—Divus Julius—it had been another grand occasion for Heliogabalus to provide spectacular entertainments and dazzling processions for the people of Roma: all day triumphal chariots accompanied by escorts of musicians and dancers had rolled through the city bearing the Emperor and his mother as well as the Senate and a number of officials from client nations around all seven hills and through every large forum, scattering coins and flowers to the people. As a result, at the end of this display the streets were still full, lit by torches at every corner, as the sun faded behind a low band of scarlet clouds in the west, and the warm, sodden night wrapped itself around the city.

Sanct-Franciscus waited with Natalis in the shadow of the Circus Maximus, where they were surrounded by a crowd of Romans following a carpentum holding three huge barrels of wine the contents of which were being ladled out into the waiting cups of those near enough to gain the attention of the serving slaves. "How many of these are there in the city tonight, I wonder?" he asked as the crowd surged after the carpentum, cups held up as if they were votive offerings.

Natalis shrugged. "Carpenta with wine barrels? A dozen or more, I'd guess, judging from the state of the populace." He found Sanct-Franciscus' polite reserve unnerving, but knew better than to mention it, for he was more troubled by what lay beneath than by the outward imperturbable self-possession. "They'll be drunk until sunrise."

"Are all the carpenta as busy as this one?" Sanct-Franciscus asked, and continued, "It is to our advantage to have it so."

"No one will remember us, or at least not too clearly," said Natalis, ducking into an alley that led northward.

"And those we seek?" Sanct-Franciscus' voice was like steel.

"If they are not out on the streets, haranguing the people, they are in their private temple, praying." Natalis paused. "I have not seen any of them about since midday."

"You are satisfied that the boy is responsible?" Sanct-Franciscus inquired.

"I am, and the Curia will be, now that one of his comrades has spoken to the Prefect of the Urban Guard. The youth who revealed their activities has accepted his punishment in the arena as fitting, which is all the more convincing that he is truthful. It takes a great deal for one of those Christians to turn on anyone in their religion. But the young man has said that he doesn't want true Christians to be suspected of the irreligious acts of a few of their number. He swore to it on his hope of Paradise, which means a great deal to Christians. The Curia has accepted his account as true, as much because it agrees with what the Urban Guard has decided must have occurred, as because they found Metsari convincing." Natalis fidgeted with the ends of his woven belt.

Sanct-Franciscus nodded, his dark eyes like black flint. "If the Curia has accepted the account, then I will, as well. I will proceed."

"Have a care," Natalis warned him as they prepared to skirt around another band of men, drunk enough to be reckless and spoiling for a fight.

They passed the crowd of men, their heads lowered like humiliora; when they reached the next street, they saw a number of Watchmen patrolling, and they hesitated, not wanting to draw attention to themselves. When the Watchmen moved on, so did Sanct-Franciscus and Natalis, going north through Roma toward the Vicus Longus.

"You will not want to go on the main streets," Natalis warned him a bit later on. "Too many patrols are out tonight, and I would prefer not to be stopped."

"You choose the way," said Sanct-Franciscus.

Natalis did as he was told, attempting to match his demeanor to that of Sanct-Franciscus. As they continued onward, the two men exchanged desultory remarks on the growing disorder they saw around them. In one narrow passage they almost tripped over two men and a woman indulging in a complicated coupling; the three paid them no heed as they passed on.

"It saddens me," said Sanct-Franciscus as they reached the next broad avenue, "to see something so precious turned into nothing more than—" He stopped. "How much farther?"

"Another four streets," said Natalis; he forced himself to ask something that had been bothering him since they had sneaked into the city. "Are you sure you won't change your mind and permit me to stand guard for you?"

"No. I must do this alone. It would go hard for you if you were detained as my accomplice; very likely you would be sent to the arena." His own recollection of facing crocodiles in a flooded arena a century-and-a-half ago very nearly shattered his calm, but he regained his terrifying composure by hard-won self-discipline. "If you will wait for me at Porta Pinciana, under the aqueduct, I will consider myself well-served." He turned his attention to the small stand of yew trees at the front of the dark-columned Temple of Mania, where burnt offerings lay on the open altar. "How appropriate, that we should come to the Goddess of the Dead for this task."

The chilly irony of Sanct-Franciscus' remark cut Natalis to the quick; he made one last attempt. "Master, what if the Urban Guard and the Curia are deceived, and they have blamed the wrong man? Shouldn't you wait a while longer, in case the Curia issues a new finding?"

"Tonight I shall find it out, and strive to make amends for my error, if I have made one, but I will not wait," said Sanct-Franciscus.

It was all Natalis could do not to growl in frustration. "If you are caught—"

"—Rugeri will know what to do," Sanct-Franciscus said, cutting him short.

They went on in silence until Natalis halted and pointed to a cul-de-sac surrounded by a dozen small, private houses. "The fourth on the right, the one with the blue wall. The one with the flower-baskets hanging by the front door."

"You know he is here?" Sanct-Franciscus asked.

"He was yesterday and the slaves said none of the four of them planned to travel. As I've old you, they haven't gone out since mid-day."

"And the owner of the house: what of him?"

"The owner of the house is a Christian who is presently in Judea; he has allowed these four young Christians to live in his house in his absence, or so the slaves have told me. Three of them are of the same gens, and one is their comrade. I had it from the cook and the steward, both, that this is the case." Natalis almost held his breath, waiting for what Sanct-Franciscus' response would be.

"Good enough," said Sanct-Franciscus, so icily distant that Natalis despaired. "Is there an alley entrance?"

"Yes; on the north side of the house. There is a common stable at the rear of the six houses on the right side, and each house has an alley on the north leading to the small bath-houses. You can enter next to the holocaust—there is a low door for loading wood that can be opened with a little patience. Once inside, there is a connecting door to the kitchen corridor." He wanted to talk, to do anything to delay what he feared would follow. "Tradesmen use the alley, and vendors of fruits and vegetables, and often members of other households, so you will not be remarked upon." Realizing he was babbling, Natalis made himself stop talking.

"And slaves? How many?"

"Four in the household; only the groom is here just now, muck-ing out stalls, and then he will have to bed the stall in straw, so he will be busy for some time. The cook and the steward and the man-of-all-work have the evening to themselves and I arranged for them to be entertained at the trattorium four blocks away. They should be there until well into the night, feasting and making the most of their time away from their labors." Natalis managed to halt his torrent of words.

Sanct-Franciscus did not smile. "Thank you. I am grateful for all you have done for me, and I have arranged a pension for you, and employment if you want it, so you need not return to thievery once I am gone." He paid no heed to Natalis' sharp intake of breath. "If I am not at the Porta Pinciana by the hour before dawn, do not wait for me; find your way out of the city and return to Villa Ragoczy."

"At least take my knife," Natalis pleaded, reaching to pull the weapon from its sheath.

"Better that I carry nothing," said Sanct-Franciscus.

"If that is your wish," Natalis heard himself say.

"It is." He tapped Natalis on the shoulder, then moved away toward the alley Natalis had indicated, his clothing rendering him almost invisible: he did not look back.

Natalis stood, undecided, for a short while, then turned to continue north in the shadow of the Virgo Aqueduct.

Sanct-Franciscus went along toward the rear of the house, pausing only to look for the door Natalis had mentioned. He found it under a partial eave, and was glad of the extra protection this afforded him. Bending down, he took a bronze pin out of his wallet and slipped it into the lock, patiently turning it until the wards released. Easing the door open, he hunched over and went into the loading room for the holocaust, relieved that it was cool. He made his way past the stacked lengths of wood to the inner door. He opened this with care, his night-seeing eyes checking out the corridor before he emerged from concealment. Most of the house was dark with only an occasional oil-lamp shining to diminish the darkness; making his way toward the atrium, Sanct-Franciscus was aware of emptiness, and for a moment he wondered if the young Christians had gone out for a night of advancing their faith. Then he heard a voice raised in argument coming from the front of the house, and he went toward it, his senses keen, his purpose set.

"—still too soon to—" one voice insisted.

"We must continue to press forward, take advantage of the impact we have made," another declared. "We have an opportunity to turn this to a—"

The third speaker was Octavian. "Why bother with preaching? I say we burn another house. That is something Romans pay attention to—fires."

"You like fires too much, Octavian," said the first voice.

"Because they're effective," Octavian responded sharply.

"But the Urban Guard is starting to detain Christians on suspicion—" the second voice objected.

"Peterines," scoffed a fourth. "Let them become martyrs—it suits them."

"Peterines and those who betray us," Octavian interjected darkly. "Your cousin has a lot to answer for."

"He didn't realize what he was doing," protested the second speaker, and almost at the same time the fourth said, "You can't blame our cousin."

"No, Octavian, you cannot," said the fourth.

"Oh, yes I can," Octavian shouted. "He betrayed me as surely as Judas betrayed Christ. They, too, were cousins, we're told."

The first speaker raised his voice. "Enough! This is no way to defend our faith."

An uneasy quiet ensued, then Octavian said, "I ask your forgiveness. But your cousin had better ask for mine before they send him to the arena."

"How do you mean?" the fourth voice challenged. "You were the one who set the fires, and Virginius Apollonius was—"

"I wasn't alone, setting our fires," Octavian interruped.

"—distressed by that. What did you expect him to do?" the fourth voice went on.

"I didn't expect him to go to the Prefect of the Urban Guard." Indignation raised Octavian's voice again. "He should have taken the matter to our pope, if he was so deeply troubled by what we've done."

"Stop it!" the first ordered.

"You speak against me because they're all your relatives and I'm not," Octavian accused. "This should be about faith, not family."

The second voice was deliberately calm. "We are all Brothers in Christ."

Another brief silence fell, into which Sanct-Franciscus stepped, opening the door quickly, and walking into the room without courtesy, halting only when the eyes of all four were fixed on him. The lamplight flickered in the slow draught from the door, touching the faces of the four with uneven shadows, and casting Sanct-Franciscus' stretched features into stark half-light.

"Who—?" demanded a gangly young man of about eighteen with thick, tawny hair and big-knuckled hands; he was in a blue-linen pallium with an embroidered pattern of fish at the knee-length hem.

"You dare to intrude!" one of the other two cried out.

"I see you have made this your temple," said Sanct-Franciscus coldly, indicating the altar with a large carving of a fish on it, and a haloed crucifix painted on the wall behind the altar; he took a step forward and closed the door. "An apt place for the glory of your god, and for your sepulchre." He regarded the four young men steadily, as if seeking to determine their degree of responsibility in the fire that burned the Laelius house.

Octavian was staring at Sanct-Franciscus, recognition dawning on him. "You! But you were dead."

"That was certainly your intention," said Sanct-Franciscus quietly.

"Then how do you come to be here?" Octavian jeered.

"Your Christ is not the only man ever to rise from his grave," said Sanct-Franciscus.

"Blasphemy!" exclaimed the gangly one.

"You *died*!" Octavian shouted.

"Not this time," Sanct-Franciscus said lightly, acidly.

"Octavian, who is this man?" the shortest of the four demanded; although he was the youngest of his relatives by three years, he was the uncle of one and cousin to the other of Octavian's companions, and exercised his seniority now. "What's he doing here? We ought to know."

"He's Sanct-Franciscus, my mother's physician. They say he got

her out of the house before she died; he was badly burned doing it."
There was as much bravado as concern in this. "A foreigner, in any
case, and not a Christian. I have no idea what he's doing here, nor do
I care."

"What's wrong with his skin?" asked the handsomest of the
three, fair-haired, hazel-eyed, with a fine, straight nose, and a sensu-
ous mouth.

"Burns—I told you, Virginius. Look at his face. He should be
dead," said Octavian harshly, and rounded on Sanct-Franciscus as if
resenting his presence. "I suppose you came to find out if I know
anything about the fire. Well, I don't."

"Not according to Gelasius Virginius Apollonius Metsari, who
has sworn that you set it, along with several others, with the help of
your companions; you have been exercising your religion by destroy-
ing lives and property," said Sanct-Franciscus in a cool, neutral tone.
"According to what I have overheard tonight, Metsari was telling the
truth." He looked away from Octavian and met the eyes of the other
three in turn. "Or were you lying to one another?"

"That! That was nothing," Octavian said, blustering. "You must
have misunderstood what we were saying."

"I did not misunderstand," said Sanct-Franciscus. "The fires
were yours: you have said it."

The shortest man brought his chin up. "Property and lives are
nothing in the face of the return of the Redeemer, which is fast
coming upon us. Who shall know the Last Day?"

The gangly fellow folded his arms. "It is unfortunate that some
must endure agony for the salvation of all, but Christ did that for us,
and those who emulate Him will be with Him in Heaven."

Octavian gestured to include the others. "What have we to fear
from you? We're Romans. You're an exile." He spat contemptuously.
"We know about you, Sanct-Franciscus."

"Do you." Sanct-Franciscus directed his penetrating gaze to Octavian. "And what is it you think you know?"

Before Octavian could answer, the gangly one stepped in between
Octavian and Sanct-Franciscus. "I am Erestus Arianus Crispenus, and
I am the host in this house, in the absence of the owner. If you have

a complaint against my guests, you should address me. By what right do you violate the rules of hospitality?"

"Yes. By what right?" Octavian seconded.

Sanct-Franciscus studied Crispenus, trying to find sympathy for this misguided youngster; he folded his arms as he contemplated, saying, "I have no enmity toward you, Crispenus, as a living man, but for what you have done you will die with the others. You will all die."

"Because of the fires?" Crispenus asked, frowning a little.

Sanct-Franciscus nodded. "Metsari has said that his cousins all supported the burning of the Villa Laelius."

"If that is so, then he will be cast into outer darkness," Octavian said confidently.

"I am of their gens and their religion; I will not abandon them," said Crispenus with a toss of his head, and in the next instant abruptly struck out at Sanct-Franciscus with a closed fist.

A cry of alarm and encouragement greeted this onslaught.

"As you wish," said Sanct-Franciscus as he dodged the blow, seizing Crispenus' arm and tugging it enough to pull him off his feet. As Crispenus went sprawling, Sanct-Franciscus ducked another punch directed at his shoulder: one of the other two relatives had attacked.

"Hold him, Rufius!" shouted the other, gesturing to the last of the three. "I'll have him begging soon enough."

Prosperus Rufius Ursinus did his best to capture Sanct-Franciscus and pin his arms to his sides, but he failed, for just as he grasped the foreigner around the chest, he was flung off with such force that he slammed back into the altar, stunning himself on the marble top and knocking over the carved fish; a smudge of blood appeared in his hair, and he moaned as he slumped against the granite slab, trying to hold onto the side of it.

Seeing his chance, Lucius Virginius Rufius gathered himself and ran at Sanct-Franciscus, head lowered to butt into his middle; Sanct-Franciscus caught Rufius' head under the chin in his locked hands and threw him back, twisting Rufius' neck as he did. There was a dull, grating snap and Lucius Virginius Rufius collapsed, his mouth now slack; he twitched, shuddered, and lay still, not more than a pace from where Octavian stood, immobile with shock.

Had he not still been recovering from his burns, Sanct-Franciscus could have ended the fight in another moment, but his skin and sinews were still taut with incomplete healing and he required a little time to steady himself against the ache his activity created, and his hesitation allowed Octavian and Crispenus a moment for recovery.

Crispenus had struggled to his feet and was now preparing for a more determined assault on Sanct-Franciscus: he took up a small footstool and raised it over his head, preparing to strike Sanct-Franciscus' shoulders and back with it, but before he could, Sanct-Franciscus swung around on one leg and used the other to slam the back of Crispenus' knees. Crispenus went down heavily, swearing by Discordia and Phobus as he landed with a cry of agony as his left knee-cap broke, and at once his leg was smeared with blood.

Octavian looked about the room for a weapon, and settled on an iron crucifix nearly as tall as he was, made of two, long, thin bars, set up in an alcove next to the shuttered window. With a steady effort, he tugged it off the wall, grasped the smaller end of the upright for a hilt, and prepared to do battle. He swung the crucifix in front of him, satisfied with the ponderous sound it made as it sliced through the air, reminiscent of a northern long-handled axe. Jaw set, he advanced on Sanct-Franciscus. "You should have died in that fire, foreigner."

"Along with your mother? Was that your intention?" Sanct-Franciscus asked pointedly as he took swift stock of the room: Crispenus was lying on his side, whimpering steadily, his left leg pulled up and clasped tight to his chest, blood running out between his clenched fingers; Rufius was dead; Ursinus was stunned, unable to stand upright without support, so he leaned on the altar with his elbows, his head cradled in his hands.

"My mother was used up. She was ready to die." Octavian took a step forward, his weapon moving restlessly in his hands. "If not for you, she would have died at least a year ago, and spared herself and us a world of suffering. If anyone caused that fire, you did! *You!*" He swung the crucifix ahead of him, trying to force Sanct-Franciscus to fall back.

"She was helpless," said Sanct-Franciscus, eluding the crucifix.

"Then she should be grateful it is over," Octavian vaunted.

"What devotion," Sanct-Franciscus marveled, stepping around Rufius' body and moving toward the center of the room, where he could act more freely.

"Better than yours. I haven't seduced any honestiora." He jabbed with the end of the crucifix. "And I haven't ruined any woman."

"Except your mother," said Sanct-Franciscus.

With a particularly vicious swing of the crucifix, Octavian rushed at Sanct-Franciscus. "You ruined my sister!" he shouted, and almost lost his footing from the power of his furious sweep.

"Only in your eyes," said Sanct-Franciscus, turning outside the reach of the end of the crucifix.

"I will never forgive you! Deceiver!" Octavian howled as he lunged at Sanct-Franciscus, missed his footing and stumbled into the altar, and striking Ursinus a glancing blow to the side of his head with the end of the cross-beam of the crucifix; this time Ursinus fell heavily, unconscious. "You did that!"

His patience used up, Sanct-Franciscus reached for the crucifix and in a sudden eruption of strength, tore it from Octavian's hands; in a single, fluid motion, he rounded on him, pinning him back against the altar. As he pressed the crucifix into Octavian's chest, he whispered, "I would drain you, but I want nothing of yours— nothing." He shoved hard against Octavian, and heard him shriek as the metal cross-arm sank deep into his arm-pit, blood welling and pumping around it: death would come rapidly.

There was panic in Octavian's eyes as he struggled against Sanct-Franciscus' implacable fury. "Let me go!" It was becoming difficult to breathe; he tried to kick, but there was no power in his leg, and he squealed in frustration and rage. He could not imagine the hot, wet swath down his side that spread on the floor, that smelled of hot metal, was his own blood.

"You are right," Sanct-Franciscus said, remote as the north wind, "this is your last day."

Octavian was feeling light-headed now, and there were cramps in his legs and hands, but he could not feel the pain, or summon up the will to resist Sanct-Franciscus, or the light-edged darkness that wavered at the edges of his vision; this troubled him in a distant way. He started to form a curse, but the words eluded him, and he realized he was cold. That frightened him. It was July, the night was warm. The weight upon him lifted, and he sighed.

Staring into Octavian's untenanted eyes, Sanct-Franciscus was at once satisfied and distressed: he had exacted vengeance on behalf of the dead, but the vindication he had felt in the past eluded him. Slowly he straightened up, setting the iron crucifix aside and wiping the blood from his hands. He would have to leave soon or risk discovery. Natalis would be waiting at the Porta Pinciana, he reminded himself; he had to join him there shortly. He would meet him and be gone from Roma. He realized that it was not yet midnight, still he had an acute urge to leave this house, as if he expected the sun to rise within the hour, or Urban Guards to suddenly appear at the door. But he could not leave the room in such a shambles. Very carefully, he laid the three dead bodies at the foot of the altar; Prosperus Rufius Ursinus he carried to the door and propped him against the wall. "Someone will find you before dawn."

Ursinus groaned; his body was clammy to the touch and his breathing was shallow.

"If you live, you will limp," said Sanct-Franciscus, his centuries at the Temple of Imhotep caring for the dying coming back to him in a rush as he surveyed the destruction around him. "And neither of us will ever forget this night."

Text of a letter from Septimus Desiderius Vulpius in Roma to Ragoczy Germainus Sanct-Franciscus in care of his scribe at Villa Ragoczy, carried by private messenger.

To my most excellent foreign friend, Ragoczy Germainus Sanct-Franciscus, the greetings of your most remorseful Roman ally on this, the 7th day of August in the 973rd Year of the City.

I most heartily apologize for my delay in writing to you, but I offer as an excuse my wish to see the conclusion of the solicitation of bribery investigation against that most officious decuria, Telemachus Batsho. I trust you will pardon my laxity in communication when I tell you that he has been found guilty on twelve counts against him for extortionate practices, and another five counts of abuse of office. I am proud to say that I was asked to give evidence before the Curia, and I would like to think that I helped bring him to justice. His sentence was handed down yesterday: he is to be sent to Vindobona in Pannonia Superior to be a factor for the Legion there. Let him take but one denarius from the soldiers' pay and he will be flayed alive. The Curia has ordered him to be branded and his tongue cut out, which should limit any mischief he might attempt: under the circumstances a light sentence, but a prudent one.

Now that Batsho is a thing of the past, I want you to know that he had threatened me with double assessments on my property if I did not reveal all I knew of your business dealings. If that caused you embarrassment or abusive taxation, I ask you to pardon me, for I was worried for my family and my gens. With Batsho making demands, I was almost unable to conclude my daughter's marriage contract with the father of Titus Gladius Cnaens, but as it is, Livia Linia will be married in three years, and on terms that will not entirely ruin me. Fortunately, the Senate has suspended for two years all commodae for those who were taken advantage of by Batsho.

When you asked that I take your servant, Natalis of Thessalonika, into my service, I admit I was dubious. The man, after all, was a thief. But you said I would discover him to be useful and willing, which he is. To my surprise, he has shown me loyalty and reliability, at least at present. Should he continue in the same manner, I, too, will provide monies for him when his working days are done. The pension you have bestowed upon him is invested in three businesses: a chariot-maker's, a trattorium, and a vineyard. All three enterprises are thriving and I believe Natalis may look forward to a very comfortable old age. I have even offered to help find him a wife.

I was sorry to hear of your decision to leave Roma, although I can comprehend it, with all you have endured here—severe burns, rapacious officials, and the disadvantage of being a foreigner. Your

*shipping business can be useful in this time, I am certain, and your
company makes it possible for our contact to continue, although we
are great distances apart. I will do my utmost to report to you regularly while you are gone: it is the least I can do, considering what
you have endured on my account.*

*The weather has been hot and close, so my wife and I will take
our family to the seashore at Pyrgi, where I hope to purchase a villa.
Now that I am not giving a quarter of my income to Batsho, I believe I can afford the villa. I anticipate that we will be gone a month,
or until the heat breaks, so if you wish to send word to me, have
your messenger come to Pyrgi and inquire of the Prosecutor where
we are staying. I will leave instructions for him to guide you to us.*

*May Fortune and Neptune favor you in your journeys, may
Mercury guide you in commerce, and may Genius grant you victories over all life's calamities. Until we meet again, may you never regret the friendship of*

*Septimus Desiderius Vulpius
by my own hand*

12

Earlier that day the report had reached Brundisium that a pair
of pirate ships were prowling the coast south of Hydruntum;
merchant-ships remained in port while a well-armed bireme set out
to hunt them down; the port city was filled with apprehension, for
pirates damaged more than business—their depredations claimed
lives. Along the docks, sailors and oarsmen alike waited and exchanged gossip, and watched the increasingly choppy waves stamp
against the docks, having nothing more they could do on this sultry
day at the beginning of September.

From his room in the merchants' inn near the waterfront, Sanct-
Franciscus gazed out the window and remarked to Rugeri, "We will

have another thunderstorm this afternoon. It may favor the pirates if the bireme does not find them."

"The storm looks likely," said Rugeri. "The horizon is black with clouds."

"And the wind is rising steadily," Sanct-Franciscus added indifferently as he turned away from the window to look directly at Rugeri. "The air is already buzzing." He rubbed his wrists where his skin remained taut and oddly thin; his face was no longer hideous to see, but it had a curiously unfinished look, with most of the lines so faint they might have been sketched in charcoal on parchment. He was dressed in a black linen chandys, its long, tapering sleeves ornamented with black embroidery of phoenixes; the garment was new, delivered by the needlewoman five days ago, just as Sanct-Franciscus was preparing to leave Villa Ragoczy in a covered carpentum, filled with chests containing his native earth. "We will be here tonight, and probably a portion of tomorrow as well."

"Captain Bion will hold the *Pleiades* ready as long as you require." Rugeri knew Sanct-Franciscus well enough to see the profound exhaustion beneath his unperturbed demeanor. "You have time to rest, to prepare for a voyage."

"Travel over water," said Sanct-Franciscus with distaste.

"We will be in Alexandria in no more than twenty days, so Captain Bion vows," said Rugeri, offering what encouragement he could.

"Make sure two chests of my native earth are in my cabin, or I will go into the hold."

Rugeri paused awkwardly, then plunged ahead. "If you find someone to visit in sleep tonight, you may spend most of our journey with your native earth, where you can restore yourself. You need not bear the full discomfort of crossing running water."

"And tides are surely running water," said Sanct-Franciscus. "Tides cross seas and oceans in their running."

"As much as any river or drain." He waited for Sanct-Franciscus to speak, and when he said nothing, Rugeri added, "It breaks your contact with the earth, or so you say."

"Captain Bion once made the voyage from Alexandria to Ostia in ten days—did he tell you?" Sanct-Franciscus remarked.

"Several times," said Rugeri, rather drily. "But he also told me it was not at this time of year."

"Thunderstorms," said Sanct-Franciscus distantly. "Rain in the streets. More running water."

"Unpleasant for you, I know," said Rugeri. "I have your pluvial ready, if you have need of it."

"Thank you, old friend: I will tell you if I do," said Sanct-Franciscus. He looked back toward the window again. "Do you think Hebseret has received my letter yet?"

"It is more than a month since it was sent," Rugeri reminded him. "I think it likely that he has."

Sanct-Franciscus nodded. "Truly."

"They will tend to you, my master. The Priests of Imhotep will consider it an honor to have the care of you. You will finally heal."

"I would do that in any case, eventually." Sanct-Franciscus laid his hand on his abdomen, over the scars there. He sighed. "But you are right—in their hands I will do so more quickly, and it will be less questionable when the scars from the fire finally vanish."

"You are certain they will vanish?" Rugeri could not keep from asking.

"Do not doubt me, old friend," Sanct-Franciscus recommended with a softening of his tone. "Worse than this has happened, and no trace remains."

"No trace but your memories," Rugeri corrected sadly.

"My memories," Sanct-Franciscus repeated. "Indeed."

A sudden shout from the street below announced the arrival of three small fishing boats laden with their catch; activity erupted along the quay as handcarts pushed by slaves, freemen, and vendors converged on the lowest dock where the small boats tied up; some of the vendors were already shouting what they were willing to pay for the fish as they attempted to beat the competition to the boats.

"I hope the rest of the fleet is in," said Rugeri. "It won't be safe to make for the harbor in another hour."

"I would not like to ride out this storm at sea, even if I did not suffer on water." Sanct-Franciscus reached into his wallet for a handful of coins. "So you may choose what you prefer for your evening meal."

"I have a plucked pheasant waiting for me already. The cook has made a sauce for it—not liquamen, but something with ground nuts and sweet onions. I will wait until the cooks are busy at the spits, and then I will eat; they would not like to see me devour a raw bird, with or without sauce." He was able to smile a little.

"No; very likely not." Sanct-Franciscus tapped his fingers together. "I ought to write to Olivia, so she will know what has happened. Perhaps tonight, when the city is asleep, and I will entrust it to a private courier in the morning. I have done all I can to secure her possessions, including her house in Roma, but she will have to inform a decuria in Roma of her intentions for the house."

"She will appreciate a word from you," said Rugeri with a singular lack of inflection.

"Meaning she will berate me," said Sanct-Franciscus with a ghost of a smile. "I expect no less of her."

Rugeri took a long, thoughtful pause. "If you have everything ready you wish loaded onto the *Pleiades,* tell me, and your possessions will be carried on board this evening, so that if all goes well, we may leave promptly when the weather clears."

"A good notion," said Sanct-Franciscus without shifting his stare from the window, although what he saw was many days and many thousands of paces distant. "I hope Ursinus lived."

"So that he can identify you to the Urban Guard?" Rugeri asked more crisply than he had intended.

"No; so that—" He stopped and went on more urbanely, "—so that none of my friends need suffer on my account."

As much as Rugeri wondered what Sanct-Franciscus had been going to say, he held his tongue. Instead, he patted the thin mattress atop a sturdy leather chest. "Are you going to nap, my master?"

"Perhaps, a little later," said Sanct-Franciscus. He came back from the window, his expression impenetrable. "I will be gone for a while—probably until sunset. If the rain becomes heavy before then, I will return, or I will wait until it is over. In either case, do not fret."

Perplexed and concerned, Rugeri said, "While you're out, I'll get your chests and crates ready for Captain Bion."

"Thank you," said Sanct-Franciscus, taking his pluvial off the back of the single chair in the room. "This, so I will be prepared."

"Of course," said Rugeri as he stepped back, allowing Sanct-Franciscus to pass.

As Sanct-Franciscus descended to the street level, he paid little attention to the noise coming from the tavern next to the inn, or to the men gathered outside at the docks, waiting for news of the pirates. He made his way back from the harbor into the tangle of streets. He walked aimlessly, ignoring vendors of trinkets and food, and small gaggles of artfully ragged children shouting for coins. Gradually the shops, brothels, insulae, and thermopolia gave way to wider streets and walled houses with impressive colonnades and iron-strapped doors. Overhead the sky darkened and the first, distant drubbing of thunder sounded; color vanished, and everything looked ochre and slate. Anticipating a downpour, Sanct-Franciscus pulled his pluvial over his head and kept on, almost enjoying the ache in his skin from his exercise.

"You. Foreigner," said a voice from a side-door of a handsome villa.

Sanct-Franciscus stopped and looked toward the voice. "Yes?"

"Where are you going?"

"To the city gate," said Sanct-Franciscus, moving forward to see the speaker.

"The storm's coming. You better find shelter." The child was about eight, in a silk tunica and with red-leather calcea on his feet; by his appearance, he was a son of the Dominus.

"No doubt I should," said Sanct-Franciscus gently. "Thank you for reminding me."

"I'd let you in, but my mother won't allow it." The boy thrust out his lower lip in disapproval; there was a glint of real fear in his eyes.

"Your mother is a sensible woman," said Sanct-Franciscus.

"She is better than anyone. No matter what anyone says." His lower lip now protruded pugnaciously.

"She must be," said Sanct-Franciscus.

"She says my grandfather's enemies are trying to kill him, but he won't listen," the boy went on, speaking more to himself than to Sanct-Franciscus. "She says that he's . . . he's—" He stopped, searching for a word.

"What?"

"Denounced. That's it. Denounced." The child grinned at his accomplishment.

Sanct-Franciscus achieved a bemused smile. "Then should you be talking to me? I am a foreigner, after all."

The boy's voice dropped to just above a whisper as lightning scissored the clouds. "No. I'm not supposed to talk to—" The rest was drowned in a ponderous roll of thunder.

When the air offered only the whoop of the wind, Sanct-Franciscus said, "Your mother will want you indoors, my lad. And I, as you warned me, ought to find shelter."

"I know," he said, and closed the gate, leaving Sanct-Franciscus alone in the road and aware of his isolation for the first time. He stared up into the sky and felt the first drops of rain on his face; he looked about him, searching for a covered gate or a recessed doorway, but saw nothing that suggested a hiding place from the storm. Ahead were the city walls, and beyond the gate, a cluster of tombs.

With thunder for company, Sanct-Franciscus made for the gate, paid his six denarii, and hurried toward one of the largest of the vaults, knowing that most had a narrow porch where mourners could keep vigil for the dead; one of these would serve to shelter him through the storm. The second tomb he found had such an alcove, and he slipped into it, hitching up his shoulders and settling back on the narrow stone seat while lightning frisked and crackled above Brundisium. In this setting of monuments to the dead, he devoted himself to remembering his own, from his millennia-lost family, to the revenge he had exacted for their deaths, to the sacrifices offered him in the oubliette, to the many who came to the Temple of Imhotep, to Imeshmit, to Tishtry, Kosrozh, and Aumtehoutep, and Led Arashnur, to Srau, to the three young men in Roma. "You cannot hold them," he said to the stones. "They will slip away, every one of them. Not even memory can keep them with you." His face was wet, but he knew it was the rain, for he had lost his tears when he had lost his breathing life: the sobbing storm would have to do for him.

For more than an hour the wind reveled, the lightning lit up the clouds, and the rain came down as if all the sky were a waterfall; the stone which sheltered Sanct-Franciscus grew damp and cold, his pluvial became sodden, and night blotted out the last remnants of illumination, save that of the lightning, and fairly soon, that, too, was gone. Only when the thunder had grumbled away to the west and the wind dropped to stiff, damp breeze filled with spitting rain did Sanct-Franciscus leave the protection of the tomb for the city gate—still open because of the storm—and the streets, making his way back toward the inn despite the slight vertigo the water running along the cobbles caused him. Around him, men and women hastened to their homes, or taverns, or inns, driven by the lingering end of the storm.

Lamps were lit and flickering in the entry to the inn as Sanct-Franciscus once again stepped through the door, and found Epimetheus Bion waiting in the vestibule, a large cup of hot wine in one hand, a folded scroll in the other, his big, leathery face creased with worry. At the sight of Sanct-Franciscus, his expression brightened. "Jupiter and Neptune be thanked!" he exclaimed, his voice rough from years of shouting orders at sea. "I feared we had lost you to the storm."

"No," said Sanct-Franciscus. "You have not lost me."

"It is not only the storm that troubled me," Bion asserted in his own defense.

"No?" Sanct-Franciscus inquired. "What, then?"

He set his cup down in the small alcove with a statue of Mercury, there to protect travelers and those in commerce. "There is a company of Praetorians just arrived at the Basilica. We saw them as we were loading your chests aboard the *Pleiades*. Word has it that they are going to be taking traitors in charge tonight." He coughed. "You, being a foreigner, might be detained."

"Praetorians? Here?"

"There are rumors everywhere," Bion began.

"That is no surprise," Sanct-Franciscus remarked.

"No. No, it's not," Bion agreed. "They say that there are conspirators in Brundisium who are plotting against Heliogabalus. They are to be arrested and sent to the arena, or so it's said."

Sanct-Franciscus thought of the youngster he had spoken with earlier, and wondered if the child had been right in his fears. "The Praetorians are at the Basilica?"

"They say they are going to arrest those suspected tonight, so that they will not be warned." Bion reached for his wine and drank hastily.

"Since no one knows the Praetorians are here, they can act covertly," said Sanct-Franciscus ironically. "Is that what brought you here?"

Bion took a second long drink of his hot wine and waved the folded scroll under Sanct-Franciscus' face. "Look at this. My scribe compiled it as we were loading. There are two chests left in your apartment upstairs, but I have them listed here, at the end of the inventory. Numbers thirty-one and thirty-two. You'll see." He flapped the scroll for emphasis.

"If you will give it to me, I will read it," Sanct-Franciscus said, checking over his shoulder to determine how much attention the men crowded together into the tavern were giving them. "Perhaps it would be best to do this in my apartment, away from the curious?"

"I take your point," said Bion, also looking toward the men. "Too many eyes, and too many ears." He gulped down the last of his wine and set the cup next to Mercury again, knowing no one would touch it while it was there. "Your manservant is out, they tell me—gone to have his meal."

"As is his custom at this hour," said Sanct-Franciscus as he climbed the stairs ahead of Bion.

"An odd hour," said Bion.

Sanct-Franciscus ignored his comment, asking instead, "What are the prospects for leaving tomorrow? Have you any useful information?"

"I am sure there will be squalls through the night, but if the morning is clear and the dawn isn't red or violet, then I will walk the beach, to see the speed of the waves, and their height, and after I have considered all I can learn, I will make up my mind." Reaching the landing, he stopped. "You own the ship, and you can order me out to sea, of course, but—"

"You are a captain and you know the sea—I am not a captain, and my knowledge of the sea is slight." Sanct-Franciscus continued his climb. "I bow to your superior judgment and experience."

"That is most reasonable of you, honestiorus." He extended the scroll again. "This is your inventory. I must submit it to the Prefect of Trade for assessment before we leave."

"Yes, you must." Sanct-Franciscus opened the door to his apartment and went in, holding the door so that Bion could step inside.

"You must sign the inventory, or the Prefect may levy a higher assessment on your goods."

"I am aware of the law," said Sanct-Franciscus as he took the scroll and opened it. "If you will light the lamps?"

"Certainly," said Bion, pulling flint-and-steel from his wallet and striking a spark at the wick of the largest of the oil-lamps. On his second attempt, flame sprouted and the shadows retreated. "You should read this. Or do you need a scribe?"

"I read well enough for this," said Sanct-Franciscus, saying nothing about the many tongues he had learned in his more than two thousand years of life. He held the length of vellum up and perused it quickly. "I have a red-lacquer chest that contains my medicaments. It is listed here in ninth place. Neither the chest nor its contents are to be sold, and so they should be taxed as property, not merchandise."

"I'll make a note of it," said Bion. "How do you plan to pay the Prefect?"

"In aurei," said Sanct-Franciscus tranquilly; he had used some of his months of recovery to make a large amount of gold in his athanor, and had accumulated coins enough to carry them well beyond the Roman Empire, should that be necessary.

"He may be greedy," Bion warned.

"Many officials are," said Sanct-Franciscus with little emotion.

"Not just the ones in Roma," Bion agreed. "Is the inventory accurate?"

Sanct-Franciscus held up his hand as he finished reading. "It appears to be. I can find nothing missing or added." He looked around for his writing-box; it contained his ink pads, styluses, quills, and a vial of water. "Shall I sign at the bottom or the top?" he asked, though he knew the answer.

"The bottom. And don't leave any room, or the Prefect may suspect that extra items have been added."

"As you wish," He located his writing-box and was about to prepare his ink when there was a rap at the door.

"May I enter?" Rugeri asked.

"Yes, old friend, you may." Sanct-Franciscus went on with the preparation of ink, and offered a half-smile as he indicated Captain Bion. "I am endorsing the inventory so that Captain Bion can file it."

"Another chore done," said Rugeri, the suggestion of worry vanishing from his face. "I have heard the Praetorians are here."

"And I; I have seen them, a company of them, entering the Basilica, in secrecy," Bion said quickly. "Which is one of the reasons I have come: to warn Sanct-Franciscus that he may be in danger."

Rugeri nodded. "A wise precaution."

"In this time, everyone must be careful." Bion watched while Sanct-Franciscus set down his name, the name of his company, and his destination, then waited for the ink to dry. When the scroll was refolded, he took it from Sanct-Franciscus, saying, "I will file this with the Prefect of Trade now, before I return to the *Pleiades,* so that if the morning is clear, there will be no delays from the Prefecture. You may pay your charges before you board. I will arrange it."

"And thus I will avoid the Praetorians? A good plan," said Sanct-Franciscus, starting to put away his writing materials. "I will not keep you now, Captain Bion. I will expect your decision on setting out an hour after dawn. May Somnus bring you sweet sleep."

"And you," said Bion, and was about to leave when he stopped. "Do you truly want to remain in your cabin throughout the voyage? Those are my instructions, but I want you to understand: it could be twenty days to Alexandria."

"Yes. I want to stay in my cabin. Rugeri will attend to me," said Sanct-Franciscus, adding diffidently. "I am prone to sea-sickness, and I fare better if left to my own devices, and my bondsman's care."

"Sea-sick!" Bion exclaimed. "You—a successful merchant, and you get sea-sick." He shook his head in disbelief. "Very well. If you must stay in your cabin, no one will disturb you unless there is trouble. This is the best I can offer you—I trust you understand."

"I will be grateful," said Sanct-Franciscus, motioning to Rugeri to open the door for Bion, who ducked his head before he left.

As soon as the door was closed and Bion had tromped off down the stairs, Rugeri said, "I think it is a good time to be gone."

"And I," said Sanct-Franciscus.

"Captain Bion—do you trust him?" Rugeri asked.

"Enough to get aboard his ship," said Sanct-Franciscus.

"Your ship," Rugeri corrected him.

"Perhaps, in the eyes of the law, but not in his heart; there the *Pleiades* is his child and his mistress," said Sanct-Franciscus. "Which is why I will be as safe on the *Pleiades* as I may be on any vessel."

Rugeri kept his thoughts to himself, saying only, "Will you go out again tonight? The storm is quieting."

"Perhaps; after midnight."

"Depending upon the weather?" Rugeri suggested as he struck flint-and-steel to light another lamp.

"And the Praetorians," Sanct-Franciscus appended, his dark eyes becoming distant once again, fixed no longer on what lay behind him, but what might lie ahead. "I will go out: after I have written to Olivia."

Text of a letter from Pax Ignatia Laelius at Roma to Sanct-Franciscus through the steward at Villa Ragoczy, and carried by private messenger to Alexandria in Egypt.

To my most valued friend of years past, the greetings of Domina Pax Ignatia Laelius from Villa Laelius in Roma, now rebuilt and once again my home, on this, the 5th day of May in the 975th Year of the City.

I cannot believe it is more than two years since I have seen you, but so it is, and I apologize for my dilatory attention. I should have written to you before now. I should have come to visit you during your recuperation at Villa Ragoczy, but the truth of it is that I was afraid that you would die, and after the death of my mother, I could not bear to contemplate another great loss. But I had one, in the death of my brother. You may not have been told, but he and three companions were set upon by unknown robbers who it seems, were caught breaking into the house where he was staying. The Urban Guard reported that they suspected a gang of three northerners operating in that part of the city, but they could not be apprehended. The Christians who are part of the group to which Octavian belonged have proclaimed him and his companions martyrs to their faith.

With all the demands of these losses, I have been occupied with attending to the changes that they have brought upon me. I am now the last of my family. I know you will understand how much a burden that can be. It is one thing to achieve old age and out-live most others, but I am twenty-seven; I may be past marriageable age but I am far from being a crone. To find myself with only my sister and her two boys left to carry on—and to lose the name upon my death—is very stark. Had I not had the wisdom and comfort of your friendship, I would find my world far more bleak than it is. You have shown me that it is possible to lose all and yet endure. As it turns out, I have not lost all, for I am now counted a wealthy woman.

My uncle has signed control of my inheritance over to my management except for the twelve hundred aurei that is my mother's dowry, to be held in trust until I marry. If I do not marry, then I may bequeath the sum to an heir of my choosing, since I have no nieces who would have a claim on the dowry. My father's aunt died last year, and left her fortune unencumbered to me, and that has doubled my wealth. The Curia has approved my mother's brother's disposal, and praised him for upholding our traditions, and my uncle, I think, is pleased to be rid of the responsibility of my maintenance. I have begun the task of setting up my household, and it is proving less daunting than I had feared. All the years I cared for my mother, I learned a great deal about how a household is run, and those lessons now stand me in good stead.

As you must have heard, wherever you are, Heliogabalus was killed by the Praetorians on March 11, for his excesses and his dishonor of the Senate and people of Roma. That is the official reason for the murder. Whatever other causes there might be, they are spoken only in whispers. His young cousin Gessius, or to use his optimistic reigning name, Marcus Aurelius Severus Alexander, is now elevated to the purple, to the delight of his mother. Julia Mamaea has a steadier hand than Julia Soaemias. The boy may last longer. Roma is wary of this child, but relief is everywhere. Even Roma was growing weary of Heliogabalus' unchecked dissipation.

There is so much I want to say to you, but as I try to express all that is in my thoughts and my heart, I cannot find the words I seek. If you and I were conversing, it might be possible to convey all I want to you. For you, who have known me better than anyone, since I cannot see you, cannot touch you, cannot hear your voice, I am mute. I ask you to pardon my stillness. You, of all men, must comprehend the reason for it. If ever you return to Roma and I am still here, I ask you to visit me, so that I may impart what I cannot express in words. Until that time, may Mercury, Neptune, Fortuna, and your gods protect you, and may Fraus and the waters of Phlegethon remain far from you.

With affection and devotion,
Pax Ignatia Laelius

by the hand of Felifanus, the scribe

EPILOGUE

*T*ext of a letter from Ragoczy Germain Sanctus-Franciscus at Vindobona to Atta Olivia Clemens at Emona, carried by private courier.

To my long-cherished Atta Olivia Clemens, Ragoczy Germain Sanctus-Franciscus, as I am known here, sends greetings.

I have your letter of January 7ᵗʰ with me, which, I am pleased to say, has actually reached me after going through Alexandria and Narona to arrive in Vindobona, where I am staying at present. I have acquired a house and suited it to my needs. It is far from lavish, but it is sturdy and the roof does not leak.

Out here at the edge of the Roman Empire, I am struck with the hard life these people are willing to tolerate all for the privilege of calling themselves citizens of Roma. This city may have walls and a Legion, but it is little more than a typical border village, a rough place under constant threat of attack from beyond the frontier. Those foolish enough to go beyond the city gates may take their lives in their hands, as many reckless Romans have learned. There are times going out of the house is enough to bring mortal danger upon one. Just a month ago, the factor of the Legion here was found beaten to death on a dung-heap, not ten paces from the Legion barracks.

Rotiger is with me still; he has this household—limited though it is—well within his command, and he has gained the trust of the local merchants in all his dealings with them, so that what few luxuries reach this place, we have first claim on them, foreigners or not.

I am enclosing with this a few new jewels toward any costs that you may encounter in pressing your claims on your Roman property when you return there next spring. I am assuming you are still planning on such a journey, and that you will find the decuriae of Roma as avaricious as I did. Think of it as a return on your generosity to me during my stay there, a decade ago.

Speaking of that time, last month I was delivered a message informing me that Melidulci has succumbed to fever and has had her body burned, supposedly in tribute to the customs of the old Republic. She left a goblet to me, as a remembrance of her, which surprised me, given her protestations of no strong attachment. It may be that over time, her affection increased, or her memories may have altered her understanding of what we had in our time together.

That does concern me, now and again. I think my memories are true, and I rely upon them to be so. Yet over the centuries, my vision of them has changed, and I occasionally fear they will become so distorted that I can no longer depend on what I recall. It is those times when I value you most deeply, for you and I share almost two centuries of memories. Between you and Rotiger, I know I will not lose my link to the past, or not completely, and that gives me solace that I thought I would never know again. From the deepest chamber of my unbeating heart, I thank you for that, and for your constant love, which I return in full measure until the True Death consigns me to the realm of memories.

Ragoczy Germain Sanctus-Franciscus
(his sigil, the eclipse)

by my own hand on November 11th, in the 983rd Roman Year

Gazetteer and Glossary

a * before the entry indicates an actual place or thing

GAZETTEER

*Achaea—the Greek Peloponnese

*Aegyptus—Egypt

*Alexandria—port city in Egypt

*Antioch—port city in Roman Syria

*Aquitania—Roman province, southwestern modern France

*Arabian Sea—still there

*Armenia—northeast Turkey today

*Asiana—Roman province; western Turkey today

*Asisium—modern Assisi

*Aventinus Hill—on the south side of Roma

*Barbary—north Africa

*Basilica Julia—Roman civil courts and records building

*Belearus Isolae—islands off southern Spain

*Bithynia—Roman Middle-Eastern province

*Bononia—Italian town, Bologna today

*Britannia—Britain

*Brundisium—modern Brindisi

*Byzantium—Roman city; later Constantinople, now modern Istanbul

*Caelianus Hill—on the southeast side of Roma

*Capitolinus Hill—upper class Roman hill, west side of the Old Walls

*Cappadocia—northwestern Turkey today

*Carpathian Mountains—fish-hook shaped range in modern Romania

*Chios—Greek Island; still there

*Circus Maximus—chariot-racing and gladiatorial arena—older than the Flavian Circus

*Cnossus—port on Crete

*Cos—town famous for linen

*Creta—Greek Island of Crete today

*Dacia—modern-day Transylvania and Moldavia

*Emona—city near the Austro-Croatian border today

*Esquilinus Hill—on the eastern side of the city

*Fars—northeastern Iran today

*Flavian Circus—we call it the Colosseum today

*Florentia—Florence now

*Forum Agricolarum—the farmers' market

*Forum Emporiarum—warehouse market

*Forum Romanum—civic center for Roma

*Gallia Belgica—Belgium and most of central France today; one of the Three Parts Gaul is divided into

*Germania Inferior—northern Holland and northwestern Germany

*Germania Superior—southern Germany, Switzerland, and Austria

*Golden House—Nero's personal palace

*Hind—India

*Hydruntum—small harbor on the heel of Italy's boot

*Iberia—Spain

*Illyricum—most of present day western Serbia and Croatia

*Judaea—roughly modern Israel and part of Jordan

*Litigianus Prison—Roman jail for minor offenders (as compared to the Mamertinus Prison)

*lupanar—Roman red-light district

*Luxor—city in Egypt

*Macedonia—northwestern region in Greece

*Mamertinus Prison—major Roman prison for major felons

*Mare Internum—the Mediterranean Sea

*Mare Nostrum—Roman nickname for the Mediterranean, meaning Our Sea

*Mare Tyrrhenum—sea west of Ostia and southern Italy

*Miletus—Asianian port

*Misenum—north-northwest of Neapolis

*Moesia—region in the southern Carpathians, between Dacia and Thracia

*Naissus—Balkan territory

*Narbo—southern French port

*Narona—Dalmatian port

*Nepete—town north of Roma

*Neapolis—modern Naples

*Nile—a river in Egypt

*Odessus—modern Odessa on the Black Sea

*Ostia—port for Roma

*Palatinus Hill—Roman upper-class hill

*Pannonia Inferior—mostly modern western Hungary

*Pannonia Superior—mostly modern Croatia and eastern Austria

*Pergamum—Asianan spa town

*Persia—today southern Iran

*Phoenicia—trading port in Middle East

*Pincius Hill—on the north side of the city

*Porta Caelinus—Roman gate on the southeast side of the city

*Porta Nova—Roman gate, immediately south of the Praetorian Camp

*Porta Ostiensis—gate on the south side of Roma, just east of the Tibrus

*Porta Pinciana—one of three north-facing gates; this one was under
   the Virgo Aquaduct

*Porta Viminalis—Roman gate, immediately north of the Praetorian
   Camp

*Pyrgi—beach-town northwest of Roma

*Quirinalis Hill—northern Roman hill

*Ravenna—Roman city on the Adriatic

*Roma—the Eternal City

*Salonae—on the Dalmatian Coast

Sapientia—Olivia's villa in Vesontio

*Stone Tower—east/west merchants' center in southeast Persia

*Syria—Syria

*Tarrraco—port city in Iberia (Spain)

*Tarsus—port in present-day Turkey

*Temple of Hercules—pagan temple in Roma

*Temple of Imhotep—temple in Egypt

*Temple of Isis—small pagan temple in Roma

*Thessalonika—Macedonian city-state

*Thracia—northeastern Greece

*Tibrus—in earlier days, the Tiberis Flumen, today the Tevere

°Vesontio—Roman town in Gallia Belgica

°Vetera Castra—city in Germanca Superior

°Via Appia—probably the most famous Roman road

°Via Castrum—Roman street

°Via Cingula—beltway on the east of Roma

Via Decius Claudii—the street of the Laelius' house in Roma

°Via Ostiensis—the road from Roma to Ostia

Via Philomena—in Vesontio, Gallia Belgica

°Via Subura—Roman major street leading to the Forum Romanum

°Via Thermae—Roman street

°Vicus Longus—Roman major street: lit. Long Boulevard

Villa Laelius—the Laelius' Roman home

Villa Ragoczy—three miles northeast of Roma

Villa Solea—Melidulci's villa near Misenum

°Viminalis Hill—northeastern Roman hill

°Vindobona—remote border city in Pannonia Superior; Vienna today

°Virgo Aqueduct—major aqueduct on the north side of the city, feeding the Baths of Caracalla and private houses, among other things

°White Fountains of Pergamum—actual spa; still there

GLOSSARY

a/ae—a copper coin, very low value—about $.05 in buying power

abolla/ae—calf-length pleated cloak

Apollo—Roman god of music, science, the sun, and masculinity

Astraea—goddess of justice and law

athanor—alchemical oven, shaped like a traditional beehive

atrium/ia—central courtyard in Roman houses

aurea/ei—Roman gold coin

Bacchus—Roman god of wine, indulgence, and madness

ballista/ae—Roman military catapult

Balus—Syrian sun-god

bestiarius/ii (m), bestiaria/ae (f)—animal trainers, usually circus slaves

biga/ae—two-horse chariot

bireme—military ship with two banks of oars

Bona Dea—the Good Goddess, often used as oath or expletive

bracae—long and short britches; riding pants

byrrus—travel-cape

calceus/ea—laced travel-boots

Carna—Roman goddess of the physical body

carpentum/a—large wagon, usually drawn by oxen

centurion—sergeant; in charge of a squad of 100 men, called a century

chandys—knee-length Persian caftan

Cherusci—barbarian eastern Germanic peoples

convivium/a—evening meal, generally with guests

commoda/ae—necessary four percent commission for civil servants and others

Consivius—god of cities and civilization

Copia—goddess of abundance

Curia/ae—Roman Senatorial adjunct; a cross between the Supreme Court and Privy Council

Daci/ii—a native of Dacia

dalmatica/ae—caftan-like Roman daily-wear garment, mostly worn by men

decuria/ae—mid-level civil servants, usually connected to the courts

denarius/ii—silver Roman coin, about $2.00 buying power in 218, reduced to about $.25 in 220 due to debasement of the coins

Diana—Roman goddess of the moon, the hunt, and feminine chastity

Dis—Roman god of death and the underworld, a name rarely spoken for fear of bad luck

Discordia—Roman goddess of enmity and strife

Divus/Diva—honorific for those made gods

Doma—unmarried adult daughter of a householder; Miss

Dominus/Domina—literally, leader of a house (Domus); later lord and lady

ecce—behold

fascae—straps, bandages; also bras

Feast of Balus—the Summer Solstice feast of the Syrian sun-god

fillia/ae—girl, daughter

forum/a—marketplace; city center

Forum Guard—paid semi-private security force for markets

Fortuna—Roman goddess of good fortune

Fraus—Roman goddess of treachery

freedman—any freed slave

freeman—any humiliorus born free

Genius—god of life; the individual spark

gens—extended family

Great Games—entertainments held in the Roman circus

Hercules—demigod hero of great undertakings

holocaust—household furnace—Roman houses had radiant heat

honestiorus/a—upper class person

honoratus/a—honorific for those in the diplomatic or governing services

humiliorus/a—lower class person

illustriatus/a—noble person

insula/ae—apartment house

Janus—Roman god of doorways, beginnings and endings

Jupiter—Roman master-god of thunder, glory, and civic pride

kalasiris—standard Egyptian male dress; one-shouldered kilt-like outfit

lacerna/ae—voluminous sleeved cloak

laena/ae—woollen cloak

lares—household gods and deified ancestors

Lictor—in 220 AD, a provincial regional military official

liquamen—ubiquitous fish sauce, the equivalent of catsup, also called
garum

lorica/ae—segmented or large-link chain-mail body armor

mafortium—hood

Magna Mater—Great Mother! Olivia's favorite oath

mal aria—miasmic fever, malaria, literally, bad air

mani/e—men's briefs attached to leggings, and women's bikini-type
underpants

Mania—goddess of death and grief

mantele—summer-weight cloak

Mars—Roman god of war

Mercury—Roman god of commerce and communication

Minerva—Roman goddess of wisdom, law, and strategy

Mithras—Middle-Eastern savior-deity

Nemesis—goddess of vengeance

Neptune—Roman god of oceans, horses, and earthquakes

numen/ina—spirits of place or specific designations of place, such as borders, orchards, etc.

paenula/ae—long, hooded cloak

palla/ae—standard female over-garment

pallium/ii—long-sleeved, knee-length tunic; usual daily wear for Roman men

Parcae—the Fates

Patronus/i—patron, an honorific for members of the equestrian and noble classes

Paulist—one of the two most prominent schools of Christianity in Roma, the other being Peterine

pero/i—ankle-boots

Persian—from central Persia (modern Iran)

Phlegethon—one of the five rivers of the Underworld; this one is made of fire

Phobus—Greco/Roman god of fear

pluvial—oiled-wool poncho, worn in the rain

Pomona—goddess of orchards, a numen

porticus—front colonnade on large homes and public buildings

Praetorian Guards—military troops protecting the Emperor and Roma; the SWAT team

prandium/ia—midday meal

Prefecture of Customs—import tax board

Prefect of the Fora—administrator of markets

Prefect of Trade—Roman merchants' courts away from Roma

Prefect of the Urban Guard—commissioner for the cops and firemen

Prosecutor—official administrator

quadriga/ae—four-horse chariot

retriarius/ii—arena fighter using a trident and net

ricinium/a—hood

sagum—pleated cloak

saie—Gallic hooded cloak

Saturn—Roman god of time and fate, the father and devourer of years

Saturnalia—five unnumbered days at the end of the year; a festival of feasting and excess, since the days, being unnumbered, do not count

Senate—Roman governing aristocratic body

Somnus—Roman god of sleep

stola/ae—standard female inner garment

Swine Fever—cholera

tepidarium/ia—swimming pool

thermopolium/ia—curbside bar and grill

tibia/ie—straight pin, part of jewelry; also a musical instrument like a straight trumpet

toga virilis—formal upper-class Roman male dress; the tuxedo and/or morning coat of the times

trabea/eae—Etruscan-style pleated and sleeved tunic

trattorium/ia—restaurant

trireme—military ship with three banks of oars

tunica/ae—Roman basic dress for males and children; occasionally worn in summer by women

Twins, the—Castor and Pollux, Gemini

Urban Guard—police force between Praetorians and Watchmen, often used in cases of violent crime and crowd control; also served as firemen

venation—a hunt in the arena

Venus—Roman goddess of sensuality and female sexuality

Verplaca—Roman goddess of domestic accord

Vertumnus—god of gardens and transformations, a numen

Vesta—Roman hearth goddess

Vestal Virgins—Roman female supervisors, traditionally six in number; for six centuries having authority equal to the Senate and capable of overruling the Emperor; by 200 AD, their power is diminished

Vulcan—Roman god of the forge, volcanos, and metals

Watchmen—Roman city patrol, the Vigilis

White Disease—leprosy